A CURSE OF FANG AND SWORD

NICOLETTE ELZIE

To all the women that get labeled with words like: "weak", "soft", "kind", "compassionate", and "delicate". Those words fail to capture who we really are and, often, people underestimate us.

That's their mistake.

Author's Note

A Curse of Fang and Sword is a dark fantasy romance inspired by the Mexican folktale of The Bear Prince and Beauty & the Beast. **This story is a creative reimagining/retelling.**

A Curse of Fang and Sword is my darkest book yet.
This book contains mature and graphic content not suitable for all audiences. Dark romance isn't black and white. What some readers may consider "light" may be "dark" for others.
Your mental health is important, and you can find a very detailed trigger warning list at https://nicoletteelzie.com/content-warnings/

CHAPTER ONE

YARI

Why is he doing this?

Tears filled her eyes, threatening to spill over and betray her emotions. She wanted to be strong and hide her dismay to better protect herself, but this was too much.

She stared down at the three men lying at her feet. They lay motionless on the cold marble floor, breathing shallowly and rhythmically—the only evidence that they were still alive.

Yari glanced nervously in Arlando's direction, her heart sinking at the mischievous glimmer in his eyes. Fear coursed through her veins, uncertain of what he would do next.

It hurt to even look at him. Yari's memories of what he'd done to her were still too fresh. She quickly averted her gaze, hoping he didn't notice.

The last thing she wanted was to draw his attention.

His white hair was slicked back, bound tightly in a neat tail at the nape of his neck. His pristine white cotton jacket and trousers were tailored to perfection and complemented by shining silver embroidery that wound its way up the legs, giving him an almost regal air. His eyes twinkled a brilliant azure against his warm, sun-kissed skin, and he radiated a kind of ethereal beauty that seemed almost otherworldly.

Yari had once thought he looked like an angel.

She shook her head at her own naivety.

She knew better now.

There was nothing saintly about Arlando Ozetero.

He was like the fruit that the Protectorate sometimes included in the weekly food rations provided to the Demon Corps.

By the time the shipments reached all the way up north, like at the camp in Norcera, nearly all the fruit would arrive bruised or rotten.

She recalled a time when Kiki had gotten into a brawl over the only apple that was still plump, red, and free of bruises. Luna had scolded her for it after, but Kiki hadn't cared. She so rarely did.

That was her favorite thing about Kiki. She set her mind to something and did it. If only Yari could be more like her.

After starting the brawl, Kiki managed to crawl between kicking feet and dodge flying fists as she scrambled away from the tussle of bodies—the apple tucked safely inside her shirt. Upon reaching Yari and Luna, she yanked them around the corner of the supply building and held out her prize with a grin.

"Here," she had said, offering the rarity to Yari first.

Yari had stared at the apple, its gleaming red surface almost too perfect to be real. Her mouth watered in anticipation, and she reached out and cradled it in her palms.

A part of her had wanted to save the fruit. If only because it was perfect and untainted, unlike everything else the Demon Corps issued.

But she knew Kiki would never allow her to waste such a treat. So, after one final moment of hesitation, she bit into it and suddenly felt filled with regret.

The taste of bitter vinegar flooded her mouth, making her gag. She held the offending apple away from herself as she turned to spit what she had left in her mouth onto the hard dirt.

"Aww, shit," Kiki said, grabbing the fruit from her hand. "It's rotten!"

Sure enough, the flesh inside was gray and squishy. Upon further inspection, there was a small hole in the bottom of the apple, near the core, where some pest had wormed its way inside.

That was exactly what Arlando was like.

On the outside, he looked decadent—full of life, unspoiled—just like that apple. But on the inside, he was just as rotten. Writhing with worms that had long ago eaten away at his soul. Leaving behind nothing but festering decay.

His firm grip around her wrist tightened as he stepped closer to inspect the three bodies on the ground.

"Well done, brother," Arlando praised, turning to Turi, who still held the blowpipe in his hands—the device he'd turned on his own brothers to put them to sleep with sedative-laced darts.

Did he have to use all the darts? She didn't think so. But then again, she didn't fail to notice the way Turi's hands shook at his side, nor how he tried to calm them by shoving them into his pants pockets.

She quirked her head at seeing the evidence of Turi's fear.

Why is he afraid? And if he is, then maybe he should have thought harder about his actions before committing such betrayal.

She forced herself to soften her expression, masking the disgust she feared she wore too plainly on her face.

Looking down at the men, she noticed the familial resemblance. She didn't know the one called Erasmo, not personally, anyway. She knew he was Arlando's twin, if only because Arlando had said as much. But also because he was the embodiment of Arlando's opposite.

Where Arlando seemed to radiate with light, a trait he capitalized on in the white clothing he always wore and the silver-white sheen of his hair—his twin wore nothing but black, his black hair bearing a single white streak near his forehead and black stubble peppering his chiseled jawline. He was also a much larger man than Arlando. Where Arlando was lean and chiseled, his twin looked heavier set and his muscles made visible divots in his shirt.

Yari didn't recognize the third man, but she suspected he had some blood relation to Erasmo, Bernat and Arlando. He shared the same shape of their eyes, if not the same color, and they all seemed to share the same sharp nose.

Next to Erasmo lay Bernat, his large muscular body spread across the ground, his arms outstretched as if he intended to shield someone right before the sedative had fully kicked in.

Guilt ripped into her heart with razor-sharp talons.

She knew Bernat. He was the second-in-command of her squad in the Demon Corps. He was a kind, gentle man, reflected in his soft tone and the way his eyes crinkled at the corners when he spoke as if there was a joke that only he knew.

His presence within the Cicatrix signaled that he had crossed the border.

But why?

That was the question she tried to get the answer to before Arlando had slithered into the room and destroyed everything.

His touch was poison. His very presence made her stomach roil. She thought she might throw up, and she secretly hoped she did. If only because she'd ruin his perfect white pants.

She had very little in her arsenal against him. He was a feral beast. A monster with the ability to change his form at will.

Phantom pains from his talons sinking into her tender flesh sent a spasm up her spine. She squeezed her eyes shut in a weak attempt to push the horrible memories aside.

The way he had rutted into her like a savage animal, bent only on his own release. The way his fangs sunk into her neck as she pleaded with him to stop—

Her stomach churned again, and she covered her mouth with her hand.

Arlando's gaze flashed with annoyance when he heard her gag. "Don't get sick on me," he growled, releasing her wrist from his grip and throwing her arm toward her to put distance between them. "Go over there if you're going to do it," he added, his upper lip curling in disgust.

Yari moved to the side, the part of her that valued survival winning out over the part of her that wanted to rebel against him. She didn't want him to punish her again. She didn't know if she'd survive it.

I'm such a coward.

Yari had always known this. Even her best friends had known it too, but they'd never say. Instead, Kiki sheltered her like a child, and Luna coddled her like a newborn lamb.

"Why are you doing this?" she asked softly, her voice still raw from her screams.

Arlando raised a brow as he turned to face her, the flames from the fire dancing across his angular features, making him look like the demon she knew him to be.

"Because I have to," he said with a puzzled expression, like he truly didn't understand why she'd even ask.

But she didn't understand. She didn't understand who this man was that stood before her. Where had the charming, caring man she'd come to know gone? How could this man, this monster, be the same person?

"You told me that you would help me." He turned to come closer, his hands clasped behind his back, his movements casual and slow. "When I asked if you thought doing anything to protect my kingdom was worth the cost, you told me 'yes' and that you'd help me."

He motioned to the bodies still laying prostrate on the floor. "This is the start."

She retreated a step back, the fire at her back lending her some much-needed warmth when everything inside her felt cold and dead. "I don't understand what you mean. How could hurting your brothers help Ozero?"

Arlando sighed heavily, his eyes raking over her from head to toe as he continued his predatory approach. "I once promised that I'd explain everything. I suppose now is as good a time as any."

He stood within a hair's breadth from her and tucked a stray strand of brown curly hair behind her ear. "Ozero is cursed. The only way to end the curse is for each of the Ozero princes to make a great sacrifice, an offering, a symbol of our repentance."

Nearby, Turi winced his eyes shut and turned his face away as if he couldn't bear to listen to the rest. Whatever it was, Turi was ashamed of his role in this. That much was clear to her.

"When I was a child, my father opened a portal to the demon realm. He summoned forth an army to defeat Ozero's enemies. But my mother did not want my father to wield more power than her.

"She was a witch, you see. A powerful witch. Respected. Feared even. She didn't like the idea of her husband having control over such a fearsome army."

He clenched his hands into fists, a vein bulging in his neck as if recounting the past infuriated him. "So she cast a spell that would punish my father. A curse. One that trapped his army within a curtain of darkness—darkness you've come to know as the Cicatrix. In her spite, she tied her curse to my father's life and the lives of his descendants.

"Like demons, we are cursed to live in the shadows, only becoming our human selves in the night. By day, we become something else. Demons that take on the shape of bears."

She shuddered at the memory of witnessing his shift before her very eyes into the creature he became. A towering beast with white fur, glowing blue eyes, talons longer than her pointer finger, and fangs that dripped with saliva as they neared her neck.

"My spiteful bitch of a mother sacrificed her life so that the curse could live. This is why my brothers and I must also offer up a sacrifice in order to break it. Blood for blood."

For a stupid moment, she wondered if she was hearing him correctly. Though he spoke simple enough words, nothing he said made sense.

"My mother was right about one thing, though," he said, his eyes gleaming with excitement, though for what reason, she couldn't discern. "Wielding control over a demon army would have made my father truly all-powerful. He would have been able to slay his enemies in a single day. The continent would have fallen to their knees in reverence and awe."

He's a lunatic. Unconsciously, Yari had started to shake her head at him. His idea for a new world was insane. No one could control the demons. They were senseless creatures. Driven by their need to feed and nothing more.

Seeing her retreating an inch, Arlando smirked, and his hand shot out. He grabbed her chin in his hand, his long fingers curling into her cheeks, pressing them together. "Do you doubt me?" he snarled.

She refused to answer him. Though she knew she'd regret it either way, the crazed look in his eyes revealed that it didn't matter what she said. Even if she lied. She'd angered him, and she'd pay for it soon enough.

Arlando released her cheeks with a growl and lifted his hand in front of her face. She recoiled, expecting him to strike her. But instead of the sharp sting she expected, she watched as he folded his fingers into a fist, leaving only the pointer finger up. A single talon pierced the skin at his knuckles, lengthening past the tip of his finger until it protruded six inches from his hand.

Please don't hurt me. A whine escaped her throat as he moved his talon toward her, inching closer and closer to her face until the tip pressed into the center of her forehead.

Sharp pain followed by blood trailing down her nose let her know he'd pierced her flesh. She held back a cry but could do nothing about the fresh tears that fell freely from her eyes and traveled in twin rivers down her face.

"Now, you can see," Arlando said, removing his talon from her forehead. He lifted the claw to his lips and drew his tongue along its length, lapping at her crimson blood.

She didn't understand what he meant. Nothing seemed different to her. Everything was the same—

Then she saw it.

At first, she thought it was just dancing shadows from the dying fire. But as her eyes adjusted, she realized that shadows did not move like that.

She whipped her head around, taking in the rest of the hall, and her skin blanched as dread pooled in her stomach.

No. It can't be. She shook her head in disbelief. Her eyes were playing tricks on her. There was no way—

Chapter Two

Yari

A creature crawled out of the shadows like it was born from her worst nightmares. There was no mistaking this beast that towered nearly seven feet tall for anything other than a demon.

The demon had the face of a wolf, and its lips curled back with a snarl while it glared out from beneath a mess of matted black hair. Blood-red eyes scanned the room as it slunk silently around the furniture, never letting anyone forget its presence.

Large goat horns sat atop its head, twisting towards the sky. Its body was human-like and covered in oil-black skin that glistened in the fire-light. Long arms hung at its sides like limp rags, its long claws stained with blood.

Feeling her gaze, the demon slowly turned its wolven head in her direction. Her heart raced as it opened its maw to reveal long, gleaming fangs that dripped with dark gooey saliva.

She stood paralyzed, unsure whether to run or stay put. Self-preservation won out, and she retreated several steps, backing into Arlando's chest on accident. She cringed when he wrapped his arms over her shoulders and pinned her into place against his body.

"Have no fear, mi amor," Arlando cooed. "They respond solely to me—complete submission. The perfect soldiers," he said, his voice laced with absolute awe.

"How is this possible?" she whispered, her voice trapped in her throat. She wasn't sure why she bothered to ask because she didn't think she really wanted to know why Arlando had a demon inside the castle. Or how it had gotten past the wards.

But it was so much worse than that, she quickly realized.

Her eyes darted around the hall, widening in fear, as the faint glow of candlelight illuminated the mostly barren hall, and she saw rows of grotesque figures lining the perimeter.

Demons stood sentinel as if awaiting their master's next instruction. Some were shaped like winged beasts, while others appeared mostly human, aside from their burning red eyes.

A chill ran through her body as she was overcome with dread, realizing that the creatures had been hiding in plain sight all along. She had to fight every urge not to run away, for she knew there was nowhere to hide from them.

I'm such a fool.

While Yari had thought she'd been quiet, slipping through the halls, eavesdropping on Arlando to know what was going on, the whole time, she'd been watched by demons!

No wonder he always knew where she was at. Why he had never seemed surprised to find her hiding in the shadows. He had spies everywhere. They probably guarded the door to her room even. Always informing him of her whereabouts.

She mustered the courage to speak, though her tongue was dry, and her skin crawled every time Arlando's breath ghosted across the shell of her ear. "I still don't understand. Why did you capture your brothers?"

"Because they are selfish and refuse to make the sacrifice required. This was the only way I could ensure the curse was broken. The only way to save my people from starvation and ruin."

Though she feared his answer. She knew she had to ask her next question. Even though everything in her body was rebelling against her.

Her stomach coiled into a painful knot, and her throat tightened as if her body refused to speak the words. "What is the sacrifice that you must make?"

She felt Arlando's smile tug at his lips as he pressed them to her ear. "The thing we love most in the world. Our mate."

There was the word again. Mate.

In the throws of passion, he'd called her his mate before. But that was back when she had thought he was someone else entirely. Now, she slowly realized what a complete idiot she had been.

"You mean me," she said softly, her words nothing more than a whisper.

"Yes," he murmured as he ran his teeth along the shell of her ear and bit down on the tender flesh, sending a sting of pain flaring at the spot.

"So this whole time. Everything you've ever said to me. It's all been a lie?" Dread washed over her, making her body feel weighed down. Her arms fell to her sides, limp and lifeless, much like the rest of her body and mind.

"Oh, but I do love you, Yari." He spun her in his arms so that she faced him. "You are my mate. I love you with my whole being."

He pressed his palm against her cool cheek, the tips of his fingers tracing a soft and tender pattern across her skin.

She wanted to jerk away from it because she knew his body had no tender bone. She knew the warmth in his eyes was a lie. As was the smile that tugged at his lips as he drank in her features. Lies. All of it.

She couldn't bear to look at him anymore. She winced when his calloused fingertips brushed softly across her lips.

He released a long exhale in what she thought might be regret. "But a King puts his people above all others, including his own selfish wants and desires. Your sacrifice will break the chains on my kingdom. My people will hail you as a saint. You and the other sacrifices, you will be Ozero's saviors."

I did not ask to be a savior, she thought sourly.

Anger and fear battled within her, both emotions so strong she felt like she might combust. Acrid heat filled her chest, and her hands trembled. She took a few deep breaths, trying to quell the tension that spread through her body like wildfire. But it was no use.

A wave of rage surged through her body that had her spinning in the direction of the man she had once considered her friend.

"You!" she cried, turning her anger on Turi. "You're okay with this? With him killing me?"

Turi's eyes seemed to drain of color as he slowly turned his gaze toward her. He looked at her with an expression of apathy before turning his attention back to the fireplace, where he stoked the flames with an iron poker. "I trust my brother," he replied, his voice like sheets of ice battering against her skin.

Yari's heart felt like it was made of ash, and his blunt words were the sharp breeze that sent it crumbling into dust.

After all these years, their friendship meant nothing to him?

She had to get out of this place. She didn't know where she'd go. All she knew was that she didn't have an ally in Turi.

When Arlando had brought her back to the castle from the cabin in the woods — incidentally, the very place that had been haunting her nightmares for weeks — she had been relieved when she saw Turi waiting for them to return.

She had wanted nothing more than to rush into his protective arms and shelter herself inside someone she trusted. He was familiar. A vestige of Kiki and Luna. A comforting balm for her weary and battered soul.

But she hadn't been allowed to do any such thing. Arlando had been keeping a firm hold on her ever since she and him returned to the castle to find Turi already here. When he didn't have his hands or eyes on her, he locked her in his room with a warning to stay quiet.

The harsh reality that her inherent trust in Turi had been so severely misplaced was like a dagger to the heart. If he refused to save her, then she would have to do it herself.

She may be a coward. May be more prone to freeze when danger first presented itself. May even be more likely to hide behind another out of sheer terror. But she refused to stand here and be a complicit bystander to the crumbling pieces of her life.

She had nothing to defend herself with. No supplies. No idea where she'd be going.

But she had to try.

With her heart thundering and adrenaline pulsing, she jerked her body from Arlando's grip and raced to the tall doors at the front of the castle. Her feet echoed on the cold marble floor as she flew across the grand foyer.

She had barely taken four steps when a hand wound in her long, dark brown curls and jerked her back. Her feet slipped from beneath her, sending her flying into the air. She landed hard on her back, feeling the breath knocked from her lungs as the force of the impact echoed through her entire body.

Arlando's eyes were icy, and his expression was a thundercloud as he towered over Yari. He jabbed a finger in her direction and said, "That wasn't very nice of you, Yarixa. You should know better than that." His voice was low, almost reminding her of a parent scolding an unruly child.

Her eyes settled on Turi, a hulking statue silhouetted by the flames that danced in the mantle. He didn't turn to look at her, but she still felt the weight of his presence and the chill of his silence.

She knew he could sense her gaze and understand her desperation, yet here he was, unmoving and unresponsive.

Her heart sank as she watched him—no—foolishly waited for him to do something. Anything.

She didn't understand why she was still looking to him for help. It was clear where he stood.

Perhaps her misguided feelings were part of some residual trust from the years she'd thought they'd been friends.

Arlando's grip was like iron, and with a violent yank, he pulled her from the floor by her hair, sending searing pain through her scalp. Her sharp cry cut through the air, and still, Turi didn't look up.

"Now I'll have to punish you," Arlando said, his voice slithering over her skin like a viper.

He dragged her by her hair. Her furious screams echoed off the walls and vibrated through her body as she kicked and tried to pry his hands from her hair to ease the ripping pain. Arlando paid no mind to her thrashing as he hauled her to the towering staircase that would take them to the upper floor.

He briefly stopped, halfway up the stairs, to glance down at the defeated forms still sprawled on the floor.

"Take them to the dungeon," he ordered the demons congregated in the hall. "Put them in the cages I showed you."

Five demons with bull-like heads and inky, leathery skin lumbered into the hall's center. They lifted the sleeping men by their feet and dragged them away.

Almost as an afterthought, Arlando spun around and added, "Don't eat them. You'll get your reward soon enough. I have something I need to take care of." He turned his feral grin on her, and she recoiled.

The demons grunted in response before continuing their task.

"Is now the best time to play with your toy?" Turi's voice echoed in the cavernous hall. He stood at the bottom of the stairs, his hand curled around the railing.

She hadn't noticed when he had moved. She frowned down at his face—a mask of hardened steel.

Arlando growled low in the back of his throat. "You're right, brother. Of course, you are. I'm letting my barbaric beastly desires get the best of me. But there is much work to do."

He pushed her up the stairs, causing her to stumble and land against the edges with a grunt of pain.

"Take her to my room and stand guard at the door," he ordered a nearby demon.

A demon with a human face but elongated limbs lurked toward her and grabbed her arm.

"Do not touch her!" Arlando screeched.

The demon released her arm as if she were the sun, and it had just been scorched by the contact.

"Never touch her," Arlando growled at the demon. "She's mine."

Out of her peripheral, she thought she saw Turi's knuckles turning white against the railing, but he removed his hand and shoved it into his pocket.

She must be imagining things.

Clearly, he didn't care for her anymore.

CHAPTER THREE

ERASMO

Erasmo shifted his weight, slowly lifting an eyelid to let in a sliver of the gray light. The room was heavy with silence and cool air pressed against his skin. His neck ached from the awkward angle at which he had slept on the hard floor.

Beneath him, prickly hay scratched his back. He cursed and rolled onto his side, wincing through half-closed eyes as the sharp straw poked at his skin.

As he lifted himself from the ground, he saw that he was in a dark dungeon buried deep within the Winter Keep.

The musty smell of mildew filled his nostrils, and the cold stone walls were damp to the touch. As he looked around, he realized there were no windows and only one wooden door with a rusted lock.

It had been many years since he'd last come here, and it looked very different now than it did back then. Still, there was no denying that Arlando had tossed him into the wretched place on purpose.

Fuck!

He clenched his teeth, feeling a deep rage boiling within him. With an angry yell, he grabbed a fistful of straw and threw it across the cage, watching with narrowed eyes as it scattered and drifted back to the floor.

He squinted, and upon closer inspection, he saw that all four sides of his prison cell were enclosed with steel bars, locked together in a crisscross pattern that ran all the way up and bolted into the ceiling.

He ran his fingers along the firm metal slats—they were too narrowly spaced apart, and even if he were a small man, not even a child would be able to squeeze through them.

Fuck you, Arlando. He sneered and pounded his fist against the bars. His brother hadn't just tossed him into a cell. No. He'd dumped him into a cage, like some kind of animal.

As he continued his inspection, his stomach pooling with dread by the minute, his eyes snagged on the two sleeping forms in the adjacent cages.

His heart skipped a beat in relief at the sight of Bernat and Mauri. They looked unharmed, if not a bit disheveled. Their deep breaths let him know they were, at least, alive, and for now, that was enough.

They hadn't come around yet, and he knew from personal experience that there was no point in trying to wake them until the sedative wore off.

He turned slowly in his cage, his gaze taking in the low burning torches spaced evenly along the walls, providing a dim flickering light.

The air was heavy with the smell of feces and fear and the unmistakable tang of coppery blood. Bile rose in the back of his throat at the stench of despair that hung in the air.

The walls of the dungeon were hewn from coarse stone held together by mortar, the surface stained with blood from previous prisoners and victims. The dripping of water echoed through the hollow space in a rhythmic pattern, setting his nerves on edge.

Metal tables lined the center of the space, their surfaces cluttered with various torture implements, most of which he'd never seen before.

Long rods with pointed ends. Wicked curved blades with sharp projections along the spine. Small phallic metal cages. It all made Erasmo's skin crawl. He did not want to know what those were used for.

But he had the nagging feeling that he was going to find out.

He clenched his jaw and balled his fists, his chest heaving as the heat of indignation rose from the pit of his stomach.

Arlando had been waiting for him. His joint attack with Turi's help was too coordinated to be anything but carefully premeditated.

The worst part was that Arlando had turned Turi against him. He felt the betrayal deep in his bones.

Family was supposed to be a safe space. Even when he and Arlando hadn't seen eye to eye, they had never resorted to imprisoning the other. Caging them like they were nothing more than animals for slaughter was a new level of low.

Erasmo felt his brother's betrayal like a dagger to his heart. It felt more painful that his own twin was doing this to him. They'd shared a womb together. They'd done everything together—

He curled his hands into fists and let out a soul-shaking roar that echoed through the dungeon as he pounded his fists against the metal bars. The veins in his arms bulged with every blow as he screamed and pounded the cold steel cage bars.

Damn you, brother. Damn you and Turi, too!

His knuckles bled, yet he continued to throw punch after punch, each shaking the metal with thunderous force. Blood coated his fists and splattered across his cheeks.

The pain barely registered in his mind; his only thoughts on how he would escape and relish in tearing out Arlando's throat with his fangs.

"Will you shut the fuck up?" a groggy voice croaked.

Erasmo whirled around to see Mauri in the cage to his right, rolling onto his side and pushing himself to a seat.

"Mauri!" he exclaimed, relief washing over him.

His cousin lifted a finger to his lips, making a 'shhh' motion against his lips.

Erasmo's eyes bowed with a lopsided grin. "I'm glad to see being caged like swine hasn't changed your sense of humor."

"Fuck, my head is killing me," Mauri groaned while he scooted himself to lean against the cage bars. He turned his head to look up at Erasmo. "Where the fuck are we?"

"The dungeon," he replied. "Though Arlando's made some alterations since we were last here."

Mauri huffed. "Clearly." He wrapped his meaty hand around one of the bars. "You think we can bust out if we shift?"

A devilish grin twisted his lips. "Only one way to find out."

Erasmo released the dark, twisting shadows that lay buried beneath his skin. Tendrils of black smoke whirled around him as his body shifted, his back bowed, and his palms slammed into the ground. The pain of the shift forced a growl to vibrate past his lips.

His nose lengthened into a snout, and black fur sprouted along his growing form. He felt his ribs breaking one by one as they expanded to reform his body.

He panted through the pain, letting it roll over him like a tidal wave until his body settled.

"You're such a showoff," Mauri said, waving a dismissive hand in the air.

"Excuse me?" He projected his thoughts so Mauri would hear.

"You heard me. You always shift like you're in some half-rate perfor-mance. All that panting and huffing. And then when you're done, you do this posing thing." Mauri shifted until he was on all fours and made a ridiculous gesture with his head.

"I do not pose."

"You kind of do, though."

"Fuck you. The moment I get out of here, I'm going to swallow your nasty ass and then spit you back out for the demons to play with."

"Oh yeah? Well, you have to get me first."

I see what he's doing. He shook his head wryly. Mauri was trying to rile him up. Get him angry so he can bust them out of here.

But he didn't need his cousin's help to get angry. He was so much farther beyond mere anger. He was furious. Pure unbridled hatred ran through his veins like molten lava.

He would make Arlando pay for this.

He took a few steps back, and with a terrifying growl, he charged the cage's metal bars.

The sheer force of his body against the steel bars caused it to rattle and quake, yet still, it stayed in place. He stumbled back a few steps, attempting to shake off the ringing in his skull and the pain in his fangs as they clattered together.

I just have to try again.

He threw his body against the metal bars, gritting his teeth and pushing with all his might. Pain shot through his shoulder as he made contact, radiating out and filling him with a rage-fueled determination.

Hollow reverberations rang through the air, but the metal was still just as impenetrable as when he started. There wasn't even a dent.

Fuuuuck!!!

A feral roar ripped through his throat as he hurled himself against the metal bars of the cell, bellowing in fury. He did it over. And over. And over.

His paws bled, and his shoulders became pulps of raw meat from the repeated impacts, but he never felt it. His fury was too much, too all-consuming to let him feel anything else.

All he could see was Arlando's satisfied expression when he'd crumpled to the ground, tricked and drugged.

With every blow he struck at the bars, a deep-seated resentment bubbled up inside.

He heard a distant voice repeating his name, but he ignored it. He had to get out of here.

A hand darted between the bars and yanked on a tuft of his fur. "Raz! Stop, you're hurting yourself."

He paused, furrowing his brows in confusion as he realized the hay was damp with what appeared to be blood.

His head spun, and he stumbled back, panting for breath. He felt a warm liquid trickle down his snout and wiped it away, only to find that it, too, was tinged red.

"They're too strong," Mauri said as he released his grip on Erasmo.

The sting of defeat coiled in his chest, and he reigned in the shadows, feeling his body shift back into his human form.

It was always the shift into a bear that hurt like a bitch. The other way around was easy in comparison.

Exhaling a painful gasp, Erasmo hunched forward in his human form, the blood from the wound on his shoulder and face oozing to the floor, soaking the hay. His mouth filled with the coppery tang of blood, and he spat it into the straw.

"What is the bastard planning?" he murmured, more to himself than directing the question to Mauri.

"Are you seriously asking that question?" Mauri asked, his brows drawn in tight. When Erasmo didn't respond, he added, "We're the bait. Obviously."

"It was rhetorical, you prick."

"Now you tell me," Mauri muttered.

Erasmo shook his head. "It's too simple. Arlando would know that we have the entire garrison at La Aguilera, and our forces would rally in a heartbeat to come to rescue us. He can't seriously think he can hold them off all by himself."

Mauri shrugged. "He's an arrogant ass wipe. I wouldn't put it past him."

A smooth and cultured voice pierced the darkness, and Arlando stepped out from the shadows of the dungeon. "It's such a comfort to see how little you've developed over the years, cousin."

Chapter Four

Kiki

The last sliver of darkness faded from the morning sky, leaving it a crisp and empty blue. A chill settled in the air as Kiki waited for Erasmo's return to camp.

She sat propped up with a bundle of furs draped over her legs and watched the campfire's orange flames dance.

She had been waiting for Erasmo to return with Mauri and Bernat, and hopefully Turi, since daybreak, and despite the way the hours crawled by, her faith in his return never faltered.

She knew Erasmo wouldn't return to their camp until he had the needed answers. She also knew that if Arlando was reluctant to provide those answers, Erasmo had no problem extracting information using force.

Or rather, his enforcer, Mauri, would be the one to do it. In any case, she didn't worry for his safety because he had taken both Mauri and Bernat with him.

Together, with Kiki and Solana's help, they had all fended off a horde of demons.

Arlando was nothing to fear in comparison to that.

Though the storm had passed, a chill wind cut through the canvas of the tent, sending goosebumps along her skin. She tucked herself tightly beneath the heavy fur blankets, snuggling deep into their soft warmth.

Luna lay with her head resting on a bundled blanket, deeply asleep on the ground beside her. Her face was relaxed, and her eyes were closed, a line of drool finding its way from the corner of her mouth to the blankets beneath her head. A soft snore rumbled from her lips, and Kiki smiled fondly at the sight.

Her friend needed as much rest as she could get. After saving Kiki's life and nearly killing everyone in order to do it, or so Mauri said, her energy stores needed replenishing. The only way a Healer could regain their strength was plenty of food and rest, no shortcuts for the very people who could save one from the brink of death.

Solana paced near the tent's entrance, her hands balled into fists and her expression filled with worry. She was a glacier of beauty in her fitted Slayer leathers, contrasting sharply against her blazing red curls cascading over her shoulders and framing her intense icy-blue eyes.

Kiki watched with increasing disbelief as the usually stoic Commander continued to pace back and forth, her hands clasped behind her back. Her jaw was set firmly, and her eyes flashed with unspoken emotion.

Kiki wasn't used to seeing the Commander express so much emotion, or any emotion for that matter. Seeing Solana pace around made her stomach lurch, and she shifted nervously, unsure of what to expect from this unpredictable display.

"Would you please sit down?" Kiki hissed, keeping her voice low. "You're making me jumpy, and you'll wake Luna if you keep strutting around like that."

Solana whirled on her heel, her hands on her hips. "I'm not strutting—oh, never mind," she growled and fixed her attention on the black pot hanging over the low-burning fire.

She grabbed a small, palm-sized bowl and dipped it into the pot. Luna's gentle snores filled the space as she maneuvered around her sleeping form and nimbly climbed onto Kiki's side of the makeshift bed, carefully balancing the bowl in one hand as she tucked herself under the heavy furs.

She held the bowl out in front of Kiki, her expression stern and expectant. "You need to eat," she said, the command in her voice unmistakable.

Kiki pressed her lips together in a tight line and shook her head. "I told you earlier. I'm not hungry."

"You need to eat," Solana said, her voice low and firm. "I'm not asking; I'm telling you—take it."

Kiki crossed her arms over her chest and turned her head away from Solana, well aware of the fact that she looked like a petulant child.

Solana huffed as she balanced the bowl of steaming soup in her lap. "Saints, Xochicale," she muttered. "Why does everything have to be a fight with you?"

Kiki's mouth curled in annoyance. "When I told you to stop pacing, that wasn't an invitation to come and mother me instead," she whispered sharply.

"If I wanted to mother you, I would have left you at La Aguilera for being woefully unprepared to go out into the field," the Commander retorted.

Kiki's jaw clenched, and her fists balled at her sides. She faced Solana, her dark eyes filled with indignation.

"Unprepared?" Kiki asked, her voice a menacing whisper. Her fingers trembled as she yanked up the sleeves of her leathers to reveal rows of stars along both wrists. Each one marked a demon killed in battle when she'd served in the Demon Corps.

"Is this what you call 'woefully unprepared'?" Kiki spat, her face flushed with rage. "What are these then? Huh? Just pretty little decorations?"

Solana's tone was heavy with disapproval as she glanced down at Kiki's tattoos. "They're a visual representation of how big your ego has gotten," she said. "Otherwise, you would have been more careful and not gotten hurt the way you did."

Kiki could still feel the stinging pain from where the demon had pierced her gut with its poison-laced claws. She remembered their sickening squelch as the demon ripped its talons from her body. The way the snow turned crimson as her blood pooled around her.

Solana lifted the bowl of soup and shoved it into Kiki's hands. "Eat. Or else Luna's efforts to heal you will have gone in vain, and we'll be stuck here longer than necessary while we wait for you to be well enough to travel."

Kiki's face heated with shame at the Commander's harsh words. Though her wounds were healed, the rest of her body still needed time to recover. Luna only had the strength to banish the poison running through her blood, but that meant removing the infected blood, leaving Kiki weak. And she hated feeling weak.

Ordinarily, Luna would be able to replenish the lost blood, but she'd used nearly all her strength and the strength of the others to rip Kiki from the brink of death.

Kiki supposed that meant that Solana needed time to recover, too, for her part in saving Kiki's life, which meant that Kiki owed the Commander. That was a sentiment she liked even less than being weak.

"Fine. But only because I want to get as far away from you as quickly as possible," Kiki snapped.

"Whatever you have to tell yourself so you can sleep at night," Solana grumbled. She wriggled further under the blankets, turning her back so she faced away from Kiki, and tucked her arm under her head.

The smell of rosemary, thyme, and oregano filled her nostrils as she lifted the bowl to her lips. She sipped the warm broth and felt it spread throughout her body, giving her a sense of comfort. With her fingers, she picked out chunks of chicken, carrots, celery, and potatoes from the delicious stew.

It seemed all the Ozero men knew how to cook, seeing that Bernat had made the food last night before heading out with Erasmo and Mauri to confront Arlando.

She certainly had a deep appreciation for men who could cook.

"Wake me if you need another bowl," Solana murmured over her shoulder, her wavering voice betraying her exhaustion.

Kiki scoffed, "I can get more myself if I need it."

"Whatever you say."

Solana slipped into sleep before Kiki could even finish the soup. Sandwiched between Luna and Solana, the lure of sleep tugged at Kiki's eyelids.

She should get some rest and recover, as Solana suggested. The rest of the trip to Arlando's estate would have to be on foot since the demon attack had scared off the horses, and none had returned. That had been a little over a day ago.

Kiki sighed and looked out through the small opening of the tent at the vast expanse of snow-covered land. Memories of her time in the

Demon Corps swirled around her like a cloud—the long nights patrolling, the grueling physical demands of training so her body could handle the life-and-death battle against a demon, and her friends supporting her through it all.

With the good memories came the bad ones too. It seemed like Kiki had been counting down the days until graduation just yesterday. Things had really gone to shit since then.

She could still see the aftermath of the demon attack on Norcera when she closed her eyes. Crumpled bodies lined the ramparts of the Wall and littered the streets of their base camp. How she stumbled through the rubble filled with broken wood, twisted obsidian, and settling ash, searching desperately for Yarixa, her tender-hearted best friend.

The stillness of the aftermath, the grim reality that Yari had been abducted by the very demons who'd laid waste to their base camp. A theory that Solana later confirmed when Norcera had been attacked shortly after and more of their people had gone missing.

To add to all of that, it was just a few days ago that she learned of her mate bond with Erasmo, the third Ozero prince. A sudden wave of emotion swept through her as she remembered the feel of his hands gripping hers tightly as she lay on the brink of death. How she feared she'd never hear his laughter again, feel his warmth wrapped around her, or kiss his lips.

Her knuckles turned white from clutching the edge of the fur blanket too tight. She pried her fingers open and sucked in a deep calming breath.

She just hoped Erasmo would return soon so they could figure out how to break the curse affecting the Ozero princes so she could resume her search for Yari.

As her mind swirled with chaotic memories, her eyes drooped, and she felt herself drift off to sleep.

She hadn't been asleep for long when agonizing pain ripped through her chest, like a demon's talons, shredding her skin and sinking into her heart.

She lurched awake, her hand frantically grabbing her chest. Next to her, both Luna and Solana sat straight up, their bodies mirroring her own. Whatever had just happened, all three of them had felt it. At the same time.

Meaning—

Another sharp pain pierced Kiki's ribs, and the breath whooshed out of her lungs. It was as if a phantom stood over her with a hot fire poker, jabbing her in the ribs.

"Something's wrong," Kiki wheezed, her eyes darting between Luna and Solana, her own panic mirrored in their expressions.

Kiki didn't know how to explain it, but a wave of fear washed over her. Erasmo was in trouble. Bernat and Mauri too.

Chapter Five

Erasmo

Erasmo crossed his arms over his chest, refusing to allow his twin to see him unsettled. Turi trailed in after Arlando, his eyes cast to the floor, refusing to look Erasmo in the eyes.

Mauri bared his teeth in a snarl, his eyes dragging up the length of Arlando's form before his lips curled back in disgust. "And you're still a lonely, blood-sucking waste of air. Guess some things never change."

Arlando chuckled darkly. "Call me whatever you need in order to assuage your own petty feelings. You're only here because I recently learned you found your mate."

A growl tore from Mauri's throat, and his eyes flashed red at the mention of Luna. "If you lay a finger on her—"

"Oh, spare me your useless threats," Arlando cut him off, waving his hand dismissively in the air. "You have no power here."

Erasmo's skin prickled at his twin's sheer confidence. It grated on him that Arlando thought he'd already won. He knew that Arlando liked to play games and that anything his twin said had to be taken with a grain of salt..

"Why are we here, brother?" Erasmo's lips curled back unconsciously at the word 'brother.'

Arlando clasped his hands behind his back as he approached the cages, stopping several feet away and out of Erasmo's reach should he try to grab him. "Your dog already figured it out," he said, jerking his chin toward Mauri.

Mauri huffed at being called Erasmo's dog. It was a derogatory term people liked to fling at him to tear him down. But Erasmo valued loyalty, and there was no one he trusted more than his cousin.

"Since you're clearly too stupid to figure it out for yourself, let me lay it out for you, *brother*," Arlando taunted, adding extra emphasis to the word 'brother.'

Arlando moved to the metal tables lined with torture devices and picked up a metal rod. He pushed a button at the bottom, and the tip of the rod crackled with lighting between two smaller nodules. "Your mates are nearby. I can sense them the same as I can sense when any of our kind is near."

Erasmo frowned, not understanding how this was possible. He was familiar with the invisible thread that tied him to his brothers, a line that he'd felt pull taut during their first shifts once they crossed the Cicatrix.

And he was even familiar with the thread that connected him to Kiki, having been able to sense his mate his whole life, especially after puberty.

But the thing that puzzled him most was this notion of being able to sense the other mates. That was something he didn't know was possible.

At that moment, Arlando turned and gave Erasmo a derisive smile. "I can tell by the dumbfounded look on your face you don't know what I'm talking about." He moved closer to Erasmo's cage, the crackling metal rod still in his hand. "You see, I've known where the mates are for a very long time. It's amazing what a little blood and the right spell can get you."

He gritted his teeth at the casual way Arlando spoke about blood magic. If it wasn't clear that Arlando had fallen off the deep end, descended into madness, and any shred of his humanity had been stripped away, then Erasmo's suspicions were confirmed by his brother's frequent use of blood magic and the way his hair had been drained of all its color. When he'd last seen Arlando, his hair was just beginning to bear silver streaks. Erasmo had thought it was because of the curse. But now, he knew otherwise.

"The best part about it was that I knew who each of your mates was before even you did. Sure, you could sense them, but you didn't *know* them. Didn't know their personalities. What they looked like. Where they lived."

He casually waved the metal rod in front of the cage, like he was having a mundane conversation over a glass of pulque. "Imagine my delight when I learned that your mates were friends. I couldn't have planned it better myself. All I needed was a way to bring them into the Cicatrix. The real problem was figuring out the right lure."

Arlando tapped his chin, exaggerating his motions to emphasize his words. "It had to be something that all of them would support. Or at least, one of them would be too stubborn to let go of."

Dread swirled in Erasmo's gut, thinking he knew where Arlando was going with this. But he had to hear it from his twin's lips. He had to know just how much Arlando had been manipulating the scales in order for them to tip in his favor.

"That's where your mate came in," Arlando said, pointing a slender finger at Erasmo. "She's bull-headed, that one," he said, a note of admiration in his tone. "There was only one way I could be sure she'd risk it all. Only one person she cared about more than her own life."

He shut his eyes, knowing what Arlando would say before he did.

When he first met Kiki, she'd revealed why she had ventured into the darkness. To rescue her best friend.

"Yarixa," Arlando crooned in a sing-song voice. "The key to it all," he added, his lips twisting into a wide grin. "I went to her camp while she was on duty one night and marked her for myself. Unfortunately, your mate made a mark on me as well." Arlando shifted his collar to the side to reveal a jagged scar.

Erasmo felt a surge of pride swell in his chest, knowing that Kiki had been the one to put it there. The Demon Slayers fought with obsidian, and it was the only weapon he and the others like him couldn't heal from if cut.

Arlando covered his scar and smoothed out his shirt. "I waited two years for your mate to leave Yari's side. I couldn't risk another wound from her. But I'm nothing if not a patient man. So I waited for the perfect opportunity."

Understanding washed over him as Erasmo came to the full realization of just how long his twin had been tugging on the strings of their lives. "You had Yari kidnapped from the Demon Corps camp in Norcera." It wasn't a question. He wanted to hear his twin confirm it...

"Indeed." Arlando strutted in front of the cell, his lips twisted in thought. "It was only a matter of time before your mate came running in after Yarixa, bringing Bernat's mate with her."

There was only one problem with Arlando's plan. Turi's mate. He still hadn't found her, and since Arlando's plan hinged on luring in Kiki and Solana, then Turi's mate, whoever they were, seemed more difficult to reach.

Relief washed over him at that. If Turi's mate stayed out of Arlando's grasp, the curse couldn't be broken, and Kiki would remain safe.

Arlando's blue eyes flashed when he noticed Erasmo's shoulders shaking with laughter.

"There is only one problem with your plan, brother," Erasmo sneered. "You don't have all the mates. You can't perform the ceremony without her."

Any sense of victory Erasmo felt quickly faded at the smile that tugged at his brother's lips. His eyes glittered like he knew something that Erasmo didn't.

Arlando drawled, "It's a good thing Mauri found his mate then. She will make a suitable substitute."

Mauri threw himself at the cage's bars, a deafening growl echoing through the dungeon.

At all the noise, Bernat groaned awake, rolling onto his back in the cage to Erasmo's left.

Seeing him wake, Arlando said, "Oh good, now we can start."

Start what? Erasmo felt a wave of dread wash over him as his muscles tensed, weighing him down like an anchor. He fought against it, hoping to keep himself afloat, but the anxiety kept rising, threatening to engulf him and drag him under.

As if things weren't bad enough, he feared what his brother had in store for them next.

"Bring her in," Arlando called over his shoulder.

A metal door groaned open, and a guard with a muddied face pulled the little woman with curly, brown hair through.

She grimaced as the guard tugged on her tresses to move her forward. Two more guards followed close behind. Their faces were equally swathed in shadows and indiscernible. The woman sobbed as the guards roughly handled her. She wasn't resisting, yet they still treated her like a spitting and hissing alley cat.

When she lifted her gaze to meet his own, the icy sting of horror washed over him, like he had been dropped into a freezing northern river and was being dragged downstream.

He had seen that hollow look before on the faces of victims of sexual violence. It was a look he never wanted to see again, but there it was, in her eyes, staring at him, pleading with him to help her.

A pit opened in his stomach at the fear in her eyes, and regret washed over him, knowing that his own twin had been responsible for her suffering.

The guard's strong arms held her around the waist as he dragged her through the dungeon's darkness. Her bare feet stumbled on uneven stones until they reached Arlando, where he released his grip, and she slumped to her knees. Silent sobs shook her shoulders as she tried to hold in her tears.

The veins in Erasmo's neck bulged, and his breath sawed in and out from his chest. He thought if he weren't stuck inside this cage, he'd rip out his brother's throat for his crimes against this woman alone.

"What have you done to her?" Erasmo asked through clenched teeth.

It sickened him to see her this way. It should have sickened his brother. The mate bond was sacred. Their mates were precious. Harming his mate should be impossible. Unfathomable.

"She is none of your concern," Arlando responded, not bothering to look at the woman puddled at his feet.

"It should disgust you to treat her this way," he spat.

"She is MINE, and I will do with her what I please, whenever I please. She belongs to ME!" Arlando roared, getting too close to the cage.

Erasmo darted his hand through the bars and latched onto his twin's jacket, balling it tightly into his fist.

He yanked Arlando forward, fully intending to bash his twin's face into the bars and hoping the impact in his human form would be enough to knock him out.

But that was a fool's dream.

Arlando quickly pivoted the metal rod in his hand and stabbed it into Erasmo's ribs.

"FUCK!" Erasmo roared as he felt a spark of purple fire stab into him, burning away his breath and spreading out through his torso like liquid flame. It felt as if he were being ripped open.

He collapsed to the ground, writhing.

Arlando adjusted the lapels of his finely tailored white jacket, and a smirk spread across his face. He gestured to the strange device in his hand.

"Very clever, brother," he murmured, and Erasmo thought he detected a hint of admiration lingering in his tone. "Pity that you had to learn how this device works the hard way. I was really hoping I'd have the pleasure of demonstrating how I intend on luring your mates here."

Arlando grabbed Yarixa's arm and pulled her from the floor, a cry of shock flying from her lips. His rough grip left a red welt on her tan skin, and he tugged forcefully at the neckline of her dress, exposing her delicate collarbones.

Looking at Erasmo, then to Bernat, and finally at Mauri, he said, "Did you know that if enough pain is endured, the mate can feel it on the other end of the bond?"

The dungeon fell so quiet that Erasmo swore he could hear the sound of his own heartbeat. His brain worked to comprehend Arlando's words.

It was hard for him to grasp his brother's ability to be cruel to his own mate, so it took him longer than the others to understand what his twin was implying.

"No!" Bernat roared, throwing himself at the bars. "Yari, run!" He yelled as he yanked and rammed his body against the bars of his cage. "Don't let him—"

Yarixa winced her eyes shut and hung limply in Arlando's grip. He pressed the button on the rod again, and purple lightning crackled between those tiny nodules.

"A demonstration," Arlando said, and before he could press the rod to her neck, he dropped her to the ground and shoved the device into his own neck.

Searing heat radiated from the metal rod and immediately caused his exposed skin to turn bright red, with little bubbles of flesh popping and hissing on contact. But he seemed oblivious to the pain, laughing maniacally with a wide grin as if he were enjoying this.

Instead, Yarixa erupted with a blood-curdling scream, her hands scrambling toward her own neck, where blood welled and gushed down her chest.

"Stop this!" Erasmo demanded, pulling himself to his feet. "Enough!"

Yarixa's agonized scream filled the dungeon, and he couldn't bear to hear the sound of it a moment longer. He couldn't understand how Arlando was even able to bring himself to do it. She was his mate. Such cruelty shouldn't be possible.

Bernat dropped to the floor of his cell and reached out his arm toward Yari, his fingers splayed against the ground as he tried to push himself through the bars to touch her hand.

"Eyes on me, Yari, eyes on me," he whispered to the woman, his eyes glistening with tears. "Focus on me, sweetie. Block out the pain."

Arlando cackled at Bernat's display of comfort, and he removed the rod from his neck, revealing a black scorch mark on his skin, his wound already healing.

Yarixa fell into a sobbing heap, blood gushing from her hands from the twin burn. She, however, was not healing, not having rapid healing powers like Arlando.

Erasmo clenched his teeth, seething with rage. "You're going to regret this, brother," he warned, his tone laced with the threat of violence.

Arlando merely grinned as he brought the rod closer to Erasmo's cage, the purple flames crackling with heat. "I highly doubt that. But I so enjoy hearing your pathetic attempts to threaten me."

CHAPTER SIX

LUNA

Pain lanced through Luna's neck like a bolt of white-hot lightning, and the scent of charred meat wafted up from her blistered flesh. Gritting her teeth, she pressed her palm against the wound and let a wave of energy course through her veins, healing the injury instantly.

A wave of dizziness assaulted her as she released the spell, and her arms fell limp at her sides. The small space within the tent swam before her eyes as she sank onto the fur pelts with a groan. The back of her neck tingled where a bead of sweat had trickled down, and she cursed herself for using her magic so soon after healing Kiki.

It had only been half a day since she healed Kiki, but the spell, combined with the amount of energy she used, had left her weaker than usual.

In the bedroll next to her, Kiki gasped and gritted her teeth, the pain of her own injury temporarily forgotten as she desperately flung aside the heavy blankets. She kicked the furs away frantically in her attempt to be at Luna's side.

Solana reacted faster than Kiki. The Commander's hard-soled boots thudded against the frozen ground as she kneeled beside Luna. She lifted the tawny furs, re-tucking them around Luna to keep her warm.

"Rest," the Commander ordered, her voice gentle but firm. Her gaze pinned Luna frozen in place like a butterfly on display, her ice-blue eyes glowing with authority.

Kiki finally freed herself of the pile of furs, yanking them from her legs with a string of curses. She scooted close to Luna, her brows tight with anxiety.

"Why'd you do that?" she asked, her voice laced with concern. She searched for a cloth and dipped it into a bowl of water that had been left out for such purposes. She wrung out the excess liquid and brought it to Luna's forehead, gently dabbing away at the beads of sweat.

Luna's voice was a dry, raspy croak. "Force of habit," she said, her eyes shut tight against the stinging thirst.

Solana moved quickly, grabbing a skin of water and bringing it to Luna's lips.

Luna sipped slowly, the cool liquid soothing her throat and helping to ease her parched tongue. She knew that taking too much at once could make her sick.

Kiki crossed her arms over her chest and shot a stern glare at Luna. "You're too weak to be using your magic yet."

Luna smirked, her eyes sparkling. "Really? I hadn't noticed."

Kiki blew out a breath and rolled her eyes, but there was fondness in the curl of her lips.

"Smartass," she mumbled before taking the cloth back and soaking it again.

Solana carefully pulled a clean, white linen from the stack and handed it to Kiki. "For your neck," she said in a gentle voice. She reached for another piece of linen, wincing as she lifted her arm, and pressed it against her own wound.

Luna couldn't help but smile at their interaction. In the short time, they'd been traveling together, the Commander and Kiki were slowly warming toward one another.

In many ways, they were two sides of the same coin. Where Kiki was a burning inferno, quick to anger and passionate, Solana was her opposite, a frozen landscape, hard to read and calculated. Despite their differences on the surface, there was one thing both women valued and honored above all else, family.

And their rag-tag group was nothing if not a familial unit. They each depended on one another and relied on each other to survive.

Though each of them had lost their family when the Cicatrix descended upon the kingdom, they'd each undertaken the challenge of filling that hole within themselves.

Luna had found Kiki and Yarixa. Solana had found the Demon Corps. But now, those families had been threatened, and the lines between the two were becoming blurred.

She thought that Kiki and Solana put up a good act in the way they paraded their dedication to the Corps. And in many ways, they were. They had the stars tattooed on their wrists to prove it. But when the dust had settled, Kiki had left the Corps to find Yarixa, and, in turn, Solana had left to find Kiki.

That the two of them were getting along in their own way brought a smile to Luna's face. Though she'd never be stupid enough to bring it up to either of them, or else she'd risk getting her eyes clawed out by Kiki and being iced out by Solana, she was glad they were softening to each other.

"What the hell was that about?" Kiki winced as she dabbed the weeping wound on the side of her neck.

"It's the bond," Solana replied, shuffling toward her pack as she began to rifle through it.

Luna knew without a doubt that Solana was right. She could feel Mauri's pain through the bond like it was her own. Her blood churned with anger that was not hers, and her heart raced with fury.

She pressed her palm to her chest, willing it to calm, sending a silent message down the bond. She wasn't sure if Mauri could hear her, but she had to try. If not, she feared what he would do.

Whatever was happening, it was clear Mauri was experiencing it alongside Erasmo and Bernat.

"How can you be sure?" Kiki asked.

"I just am," came Solana's terse response. Solana's jaw was set, and her eyes were hard. She reached into her pack and pulled out two leather bandoliers, adjusting each one across her chest in swift movements of practiced precision.

Kiki rolled her eyes. "Thanks, that cleared things up."

Solana paused, her jaw clenched tight as she heaved in a deep breath before turning to continue her task.

Inwardly, Luna winced. Kiki sure had a knack for riling the Commander up.

"Sol is right," she offered, hoping to keep Kiki and Solana from each other's throats. "We can feel it more because we sealed the bonds. You and Erasmo didn't, so you don't feel it as much."

"Whatever this was," Kiki motioned to the burn on her neck with a scowl. "I felt it plenty, thank you very much."

Solana stopped tightening her straps and rounded on Kiki, her cool demeanor slipping. "You felt NOTHING if you can just sit there and act like everything is alright! I feel him! Bernat is in agony, and not just of his body. His soul. I can feel it right here," she pounded her fist against her chest. "You—" she groaned, curling her hands into tight fists at her side, visibly struggling to regain control. "Just be quiet for once in your life and gear up," she added through clenched teeth.

Luna grimaced, and Kiki glared daggers at Solana's back but turned an apologetic look toward Luna. "Is she right?" she muttered. "It feels like that?"

"I feel it like I feel my own breath in my lungs. Like I can hear my own heartbeat. It's in the very marrow of my bones," Luna said softly, pressing her hand to her chest the whole time.

"She's right. I don't feel it that way," Kiki said, casting her gaze away. "Sorry if I came off like a jerk."

"It's fine. Just help me up."

"Excuse me?" Kiki asked, her black brows furrowing tightly together.

"You heard me just fine." Luna rolled her eyes and pushed the thick furs away. "Obviously, the guys are in trouble. We can't exactly help them from here. So either help me up or get out of my way. Because I'm not staying here."

Kiki's eyes widened. "Uhh, no. You're not going anywhere." She placed her hands on Luna's shoulders and gently forced her to lay back down, ignoring her huff of indignation. "You quite literally just brought me back from the brink of death. You're not ready to go out into the field yet."

"Like hell I'm not," Luna snapped, smacking Kiki's hands away from her shoulders. "Mauri is in danger. Bernat is in danger. Erasmo is in danger! What about that don't you understand? My mate is in agony, Kiki. I'm not just going to sit back and wait to see what happens."

Kiki's dark brown eyes narrowed. "I understand the situation about as well as any of us do. Which is that we know nothing."

Luna scoffed. "You pick now of all times to be the level-headed one? That's a first."

Kiki ran her palms over her face. "I'll go to Arlando's castle and see what I can learn. But you need to stay here and rest."

Luna pushed to her feet and wobbled where she stood. "Well, you can't stop me. I'm going whether you like it or not."

Behind them, Luna saw Solana holding her machete out before her. She carefully ran her fingers along the blade before flipping it back and sliding it into its sheath at her belt. The sound of metal on metal rang out as she secured it with a satisfied nod.

She recognized the determination burning within the Commander's gaze, for it reflected her own feelings. Solana gave her a grim nod and said, "We're not leaving her behind, Xochicale. I'll help the Healer. Get your gear on."

"No," Kiki spat, getting to her feet to stand toe to toe with the Commander. "She's in no shape to go traipsing around out there."

Kiki gestured to the tent's entrance, where a thick layer of snow had built up around its edges. Through the opening, a pristine white landscape—trees dusted with fresh snow and rolling hills in the distance—greeted them.

Luna forced a smile and tried to hide the pain as she moved toward her pack to dress for the weather. "I'm fine," she managed to say.

Kiki huffed. "Your labored breathing says otherwise."

Luna's nostrils flared in irritation.

Solana cut Luna an assessing glance before looking around the tent. "Then we'll fashion a sled out of the tent's canvas and poles and drag her along with us. But I won't leave her behind."

Kiki sputtered, "I wasn't suggesting we leave her behind—"

"Oh, trust me. I know exactly what you want to do. You want to go out alone and investigate," Solana cut Kiki off. "Don't give me that look. I know you better than you think. And if anyone is going out there, it's going to be all three of us. Together. We're not losing any more people by splitting up."

Luna released a pent-up breath, grateful that Solana had regained her calm composure and was thinking with a level head.

Kiki stamped her foot. "But that will take hours, and I can easily go and be back in half the time—"

Anger rose in her chest at hearing Kiki still pushing back. As much as she loved her best friend, sometimes she hated how headstrong she was. "Can everyone stop talking about me like I'm not here?" she snapped.

Kiki approached her slowly, stepping over the crumpled furs, her hands held out in front of her as if she were approaching a skittish deer. "I can be back in no time. Just let me—"

She curled her hands into the thin layers of her linen dress. "No! Your mate isn't the only one out there. Mauri—" Her voice cracked on his name, and she fought the burning feeling of tears threatening to fall. "I feel his pain. He's not in a good place. He's losing himself. I can feel it, and maybe if I'm closer, maybe he'll sense it and calm down. I can't lose him, Kiki. Not him too."

Kiki dropped her chin to her chest, her shoulders rolling forward in defeat. With a sigh, she gently reached out for Luna's hand and wound their fingers together.

"Okay. I hear you," Kiki rasped, her eyes clouded with emotion.

Luna could see that Kiki was more worried than she was letting on. "We'll go together, then."

Chapter Seven

Turi

Turi sprinted out of the dungeon, his feet pounding against the cold stone floor. His breath came in ragged gasps as he stumbled up the winding staircase and charged through the wooden door at the top. He raced down the hallway, pushing past yellowed tapestries with wild desperation, until he skidded to a stop in front of an ancient stone pillar.

Gulping stale air, he staggered forward and vomited onto the white marble tile.

I can't do this.

But he knew the choice he'd made. A choice he couldn't go back on. Not if he wanted to break the curse. Not if he wanted to save everyone.

And he did. He wanted to save all of Ozero from the impending doom—because that's what was coming for them should the curse continue to plague the kingdom.

It was already happening.

People were going missing. Straight out of their homes. Gone. Without a trace.

And he knew why.

He knew because his brother had told him so.

The thing about Arlando was that he had a loose tongue when he was in a good mood and drunk from celebrating.

He wiped his mouth of vomit and then immediately regretted it for the sour smell it left on his sleeve.

He glanced behind himself, making sure that Arlando hadn't followed him. His thoughts went back to three nights ago when he'd first arrived at the Winter Keep.

*T*uri shivered as he approached the towering stone walls of the Winter Keep. Icy gusts brushed his wild, unkempt black hair across his forehead.

He paused before the drawbridge, his breath misting in the frigid air. Above him, skeletal tree branches silhouetted against an emerald-blue sky, and snow crunched beneath his feet. He inhaled deeply, filling his lungs with crisp winter air.

There was a certain beauty to the winter season. To many, winter marked the end of all things green and teeming with life, but he saw it as merely a precursor to spring and the blooming of rebirth.

It signaled that there was always hope when everything seemed like it had come to an end. At least, that was his whimsical way of looking at things.

The white stone of the Keep was covered in thick, twisting vines that clung to the walls like murderous serpents. Dead trees lined the castle's perimeter, their branches blackened by winter frost and weighed down with the weight of snow. An errant raven darted between two gnarled branches, singing a mournful tune.

Turi didn't think the Winter Keep had always looked like this. Now that he'd crossed the Cicatrix, his memories of his earlier life were starting to come back in spurts of clarity. Still, he'd only been six when he was sent away before the Cicatrix slashed its way across the landscape and swallowed the center of Ozero.

Joyful ignorance had a way of distorting the truth of the world around a child. In place of an ugly, deteriorating pile of wood, a child had the unique ability to see a magnificent ship instead, complete with billowing sails and swashbuckling crewmates.

But Turi wasn't a child anymore, and the castle no longer seemed full of the grandeur he had once believed it to hold.

He stood in the cobweb-coated ruin of the castle, and every glance seemed to bring a new sign of neglect. He stepped closer to the once grand southern tower, its stones crumbling and moss-covered. There were busted-out windows along the western walls, and the stench of mold and rot assaulted his nose.

He crossed his arms against the chill that had crept up his spine and tried to ignore the ever-growing knot of dread in his stomach.

Turi knew he should go back to the eyrie. That it was stupid of him to leave the way he did. He was fully aware that he had let his anger and jealousy get the best of him.

He also knew it wasn't Erasmo's fault the curse bound him to Kiki.

Nor was it Kiki's fault.

Still, the pain that wrenched through his heart upon hearing his brother speak the truth—he didn't think it was possible to feel like his heart could actually implode, but that's what he felt then.

Like his heart was nothing more than fragile glass, and when the hot coal of betrayal had struck it, it had disintegrated into fleeting motes of sand. Leaving nothing in its wake but a black pit of emptiness.

The beast within had no problem filling that void with rage. It had taken every ounce of self-control that Turi had to stop himself from shifting right there in front of Erasmo and ripping out his throat.

Turi clenched his hands into fists at the sickening thought.

I love my brother. I would never do that.

Are we sure? *Another part of him spoke aloud—the beastly part.* **His blood would have been sweet. His heart is full of desire for his mate. We could have done it, you know.**

Turi clenched his jaw so hard that it hurt. Go away!

The beast within shook its burly head and huffed indignantly before Turi sensed it retreating deeper within. Hiding. Waiting.

He winced at the constant reminder that something lived within him. Something that hungered for things Turi had never yearned for before.

But that was a problem for another day. A problem that would cease to exist once the curse was broken.

There were more pressing problems that he had to figure out. The first among them was that he shouldn't be here at the Winter Keep.

He knew that he should go back. Every part of him wanted to. But there was also a part of him that was afraid.

Erasmo will never forgive me. Why did I say those things to him? Why can't I just be happy for him?

It's not like Turi didn't know he and Kiki were over. Nor was it because he couldn't get over her. It was the fact that she had been the first person he'd felt he could call his friend.

She'd been a fearless and sometimes reckless advocate for him when they were kids. But he wasn't unique in that way. Kiki had stuck up for Yarixa similarly.

There was something about Kiki that drew people like him and Yarixa to her. Her strength was like a magnet to their hearts, a comforting balm for their fears. She was fearless in ways they were not.

I was afraid to lose her.

Turi dropped his head to his chest. But now I've ruined everything.

Turi had to force his feet to take one step and then another. His legs felt like lead as if he were slogging through a swamp. Each step was an act of sheer willpower, and he gritted his teeth with each movement forward.

I've come this far. I might as well speak to Arlando before I go back to La Aguilera and beg on my hands and knees for Kiki and Erasmo to forgive me for being an idiot.

Or we can eat him.

Turi ignored the beast's suggestion. The beast had a habit of saying the most depraved things and often the best response was silence.

His feet dragged across the cobblestones, leaving small marks in the dirt. Finally, he reached the large wooden doors of the castle.

All of Erasmo's, Mauri's, and even Yasir's warnings about Arlando sounded off in his mind.

I'll be careful. I just want to ask Arlando some questions.

He sounded naive, even to himself. But, at the very least, he needed a place to stay for the night. The storm was only worsening, and he hadn't appropriately planned to camp out in the woods.

Not that he'd even try something so foolish. Though he hadn't encountered a single demon during his trip, that didn't mean they weren't around.

He'd heard the crunch of dried leaves underfoot, coming from some-where deep within the shadows of the trees. He'd felt their red eyes upon him, the musky scent of danger heavy in the air. The demons had been watching him, lurking and prowling. Waiting.

Why they didn't attack, Turi hadn't the faintest clue. He had theories because all his time walking had left his mind to wander down rabbit holes and chase tangents, but he wasn't sure.

Inhaling deep through his nose, he raised his fist to the door and knocked three times. The reverberations were loud enough to break any silence, echoing through the darkness like a warning.

The door opened slowly, the groaning and grinding of the rusty hinges echoing in the night. Turi cautiously peered inside and was warmly greeted by a fire roaring in the hearth. Soft shadows danced on the walls as sparks flew from the burning logs.

A strange feeling slithered around in his chest, and he had to squash it down to force himself through the door, or else he feared he'd lose his nerve entirely.

As he stepped inside, the door slammed shut behind him with an uncannily loud snick.

Turi's brows furrowed as he stared at the door that had moved on its own. What the hell?

"Arturito," a voice crooned. "You've come at last."

His brother was clad in an all-white pantsuit, and elaborate rose-gold embroidery embellished his sleeves and down the sides of his legs. He lounged against the cushions of a plush red velvet sofa, a crystal glass of wine in one hand and the other raised in greeting. His booted feet were propped up on a low-sitting table, the mud on his soles flaking off onto the polished surface.

Turi paused momentarily, unsure if he should keep going or turn back and go the way he'd come.

His brother must have sensed his hesitation because he added, "Aurelia told me you'd be coming." He flashed Turi a brilliant white smile and gestured to the sofa opposite him. "Come, join me. I was just celebrating."

Turi approached slowly, his boots quiet whispers against the marble floors.

Flickering flames danced in the hearth, bathing Arlando's figure in an ethereal golden light that seemed to emphasize the intricate details of his outfit. His long silver hair was pulled back into a neat ponytail, and a silver circle adorned with gold roses rested atop his head.

"My, my, I haven't seen you in two years," Arlando said silkily, uncrossing his ankles and setting his boots on the floor with a thud. He grinned from ear to ear, his eyes twinkling with delight.

Still, Turi couldn't shake the feeling that he was a mouse that had just stumbled into the path of a very pleased tom cat.

Turi forced himself to smile as he drew closer. "Why do you say two years, brother? I haven't laid eyes on you since I was six years old."

"Ah! But, of course, how foolish of me. I should explain." He stood and walked over to a table with a silver tray of crystal glasses and a decanter of red wine. "Come, come, sit!" he motioned to a red velvet lounger opposite the sofa as he poured the wine into a glass and refilled his own.

Turi hesitantly took a seat on the edge of the lounger, his eyes darting around the dimly lit hall.

The fire of the hearth crackled, and its embers illuminated the room's dark corners, casting a mysterious array of shadows that swirled around like dancing figures.

Arlando handed the glass to Turi and took a seat opposite him. Once he settled into a comfortable position, his lips spread into an unsettling grin.

"Now, where was I?" he tapped his chin in a contemplative gesture. "Ah, yes. You were wondering how it is that I've seen you, but you haven't seen me."

Turi nodded. He wasn't sure if his brother was drunk or if he always talked like this. In any case, he decided it was best to keep his guard up.

"Well, you see, I've been keeping an eye on you for your whole life. I used to leave the Cicatrix quite often just to see how you were doing. That is, until two years ago when I had a rather nasty encounter at the Wall. Believe it or not, I actually lost a tooth! Thankfully we regrow those kinds of things."

Turi found himself rendered speechless and his brows pinched in confusion. There was so much to process, but one thought kept recurring. "You were able to leave the Cicatrix? To see me?" Turi shook his head disbelievingly, his eyebrows knitted together as he attempted to make sense of it all. "Why didn't you ever say anything?"

Arlando waved his free hand in the air in a dismissive gesture. "Sadly, when those of us affected by the curse decide to cross the border, we get stuck as bears." He tipped his glass at Turi before he took a sip. "I couldn't exactly go up to you in such a state, now, could I? You would have soiled your pants on the spot. Not to mention you wouldn't have understood a word I said."

That feeling of unease churned in Turi's stomach again, and he looked down at the glass of red wine in his hand. A sharp coppery tang flitted under his nose as he stared at the liquid.

"No, I guess not," he mumbled, his gaze glued to the contents of his glass.

"Go on, take a sip."

Turi met his brother's gaze, and he had the unsettling feeling that this was some kind of test and that he was moments from failing it.

Turi raised the glass, the cold rim chilled his lips, and metallic notes whirled from within. When he sipped the wine, he was overwhelmed by the briny, copper-like flavor on his tongue.

It's blood!

His fingers strained around the delicate stem of the glass. More than anything, he wanted to throw it from his grip. But one look at Arlando told him that he wanted Turi to enjoy it. His brother's eyes flickered with excitement, his irises blooming crimson.

Turi silently cursed himself and brought the glass back to his lips as he slowly tipped it back and swallowed the bitter liquid, feeling it burn its way down his throat. He felt a heavy weight in the air, knowing that his brother was watching him intently, and tried not to react as he drained the glass with one final gulp.

With measured movements, Turi calmly set the glass down on the low-sitting table between them, not once flinching away from Arlando's gaze.

He knew this was a dangerous game he was playing and that, at any moment, he could find himself the loser.

Arlando's lips curled into a satisfied grin. "I knew you were like me. I just knew that you couldn't truly be as weak as you pretended to be."

He stood quickly and began to pace in front of the hearth. "I thought to myself, 'He must be hiding his true nature. He must fear what others will do should they see beneath the mask.' Trust me, I'm all too familiar with putting on such a show. The scraping and deference. The civility and propriety." He stretched his neck like he had a pain in it, his shoulders rolling as he tried to work out the kink. "It's suffocating."

Turi was thankful that he had passed Arlando's test, even if the act made him want to crawl out of his own skin.

A small part of him still feared his brother would be able to sense that he wasn't genuine. But for the moment, Arlando seemed too caught up in himself.

"Now that you're here, my plan can move forward. You understand what must be done?"

Turi nodded. "Yes, but I haven't found my mate yet."

Arlando slashed his hand in the air dismissively. "Not to worry, I have a plan for that. A substitute."

"A substitute?" Turi asked, feeling something oily crawling along his skin.

"Yes, it will work. I've done a similar spell before." Arlando turned and barked, "You, fetch us more blood from downstairs. We're going to need it."

Turi glanced in the direction Arlando spoke but saw nothing but empty space.

Wonderful. He's seeing things. As if he wasn't insane enough.

Arlando ran a hand over his face as he threw himself back into the sofa cushions. "It's so hard to train them."

"Them?" Turi asked, his eyebrows raising into his hairline.

Arlando quirked his head in puzzlement. "The demons," he said, his tone matter-of-fact, as if they were merely discussing the weather and that the sky was blue.

Turi didn't think Arlando could possibly mean what he had just admit-ted aloud. Demons? Here? In the Winter Keep?

Turi slowly raked his eyes around the hall, the hair on his arms rising as the sensation of being watched washed over him. It was the same feeling he'd had during his travels, the sense that he was being followed by red glowing eyes just past his vision.

Arlando barked out a laugh. "How silly of me, I forgot to lift the spell." He lifted a finger, and a black talon extended past his fingertips, the point sharp and reflecting light from the nearby fire.

Turi had to resist the urge to flinch away as his brother approached. Everything up to this point would be in vain if Arlando started to suspect him now.

"This will only take a moment," Arlando assured with a honeyed tone. He lifted his finger and pressed the sharp tip into the center of Turi's forehead.

A pinprick of pain drew a sharp gasp from him as a trickle of blood slipped down his brow and trailed over the ridge of his nose.

When Arlando removed his talon, bright crimson blood glittering on the tip, he smiled and motioned with his arm as if showing off the room.

Turi felt like his sight had become crystal clear; everything seemed more detailed and tinged with a strange sort of shadowy mist of cor-ruption. It took him mere moments to notice the slinking figures in the shadows, their elongated skeletal bodies, their lidless eyes, and snarling mouths.

He knew that Arlando was watching him with the eyes of a hawk, taking in every minuscule reaction. He knew he had to say something. Anything. Or else his brother would pounce.

Turi cleared his throat to hide his discomfort. "How do you control them?" he asked, turning to examine the rest of the room and the demons stationed sentry along the walls. He counted a total of ten in this room alone.

His eyes roved along the grand staircase that led to the upper levels of the Keep where the living quarters were and counted another six along the marble stairs.

Arlando clapped a hand on Turi's shoulder and made a noise that sounded like an inhale of pride. "Aren't they wonderful? I tell you, it took me several years of experiments to get the spell just right. So many failures," his tone turned dark, but he quickly recovered and turned his bright gaze on Turi. "But it was all worth it. Fitting, don't you think? That I have bent the very source of our troubles to my will?"

But how? That's the question.

Arlando was either evading the question, or he was too caught up in his supposed victory. It didn't matter to Turi which it was. He needed to know how his brother was doing this.

"Will you teach me?" Turi asked, forcing a note of sincerity in his voice. He turned his gaze to his brother and tried to recall any happy memories he had of Arlando. Anything that might resemble the shine of adoration that Arlando so clearly fed off of.

Arlando's lips curled into a brighter grin, his hand on Turi's shoulder gripping tighter. "Gladly, brother. Most gladly."

Chapter Eight

Luna

Hours later, Luna sat in the makeshift sled that Solana and Kiki had fashioned out of the tent. Two long poles were bound together with the thick canvas, and a cross-section of shorter rods had been lashed together to give the sled structure. The bottom portion dragged along the snow while Kiki held the two poles at the top in each of her hands.

Kiki had insisted on carrying the entire weight of the sled with Solana by her side, adamant that Solana acted as their scout, guiding them through the snow-laden woods.

The color of the blue sky was fading from a vibrant cerulean to the deep blue of twilight. The sun slowly sank below the horizon, and ashen clouds replaced the remnant daylight overhead. The entire world seemed to wilt in sadness as night crept upon them.

Each step felt like a lifetime as Luna felt her bond with Mauri slowly fading in her chest. She squeezed her fists together and tried to remember when she last spoke with him, trying to recall the warmth of his voice and his smile. But it was all too distant, too far away...

The late evening air grew colder, but they continued on. Solana jogged ahead of them, scouting out potential dangers and marking their route for when it would be time to head back. As Luna watched the Commander's red curls bouncing in the wind, she whispered a silent prayer for Mauri's safety under her breath.

Kiki stumbled forward, exhaustion etched deeply into every line of her body. Luna thought her friend must nearly be at her breaking point from carrying the stretcher alone. But Kiki still hadn't uttered a single complaint since leaving their camp. As if sensing Luna's appreciation, Kiki looked over her shoulder and gave a small smile before pushing onwards.

Solana navigated them around some of the dangers in the forest—roots hidden beneath snowdrifts or rocks jutting up from beneath their feet—and eventually, their path widened at a trailhead which led to a winding path that followed the ridges of mountains below. The cliffside was sheer, and when they stopped walking, the only sound she could hear was wild brush scratching at the bare rocks below.

Kiki stopped in front of them and set down the stretcher carefully before turning around with an exhausted sigh. "I need a break," she said simply, her heavy breath misting into white clouds before her face.

Luna looked around, taking in the deep purple sky and the rolling hills that seemed to stretch forever below them.

Her heart twinged with regret as she took in the beautiful colors and the white landscape. There was something breathtaking about this part of Ozero. As if it had been untouched by humankind, unmolested. Uncorrupted.

She wished at that moment that she could share this moment with Mauri. He lived in so much darkness that he deserved to come into the light once in a while.

After a few moments, Kiki slowly pushed up to a stand and lifted her arms, stretching them above her head before clasping her hands behind her neck. Her chest rose and fell with each breath, and a subtle tension built in her shoulders. "What do you feel now?" she asked, a glimmer of anxiety sparkling within her eyes. "Anything new?"

Luna knew what she was asking about. The bond. "Nothing in a while. A few flashes of pain. Some feelings of anger here and there."

Kiki chewed at her bottom lip, her eyes staring off into the distance. "But alive, right?"

A tremor of fear rushed through Luna's heart. She didn't want to think like that, but she understood why Kiki did.

She nodded, the silence wrapping around them.

Solana joined them a moment later, her eyes cast to the sky above. "We're almost there, but we're cutting it close. The days are growing shorter. Sunset is only a few hours away."

Kiki rolled her neck, audible popping noises filling the air. "Then we better get moving. I'd like to make it to the Keep today and not be forced to make camp."

They pushed on, the wind growing stronger the closer they got to their destination.

Luna hated feeling so useless as Kiki and Solana pulled her behind them. When Kiki needed another break, Sol chided her stubbornness and insisted on helping.

Kiki had relented, but not without saying that she was more than capable of doing it alone.

Luna shook her head. *So stubborn. Can never admit that she needs help. Always has to go at it alone.*

Except when it came to Erasmo. They seemed to work well together.

Luna was glad about that. Kiki needed someone as strong-willed as her to keep her grounded. Someone unafraid of her temper and able to match her strength.

Lost in her thoughts, Luna didn't notice when Kiki had come to a stop.

It wasn't until Kiki muttered, "Shit," that Luna angled her head to see.

"What?" Luna pushed up to her elbows as best she could, trying to stretch her neck to see behind herself.

Wordlessly, Kiki and Solana lowered the stretcher and pulled Luna to her feet.

At the bottom of the hill, an ancient fortress loomed in the distance. Stone walls, several meters high, enclosed the estate, their icy gray hue contrasting against the darkening sky. The vast courtyards were dotted with stunted trees, their branches a frozen lacework beneath blankets of snow.

A thin sheet of ice had formed atop a small river that encircled the small island on which the fortress was built, and a rickety wooden drawbridge connected it to the mainland.

Shrouded in a dark mist, shadowy figures lumbered through the court-yards, their tortured shrieks and caws bouncing off the silent walls.

"Demons?" Luna hissed. "Are they under attack down there?"

Solana ran her hand along her chin, her eyes darting over the scene before them. "If they were under attack, there would be more chaos."

"I've never seen demons act so calm," Kiki mumbled, her hand wrapping tightly around the pommel of her machete, her other hand toying with a tlazon strapped in her bandolier.

"That's because they're mindless beasts without a conscious. They don't kill for survival. They hunt for the thrill of it," Solana said, her head tilting as if in thought. "Or so we thought."

Kiki snapped her focus onto the Commander. "You don't think they're being controlled, do you?"

Solana's jaw clenched as she flicked her gaze to Kiki. "That's exactly what I think. And I think we finally know who's been controlling them. Or at least these ones."

The reality of their situation hit them like a slap to the face. This was worse than any of them had imagined. And their mates were inside. Being hurt and tortured, and who knew what else.

Fear and anger made a dangerous mix inside Luna's stomach. She wanted to howl in sorrow and rage at their predicament. "Well, we can't just do nothing. So what's the plan?"

Kiki and Solana exchanged a look, each of their gazes trailing over the other as they took silent inventory of each other's weapons.

When they didn't immediately respond, Luna huffed. "Don't everyone talk at once."

Solana was the one to face her. "Xochicale and I may be the best Slayers in the Corps, but even we have our limits." Luna opened her mouth to protest. "I've counted fifty demons outside alone. We have no idea how many are inside, nor do we have knowledge of the interior layout. We can't just go storming down this hill and cut our way through. We won't make it."

"What are you saying?" Luna whispered, fearing the answer. Knowing logically what Solana's response would be, but hoping she'd have some daring solution that would free their mates now. Today.

All she wanted was to wrap her arms around Mauri, to smell his scent that seemed as if it was ingrained in her, as if his blend of cedarwood had always been the smell of home.

She wanted to feel his warmth wrapped around her as she hid from the darkness that shrouded them all. She wanted to press her lips to his and feel him sink deep inside her, filling her to the brim with his passion and fire.

She realized that Solana and Kiki were staring at her, waiting for her to understand their unspoken answer. The words none of them wanted to say aloud because saying them would make them real.

She shook her head slowly, backing a step away from them both. "We can't—"

Kiki winced. "We must."

Luna continued to backpedal away, her heart lurching into her throat. "No."

Kiki's grip on the pommel of her machete tightened. "We have a choice here, Luna. Go down there and get torn to shreds by those demons, or go back to La Aguilera and get some help. Only one of those choices gives us a real chance at rescuing the guys. Only one of those choices doesn't equate to certain death. If there is any chance of rescuing them, then that's the choice I'm going to make."

Luna sank to her knees, the snow beneath seeping into her pants and sending a shiver up her spine.

She knew Kiki was right, but that didn't soothe the aching in her heart. She turned her face toward the castle, taking in the blackened vines crawling up the stone walls and the crumbling parapets. Somewhere inside that hellhole was her mate, and he was being tortured by a madman.

Though it didn't sit right with her, she slowly nodded her agreement, all the while holding onto the flame of rage that was simmering inside her chest. She could hold on to that spark for as long as she had to until she had Mauri in her arms. She wouldn't let it flicker out.

She whispered a promise from the deepest part of her heart. "No matter where you are, how far you are, how dire everything around us seems, know that my love for you has no bounds. That I will find you even if I have to dive into the deepest depths of hell to yank you back to me."

She didn't know or care if Solana and Kiki heard her declaration. The only person she wished could hear her was just beyond her reach.

Then, with a heavy heart and a burgeoning flame of anger, she turned in the direction they had come.

Chapter Nine

Turi

The problem with living a double life wasn't the pressure Turi felt to maintain the cover he'd created to make Arlando trust him. Nor was it the constant vigilance and caution he had to take with his words and actions. Not even the isolation really got to him too much. He'd always been a loner and was used to not sharing his feelings with another person.

He clamped his hands into tight fists and felt tension ripple throughout his arms as he tried to repress the memory of his first night with his brother.

What bothered him the most was having to partake in activities that he found abhorrent. Doing things that he knew were morally and ethically wrong. That bothered him the most.

His eyes darted to the floor, taking in pieces of half-digested food and a splatter of yellow vomit where he had thrown up. His stomach churned as the pungent smell of acid filled his nostrils.

Great. Now what do I do?

He tugged at his black suit jacket, straightening the lapels and pulling them tight against his broad chest. He adjusted the collar, revealing a crisp white dress shirt underneath. With a deep sigh, he ran both hands over his dark curls to flatten the stray strands.

He knew he couldn't leave his sick here for his brother to find. If Arlando had seen him or had any inkling that Turi was wavering, he had no doubt that he'd be in those cages with Erasmo, Bernat, and Mauri.

His lips curled back in a snarl, and he squeezed his eyes shut.

I have to do it. I can't leave this here.

I don't like how it feels. Let's leave it.

You think I enjoy doing it?

The beast didn't reply and Turi was thankful. It was bad enough feeling like a stranger lived beneath his skin. The effect was compounded by the fact that the stranger was a psychopath.

His index finger trembled slightly as he slowly extended the pointed black talon that lay burrowed deep in his flesh. With a deep breath, he pressed the tip of the talon into the center of his other palm, feeling the skin give way under its sharpness until a single drop of blood emerged.

His stomach churned with nausea as his blood called forth a deeper power within.

According to Arlando, blood magic didn't require the shedding of blood for every spell. Only amateurs needed the physical presence of blood. Arlando could easily draw on the dark powers because the blood in his veins was enough to propel most of his spells.

But Turi had just learned to use blood magic just a few nights ago. So he had to draw on his own life force to do it.

He hated using blood magic. Everything within him wanted to rebel against the slick feeling of it as if it were a physical thing coiling around his chest, wrapping tighter and tighter like a boa constrictor, slowly suffocating him.

But he knew he needed to get this mess cleaned up, and the only way to control the demons was to use blood magic.

Taking his thumb, he smeared it across his brow and turned to the nearest demon lurking in the shadows.

Adopting his most commanding voice, he called out to the beast. "You, clean this mess up before your master sees it."

The demon made a gurgling noise that he took to be acknowledgment. Within moments, the creature lumbered over, its skeletal arms dragging behind it, bringing cloth and a bucket with it.

Satisfied, Turi pressed his shoulders back, strode through the hall, and vaulted up the stairs.

He passed the decorative tables that lined the second-floor hallway. Their surfaces were barren of ornaments and bore only flickering candles to light his way. Upon reaching his room, he shoulder-slammed through it and quickly locked the door.

Clenching his fists, he rushed to the floor-length mirror adjacent to his wardrobe. He yanked the high collar of his jacket down, revealing a quickly fading black scorch mark against the lower part of his neck—a twin to the wound burned into Yari's skin.

That was the other thing that made everything so complicated.

Turi's thoughts raced back to three nights earlier when everything he thought he knew was turned upside-down.

The sound of a rusty door hinge roused him from his slumber.

Turi bolted up, his hand instinctively shooting to the hilt of a dagger tucked under his pillow. His heart pounded wildly in his chest as he stood to face the intruder. The blade felt icy and heavy in his grip, providing some sense of security.

I want to bleed him. The beast within rumbled. ***I don't trust him.***

Welcome to the club, genius. Now shut up.

The beast growled at him but did as it was told. Turi could feel it curl around itself as if settling down for a nap.

Arlando entered his bedroom, a faint glow illuminating his face. He held a single sheet of off-white paper in his hands, the edges neatly folded.

"At ease, little brother," he purred. "I did not wish to wake you. After our long night, I thought you'd like to sleep in."

Turi rubbed his eyes and squinted to focus. His brother spoke in a low, steady tone, but the softness of his voice made it hard to discern if he was being sincere or hiding an agenda. Turi couldn't help but feel like it was the latter.

Turi forced a smile and tried to sound nonchalant as he replied, "It's fine," before easing the dagger onto the bedside table. He could still reach it quickly if need be, and he ensured it was within arm's reach just in case.

"Well, there's no use for this then," Arlando said with a laugh as he tapped the paper. "I was going to leave it here for you to find, but seeing as you're awake—Anyway, I have some very pressing business to attend to. I have some loose ends to deal with, and I need to fetch my mate."

Turi's ears perked up at the mention of Arlando's mate. His brother hadn't mentioned her last night, and he was reluctant to bring her up and risk putting Arlando in a foul mood. He also couldn't shake the sense that

Arlando was hiding something. Not hard to believe since his brother was cloaked in secrets.

But this business that Arlando had to run off and take care of had something to do with his mate. Arlando wasn't telling the whole story, and it was clear he didn't want to fill Turi in.

"I understand." Turi nodded in understanding. He turned towards the mahogany wardrobe and opened both doors, revealing neat rows of collared shirts and crisp trousers.

Blazers in shades of charcoal, taupe, and beige hung carefully on solid wooden hangers. Turi's fingers slid across the fabrics as he browsed through the wardrobe, tracing the looping patterns of silver and gold embroidery.

Knee-high boots in white, black, and shades of brown lined the bottom of the wardrobe, their glossy leather shimmering in the light.

Feeling Arlando's eyes carefully taking inventory of his every move, he looked up and said, "I'm sure you already know that I'm not going anywhere."

"I didn't know what colors you liked best, so I picked a generally appealing pallet. Of course, if you don't like anything, I can have the demons fashion a new set."

Turi turned to his brother, mindful to keep his mouth shut or else he'd be gaping. "The demons made these?" Turi asked, motioning to the closet.

"Oh, yes. The demons who have retained most of their humanity do all sorts of things for me. You've met most of my guards already. They look very human in aspect, but they're far from it," he said, a prideful gleam in his blue eyes.

The guards are demons, too?

Turi felt as if his world were tipping on its axis. His mind swarmed with this new information and the fact that Arlando had command over so many.

Turi started to think that maybe he was in over his head here. It was clear that Arlando was orchestrating far more than Erasmo and Mauri had initially feared.

I knew something was off. The beast within grumbled.

Liar. You never said anything.

You're always telling me to shut up, so I kept my suspicions to myself.

Annoyance bloomed in Turi's chest at the beast for how fickle it was.

"That's very impressive," Turi said, trying to appeal to Arlando's oversized ego.

His brother beamed at the compliment.

To think, soon, Arlando's mate would be joining them. He could only imagine how awful she'd be. She'd have to be just as conniving and manipulative if she were Arlando's mate.

He knew that he'd have to keep his guard up with two master manipulators around. Or else he'd find himself at the end of their wrath, which was not where he wanted to be.

All he wanted was to end the curse without any of his friends being sacrificed for it.

It made no sense that the only way to break the curse was to shed the blood of one's mate. Not when his own mother set the curse as a punishment for his father's betrayal.

She wouldn't want to wish that kind of pain on another. Would she?

Turi vaguely remembered his mother. She'd been soft and warm, loving, and made him laugh.

He flicked his gaze to Arlando, but he supposed that could have been a mask his mother wore, much like the one Arlando wore.

Turi tugged a dark grey blazer from its hanger and picked a pair of simple black pants. "You said you'd teach me how to control the demons like you do."

Arlando's grin widened as he stepped closer and clapped a hand on Turi's shoulder. "All in good time, little brother. I keep my promises. Upon my return, I'll show you everything I know."

His stomach churned at the thought of such a macabre spectacle, but he didn't let the disgust show on his face. Instead, he returned Arlando's smile and said, "Then I wish you good luck and safe travels, brother."

Arlando moved to the door and paused on his way out. "If all goes to plan, I should be back by tonight. If not, expect me by tomorrow afternoon."

Turi didn't fail to notice how Arlando's hand tightened around the doorframe. Once he was gone and it had been several minutes, Turi inspected the wood. Gouge marks from Arlando's talons pressed into the wood, revealing brown timber underneath the white paint.

He snorted. For all of Arlando's attempts to seem composed, he was anything but.

Turi washed in the oversized bathroom, soaking in the tub sunken into the floor until his skin was puckered and the water had turned cold.

Afterward, he dressed and walked around the castle, carefully examining the demons he saw tucked into the corners and even sensing the ones he couldn't see.

If Arlando indeed controlled the beasts, then the demons scattered throughout the castle were nothing more than carefully placed spies.

He'd have to be extra careful when he left his room. Any action had the potential to be reported to Arlando.

When Arlando did not return after dinner, Turi guessed that his brother's business had not gone according to plan. He shuddered to think what that might mean and who'd have to pay for it.

Perhaps Arlando's mate was helping him. From what he'd seen, the mate pairs seemed to compliment each other. They were two sides of the same coin, equal in every right but distinct personalities.

Perhaps Arlando's mate played more of an active role, the executor of Arlando's will in the opposite and complementary way that he was the master planner of it all.

Later that night, he tossed and turned, his stomach churning with anxiety at the promise of his brother's return. It had only been a day since his arrival, and already he was questioning whether or not he could see this through.

The next morning, Turi was awoken by a light tapping at the door. He groaned and rolled over, finding his breakfast tray balanced on the edge of the bedside table. He sat up to inspect it, avoiding looking into the hall where he knew a line of demons would await him. The smell of freshly cooked eggs wafted through the room, and while hunger tugged at his stomach, he felt his skin crawl with repulsion.

As the sun reached its peak, he slowly descended the grand staircase. His footsteps echoed off the stone walls, and a chill hung in the air. He shivered and ordered a guard to bring him a fur-lined cloak from his room. The hearth was cold, so he took a fire poker and carefully built a blaze in the fireplace.

Arlando was due within the next few hours, and he wanted to seem like he'd made himself at home. He thought Arlando would like that and see Turi as an ally. He needed to gain his brother's trust. For the first time in his life, he was diving headfirst toward danger instead of away from it.

He stood by the fireplace, his back against the mantle. The gold and bronze flames flickered and popped playfully, but even the roar of the inferno couldn't fill the void inside him. His guard had brought his cloak, a soft sable fur lined with ermine, but it rested heavy and cold on his shoulders and failed to drive away the chill in his soul.

A feeling of icy dread pressed against him, like the weight of a supply crate in receipt. He smirked to himself at the reminder of simpler days. He had enjoyed his post in Norcera. He enjoyed working with the supply equipment and keeping accurate records of everything that came in and was issued out.

But even the memories of better days did little to chase away the hollow feeling spreading from his chest and outward to the rest of his body. Shivering, he pulled his cloak around himself tighter and lifted the cowl over his head.

Everything about this plan was dangerous, yet he saw no other way around it. The curse had to be broken. He could feel his humanity at war with the beast inside.

The longer he was under the pull of the curse, the less of himself he'd have at the end of it all.

Lost in his thoughts, he didn't immediately notice the doors to the castle open, not until Arlando's voice echoed through the empty halls saying, "Brother, come meet the love of my life. My mate."

Steeling himself, he spun on his heel to greet his brother's mate.

His eyes widened when his gaze fell upon the petite frame held tight to Arlando's body. He instantly recognized her heart-shaped face, soft brown eyes, and warm brown curls cascading down her shoulders.

He didn't recognize the feeling of something tugging him toward her. Like an invisible thread had coiled around his throat and was being jerked in her direction.

Mate, the beast within rumbled. ***She is ours.***

He forced himself to a halt, his jaw slackening in disbelief as the beast within continued to growl with anger.

He has his hands on our mate, the beast snarled.

Shut up; you're going to get us killed! Turi chided the beast.

He was still staring at her in disbelief. He knew he should say something. Anything. But all he managed to say was her name.

"Yari?" he choked out.

For her part, she looked equally shocked to see him, here of all places. "Turi?" she said in her soft, sweet voice.

His name on her lips sent a rush of lightning through his body. He'd known Yari his whole life. Had even dated her best friend. But he had never felt this way toward her before. She'd uttered his name more than a hundred times before.

But her voice was currently calling to him, like a siren song, luring him closer to a demise he'd welcome with joy.

Because none of his past mattered anymore, nothing he'd said or done, no one he had loved compared to the feeling of seeing his mate standing before him.

There was no denying it. The very fabric of Turi's being seemed to hum with glee at being near her. At her eyes on his. At the shape of her mouth and the softness of her eyes.

Yet, there wasn't something right about the way she stood. Like she was curling in on herself. Or the way she flinched as Arlando yanked her closer to the side of his body.

Spill his blood. Tear out his throat. Eat his heart, the beast within raged. ***His scent is all over her. He has taken our mate for his own!***

Inside, the beast was pacing back and forth, shaking his head, his fur standing on end as he howled in fury.

Kill him where he stands. Let his blood run free. Let us bathe in it. Let us split him from cock to sternum!

Turi felt like he was being cracked open. *How can Arlando do this?* No, that wasn't the right question. *How did Arlando do this?*

That's what Turi didn't understand. The mate bond only snapped into place between two mates.

So why is Yari here with Arlando? And why does she look like she'd rather be anywhere else but here?

We will carve him to pieces with our fangs and then fuck our mate in the offal of his body. We'll bury ourselves so deep inside her sweet pussy, that we'll forever rid her of his scent and his seed.

We'll feast on her cunt like it's our last meal and never eat anything else again.

The beast was uncontrollable, but what was worse, Turi felt his pants tightening around his cock at the beast's filthy words. The picture the beast painted was depraved and wrong, and it was everything Turi wanted.

He had to force his breath into a steady rhythm to stop himself from doing exactly what the beast demanded. Because he wanted to do all of those things.

He wanted to wrap Yari into his arms and make her feel safe. He wanted to lick away the tears that streamed down her cheeks and replace them with his kisses. He wanted to whisper sweet nothings in her ear and watch her shiver at his hot breath trailing across her skin. He wanted to erase his brother from her mind and ease her troubled heart.

He knew that he could do none of those things, though. Because it was clear that Arlando was playing a very dangerous game.

He realized with absolute clarity that this was a test. If he had to guess, Arlando was putting Yari before him to see his reaction. To get a gauge on him.

But Turi would not be played so easily. If Arlando wanted to play games, then so could he.

Inside, the bear was still muttering his raunchy fantasies about Yari.

Calm down, you idiot. If we act rashly, he could hurt her. And we don't want that, do we?

That seemed to stop the beast in its tracks. The rage he felt unfurling in his chest faded to a simmer.

I make this vow: by my fangs or your sword, our brother will fall by our hands.

He felt the beast curl in on himself, waiting patiently for the moment he'd get to keep his promise.

He made sure the beast was contained before he let a false smile tug at his lips. "Where have you been all this time, Yari? We've been looking for you."

Chapter Ten

Yari

"Where have you been all this time, Yari? We've been looking for you."

She shuddered as she remembered when Turi first came to the winter keep a few days ago.

Had it really only been a few days?

Time seemed to be creeping forward with tortured slowness.

Each moment she had to endure with Arlando, she felt like another piece of her soul was breaking off and scattering on the wind.

She winced as she remembered the hope that filled her chest with the warmth of the blazing sun upon seeing Turi. He'd come to rescue her! And he'd have news of Kiki and Luna, too!

But Turi was not her friend. He didn't care what happened to her. He hadn't stopped Arlando from using that rod and pressing it into his own flesh just so he could show how his pain would blossom against her own skin.

Turi hadn't helped her when Arlando had ordered the demons to return her to his room. Turi hadn't even flinched. He'd merely left the dungeon as if nothing could rattle his walls of stone.

At the moment, she sat curled in the corner of Arlando's suite, her dress still torn at the front, the collar ripped open at her breastbone. The burn on her neck stung, and she was sure she had bruises on her arms from the human-looking demons that had dragged her into the dungeon.

Her body still ached from Arlando's attack days ago. Though he had healed all the wounds he'd opened on her flesh, this bone-deep pain still lingered like a shadow over her heart.

A gaping wound in her soul that refused to close. A seeping, festering wound that she hoped would consume her entirely and leave behind nothing but dust.

She wanted to disappear. Be anywhere but here.

But wishing for something didn't make it true.

She choked back a sob and curled her arms tighter around her body.

She wished for her friends. For Kiki and Luna. She wished she knew they were safe. She wished that Turi would talk to her. Tell her how he came to be inside the Cicatrix. She wished she'd been able to talk to Bernat. At least *he* would have spoken with her.

But she hadn't gotten that chance. The only good thing about Turi's presence was that he was occupying all of Arlando's time.

The two brothers stayed up late drinking and recounting decades-old stories about their childhoods. They laughed and made a mess as they played vulgar games involving the demons.

Arlando hadn't even returned to his room, despite ordering her to remain within the confines of these suffocating walls.

She was grateful for that, at least.

Not that she was grateful to Arlando for anything. Not anymore. She was just relieved that he hadn't returned to take her again. She didn't think she'd survive it if he did.

Anger swirled in her chest as the memory of that night resurfaced. She didn't want to remember his fangs sinking into her flesh or the way he pressed between her legs, the way she'd cried and sobbed for him to stop. But it was like a recurring nightmare, haunting her every moment.

She shook her head, knowing full well that doing so couldn't remove the memory from the trenches of her mind. But she had to do something. Anything.

What would Kiki do in this situation?

Well, to start, she wouldn't have gotten herself into such an awful place to begin with. But if she somehow were in Yari's shoes, she wouldn't take this abuse lying down.

No. Kiki was the flame of an inferno. She was hardened obsidian. A powerful gale whipping through anything in its path. She would fight Arlando until she had no more breath left in her body.

At that moment, Yari knew without a doubt that she needed to be like Kiki. And since she had no strength of her own, she would call upon Kiki's strength to see her through this.

Inhaling a deep breath, Yari resolved that if she wanted to survive, she had to think and act more like her best friend.

And that started now, with picking herself up off the floor and cleaning up the mess Arlando had made of her neck.

Though she'd bathed many times since he had assaulted her at the cabin, she thought she could still feel his release leaking along the inside of her thighs.

She swore she could still smell his saliva along her skin, where he'd licked and healed her wounds.

She still felt polluted by him, and no amount of washing seemed to rid her of his taint.

She wanted to be rid of any trace of him. She'd burn it away if she could.

But another bath would have to do. Perhaps if she scrubbed hard enough, she could finally rid herself of him.

She steeled her spine and pushed up to a seat on trembling arms. She swiped at the hair sticking to her forehead, wincing at the crunchy feel of dried blood that soaked through her brown curls. Then, with a whine, she tucked her feet beneath her knees and stood up.

Her legs wobbled, and she grabbed onto the nearest surface for balance. Once she felt sure she wouldn't collapse in a heap on the floor, she limped toward the bathroom.

The bathroom looked different now that she saw Arlando for what he really was.

What she had once regarded as a beautiful and lush space full of candles sitting on pedestals, baskets filled with scented soap, and glass jars with aromatic oils, she now saw as just another mask that the monster hid behind.

The tub was sunken into the floor and had three steps leading down into the basin. She turned the faucet, letting the water run at its hottest setting. A fragrant mist rose from the stream as she picked a jar of oil that smelled like lavender and lemon and poured a trickle into the water.

Soon the soothing sweet aroma of lavender filled the room, and she stripped off her ruined clothes, discarding them in a corner. Then, using the steps, she lowered herself into the tub.

The hot water wrapped around her naked body like a soft blanket, with a comforting warmth that shifted to fit her shape.

She felt her muscles relax as she sank lower into the tub.

Dried blood sloughed off her skin, turning the water pink. She dunked her head under the water and winced when the burn at her neck stung from the heat.

She didn't relish in the warmth of the water as much as she had once done when she first arrived at the Winter Keep.

She would trade this luxury for the ice-cold showers at the Demon Corps basecamp in Norcera any day.

She reached over the rim of the tub for the bottle of shampoo when she noticed a rather large candle sitting on an iron candle holder with a round circular base.

Forgetting the shampoo, an idea formed in her mind. She stood up, grabbed the white candle, and yanked it from the base.

In the center of the iron base was a central spike at least two inches long. She set the large candle aside and picked up the candle holder, testing the weight in her palm before wrapping her fingers around the long tapered base.

Arlando had removed all items that could be used for weapons. But he hadn't thought to consider the candles and their spiked holders.

She knew Arlando could walk in on her any minute, and she didn't want him to catch her with the large metal spike. So she quickly replaced the candle on the base and returned it to its spot with the other candles.

It wasn't much of a weapon, and she doubted it would do much good. But if she caught him off guard with it, she might buy herself enough time to run.

She didn't know where she'd go if she did get away. But anywhere was better than here.

The loud, persistent banging at Arlando's door reverberated through the walls, shaking her to the core.

She stumbled out of bed and scrambled across the floor, darting her hand beneath the frame and feeling wildly for the iron candle holder. Her frantic fingers brushed against the waxy surface of the candle, tipping it over with a clatter to the floor.

She winced, hoping Arlando didn't hear it when a familiar voice called to her beyond the door. "Yari? It's me."

Her hand froze mid-air as she recognized Turi's voice. Slowly, she turned towards the door and stepped away from the potential weapon.

She hesitated, her hand inches away from the ornate door knob.

Why would Turi come to her now? He had no care for her. He had let Arlando hurt her in the dungeon just hours ago. She knew she shouldn't trust him. He was working with Arlando, but something inside her tugged her hand closer to the knob.

She opened the door a crack, angling her body so she could peek out the smallest bit. "What do you want?" she whispered, her throat still hoarse from screaming. An unconscious hand flew to her throat to quell the stinging pain.

Turi stepped closer, his gaze skimming over the curves of her face until it finally settled on the bright red burn at her neck. "I found this in the old

infirmary," he said, reaching into his pocket and pulling out a palm-sized tin. "It's aloe—thought it might help."

She narrowed her eyes into thin slits and measured him up and down as if he were a specimen under a magnifying lens, trying to find any trace of deceit.

But she could find none.

Finally, she let out a soft sigh. She was still unsure if she could trust Turi, but she did really need the aloe.

"Can I come in?" He motioned past her to the room beyond.

She clenched her lips, cast her gaze downward, and slowly shook her head. "Arlando wouldn't like you being in here with me."

She hated how the words felt on her tongue, heavy like stones and hard to push back into her mouth. Still, she knew they were true.

Turi leaned in towards her and whispered, "He's passed out down in the main hall."

"Oh." It wasn't even nine o'clock yet. Had he really drunk himself into a stupor while the night was still young?

She was aware of Turi's steady gaze, unyielding, seeking her permission to enter. With a subtle nod, she allowed the door to swing open and stepped back to let him in.

Turi entered the room, his long strides careful and deliberate, his height and broad shoulders blocking the light from a flickering candle. He lifted the tin and extended his arm toward the bed. "You might want to sit."

She padded to the bed, wrapping her arms around her narrow frame for warmth. As she settled onto the edge, Turi unscrewed the lid of the

tin, placing it next to her thigh, then reached in to scoop out a dollop of aloe with two fingers.

"This will sting," he warned softly, bringing his fingertips closer to her skin.

Before she could stop herself, she said, "I've endured worse."

Turi's jaw tightened as he clenched his teeth together, his nostrils flaring ever so slightly as he brought the cool ointment to the wound. His fingers trembled ever so slightly as he carefully applied the salve. "I'm sorry," he whispered, his voice dipping low into a deep, gravelly tone.

She watched him carefully, noticing how his throat bobbed when he swallowed, the furrow of his dark brows, and the hairline muscle twitching in his jaw.

"Why are you here, Turi? You've ignored me ever since you arrived. You've made it painfully clear that you don't see me as your friend any-more—"

He stopped what he was doing and leaned forward, bringing his bril-liant blue eyes to meet her gaze. The air crackled with lightning as he watched her intently. His hand hovered over her cheek, fingertips a hair's breadth away, poised to cradle her face in his palm.

"That's not true—"

Her nostrils flared, and her eyebrows knit together as she spat out each word. "What's not true? You let your brother hurt me. You allowed him to inflict pain on me and did nothing to stop him! Did you or didn't you?" Tears spilled down her cheeks as she yelled. "Is that something you do to all your friends?"

Turi palmed his face. "No, I meant—what I mean to say is—" He let out a primal growl from the back of his throat and retreated several steps

away from her. "I have ignored you. Yes. That is true. Because I thought if I did, I'd get Arlando to trust me."

She didn't understand what he was saying. Why would he need Arlando to trust him? Weren't they working together?

From the moment she saw him, she thought he was acting weird. For three days, she had believed him to be indifferent to her.

Turi spoke up, breaking her whirling thoughts. "I wanted my brother to trust me because I believed I could stop him. I thought that if I pretended like you meant nothing to me, he would leave you alone and reveal the full extent of his plans."

Something wasn't adding up. Of course, Turi would care for her. They'd been friends for their entire lives. "Why don't you want Arlando to know we were close? Doesn't he know that already?" she asked, pushing from the bed to stand before him.

She didn't know why she was moving toward him, just that she felt an invisible thread tugging her closer. She thought perhaps it was so she could be close enough to slap him like he so clearly deserved.

Turi retreated a step as if sensing her anger coiling within her, readying to strike. "Because he's testing me. Seeing if I react to you." He inhaled a breath deep through his nose, his shoulders rising and falling as he rubbed his face with his hands. "He's not your mate, Yari."

That word again! She was sick of hearing it. That word meant nothing to her, and she was tired of everyone around her seeming to know its significance but not bothering to tell her.

"What is that? What's a mate? I don't understand what that is, why he calls me that, or why it's important!"

Turi's face turned ashen. "You don't know?"

"Know what?" she hissed, the flames within rising higher and higher by the minute. With enough pressure, she knew she'd combust and nothing would be left of her.

She couldn't let this break her. She had to be strong like Kiki. But if Turi didn't start explaining things, she would retreat so deep inside of herself that she would never resurface again.

All her life, she'd been sheltered and coddled and protected—from the truth, danger, everything. And while Kiki and Luna had meant well, their protection didn't follow her everywhere she went.

She'd had to endure the last several weeks by herself, without Kiki and Luna by her side, shielding her from the brutal edge of reality.

But that was the problem. Yari had allowed herself to be tucked into a corner by everyone in her life. By Kiki. By Solana. And, apparently, by even Turi.

She'd always thought he understood her more than the others. If only because he, too, didn't relish in the fight the same way people like Kiki and Solana did.

He'd taken the logistics route, safe behind the Wall. Yari should have taken that path too, but she'd feared what would happen if she, Luna, and Kiki all went their separate ways. So she'd performed poorly on the tests required to exit the Slayer Corps and followed Kiki's footsteps as she had in every other aspect of her life.

She'd thought his quiet nature matched her own, and his tendency to contemplate a situation before jumping into action. He was kind and sweet in ways that Kiki had never appreciated or noticed, but Yari had.

A sharp pang of regret ripped into her chest like an eagle's talons. It was those same qualities that she'd thought Arlando had. Qualities which she'd fallen in love with. Qualities that turned out to be nothing but lies.

As Yari slowly unraveled, Turi had been pacing back and forth, muttering under his breath. "No, no, no, this isn't right. How do I explain this? No, don't start with me. You have no say in this. You don't know her like I do. I will not say that to her."

Yari tilted her head in confusion. She looked around the room, wondering if there was someone else in the room that she wasn't aware of. Another demon, perhaps? This one kept invisible to her?

When she couldn't bear his muttering any longer, she snapped, "Who are you talking to?"

Turi whipped around on his heel, his eyes wide. "If I tell you, you're going to think I'm insane."

She crossed her arms over her chest. "Honestly, anything you say at this point will be better than what I'm thinking."

Turi pulled his bottom lip between his teeth and moved to the other side of the room, where a pair of chairs sat on either side of a low sitting table.

He lowered himself into the plush red velvet chair and dropped his face into his hands. "Where do I start?" he groaned.

Feeling like this was the Turi she had come to know throughout her life, she laid her suspicions down and sank into the chair opposite him. "How about from the beginning."

Chapter Eleven

Kiki

The night was quickly approaching, and with it, the promise of prowling demons. Kiki and Solana worked together to pull Luna atop the heavy wooden sled. Snow crunched beneath their boots as they trudged forward, their breath visible in the frigid air.

Their breaths came out in puffs of white smoke, sweat beading their brows. They were close to their original campsite, and there was no point in stopping now.

"Just a little farther," Solana said, the strain in her voice the only evidence that betrayed her exhaustion.

Kiki nodded in silent agreement. It wouldn't have mattered if they were still hours away. She'd run through the night to get to the campsite if needed.

The site still bore the rune markings that warded the space from demons. It was the only safe area within fifty miles they knew of.

Suddenly, a sharp crack pierced the air, causing Kiki and Solana to pause.

Kiki shared a long stare with Solana, noticing how the Commander's irises grew bigger as fear surged through their veins.

"Don't say it," Solana warned, giving Kiki a subtle shake.

Fine. Kiki wouldn't say it out loud, but she needed to confirm what they were both thinking.

Demons.

With neither of them saying it, they picked up the pace with renewed vigor, running headfirst toward the camp.

The darkness grew thicker around them as the sky slowly transitioned into deep navy hues, and the stars began to twinkle in the heavens like distant fireflies.

A chill ran up Kiki's spine as the rush of anticipation slithered over her skin. It was in these brief moments before a battle that set Kiki's senses on high alert. Everything seemed to sharpen into focus, her sight heightened, her hearing sharpened, and even her sense of smell became more astute.

The shadows of the trees began shifting and moving in ways that were not natural.

Kiki spotted them first. Several dark shapes emerged from the darkness, their forms tall and lanky with long arms that almost dragged on the ground as they moved.

They prowled like a pack of wolves, stalking their prey with coordinated movements and silent steps.

"Get ready," Solana said through clenched teeth, her voice low yet authoritative.

Kiki counted the demons nearest to her, five and another four crowding toward Solana. What she couldn't see was how many demons lurked in the trees and why weren't they attacking with blind blood lust. What were they waiting for?

Kiki didn't wait a second longer to find out. She dropped the sled's handle to the ground and leaped forward in front of Luna, keeping her safely behind her, her machete held tightly between her hands.

"What are you sorry wastes of air waiting for? If you want us, you're going to have to come and take us," Kiki yelled, her brows furrowed in determination.

The nearest demon hissed at her taunt and lunged forward. Kiki was ready for the first assault and expertly sliced through the air with her machete, creating an arc of shimmering obsidian as she spun around and followed through on her swing.

At her elbow, Solana was already engaged in warding off a set of demons, hacking at their elongated limbs, working her way to their necks, or a straight shot to their hearts.

The demons screeched in response to their joint defense and began surging forward as one mass.

Kiki let out a battle cry, shaking the air with her fury as she sliced at each demon that came close.

With each swing of her machete, she would separate a demon from its head or pierce it through the heart.

Ichor splattered against her face as she took out demon after demon, each strike finding its mark.

But it wasn't enough. More demons poured from the trees, their awful screeching filling the night air.

Between the two of them, it was taking everything Kiki and Solana had to keep the demons from Luna.

"Luna, can you run?" Kiki called over the sound of the screeching demons.

Luna shook her head.

Damn. Kiki had hoped that at least Luna could run to the camp. If anything, she and Solana could give her a head start and follow after, the demons hot on their heels.

"What about your little fire show, Commander? Think you can help a Slayer out?"

Solana scrunched her face as she tried to call forth her newfound fire magic. But after long moments passed and more demons rushed from the trees, she felt a sense of dread fall over her.

Kiki didn't often feel hopeless during battle. Still, her arms were already fatigued from lugging Luna on the sled. She was quickly running out of her last vestiges of energy reserves.

Just when all hope seemed lost, a bright light came hurtling at them.

"Get down," Kiki yelled, lunging forward, taking Solana by the waist, and tackling her to the ground.

The glowing ball exploded into a spray of molten light, coating the demons nearest with a luminescent splatter. The demons screeched as their skin made contact with the light from the orb and scattered in all directions.

Two figures astride a pair of horses galloped closer, their sable fur cloaks billowing out behind them in the wind. Alongside them ran a pair of horses following along on leather leads.

Kiki instantly recognized Erasmo's cousins, Yasir and Guille, the closer they came.

"There you are," Yasir cried in relief as he pulled his horse to a stop. He jumped from the saddle and held his hand to Kiki and Solana, still sprawled on the ground. "Where are the others?" he asked, looking around for his cousins.

"It's a long story," Kiki said, accepting his help.

Guille moved to Luna, his brows knitted together in worry. He produced a glass vial from his robes and had her sip from it.

"We noticed your camp a few miles from here. We started doing a perimeter sweep when we heard all the commotion," Guille said, turning to Kiki.

"Thank the saints you came when you did," Kiki said with relief as she wiped the sweat from her brow.

"Mount up, ladies," Yasir called, tugging the two extra horses toward them. "Let's get out of here before that horde decides to come back for seconds."

Kiki spun to help Luna out of the stretcher while Solana bundled up the furs and strapped them to her horse's back.

"She can ride with me," Guille offered, helping hoist Luna from the stretcher to a stand. "My horse can handle both of us. We'll be fine."

Kiki turned her attention to Luna, unsure how her friend would feel about riding with Guille now that she and Mauri had sealed the mate bond.

Luna gave her a reassuring grin, albeit it barely ghosted across her lips with her fatigue. "It's okay; Guille's my friend."

Trusting Luna to handle herself, Kiki moved to mount the remaining horse. As she approached the beast, she patted its nose while notching her foot in the stirrup. "Alright, friend, I don't like this any more than you, so let's take this nice and easy."

Kiki wasn't used to riding horseback. Her time in the Cicatrix was the most exposure to the beasts than she'd ever had.

Horses were expensive to properly care for, and the Demon Corps was nothing if not cheap and stretched for resources.

Horses were a luxury saved for the Protectorate and the upper classes hidden behind their mile-high stone walls.

Though she'd never admit it aloud, least of all to Erasmo, she didn't like riding horseback. She always ended up feeling sore in places she didn't think could get sore.

Once Luna was seated in front of Guille, Yasir nudged his horse forward and led them toward their camp at a gallop.

Soon enough, they made it back to camp, and when the rune markings became visible once more, Kiki allowed herself to relax for what felt like the first time in days.

Two tents remained standing, the canvas stretched taught between stakes driven into the cold ground. The third and smallest tent sat off to the side in a pile of ripped shreds and discarded rope—the aftermath of her and Solana's attempts to fashion the canvas and poles into a sled.

She exhaled deeply as she slid off her horse, giving it a gentle pat on the side. "Thanks for not bucking me off." The horse made a chuffing sound that Kiki took to mean 'You're welcome.' "The first chance I get, I'm giving you the biggest bag of apples."

As if the horse understood her, he made a pleasant nickering sound and nudged her with his nose.

Kiki moved toward Luna and Guille, offering her friend help down, and together they meandered into the safety of the largest tent and sank to the ground with relief.

Yasir moved to unpack the horses while Guille set about making a fire to warm them.

As Guille set about gathering wood, he said, "How does a nice meal sound?"

Kiki hadn't realized how hungry she was until she'd collapsed into a pile of furs they'd left behind.

"That sounds like heaven," Kiki murmured, her eyes drifting closed at the promise of food.

Guille chuckled at her response and smiled warmly. He set about preparing the meal with practiced ease.

"What are you and Yasir doing here?" Solana asked as she tugged off her twin bandoliers and unlaced her boots.

"We got worried when you didn't come back as planned. We expected you back yesterday, and when we didn't see you approach, nor did our scouts spot you, we feared the worst."

"Thank you," Solana said solemnly, her head bowed. "We're grateful for your due diligence."

Guille gave her a soft smile, "Anything for family," he replied like it was a mantra.

He turned his attention back to his task, and Kiki couldn't help how her heart ached at watching him pull vegetables from his knapsack and a small cutting board just large enough to cut one onion at a time. Seeing his ease around preparing a meal reminded her too much of Erasmo and the meal he'd prepared for her at the inn.

The way he'd hummed a sad melody as he worked, the way his shirt had ridden up, revealing his delicious abs. She resisted the urge to groan in frustration, the events of the last few days jostling against one another for her attention.

But she didn't want to think about any of that now. The exhaustion of everything that had happened washed over her, and before she knew it, she'd fallen to sleep.

Chapter Twelve

Erasmo

Erasmo slumped against the stone wall of his cell, his breaths sawing in and out of his lungs. Glancing to his left and right, he saw that he had fared no better than Mauri or Bernat.

Arlando had ordered his guards to torment them while he lounged in the corner of the dungeon, a decanter of red wine at his elbow and a smug smirk on his face.

Fury rose in his gut and unfurled in his chest. He was going to enjoy ripping his brother apart limb from limb. Family was the one boundary that no one should ever be willing to cross because family was blood. Family was what one was born with; no matter what, family was supposed to hold those bonds sacred.

What was worse was that Arlando was Erasmo's twin. They'd shared a womb together. Been born minutes from each other. They'd taken their first steps together. Played together. Cried together.

It was as if a lance pierced Erasmo's heart at the foolish hope he'd harbored. A hope that had cost him his freedom and could very well cost Kiki her life.

He glared at his brother's pallid skin and silver-white hair, barely recognizing his brother as his twin. At one time, they'd been nearly impossible to tell apart. They had the same features, the same height, and the same muscular build. They even used to walk with the same gait. But now... Now he didn't recognize the man smirking at him.

Erasmo grabbed at his chest, right above where his heart beat violently against his ribs, where the pain of this betrayal took root and festered.

Arlando had violated the most basic tenant of familial bonds. For his betrayal against his own flesh and bone, Erasmo would render pain from his body until he was sated.

He just had to get out of this godforsaken cage before Kiki tried storming into the Winter Keep, machetes in both hands and the fire of hell in her eyes.

Not that he wouldn't enjoy such a sight. Just the thought of her in such an inferno of glory made his cock harden in his pants.

Gods, how he wanted to pull her body against his own. How he wanted to dip his tongue into her sweet cunt and lap at her until she came so hard, the whole earth shattered around them. Already he missed the little sounds she made beneath him as he drove his cock deep inside her tight little pussy.

Now his dick was painfully pressing against his pants, aching for the only one who could stoke his flames and send his soul soaring.

With a grunt of pent-up frustration, he curled his hands around the bloody hay at his fingertips and tossed it toward the bars of his cell.

"Nice," Mauri deadpanned to his right. "Just keep doing that, and we'll be out of here in no time." He adjusted from his position, sprawled on the ground until he came to lean against the wall, mirroring Erasmo.

Erasmo rolled his eyes, knowing full well that Mauri dealt with bad situations with humor. But Erasmo wasn't in the mood. He wanted Kiki. He wanted her so bad that his heart ached.

Despite how much he yearned for her, the last thing he wanted was for her to actually come for him. That would be walking right into Arlando's plan, and he couldn't bear to see her suffer at his twin's hands.

No. He needed a plan. Something that Arlando wouldn't see coming. Or, perhaps, *someone*...

"Hey, Mauri," Erasmo called.

"Literally right here, jackass," Mauri grumbled.

Erasmo heaved a breath, fortifying himself with the patience needed to deal with his cousin's mercurial nature and the need to diffuse every situation with humor. "Any theories on why Arlando can harm his mate? Shouldn't the bond make that impossible?"

Mauri shrugged. "He shouldn't be able to stomach the thought," he growled. "If I think of any harm coming to Luna—" He clenched his jaw and curled his hands into fists. "I feel like I want to murder something, then bathe in its blood, drape its entrails across my shoulders, and offer the bastard's heart to her in the center of my hands. Then I want to fuck her while we're covered in the blood of our enemies." He was breathing heavily now, his eyes shifting from deep brown to crimson.

"Thanks, psycho," Erasmo groaned. "That image is going to haunt me until the day I die."

"You're welcome. Can't let you grow soft on me."

"Right, because we're in such a state of luxury, the threat is real," Erasmo said, his tone full of sarcasm.

"Exactly," Mauri grinned, his smile lopsided from a busted lip.

"What's in your head, Raz?" Bernat spoke up, his baritone a deep rumbling growl.

Thankful for the conversation being steered back into focus, Erasmo turned to his older brother. "I'm just wondering how Alando can do it. The bond is sacred. The merging of two equal souls into an unbreakable thread. He shouldn't be capable of causing her harm."

"Should or shouldn't doesn't make a difference," Mauri snapped. "He did, and that's the end of it."

Erasmo rolled his eyes. "Yes, but how?"

"What difference does it make?" Mauri grumbled. "Is the answer to your question going to magically bust us out of here? Are we suddenly going to be able to save our mates from their fate?"

"Fate?" Bernat pushed in, his brows raised. "Are you saying you believe the prophecy?"

"I don't know what to believe. All I know is my mate is out there," he pointed in the direction they could all feel the threads tugging their hearts. "And I'm stuck in here. I know she will come for me, and I don't want her to. I know that Arlando can't lay a finger on her if she is far away from here. And I know that there is nothing I can do to stop him. That's what I know. Everything else is just bullshit."

Erasmo opened his mouth to tell Mauri off for spiraling into doom and gloom, but Bernat caught his eye and shook his head, stopping him.

Scooting closer to the bars adjoining their cells, Bernat leaned in and whispered, "Yarixa being Arlando's mate doesn't make sense. I've known her for years. She's been Kiki's shadow for even longer. She's the gentlest, sweetest person you'll ever meet. So, if you're thinking what I'm thinking, then I think we found a way out of here."

Erasmo nodded. "The only problem is how to talk to her."

None of them could contrive a way to bring Yarixa back to the dungeon. The last thing any of them wanted was for Arlando to bring her back for the sole purpose of torturing her again.

So they agreed to get what rest they could, not knowing what Arlando had in store for them next.

Erasmo shifted in the pile of hay underneath him, the dry straw poking him through his pants and shirt. He wished he could remove his boots, but he didn't like the idea of his feet being tickled all night.

He wasn't so spoiled that he couldn't handle sleeping on the ground, let alone in this cage. That was the least of his worries.

Right now, he was concerned about how close he could sense Kiki. She wasn't as far as she had been earlier in the day. He figured she had felt his pain through the bond and come running.

Relief had filled him when he sensed her presence fade once more as if she'd come close and had retreated to regroup.

He wished he could speak to her. Communicate in some way. That's why Yari was so important to his plan. If he could get Yari away and to the safety of La Aguilera, back with Kiki, Sol, and Luna to protect her. The four of them would be safe and untouchable by Arlando.

The ache in his body and the pounding in his head wasn't enough to stave off the exhaustion that washed over him, and before he knew it, he had fallen fast asleep.

He stood in a training yard, the ground scuffed with the heels of too many boots and the dried stains of blood from one too many broken noses.

He smiled as he slowly spun around, taking in the familiar space of La Aguilera.

The sound of a woman screaming and the distinct clunk of metal against wood lured him toward the area where they kept the training dummies.

Only one person he knew took her anger out on inanimate objects.

He smiled as he rounded the corner, getting a full view of Kiki as she spun with her machete in the air and sliced off the dummy's wooden head.

Her brow gleamed with sweat, and her hair stuck to her neck. Her black Slayer leathers molded to every perfect curve of her body, teasing him with the knowledge of what he knew waited for him underneath.

He leaned his shoulder against the weapon's shed, off to the side where he could see her in all her glory.

This was a nice dream to have. He just wished it were real. He wished he could hold her in his arms, breathe in her scent of cinnamon and apples. Kiss her soft lips.

There was an array of other more depraved things he wanted to do with her body as well, but since he wasn't really here, he'd have to settle for admiring her from afar.

Kiki wiped her brow with the back of her hand and kicked the remains of the dummy to the ground, its wooden body hissing into mist in a *way that could only ever happen in a dream. Another wooden dummy, head and all, quickly materialized to replace the first. She examined her machete and the nicks in the obsidian and tossed that to the side too. Her empty palms were quickly filled with a pair of brand-new shining blades.*

Erasmo chuckled. Only Kiki would dream something like this—an endless supply of weapons and objects to pulverize. He expected nothing less of his little demon slayer.

Kiki whirled around and faced him then, her mouth agape at seeing him. "Erasmo?"

He blinked in confusion.

"Saints, it is you!" She tossed both machetes to the ground and sprinted toward him, her hair catching the wind and fluffing up behind her head. Her eyes glistened with unshed tears as she raced closer, and before he knew it, she threw herself into his open arms.

He wrapped her in his embrace, his instincts kicking in before his mind could catch up.

How was this possible?

Her familiar scent filled his nostrils as she dove her nose into the crook of his neck, her hot breath fanning across his skin. She wrapped her legs tight around his waist and clung to him like a coati on a tree.

"What happened? Are you okay? How are you here in my dream? Where's Turi?" Her questions rushed from her mouth so fast he barely heard them all.

And answering them was the last thing on his mind, not while he could feel her soft curves pressing against him and the salty perfume of her sweat just within licking distance.

He stopped her barrage of questions with his mouth. Because his tongue needed to answer her first, his body needed her more than he needed air, more than life itself.

He yanked her mouth to his, diving his tongue into the sweetness of her mouth, his kiss full of all the fiery passion he possessed for this woman. His mate. His whole world.

He felt her melt into him, surrendering to his embrace as their tongues clashed together. He could feel the buzzing energy between them; every inch of his skin felt alive with anticipation for what was to come.

He tightened his grip on her waist as he pulled her closer, deepening the kiss further as if doing so would sync the beats of their hearts and join them into one being for the rest of eternity.

The world around them faded into nothingness, and he was lost in her, consumed by her. He ran his hands over her body, savoring the feeling of her soft skin beneath his touch.

They parted, gasping for air, their foreheads touching as they looked into each other's eyes. He could see the desire and longing in her gaze, and he knew with certainty that he wanted nothing more than to pleasure her in every way possible.

He trailed kisses down her neck, nipping at her earlobe before whispering, "I need you, now."

"Yes," she moaned in response, her hands tangling in his hair as she pressed herself closer to him.

"I'm not asking you. I'm telling you," he growled.

Without another word, he carried her back into the manor house, the details of his home fuzzy and incomplete in the space of her dream, and followed the familiar path up to his room.

He kicked open the door and didn't bother to close it. No one else was here to see them anyway.

He laid her down, his lips never leaving her skin as he tugged down the zipper of her leathers inch by agonizing inch.

She was his, completely and utterly. And he was going to show her just how much he loved her, worshiping every inch of her body with his lips and tongue. He took his time, savoring every moment, until she was writhing beneath him, lost in the pleasure he was giving her.

"Now, be a good girl for me and take off those fucking leathers before I shred them into pieces."

The corner of her mouth lifted into a smirk as she shimmied her arms out from the skin-tight leather and did a little wriggle to bring her legs out as well.

He knew it drove her wild when he told her what he wanted, and he had every intention of telling her tonight.

With her completely bare before him, he couldn't resist the urge to take a nipple into his mouth, tasting the saltiness and sweetness of her skin.

"Fuck, these tits are so perfect," he said around a mouthful of her hard nipple.

"Please, Erasmo," she whined, "I need you."

Her hands fumbled with the buttons of his shirt, desperate to feel the hard muscles under his clothes. He broke the kiss, nibbling on her bottom lip before trailing his lips down her jawline to the spot just below her ear that he knew drove her wild.

She gasped as his teeth grazed the sensitive skin, and he felt her nails dig into his back, urging him on. His hands ran down her body, cupping her curves and pulling her even tighter against him.

He could feel the heat radiating off her body, and he knew he couldn't hold back any longer. "I have to be inside you," he growled.

"Then take me, you fool," she snapped, yanking at the belt around his waist and freeing his hard cock from his pants.

She encircled him with her hand, and he stifled a groan.

"Just fuck me, already!" she demanded, adding a gentle stroke to the command.

"Just a needy little whore for my cock, aren't you?" he whispered against the shell of her ear. He thrust into her hand, a groan escaping his lips from the friction. "Tell me who you belong to."

"You," she panted, trying to angle her body so she could rub her pussy against him. "Only you."

"That's right, princess. You're mine." He pulled her legs wide open, positioning himself at her entrance. He paused for a second to take in the majesty that was her splayed out before him like a fucking feast.

Without waiting for another second, he thrust into her with one swift motion. He stilled, relishing in that first moment of connection, that feeling of coming home.

"Don't hold back. Give me all of it," she whispered.

He smiled, knowing full well that his mate was a little minx. She wrapped her legs around his waist, pulling him deeper into her.

His eyes rolled back in his head as he felt her hips move against him.

He groaned, holding her tighter as he thrust into her hard, her body taking every inch and begging for more. "Fuck you feel so good..." he managed, his voice straining.

She started rocking her hips against him, her beautiful brown eyes locked onto his as he pounded into her.

"Yes, yes, yes!" she chanted between each thrust, her orgasm building. "Fill me up, Erasmo, fill me with your cum."

Fuck. He couldn't take it when she talked dirty to him. The pressure in his balls was building as his orgasm threatened to consume him.

"I love when you're like this. So needy for my cock," he moaned.

He brought his lips to hers, kissing her, dominating her mouth until she was clinging to him. He pulled his mouth away from hers.

"I. Own. You," he growled, punctuating each word with a thrust of his hips.

"Yes," she moaned in reply, her inner walls tightening around him.

He reached between them to play with her clit, rubbing and pinching it.

"Oh saints, I'm going to come," she whimpered, her head arching back as she neared her own orgasm.

"Give it to me, baby," Erasmo growled, thrusting harder. "Let me feel you come around my cock."

Her body tightened around his, her pussy pulsing against his cock as he felt her orgasm rack through her body. He thrust into her a few more times, his own orgasm building with each stroke.

"Fuck, you feel so good," he growled in her ear, thrusting deep into her one last time as his cum filled her pussy until he felt it leaking from her and onto his balls.

He collapsed on top of her, his heart hammering in his chest from how hard he'd just come. He kissed her, a satisfied grunt from his throat as he savored the feeling of their bodies pressed together.

He took a moment to catch his breath before rolling off her. Her skin was covered in a fine sheen of sweat.

When he pulled her into his arms, he could feel the beating of her heart next to his, and he knew that no matter what happened in the future, he would do anything for this woman. He'd die for her as much as he lived for her.

"That was the best dream sex I've ever had in my life," Kiki said, a satisfied smile on her face.

Erasmo quirked a brow at her. "I take it you've had many dreams like this before."

She nodded, nuzzling her nose into his chest. "Oh yes, but never one this vivid. Never one where I could actually see anything."

Erasmo couldn't help but laugh. "So you just let some shadow fuck you silly? That sounds about right."

"Hey! Not some shadow, asshole. Someone, but I never saw their face." She adjusted herself so she was propped on his chest. "Come to think of it, I think it might have been you this whole time."

"Me?" He liked the sound of that, her dreaming of him all this time without even knowing it.

"I mean, we're mates, right? Maybe when I was dreaming of you, you were dreaming of me," she said, lowering her mouth to kiss the space above his heart.

Now he really liked the sound of that.

She sighed heavily. "Are you really here, or is this just my mind's way of coping with all the shit that's going on."

Erasmo shrugged as best he could, with her perched on top of him. "How would I know. You feel real to me. Do I feel real to you?"

She nodded.

"Then maybe this is real. I was asleep one moment, then here the next."

Kiki chewed the bottom of her lip, and he had to resist the urge to take that lip between his own teeth. "Maybe it's the mate bond."

"That's the only explanation I can think of."

Seeming satisfied, she lowered herself back down so her breasts were pressed against his chest.

They let the silence of their shared dream drift around them, the only sound that of their breaths and beating hearts.

But after a few peaceful moments, Kiki's arms tightened around him as she whispered, "Are you okay?"

Erasmo wanted nothing more than to bask in the afterglow of mind-blowing sex with his mate, but he knew she needed answers as much as he needed to protect her.

"I don't even know where to begin," he muttered, his mind flashing with every betrayal he'd endured within the span of a single day.

He figured the best place to start would be the moment he realized he'd made a huge mistake. The moment he'd met Yarixa.

"I'm going to tell you something, but you have to promise me that you won't do anything rash."

Kiki snorted. "Yeah, okay," she said, her tone full of sarcasm.

He couldn't help but smile. Of course, he'd expect nothing less from her. "I found Yarixa."

It felt like the air had been sucked from the room. Everything seemed to freeze. Even Kiki seemed to hold her breath.

Then, quick as lightning, she bolted upright, her breasts bouncing as she adjusted herself to straddle his waist. "What the hell are you talking about?" she demanded, her brows knitted tight together.

"I found your friend. She's been with Arlando this whole time."

Kiki's mouth dropped open in shock, and Erasmo had to quickly tell her everything else before she could pepper him with more questions that he didn't have answers for.

After he told her everything, she shifted off him and sat on the edge of the bed, her eyes unfocused as she took a moment to process everything.

"And you said Turi helped Arlando?" she asked, turning to look at him over her shoulder. "You're sure?"

"Unless he thought he was playing the flute, then, yes, Kiki, I'm sure. He hit me with four to five darts filled with the same sedative Tomás had used, then did the same to Mauri and Bernat."

She shook her head. "I don't understand. Why would he do this? And to Yari as well." She stood up, her naked body on full display, not that he was complaining, as she began to pace at the foot of the bed. "It doesn't make sense. That doesn't sound like the Turi I know."

"Well, get used to it because he's in league with Arlando and helping him draw you, Sol, and Luna in."

Her shoulders sagged. "We came after you all, you know. You probably felt it," she added, pressing her hand over her heart. He nodded. He had indeed felt when she'd drawn near.

"But we realized we couldn't take on your brother by ourselves. Not with that army of demons; he has the place surrounded."

"Demons?" he asked, sitting up as well. "What do you mean?"

"You didn't see them?" she scoffed. "The castle is full of them, all the outer walls and inner gates too. He's got full squadrons of demons, just lurking around, patrolling the area."

His heart thundered in his chest at the news. Standing up, he rushed toward her and clapped his hands on her arms. "Promise me you won't come back," he said, his eyes wide with fear. "If what you say is true, then Arlando is far more powerful than any of us thought. You need to get yourself, Luna, and Solana as far away from here as possible. Pack up your camp right now and run."

Kiki yanked herself from his grip. "I will do no such thing. We're going back to La Aguilera, yes, but then we're coming right back with an army of our own."

Erasmo laughed without humor. "La Aguilera doesn't have that type of army. You'd be slaughtered."

Kiki crossed her arms over her chest, her breasts pressing together in a most distracting way. "Thanks for the vote of confidence, asshole."

"I didn't mean it like that, Kiki, and you know it."

She rolled her eyes. "Well, I don't have to listen to you. You got yourself captured, and now I have to do what I always do, rescue you."

Erasmo couldn't help the laughter that peeled from his chest. "You're such a piece of work, Kiki," he said as he crossed the distance and took her by the waist, pulling her close. "Last time I checked, we're even in the saving each other department."

She wriggled in his arms, barely trying to get away from him. "Then you really need to go back to school because you suck at counting."

"Do I now?" he hummed, running his hands down her spine to the curve of her ass. "How many orgasms did I give you that one time? I forget. Four? Five?"

She lashed out with her fist and pegged him in the chest. "It was six, you self-righteous bastard, and you'll never let me forget it."

"No," he grinned. "I won't. Not until I beat my own record."

She rolled her eyes. "You're a bigger idiot than I thought if you think I'm going to leave you to rot in some cage while your maniac of a brother tortures you to death."

He exhaled deeply, pulling her closer. "I wouldn't be able to bear it if you got hurt because of me. I wouldn't survive it if Arlando got his hands on you and sacrificed you for the sake of the curse. There is no world that I could live in if you're not in it, Kiki. You're it for me. Forever. I will never love another like I love you. I never have."

Her brown eyes searched his own, her teeth chewing at her bottom lip. "Don't you think I feel the same way? Don't you know how much I love you? That I'd do anything to save you? That I'd die trying if that's what it took?"

"NO!" he growled, gripping her even tighter until she made a sound that had him loosening his hold.

"Don't think I don't know you as well as I know myself, Erasmo Ozetero. If I've thought about it, then so have you. Why should you be the only one willing to lay their life on the line?"

He couldn't bring himself to argue with her, not when he knew she meant every word.

"You can't ask me to leave you behind, Erasmo," she said softly. "Don't ever bring it up again."

"Lo que quieras, mi amor," he said, pressing his lips to her forehead. "You win."

"Of course, I win. Did you really think you had a chance?"

He felt his lips tugging into a grin. "Not in a million years."

As if sensing his time with her was quickly coming to an end, he attacked her lips with his own, putting everything he'd left unsaid into the kiss.

"Please be safe," he whispered before the dream collapsed into swirling mist, sending him tumbling down into a black abyss of perpetual falling.

When he jolted awake, he was once more back in the confines of his cage, the dungeon dank and smelling of rot. But his heart was full, and for now, that was enough.

Chapter Thirteen

Yari

Yari stared out the window with a vacant stare as she took in all that Turi had explained.

As she listened to him tell the story of her abduction and the journey that led him to the Winter Keep, a whirlwind of feelings and thoughts raced through her mind, leaving her uncertain about how to handle them all.

She was relieved to learn that both Kiki and Luna were alive, even if they weren't exactly safe, not with Arlando hell-bent on capturing them so he could end the curse that plagued the males of the Ozetero lineage.

She was still surprised whenever Turi spoke about Bernat as his eldest brother. They'd been in the same Demon Corps company for years if not their whole lives, and no one had put two and two together.

Not even Bernat. But by the sounds of it, he'd assumed his entire family had been swallowed by the Cicatrix and hadn't held onto the foolish hope of ever seeing any of them again. He'd been so young when it had happened, not younger than her, of course, but still, losing everything one has ever known is traumatic at any age, let alone while still a child.

However, what brought her grief was the knowledge that in his foolish attempt to get Arlando to trust him, Turi had helped his brother capture Erasmo and Mauri alongside Bernat.

Though she didn't know Erasmo or Mauri, it was enough to know that Erasmo was Kiki's mate and that Mauri was Luna's.

That status alone made them important to her. They were men her sisters had fallen in love with—or rather, been bonded to through this mate bond thing. For that reason alone, she cared for their welfare and grieved for the pain they undoubtedly endured while Arlando tortured them.

All to bring her friends running. So he could sacrifice them.

It made her sick.

The man she'd thought Arlando to be was nothing but a lie. She'd accepted that fact. But it didn't stop the sting of betrayal from burrowing deeper into her chest.

"Please say something," Turi whispered, leaning forward in his seat, his elbows propped on his knees as he stared at her.

She was fully aware that he was waiting for a response. But she'd remained silent during his entire confession as she tried to process every-thing.

She had no words to express the chaos within. She felt like her insides were in knots. Her heart raced, and her stomach churned as conflicting emotions swirled around her, battling for control.

She turned to face him and noted the dark circles beneath his azure eyes. "I don't know what you want from me, Turi," she admitted. "I—why are you telling me all of this now? What does any of this have to do with you treating me like dirt beneath your boot?"

Turi ran a hand through his black hair, further tousling it. "I need you to understand that the mate bond isn't a choice. It just is. Destiny or fate or whatever you want to call it forges the bond without a care for what we have to say about it."

She shook her head sadly, gazing at her hands in her lap. "Fate must have it out for me then because it has a sick sense of humor to bind me to Arlando."

Turi reached out his hand slowly and paused midway as if hesitating before enveloping her hands in his much larger one. "I'm sorry he hurt you."

She couldn't bear the touch of another man, not when her heart still bore the scars of what Arlando had done to her. She twisted her hands from Turi's grasp and moved them to either side of her chair.

"Hurt isn't the word I'd use, Turi," she said quietly, those feelings of hatred and anger flaring to life like embers in a fire.

Turi swallowed the lump in his throat as he searched for words.

But there was nothing he could say that would bring her any comfort. Nothing short of Arlando's still beating heart laid out on a platter for her would make anything right again.

Whoa, where did that come from?

She had never been one to relish in the thrill of battle, so why was she fantasizing about Arlando's blood spilling into a puddle at her feet? Why did her heart race when she pictured him begging for his life and her standing above him, dagger in hand, as she plunged it right into his cock? Why did that thought fill her with so much exhilaration?

"He isn't your mate, Yari," Turi said softly, his brows knitting together as if he were in agony over what he was about to say.

"Aren't I? Isn't that why he used that awful device on himself today? To show your brothers and cousin that he'd do the same to them in order to draw in Kiki, Luna, and Solana?"

"Yes, but you're not the only one who felt the burn against your skin." He tugged at the high collar of his jacket, revealing a black scorch mark in the same place as her own.

Unconsciously, her fingers drifted to her protruding collar bones, inches away from her twin wound. "How?" she whispered.

"I don't know," he admitted sadly. "But I don't believe he is your mate."

He left the implication unspoken, allowing her to come to the realization in her own time.

"You?" she asked, feeling a distinct pull in the center of her stomach urging her to draw closer to him. But she didn't want that. She just wanted to sink into the very fabric of the chair and disappear forever.

"No," she said, standing in a rush and backing away from him slowly. "I don't want this," she murmured. "I didn't ask for this. For any of it."

Turi watched her with wary eyes. "I know you didn't. None of us did. But you can feel it, can't you? That feeling like there is this inescapable tug, reeling you in, like a thread wrapped around your heart, winding round and round a spool the closer you get?"

That thread tugged on her heart sharply as if responding to his words.

Tears stung her eyes as she realized the truth of his words. "Yes," she whispered. "But I can't be that for you, Turi. I can't."

"But you already are, Yari. That's what I'm trying to tell you. You're my mate."

She didn't realize she'd backed all the way toward the door, her back pressed against the wood. "I can't be anyone's mate now, don't you understand?" she hissed. "I'm worthless. Ruined. Spoiled."

Turi rushed forward, a growl on his lips. "Don't you dare speak about yourself that way."

"Do you even know what he's done to me? Truly?" she whispered, blinking away the tears welling in her eyes.

Turi's eyes flashed red before returning to their normal blue. "Yes," he rumbled. "And he will pay for what he's done if it's the last thing I do."

"Then how could you possibly want anything to do with me?" she asked, her heart aching with the pain of her trauma and the foolish hope that anyone would find her worthy of real all-consuming, self-sacrificing love.

"Because mate bond or not, you are precious, Yari. You always have been. You're the sweetest, kindest, most caring person I've ever met. You see the best in people, even when they have very little good in them. You trust with your whole heart, even if that means your heart will just get broken. You don't give up on people, and you've never given up on hope. You're the stars shining bright on the darkest night. And you are more than anything I could ever deserve, but I am willing to spend the rest of my life doing anything I can to prove to you how worthy you are of love and kindness and care."

Tears slipped from her eyes as if each word were a balm for her battered soul.

He reached out to wipe them away, but she ducked her head away. "Please don't," she said in a soft voice. "I—I can't."

His eyes winced shut, knowing why she couldn't bear his touch. When he opened them again, he said, "I make you this promise, Yari. Even if it kills me. I will bring him to his knees and offer him as a sacrifice at the altar of your feet. That will be my sole purpose in this life, to one day watch with pride as you cut out his cold, shriveled heart and hold it still beating between your precious hands."

She stared at him in shock, wondering how he had been able to discern her deepest, darkest desires. She wanted Arlando to pay for what he had done to her, and here was this man making a solemn vow that he'd ensure vengeance would be hers.

She wished she could throw her arms around him in gratitude, but the thought made her stomach flip over itself and twist into a knot.

"But first," Turi added. "We need to get you out of this castle and to safety."

He turned and began looking around the room. "I can draw a map leading you to La Aguilera. If you leave tonight and take one of the horses from the stable, ride through the night, and don't stop, not even to rest, you can make it to the eyrie before nightfall tomorrow."

The thought of escaping this living hell sent a rush of relief through her. This is also what she wanted. She couldn't bear to be around Arlando a minute longer. What if he came barging into her room again, drunk and ravenous for her flesh? What if he took that which she was not offering once more? She didn't think she'd survive it. Once was enough.

But then she thought of Kiki and Luna and their mates lying in the filth of the dungeon, their bodies covered in welts and oozing wounds.

She wouldn't be able to live with herself if she knew she'd left them here to rot. She wouldn't be able to look Kiki in the eyes, knowing that she'd saved herself and done nothing to help the man Kiki loved.

It warmed her heart, knowing that Kiki had not hesitated for a moment when she deduced that Yari had been abducted. Deep down, she'd held onto that secret hope that Kiki would save her. She'd even prayed for it, not knowing that her prayers had been answered.

Kiki had stomped into the face of the darkness itself and didn't waver. All because of a hunch. No real evidence. No real hope, even.

Yari steeled her spine and stood taller, remembering her promise to herself. That if she wanted to survive this hellscape, she'd have to think more like Kiki.

Turning to Turi as he searched the room for pen and ink, she realized that she had decided.

"I'm not leaving," she said, her tone firm and unwavering.

Turi's mouth dropped open. "No, you can't stay. I won't be around all the time to protect you from him. I slipped some of the sedatives he used on my brothers into his glass tonight, but I bet my life that he'd notice if he were to pass out every night like that."

She chewed on the inside of her cheek in thought. Staying meant that she might face Arlando's cruel brand of punishment. But if she left?

She shook her head. "I can't just save myself. I'd never be able to face Kiki and Luna ever again. Even if they forgave me, I wouldn't. I'd have to live with that. I'm tired of being sheltered by everyone around me. Let me do this, Turi. Trust that I can handle it."

His gaze darkened as his eyes roved over the delicate features of her face. "You know, you're much stronger than you think, Yari. I don't think you've ever given yourself enough credit for that."

She scoffed. "I'm nothing like Kiki and Luna. I don't run into the face of battle with a smile on my face. I'd never rush forward to help the wounded, not once flinching in the face of their agony and their destroyed flesh."

"No, you're not like either of them in that way. But you're no less brave than them, either. You've always had the courage to be kind, even if you knew it would amount to nothing, even if you'd just get dirt kicked in your face. You've always had the courage to hope, even when there seems to be none at all. You've always held on to that spark you have inside, and I think that takes the most courage of all."

She didn't know what to say to something like that, so she ducked her head and pushed an errant brown curl behind her ear.

Turi moved until he stood in front of her, and though he leaned forward as if he couldn't control himself and the urge to be close to her, he didn't push her boundary by trying to touch her.

"I'll do everything I can to distract Arlando. I'll slip him the sedative every night, even if he figures it out. We have until then to come up with a plan."

She nodded, her heart racing at the prospect of what they were going to try to do. "How do we open those cages?"

He shook his head sadly, "That's the first problem we'll have to figure out. In the meantime, we need to map out an escape route that will get us past the demons and out from under Arlando's nose."

"I'll start working on it," she said, feeling braver than she ever had in her life despite what Turi said.

Turi lingered for a moment, his hand twitching at his side as if he was fighting an internal battle to reach out and touch her. But he pulled himself out of his trance and slipped from the room.

She returned to the bed and wriggled under the covers, but she knew she'd get no sleep this night. Her mind was abuzz with plans to escape and save the men in the cages.

CHAPTER FOURTEEN

KIKI

"Quiet!" Yasir roared.

The dining hall was a swirl of people yelling and arguing, their voices bouncing off the wood-paneled walls and high ceiling.

The taste of unease and disappointment poured from the room like chicha that's gone sour, full of bitterness and regret.

Yasir pounded his fist on the table, making the glasses and dishes rattle.

"I said be quiet!" he bellowed.

But the room of men refused to listen, too engrossed in their rescue plans, revenge plots, and general descriptions of vengeance against Arlando for capturing Bernat, Erasmo, and Mauri.

Kiki stood next to Luna and Solana with her arms crossed over her chest, frustration furrowing her brows at the male display before her.

Their return to La Aguilera had been nothing but a chaotic mess of questions, outraged males, and far too much shouting to make any real decisions.

Everyone knew why they had called this meeting—to plot a rescue attempt.

Yasir retreated a few steps, rejoining Kiki and the others. "It's no use. Everyone's blood is boiling right now. We'll never get them to shut up long enough to go over ideas, let alone any real strategy."

At Luna's elbow, Guille leaned forward and said, "We're without a leader. Erasmo has filled the role of the family head since the exodus from the Winter Keep. Things were looking brighter when Bernat returned. No one questioned him or even dared to think it. But now? We don't have anyone that the whole family will unanimously get behind."

Kiki quirked a brow at that. "I can understand that, but why Bernat?" she asked, uncrossing her arms and motioning to the rest of the Ozero family. "Everyone has known Erasmo for their whole lives. Why did they suddenly listen to Bernat after he'd been gone for over a decade?"

Yasir and Guille exchanged a look as if the answer were obvious.

"Bernat is the rightful king of Ozero," Yasir answered. "The throne is his birthright. We have followed the line of succession from the beginning. Arlando was the second oldest, so he was our leader by default. But we all looked to Erasmo when it became clear that he was losing his sense of reality. If Bernat had never returned and something had happened to Erasmo, we would have looked to Turi. It's the order of things. It's what keeps us all in line. No one would dare question it."

"Except perhaps Arlando," Guille muttered.

"True," Yasir admitted. "Bernat is our brother and our king. It's our honor to follow him."

Kiki didn't have a whole lot of personal experience with such strong familial loyalty. But she understood the concept just fine, having long been committed to the Demon Corps.

A pang of regret pierced her stomach at the thought of the Corps.

I guess I wasn't as loyal as I thought since I jumped ship the moment one of my own was in danger.

A wild thought occurred to her. If the Ozetero family held the idea of loyalty and lines of succession in such high regard, then perhaps...

"Solana is Bernat's mate. What does that make her to everyone else?" she asked, pointing a thumb toward Sol.

The Commander quirked a red brow at Kiki but looked to Yasir and Guille for their response.

Guille rubbed his palms together. "Well, technically, that would make you the equivalent of Bernat's wife, which would make you his queen, which, in turn, would make you *our* queen."

He exchanged a look with Yasir as if checking that what he was saying was true. Yasir only nodded, nonplussed.

Kiki could only blink at the Commander. It hadn't occurred to her that Solana might now be considered their queen. But it made complete sense now that Guille and Yasir pointed it out.

Solana seemed unfazed by this revelation and merely nodded her head like someone had just told her the weather for the day.

Squaring her shoulders, she stepped forward and glided into the middle of the room.

The room suddenly filled with murmurs as everyone noticed her pull out a chair from one of the tables, the legs screeching across the floor, and she stepped into the center of the table above all the others in the room.

"The time for bickering is over," she began, her voice low yet full of power and authority. "The fact is, Arlando has taken captive your king, your prince, and your cousin and has done so without provocation."

The room went completely silent as everyone waited for Solana to continue.

"What we need now is to come together and act as one. There are several problems that we need solutions to, and any in-fighting is only going to lead us to defeat."

Kiki could feel the shift in the air as the men in the room listened to Solana with rapt attention.

"I need three working groups to brainstorm ideas and solutions to the following problems—"

Solana then described the problem with breaking the curse and the prophecy and the need to find another loophole that would break the curse. She then laid out the situation in the north with the demon army guarding the Winter Keep and the need to assemble a fighting force that could infiltrate the castle, rescue the guys and capture Arlando in the process. Finally, she explained the need for a logistical team to coordinate the necessary supplies for the various ventures and act as a central information hub.

"Yasir will lead the team that's working the situation in the north," she announced to the nodding heads in the crowd. "Guille will take point on the curse breaking as he is our resident magi. That leaves the logistics."

A very large man in the back of the room raised his hand and stepped forward. "I'll take the lead on that, mi reina. I manage the receipts and storage of supplies to La Aguilera and have been teaching my brother how to manage things for when—"

He paused, and the energy in the room turned sober.

He swallowed the lump in his throat. "For when I don't return from the shift."

A young man, likely his brother, gave him a comforting pat on the shoulder.

"He can manage La Aguilera. I'd like to manage everything we need to return our king to his rightful place and the plans necessary to end this curse once and for all."

Solana gave him a firm nod. "What's your name, sir?"

"Ramón, mi reina," he replied with a reverent bow of his head.

"Ramón," Solana repeated, mulling the name over her tongue. "I can think of no one better to be the operational mind of our efforts than a man whose name means 'resolute protector'. Thank you for your service."

"Mi reina," he answered and clapped his fist to his chest over his heart.

Next to him, his younger brother mirrored the salute, and one by one, the rest of the men in the room had done the same, the air echoing with the reverberations of heavy claps over their chests.

Then, as one, the men dropped to one knee, their heads bowed.

"Solana, La Reina Suprema," someone in the crowd said, and the rest of the room repeated the phrase until it became a chant that filled the room.

A strange feeling washed over Kiki at seeing how the Ozetero family so readily bowed to the mate of their king. So readily accepted Solana as their queen.

Solana stood atop the table, slowly turning as she took in the men chanting her name and newfound title. The Supreme Queen.

Despite her past with Solana, Kiki couldn't deny that there was no one more qualified to take on the weight of responsibility that was being thrust upon her.

No one commanded attention and respect quite like Solana Ramirez. She was a force to be reckoned with, and anyone who knew her for three seconds could instantly tell that she was exceptional.

Next to her, Luna and Guille dropped to their knees, Yasir having been on his knee since she'd given him command over the military aspect of their plan.

Oh, what the hell.

Kiki dropped to her knee and clapped her fist to her chest, dropping her head to her chest as well.

When she peeked a glance up, she caught Solana's gaze trained on her. The Commander gave her the faintest of smiles, a silent 'thanks' before turning to the crowd to begin preparations.

Kiki stood along with the rest of the room as people started moving toward their respected leaders, choosing the groups that would most use their skill to the fullest.

Finally, now we're getting somewhere!

The need to act and rip into something was overwhelming. Kiki hated waiting around and doing nothing. She wasn't known for her patience, and now, more than ever, she wanted to return to the Winter Keep and say, 'fuck it' and try to beat through the demon army all on her own.

Logically, she knew that was a stupid idea, and she'd only get herself killed.

But that didn't stop the rage-filled fantasies from occupying most of her thoughts.

"Kiki!" Luna's voice penetrated through her reverie.

She blinked at her friend. "What?"

"I've been talking to you," Luna said, her tone full of annoyance.

Kiki gave Luna an apologetic smile. "I'm sorry, I sort of went to a dark place in my mind. What were you saying?"

Luna nodded understanding and motioned to Guille, "I will work with Guille on the curse. I assume you want to work with Yasir and the battle plans."

Kiki nodded. She hadn't thought that far. But yes, that made the most sense. She knew nothing about magic and trusted Luna to look for a solution to the curse that didn't involve sacrificing their lives to end it.

"Okay, well, Yasir took off that way with a group of people. Just thought you should know."

Kiki glanced over her shoulder, and sure enough, most of the room had cleared out, along with the blondish rogue. "Damn it!" Kiki spun on her heel to rush after him. She quickly spun around and shouted her thanks to Luna.

"Get your head on!" she responded with a playful grin.

Chapter Fifteen

Turi

Turi surveyed the table of food, illuminated by a row of taper candles that were nearly melted down to nothing. Yari's silver dress glittered beneath the light, and he noticed a hint of sadness behind her pasted-on smile, which was partly concealed by the luxurious fur shawl draped around her tiny frame.

She had carefully pinned her hair back, leaving tiny tendrils framing her face, only adding to the softness of her already delicate features. Her golden brown skin had grown pale from her time so far up north. Still, she had painted her cheeks a rosy hue and had added something to her naturally alluring pout that only made her lips even fuller and more inviting.

Rows of tamales were stacked twelve high, their cornhusks gleaming in the flickering candlelight. Soft flour tortillas and bowls of steamy chicken mole, cabrito, and red rice lay invitingly along the table, filling the air with a medley of aromas: rich chile powder, masarina, and green chiles. Turi's mouth watered at the smells wafting under his nose as his stomach growled in anticipation.

He knew that Yari always compared herself to Kiki and Luna, seeing her best friends as superior to her in every way. But he'd never viewed her in such a way. Each of the three women were strong in their own ways.

Yari was clever and calculating when she wanted to be. She was also kind and her heart ached for those who were treated unfairly and been handed the short stick in life.

He also found her breathtakingly beautiful. He'd never let himself see her in a different light before, but now that the mate bond tugged on his heart anytime he looked at her, all he wanted to do was admire her delicate features.

He did his best to keep his attention on the platters of food before them rather than gluing his gaze to her. Though he'd much rather stare at her, he couldn't afford for Arlando to catch him staring—that was out of the question, and doing so would only put her in danger. Openly admiring her was not an option.

We can smell her soap. The beast within rumbled.

By the Saints, shut up already!

We want a taste. Just a little one.

What part about the fact that she's been raped do you not understand, you sick fuck?

Turi hated the beast that spoke to him. He wished the bastard would just curl up and die.

We can help. The bear said, pacing back and forth now. **We can rid her of his taint and fill her with our cum—**

That's it. You're done for the day. Shut the hell up, or I'm going to get rip-roaring drunk just so I can't hear you. And then that'll put her in danger because I won't be sober enough to look out for her and distract Arlando. Is that what you want?

No.

Then shut your muzzle and stop telling me all the dirty shit you want to do to her.

We want to do it. You and I.

Last warning, beast.

Fine. We be quiet.

Turi sighed in relief.

Yari slowly moved her lips, barely forming the words. "Are you okay?" She kept her gaze focused on the food in front of them as if, at any moment, Arlando would appear and catch them doing something they shouldn't.

The fire in the hearth crackled as Yari and Turi waited for Arlando to make his entrance.

He'd spent the rest of the night sleeping in the main hall and had woken in a foul mood.

Yari had wisely escaped to the safety of the library before he had made it to his suite and hadn't bothered to go look for her himself.

Instead, he'd ordered Turi to look for her and inform her that breakfast would be in the main hall and that he expected her presence.

"Turi?" Yari asked.

"I'm fine," he said, not wanting to worry her and definitely not wanting to admit that there was a beast inside of him with a mind of his own and a set of wicked intentions where she was concerned.

She scanned the empty foyer, eyes darting up the staircase. Her voice a barely audible whisper, she asked, "Where is he?"

Turi glanced sideways at her with a mischievous glint in his eye. "With any luck, he fell asleep in the tub and drowned," he said darkly.

A glimmer of a smile tugged at one corner of her mouth before she quickly suppressed it and smoothened her features.

But when did either of them ever have such luck?

"Turi!" Arlando bellowed, his voice reverberating throughout the deserted hallways of the castle.

Yari flinched in response, the faintest beginning of a frown furrowing her brow before she quickly wiped it away.

Turi screwed his face into a mask of long-suffering, making the corners of Yari's mouth twitch again. He liked seeing her smile, or the ghost of it. He wished she'd smile for real, though.

Knowing they were navigating dangerous waters where Arlando was concerned, he lifted himself from the ornate chair that scraped against the polished marble floor and reluctantly moved away.

"Turi, where are you?" Arlando's deep voice echoed throughout the castle like a cannon blast as he yelled Turi's name. His boots clunked rhythmically against the hardwood floors that lined the upstairs as he stomped down the hallway, rage intensifying with each step.

"Right here, brother," Turi called, his voice echoing off the vaulted ceiling. He dashed through the archway leading to the grand staircase as he desperately tried to intercept Arlando before he swept into the dining hall like a hurricane and caught Yari in his storm.

"The horde we sent last night failed. I need you to gather all the demons around the grounds and bring them here. The women are getting away and are getting farther and farther the longer we stand around and do nothing about it!" Arlando screeched, his eyes wide with fear. "We're going to lose them, and everything I've done will mean nothing!"

Turi hid the relief that heated his blood at knowing the horde of demons Arlando had sent last night to track Kiki, Luna, and Solana had failed to capture them.

"As you wish, brother," he said, adding a respectful bow of his head. Arlando would take it as a sign of Turi's deference, even though that couldn't be farther from the truth.

"All of them," Arlando repeated. "I need every last one of them, Turi. I need them now!"

Arlando's eyes were wide, and his pupils were dilated with fear. His hands shook violently at his sides as he paced.

"Of course. I'll make sure that all the demons are on the prowl. They won't be able to hide from us."

Arlando nodded, giving Turi a pat on the shoulder as he brushed past and headed straight for the dining hall, not bothering to wait and see if Turi followed.

The fact that Kiki and the other two had managed to escape the first horde of demons was a miracle. He hadn't been able to sleep for fear that they'd be captured and dragged back here, where Arlando would be waiting for them.

He didn't think Kiki and Solana would have recovered enough to fight off a second horde. Especially one the size that Arlando was asking him to pull together.

He thanked the Saints that Kiki and Solana were so skilled and clever, but such traits wouldn't help them if they were fatigued and caught off guard again.

He had to do something to stop this.

His thoughts turned to Yari. If he could only convince her to leave, he wouldn't have to worry about her being in danger. She'd be safe, and he'd be able to concentrate his energies on breaking his brothers out of the dungeon and stopping Arlando's attempts to capture Kiki, Luna, and Solana.

If only there was some way to get her away from here. Some way for him to protect her.

He could feel her gaze boring into the back of his skull and instinctively knew that she'd be able to read the turmoil that was painted on his face. Somehow, she was always able to do that. To know what he was thinking when he tried so hard to hide everything from her.

An idea started to form in the back of his mind, and he hid the grin that gently tugged at his lips.

He didn't have control over the demons as a horde the way Arlando did, but he could order them around one at a time.

He made his way toward the main doors of the castle, his plan beginning to grow wings.

The demons were also fairly stupid. He'd witnessed them snarl at one another for the slightest grievances. Perhaps he could make it look like the demons' fault?

It would take him longer than he was sure Arlando was willing to wait, but if he tried two demons at a time, he might just be able to make this work.

He quickened his pace as he made for the courtyard.

Turi watched from the balcony as a pitiful group of demons gathered outside the castle gates. Arlando had been pacing and ranting orders for the last half hour, demanding updates from the guards.

When another hour passed, and Arlando's horde didn't show, anxiety began to unfurl in Turi's stomach.

Would Arlando see through this ruse? Would he immediately suspect Turi?

Turi's chest grew tight as he watched Arlando pace, his hands twitching at his sides, his face red with anger.

Turi knew he had to be very careful. He had to let Arlando believe he was in league with him, that he had every intention of finding the women and bringing them back here.

"Useless, unreliable, disgusting creatures!" Arlando growled, turning to face the smattering of demons that had gathered in the courtyard below.

Turi held in his exhale of relief. His plan had worked.

It had taken every ounce of strength he had to work the blood magic on two to three demons at a time. But sending them all running in multiple directions like packs of idiots had been its own simple entertainment.

Next to him, Arlando roared with frustration, and the demons below them flinched and chittered with unease.

Taking his dagger from his belt, Arlando slashed a deep gouge in his hand and let the blood flow freely in a gushing stream onto the cobblestones below. "Find the mates," he bellowed. "Find them or suffer a fate worse than death."

The gathered demons looked at one another before skittering off toward the south.

Turi could feel his brother's assessing gaze on him, knowing he only had one chance to throw off Arlando's suspicions.

He cleared his throat, "If the demons are really so stupid, perhaps it would be better if we go after the mates ourselves. I'm a decent enough tracker, and you know these lands better than any mindless demon. Perhaps, together, we can bring them back faster."

Turi sent a silent prayer up to the saints to let this work. If he and Arlando were away from the castle for a few days, Yari would be safe, and she'd be able to search for a way to open the cages.

Arlando studied Turi for a long moment before finally giving a curt nod. "You're right, brother. I should never send those beasts to do something that I can do better myself," he said gruffly. "We'll leave at once."

Arlando pivoted on his heel and stormed through the balcony doors back inside, his strides long and full of wicked purpose.

Relief coursed through Turi's veins as he followed after him.

Chapter Sixteen

Kiki

Kiki slashed her machete through the air with a frustrated growl. Today, she was in the training yard working with Yasir on proper Slayer technique. Since the shift wasn't reliable, and the blood lust could just as quickly turn into a bloodbath that wiped them all out, including the demons, it had become painfully clear that the men needed to learn different techniques that didn't rely on fangs and talons.

As the only Demon Slayer in La Aguilera, besides Solana, of course, who was much too busy to be doing something so mundane, the exciting task had fallen to Kiki.

This is not what she had in mind when she joined Operation Fuck-ShitUp, which Yasir had decided to call his little cadre of warriors who would fight the demon army and rescue the guys.

"Come on, Kiks, lighten up!" Yasir joked, swinging his sword behind his head and grasping the other end in his hand so that his arms were bent behind his head.

Kiki growled and pointed the tip of her machete at his face. "Call me Kiks again, and I'll cut your balls off," she snapped.

The cold wasn't helping her mood either. Snow had started to fall and covered the training ground in slippery patches of ice.

She'd fallen one too many times on those little bastards and had the bruises to prove it.

Yasir had a devious expression on his outrageously beautiful face. "You plus my balls sounds like a party," he said with a wicked grin.

Kiki glared at him, knowing full well that he was only trying to get her to stop pouting. He was a shameless flirt and chased after anything with legs. She was convinced that Yasir would fuck the wind if it'd let him.

The real reason for her foul mood was that, after taking stock of their supplies and their numbers, they'd come to the conclusion that La Aguilera simply didn't have enough of either to launch a full-on assault on the Winter Keep.

So they'd sent messengers to all the other territories of Ozero that resided within the Cicatrix.

Arlando's and Erasmo's territories counted for two of the thirteen territories, meaning they'd sent off eleven messengers to call for a multi-territory meeting.

There was no guarantee that the other leaders would respond to the call, let alone want to participate in any kind of assault.

It was a long shot, and every day that went by was one more day that Erasmo was trapped in that awful cage being tortured by his brother.

That was a week ago, and she was getting anxious. She hated not being able to do anything. She felt useless and backed into a corner. A deadly combination.

The only thing that made the passing days easier was the nightly hope that Erasmo would revisit her dreams.

She'd seen him again last night and had learned that Turi and Arlando had been gone for the last few days, giving him and the others a break.

She touched her fingers to her lips at the memory. Though her interludes with Erasmo were only in her dreams, they felt real enough, and she swore her body bore the phantom evidence.

Like today, her arms felt particularly sore from how Erasmo had pulled them behind her back and held them down as he rammed his delicious cock deep inside her until she cried out his name.

"Hey," Yasir's voice cut through her daydream. "We'll get him back. Don't let doubt cloud your mind."

Kiki rolled her shoulders to rid herself of the stress there. "I'm more concerned about all the time we're wasting. I understand why we need to call the other territories, but why would they answer our call? What do we have to offer them? I just feel so stuck. I want to act. I want to shove my machete so far up Arlando's ass that it comes out the other end." She pierced the air with her machete to punctuate her words.

Yasir's face pinched together in a wince. "Remind me to never piss you off," he said with a grin.

"I'm serious," she said with a defeated sigh. "I can't stand doing nothing."

"This isn't nothing," Yasir motioned to the rest of the training yard where men were sparring with machetes, swords, lances, and rows of men were practicing their aim with tlazons. "We're doing really good here. This is important and will mean the difference between our success and failure in the assault. If even one of them bears-out, that could create a chain reaction, especially among the younger ones."

"Do you ever wish you were them?" she asked wistfully, looking at the men training.

"Not in a million years," he breathed out heavily. "Sure, the strength, the speed, the heightened senses, that's all great. I hear that most of them don't even have a refractory period, which sounds fun," he added with a mischievous wink before he sobered. "But the rest of it? The blood lust? The shift itself? The whole losing oneself to the beast within? Yeah, hard pass."

When he put it that way, she couldn't entirely blame him. However, if it were up to her, she'd take the enhanced physical abilities any day and worry about the not-so-great side effects later. "How old was Erasmo when he first shifted?" she asked, curiosity getting the better of her.

"Oh, saints, I dunno. Ten? Eleven, maybe? It's been so long. He and Mauri shifted around the same time. I think that made them closer. It was something they both understood at the time they were going through it."

Kiki knew that feeling, bonding over trauma was something she was an expert at.

"Hey, you want to know something funny about the bears?" he asked, that same devious glint returning to his eyes.

"Do I even want to know?" she deadpanned.

"Oh, I think you do," he laughed and threw a conspiratorial arm over her shoulder as he walked her through the training yard. "So you know how they shift and retain some aspects of their human selves?"

Kiki nodded. "Sure, Erasmo's bear has silver streaks in his fur. And Bernat's bear was so massive, it was terrifying."

Yasir chuckled. "Have you ever wondered why Mauri's bear has all those silver streaks in his fur, but when he's human, his hair is all black?"

Kiki hadn't really thought much about it. "Yeah?"

Yasir started to chuckle. "Well, it's because he dyes his hair to hide the silver. Says it makes him look like an old man."

Now Kiki was resisting the urge to laugh. "I never would have guessed that psycho was so vain," she said with a smile.

"Oh, that's nothing. If you think Mauri is an ass now, you should have seen him as a teenager. Completely unbearable. Raz was the only one who tolerated him."

"Well, Erasmo certainly has more patience than I do." Longing lodged itself in her throat, choking off any further words. She pushed it down so she could revisit it later when she was alone and away from curious eyes.

Yasir led them to a pair of men sparring and leaned down to whisper in her ear. "Want to know something else?"

She knew what he was doing. So she played along and rolled her eyes. "You're going to tell me regardless."

"True," he laughed. "Okay, you know how some of the bears are bigger than the others?"

"Mhmm?" she hummed, with a nod of her head.

"Have you ever wondered why?"

"Nope. But I have a feeling you're going to tell me anyway."

"Let's just say that paw size matters," he said with a wicked chuckle.

Paw size? What the hell was he talking about—

Oh!

Her eyes widened as she realized what Yasir was implying.

"Yeah," he barked. "You know what I'm saying."

"How would you know something like that?" she asked, rounding on him.

"I literally live in a house full of horny ass guys. What else do you think we talk about?" he said, his face completely serious.

At that, Kiki threw her head back and laughed. She hadn't laughed or truly smiled since losing Erasmo. It was a bittersweet feeling, having the capacity to laugh and to smile without him near.

Her laughter died down, and she gave Yasir a grateful smile. "Thanks, I needed that."

"I'm here all week," he said with a grin, throwing his hands behind his head again. "Just do me a favor and don't tell Raz I fake-flirted with you. He'll eat me." A laugh slipped past her lips once more. "I'm not kidding. He will quite literally eat me. And I'm very attached to this body. I mean, look at me," he gestured to his lean, muscled frame. "I'm a verifiable work of art."

She shook her head at his antics. "Your secret is safe with me."

L ater that night, the scent of peppers and cumin filled the air while everyone enjoyed a meal of red rice with shredded chicken, soft corn tortillas, and heaps of delicious refried beans.

Kiki sat next to Yasir, tuning out his most recent sexual conquest. There was only so much she could listen to without missing Erasmo terribly.

Near the end of dinner, Guille entered the hall with a pile of books in his arms and Luna at his elbow.

"Kiki, look!" Luna exclaimed, her eyes shining. "We've found some books that might help us break the curse."

Guille placed the pile of books on the table and began to sift through them.

"This one seems very promising," she said, pulling open an ancient tome bound in dark leather and inscribed with a mysterious script. "According to this, there is an artifact from the time of the Saints that contains such pure and powerful magic that it could potentially break the curse and banish the demons for good."

"That sounds great, but if it's so powerful, why hasn't anyone gone looking for it before?" Kiki asked, her brows furrowed as she slowly flipped through the coffee-colored pages.

Guille answered for Luna, his hand snaking out to flip to another page in the book with delicate calligraphy. "This is why," he said, pointing to an intricate map.

The drawings depicted a part of Ozero that Kiki had never seen on any maps before. Thick, dark lines marked a wide swamp covered in mangroves, surrounded by a murky mist. The mountains didn't look familiar either, their jagged peaks marked to show their high elevation.

Kiki pushed the book away. "Well, that idea is out."

Luna huffed in frustration. "I know how it looks, but this map is hundreds, no, thousands of years old. The terrain has likely changed, but that doesn't mean the artifact doesn't exist."

"I'm not going to argue with you on that front, Luna. But a theoretical object hidden in an unknown place isn't really helping our current problems. It's just adding another."

Luna scowled, pulling the book to herself and cradling it to her chest as if it were precious to her. "Fine. We'll put this idea on hold. Guille, show her the other stuff we found."

Guille pulled forward another book filled with illustrations of strange rituals and arcane symbols—enough to make Kiki's head spin.

The worst part was that the text wasn't even in a language Kiki recognized. "What is this written in," she asked, skimming her fingers over the aging parchment paper.

"We think it's a dialect from the time of the Saints," Guille explained. "But I think we can translate it. Our library has some texts with these symbols, and if we use those books and cross-reference them, we'll be able to decipher this script."

Kiki leaned back in her chair with a groan. "That sounds time-consuming."

Luna made an annoyed sound out of her nose. "There are no easy solutions here, Kiki. If there were, the Ozeteros would have done it long before now."

Kiki hated the idea of chasing some artifact that might not even exist, but she hated the idea of sitting around translating thousand-year-old texts even more.

They were running out of time, and the longer Arlando was left to his own devices meant the longer he had free reign to torture Erasmo, Bernat, and Mauri.

There was another idea. One that was burning brightly in her mind and wouldn't let up. Erasmo had said the price was too high, but the alternatives were too tiresome for her. They'd take too much time, time none of them had.

"What about the Spirit Woman?" she asked, her focus entirely on her nails as she picked at some dirt.

Their table grew uncomfortably silent, and Kiki dared to glance up. Yasir and Guille were looking at each other, their expression communicating the fact that they both thought her idea was crazy.

Kiki stood up in a rush, her chair screeching across the floor. "Ugh!" she growled. "I don't get the big deal. So, the Spirit Woman demands a price. I'll pay it. I don't care. What I do care about is the fact that my mate is trapped in a cage and being tortured to death. That's what I care about!"

Yasir wrung his hands together. "You don't know her like we do," he said carefully. "The prices she demands are too high."

"That's what everyone keeps saying, but no one has told me what those totems around all of the Ozetero male's necks cost. I only know about that snake, Aurelia, and her silver eyes, which don't seem so bad, by the way. She can see the paths out of the Cicatrix, which, by Erasmo's own admittance, you all had no problem using to smuggle supplies."

Yasir winced, casting a glance at Guille, whose face had drained of color.

"My mother's life. That was the cost of the totems," Guille answered, his eyes wide and unfocused as if he was seeing the events play out once more. "My mother was one of the four Ozetero sisters. The eldest, in fact. She hated seeing the pain that the curse inflicted on her brothers and her nephews, so she sought out the help of the Spirit Woman. In exchange for the totems that would allow them to shift at will and slow down the progression of the curse, the Spirit Woman demanded my mother's life."

Kiki felt like someone had punched her in the gut. It was like all the air had been sucked from her lungs. "I'm sorry," she whispered, feeling like an insensitive jerk.

"You didn't know," Guille said kindly. "And, understandably, no one likes to talk about it. She knew the Spirit Woman might demand any price, and she was willing to pay it if it meant that she could buy her family time."

Time. The very concept that had been against them from the start. Time was their ever-present enemy, bowing forward toward their inevitable fates, uncaring, unfeeling, and unknowing to those it destroyed along the way.

She sat back down, her shoulders rolling forward in defeat. "So what now?" she asked, glancing around the table.

Luna pointed to the open books on the table and tapped her pointer finger along the foreign script. "We start with this," she said with resolve.

CHAPTER SEVENTEEN

MAURI

Mauri stared up at the ceiling of his cell, the sound of Bernat's gentle snores filling the air. In the cell next to him, Erasmo tossed and turned as if he were fighting off some demon in his sleep.

All Mauri could think about was Luna. Her soft lips, her sweet smile, the way she held her breath when he pushed his cock inside her...

Fuck, he was so horny.

He opened one eye, checking that both Erasmo and Bernat were asleep, and quietly repositioned himself so that his back was to them.

Neither of them was going to want to see what he was about to do.

He unlaced his pants and slipped out his already hard cock.

***

Closing his eyes, he thought of Luna and began to stroke up and down his shaft.

He pictured her vividly in his mind, recalling all the tiny details about her that he adored.

When she formed completely in his mind, she reached out and pulled him close, wrapping her arms around him as she attacked his mouth with her own.

"I've missed you," she gasped, pulling away for air. "How are you?"

"Later," Mauri growled. "First, I want to sink my tongue inside your sweet little pussy and make you scream my name as you come."

Luna moaned. "I want that, Mauri. I want that so much."

"Then spread your legs and lift your hips, chiqui," Mauri instructed, his voice deep.

Luna eagerly followed his command and shifted so her legs rested on either side of his thighs and her hips raised up into his face.

Mauri groaned, closing his eyes as he moved his hand faster over his cock. He could almost smell the sweet scent of her perfume, and it was making his cock so fucking hard.

"Don't stop," Luna begged, her voice soft.

"I won't, baby. I'll make you feel so good."

As he started to lick at her wet pussy, he felt his cock begin to throb. Mauri's grip on his cock tightened as the ache grew more intense.

"Fuck, Luna, you taste so good," Mauri growled, releasing his dick to wrap his arms around her thighs and dig his fingers into the flesh of her ass. "I love how wet you are for me."

His cock was hard as a rock, and he quickly wrapped his fingers around it and began to stroke it again, wet with his own precum, his hand moving up and down his shaft at a furious pace.

Her skin flushed, and an exhilarated smile spread across her mouth.

"I've been thinking about you all day," she whispered.

Mauri's mind raced, his own breathing growing heavy with anticipation.

Her thighs quivered around his head as she said, "I couldn't stop thinking about you last night either. I dreamt about you all night. Every time I closed my eyes, I saw you towering over me with your cock in my mouth. I felt it sliding inside me, that warm, delicious feeling when you fill me up, taking me, possessing me..."

Fuck, he was so close already.

As if needing to relive that fantasy, she pushed him off of her and fell to all fours in front of him. She took his cock in her hand, stroking him gently. As her eyes locked with his, he watched through a silent gasp as her tongue snaked out, and she slowly pressed it against her soft, pink lips.

Fuck this was the best wet-dream he'd ever had in his life. He didn't want it to end, but he could feel himself reaching climax.

She pulled her hand away, and his cock sprang free of her touch before he found her lips on his again.

He couldn't take it anymore. Suddenly, her lips weren't enough. He needed more.

With a feral growl, Mauri launched himself back into a seated position, his fingers digging into her waist as he pulled her down to straddle his lap, their mouths still connected. He moaned against her lips, his cock rubbing against the lips of her pussy.

"Fuck, Luna," he groaned, breaking their kiss. "I want you so much."

This was the best dream of his fucking life, and he was going to take full advantage of it.

He grabbed her hips, positioned his cock at her entrance, and thrust up into her, his cock sliding inside her with ease.

Mauri moaned softly, his lips on hers as he began to rock his hips, sliding his cock in and out of her.

With a cry, she broke their kiss and buried her face in his shoulder, her fingernails digging into his chest as he pummeled her pussy, her hips bouncing with his movements. It wouldn't take long for him to finish if he kept up like this.

"Fuck !" he cried out as she arched her back, her pussy tightening around his cock.

"Mauri, oh Saints, I'm going to come...." she breathed, her mouth against his shoulder.

"Yes....come for me...." Mauri breathed desperately. He was close, so fucking close. He rocked into her, the base of his cock rubbing against her clit.

"Yes, please, yes...." Luna cried out, her pussy quivering as she started to come. Her pussy clenched around his cock so hard, and the sound of her moans pushed Mauri over the edge, and he grunted loudly as he began to cum, thick spurts of his warm cum filling her up.

When his orgasm ended, he dropped his head into the crook of her shoulder, their bodies still joined together.

He felt as if his heart was trying to beat its way out of his chest.

He had never come so hard in his life, let alone in a dream before.

Luna kissed his hair, nuzzling him gently. "I love you."

"I love you, chiqui." He kissed her shoulder. "I miss you."

They stayed just like that for a few minutes, her straddling his hips, his arms wrapped around her waist.

When they had calmed down, Mauri slowly lifted her off his lap, his cock softening and small spurts of cum slipping from her pussy.

He sighed, "Fuck, I wish this was real."

"Me too," she said with a lazy smile. "Best dream ever."

Mauri looked deeply into Luna's eyes. The connection between them was palpable, lacking all the telltale signs of a dream.

"This is my dream," he said hesitantly.

"No," she tilted her head in the way she did, the one that made her look so unbearably adorable. "It's my dream. I was sleeping."

"I was—" Mauri started to tell her what he'd been up to but stopped, suddenly feeling embarrassed.

She chuckled knowingly and reached up to caress his cheek. "Were you playing by yourself, my love?"

"Yes," he admitted as he nuzzled into the warmth of her palms. Palms made rough from working with cleansing agents as she worked to heal the wounded and sick. Palms that she used to hold him as she writhed beneath him. He pressed a kiss to the center of her palm, cherishing her touch.

She grinned wider. "And you were thinking of me?"

"I think of no one else but you," he said, his voice little more than a rasp.

"Then I don't think either of us are dreaming, not really."

Mauri reached out and ran his fingers through her midnight black hair, the strands so soft, they slipped through his fingers. "Then what is this?"

"I'm beyond wondering what the mate bond can do. I'm just happy to see you again."

He pulled her close. If this was real, he didn't want to wake up and find her gone.

"Mauri?"

"Hmm?"

"I can't breathe."

Mauri loosened his grip on her immediately. "Did I hurt you? Are you okay?"

"I'm fine, you sweet fool," Luna said, pressing her lips to his mouth. "I promise that I'm going to get you out of there, and if Kiki and Sol have any say in it, they're going to make Arlando wish he'd never been born."

Fear twisted his insides. "No, chiqui. You can't. Don't come for me."

"I will do what I want, Mauricio Ozetero," she scolded. "I'm not leaving you there to be tortured and maimed and possibly even killed."

"But Arlando," he pulled away from her, the panic in his heart making it race. "He's too powerful."

Luna reached for him again, and he couldn't resist melting into her arms. "Arlando doesn't have the entire eyrie behind him," she whispered as she ran her fingers through his hair. "He doesn't have the loyalty of an entire family behind him. He may have those demons, but they're no match for all of us."

While all of that may be true, it didn't change the fact that La Aguilera didn't command a large enough military force to win such a conflict. Fear wormed back into his heart, making his next words come out in a choked whisper. "The eyrie can't take on a demon army alone."

"We won't. We've sent messengers to the remaining eleven territories calling for a war council."

Mauri scoffed and regretted it instantly when Luna leveled him with a stern gaze. "Sorry, chiqui," he said sheepishly, nuzzling his face into her neck. "I just don't see how that'll help. The other territories have no reason to answer the call. They're more likely to laugh in your faces than to raise arms against Arlando."

"I love it when you're so optimistic," she answered dryly.

Mauri nipped at her shoulder and then pressed a kiss to her skin. "I'm just saying not to put all your hopes on the other territories."

"I'm not," she answered, matter of fact. She explained her search for the artifact and the painstaking translation process. His head hurt just listening to her talk about it.

"If I asked you to stop and give up on me, would you do it?" he asked.

"Never," she said, her hands reached up and cradled either side of his face. "I'd face all the demons in the world for one more chance to be in your arms. Nothing will stop me from trying to get to you. Not even death itself."

Mauri sighed heavily, "I was afraid you'd say that."

He kissed her again, gently at first, before his heartbeat began to race again. He'd never get enough of this woman. If he could keep his cock buried inside her for the rest of eternity, he'd do so.

Now that sounded like fucking heaven to him.

He was so caught up in the fantasy that he didn't realize the dream had ended, and there was a very loud and obnoxious sound roaring around him.

"Cut it out, Mauri," Erasmo growled. "You've been yanking your chain for the last hour, and I'm tired of hearing it. Go the fuck to sleep, you sick fuck."

Mauri glanced around, taking in the bars of his cell and the cum he'd spilled all over the hay.

An idea popped into his mind, and he tucked his dick back into his pants and started to collect all the sticky hay into a pile.

"Now, what are you doing?" Erasmo groaned.

Mauri's lips curled into a smirk. "I'm making a present for your brother," he said as he began to form the cum filled hay into a ball.

"Which one?" Erasmo deadpanned.

"Does it matter?"

Erasmo's lips curled into a conspiratorial grin. "Not even a little."

"Didn't think so," Mauri chuckled as he continued to bundle the sticky hay into a ball. He'd make sure to deliver his nasty little gift, preferably in Arlando's face. But he'd be fine with leaving it somewhere for Turi to find, too.

Chapter Eighteen

Turi

Terror glued him to the spot. He dared a glance at Arlando to see the corners of his brother's lips lifting into a smile.

A small village lay immobile in the valley below as if frozen in time.

In the village center, a woman selling flowers stood with her arm raised in the air, a rose uplifted. Her mouth open in the middle of her hawker's call.

Next to her, a little boy chasing a ball stood still, his smile frozen on his face, his chubby cheeks red from the cold.

The whole village was in various states of halted motion; their activities paused as if captured by a painter's eye.

"Isn't it marvelous," Arlando cooed, his eyes twinkling with glee. "They make the most perfect decor, the perfect ice sculptures."

Turi mustered the strength to nod his head, his heart racing in his chest. He hoped the rapid thumping against his ribs was inaudible to Arlando because his ears were full of the rushing sound of blood.

"Come," Arlando motioned with a jerk of his head. "We need to replenish our numbers after the losses we suffered."

When Arlando's back faced him, Turi couldn't resist the urge to smile. Kiki, Solana, and Luna somehow survived the small horde of demons Arlando sent after them. Not only that, but they'd eliminated almost all of them, both angering Arlando and necessitating lengthening their time away from the castle.

The latter suited him just fine. The longer Arlando was away from the Winter Keep, the more time that gave Yari to solidify their plans.

What Turi hadn't planned on was this macabre display of Arlando's blood magic.

He followed Arlando down the ridge, and together, they walked along the dirt road that ran through the center of the village.

The sight of people frozen in mid-motion was even more disturbing up close than it was at a distance. A mother with her young daughter stopped mid-step, a man rifling through his bag, and two people mid-laugh over a shared joke—frozen in time.

"What are you going to do to them?" Turi asked, pausing before a shoemaker's shop and peering inside. Guilt flooded his veins as he stared at a family of four hunched over their workstations, tools in hand, smiles on their faces.

"Not me, brother. Us," Arlando clarified, coming up to Turi's elbow and peering inside. "They will become part of our army."

Turi was about to ask for an explanation when he gagged on the stench of sulfur and burning ash filling the air, announcing the demons' approach.

They lumbered through the village, their clawed feet dragging through the snow, leaving gnarled tracks in their wake. One by one, the demons flooded the village and pushed through the doors of each shop.

A demon with bat wings and the horns of a ram curling around its head entered the shoemaker's shop and stood over the family as if waiting for direction.

"Give me your hand," Arlando commanded, his eyes bright and full of wicked glee.

"Why?" Turi asked, his stomach churning with nausea.

"Together, we can make them stronger. But even better, together, we can make them smarter."

Before Turi could object to this insane idea, Arlando grabbed his hand and, with lightning speed, pulled out his dagger, slashed it deeply across Turi's palm, and did the same to his own.

He clasped their bleeding hands together, the snow at their feet blooming crimson as the blood trickled down.

Arlando began to chat in a guttural tongue, the language harsh to the ears.

The demon inside the shop started to writhe as if it were in immeasurable pain before it shattered into a black swirling mist.

The mist formed a black cloud in the shop and then split into four turrets as it shoved its way into every available open orifice—mouths, ears, noses, and eyes.

Once frozen by Arlando's spell, the people woke, their screams filling the village as the dark mist engulfed them.

Turi's yell of shock died in his throat.

The people began to change everywhere the cloud touched, becoming something else, something not of this world.

Reptilian scales grew over human flesh.

Wings sprouted from backs and necks.

Limbs elongated and grew slick with oily flesh.

Lips curled back to reveal pointed teeth and whipping tongues.

Turi's stomach roiled. He wanted to howl in rage and confusion and horror. He wanted to rip the world apart, rend Arlando limb from limb, go back to the Winter Keep, and take Yari away from all of this.

Inside, the beast battered his burly head against the stone cage of Turi's heart, a roar of fury echoing through Turi's mind.

We cannot let him do this! Let's finish him and be done with it.

As much as Turi wanted to give in to the beast's demands, he knew that anything he did now wouldn't matter. These people were forever changed. Their deaths marked their rebirth into the demons of Arlando's army.

Instead of succumbing to his anger, he stood in stony silence as Arlando took their clasped hands and led him through the village, stopping at each shop and repeating the same ritual with the same sickening results.

The screams of the victims haunted Turi. He couldn't shake the feeling that the screams were the last vestiges of their humanity echoing through the air before being swallowed whole by Arlando's magic.

The new demons stirred, looking around themselves as if confused, and Turi's skin prickled with goosebumps.

Arlando turned to him with a satisfied smile, his eyes glowing red. "They're magnificent," he said, pulling a white handkerchief from his pocket. "They will be the building blocks on which we'll build our army. The dawn of a new age of magic and power."

He wiped the blood from his hand and tossed the soiled rag to Turi, turning to the demons as they stalked out of the shops, down the streets, and from all corners of the village to stand before him.

Bile rose in Turi's throat at the evidence of what he'd done. What he'd helped Arlando do.

He'd made his choice to be here, to act as a spy on Arlando, to learn what he could to stop this curse without sacrificing the mates. But this had been the cost.

The only alternative would have been to fight Arlando early on, which would have put Yari in danger, which would have meant Turi would be in a cell next to his brothers and Mauri, leaving no one to look out for Yari and the other girls he'd known his whole life—the only family he knew.

That he couldn't allow. He would do anything to protect her and the rest of his family, to save them from the fate Arlando planned.

If this was the price, then he supposed he'd have to find a way to live with it.

He winced, his eyes shut, and steeled his spine because he had a feeling things were going to get a lot worse.

"Come, we have three more villages to visit today," Arlando said, already walking away from the horde, their talons clicking against the frozen ground as they dutifully followed him.

Oh yes, things were going to get a lot worse.

Chapter Nineteen

Yari

The thing about living her life in the shadow of others meant that she'd grown accustomed to the shadows. They greeted her as she slinked through the castle, slipping by the demons unseen.

Her heart pounded in her chest as she approached a bend in the hallway where a pair of demons stood sentry before a single door.

That's exactly where she wanted to go—Arlando's office.

He'd only let her in one time, and she'd spent the day watching as he read reports and created orders to send aid to struggling villages in his territory.

She scoffed at the memory. She suspected that everything he did that day had been for show. No villages were calling for his aid. Or if there were, he wasn't sending them any help.

She felt like such a fool for falling for his spell and ignoring all the warning signs.

She took a silent step back, her bare feet a whisper against the cold stone floors, and let the shadows wrap their comforting arms around her. She needed to know the castle's layout, and Arlando's office seemed the most logical place to look first.

She'd made herself a crude map of the places she'd explored, marking areas that the demons seemed to patrol and the places they stood guard.

Keeping to the shadows, she navigated herself back to the library, where she felt the safest.

Slipping between the partly opened double doors, she rushed to the farthest corner of the library, where she'd stacked some books and strategically moved over some books on the shelf to create a makeshift ladder.

She climbed up the bookshelf, careful to place her toes on the very edge of each ledge, mindful not to leave any footprints on the surface.

So far, the demons had not found her hiding place, and she wanted to keep it that way. If they didn't know where she ran off to, then neither would Arlando.

He and Turi had been gone for a few days already, giving her time to start working on finding an exit route.

Once she was on the top of the bookcase, she reached up and grabbed the wooden beam overhead. Taking in a deep breath, she hoisted herself up, careful not to make a noise as she struggled to pull her own weight up.

A month ago, such physical activity would have been easier, but she'd stopped any kind of training, and her body had grown weaker.

She was thankful that she'd retained some of her strength, not that she'd had much to begin with because it would have been nearly impossible for her to pull up and over the beam.

Once on top, she held out her arms so they were parallel to the ground below and took a careful step along the joist.

Small footprints from her previous trips marked the way as she slowly crossed the length of the library across the wooden support. She was grateful for the high-vaulted ceilings and that she could do this while standing; she didn't think she'd be as silent if she had to shuffle around on her hands and knees.

Once across the beam, she pressed herself against the wall and stepped sideways until she reached a small alcove where the ceiling and wall met. She set her palms along the bottom of the alcove and lifted herself up, diving into the space like a field mouse into its burrow.

Once safely inside, she pulled out her map and drew out the new hallways she'd gone down along with the demons she'd seen.

Finished with her map, she tucked it back into the pocket of her dress and grabbed for her rucksack. She pulled out a small pouch containing a few pieces of bread and took a bite of the stale morsel, hoping it would give her the energy she needed.

Just as she was about to take her second bite, she heard someone enter the library loudly. She dared a peek out of the alcove to find Arlando's cousin, Aurelia, down below.

She watched as Aurelia frantically searched through each book as if looking for something specific. After a few minutes, she let out a huff and slammed the book in her hands shut before throwing it across the room with a loud thud.

Sheer panic raced through her veins as she saw Aurelia's eerie silver eyes scan the room. She watched in horror as Aurelia started walking closer and closer to where she was hiding, seemingly aware of Yari's presence.

She willed herself not to make a sound or move, the fear racing through her veins keeping her rooted in place.

As if sensing something amiss, Aurelia suddenly stopped and spun around quickly towards the alcove, where Yari watched in fright.

"What are you doing up there?" Aurelia asked, quirking her head in confusion.

"Hiding," Yari squeaked. She didn't know if she could trust Arlando's cousin or not. Aurelia didn't seem like a bad person, but Yari had thought the same thing of Arlando once, too.

"I can see that," the silver-eyed woman said with a roll of her eyes. "Why are you hiding?"

"I don't like the demons," she replied, deciding on a half-truth. Surely, no one could blame her for not liking the demons. They were foul creatures with lifeless, ever-watching eyes.

She didn't want to tell Aurelia that she was hiding from Arlando because she'd likely tell him, and that wouldn't mean anything good for Yari.

"You can see them now?" Aurelia asked, her eyes wide with shock. "So he's told you then."

Yari nodded, thinking she meant the part where he planned to sacrifice her to end the curse.

Aurelia nodded contemplatively. "Then you know they're a necessary evil. But don't worry, it won't be for long. Before you know it, Lando will have this whole curse thing figured out, and you'll be able to enjoy your time here without having to worry about the demons anymore."

Yari's brows furrowed at that. If Arlando's plans went the way he wanted, she wouldn't be alive to enjoy the castle demon-free.

The woman ran her hand through her hair and found a plush red chair to throw herself into. With a sigh, she rearranged herself so her legs were tossed over one arm and the other supported her back.

"Where have you been?" Yari asked, feeling bold as she leaned out of the alcove to see Aurelia better.

"Running errands for Lando," she replied, her focus on picking dirt from under her nails. "He sent me to look for Tomás. Apparently, the smuggler has been dodging Lando's messages. But I checked all his usual haunts and couldn't find Tomás anywhere. He must have screwed over someone real nasty for him to go underground so completely."

Yari frowned, confusion swirling in her mind.

Aurelia had been gone for weeks, ever since returning to find her mother had gone missing. Yet, here she was, claiming that Arlando had sent her to look for Tomás.

Except Tomás was dead. Arlando had ripped his heart out from his chest and left him to rot.

Aurelia's voice yanked her from her chaotic thoughts. "So, how was the manor? I haven't been in years, but I do miss the hot springs."

Now, Yari was well and truly confused.

At her silence, Aurelia looked up at her in the rafters again. "Lando said he took you up there to get away for a bit as a nice treat before his focus had to go back on breaking the curse. Didn't you like it?"

Yari opened her mouth to speak but couldn't form the words. What lies had Arlando been telling his cousin? How deep did those lies run?

Aurelia chewed at her fingernail, biting off a piece before spitting it out. "You really don't talk much, do you?" She shrugged at Yari's continued silence. "Well, I hope he at least had the staff prepare you some tres leches. Our housekeeper, Neli, makes the best sweets. How is the old bat nowadays, anyway?"

Yari swallowed the lump in her throat. "I don't know anyone named Neli," she said quietly.

"Really? She's usually there all year. Must have had some family stuff come up."

"No, I mean, I don't know anything about a manor, or hot springs, or tres leches cake."

Aurelia stared up at her, her silver eyes narrowing. "What are you talking about — Hey, you look different," she mumbled, swinging her legs off the arm of the chair and setting her feet on the ground again. "Come into the light," she said, blinking rapidly. "I can't see you right."

"That's sort of the point," Yari replied, slipping further into the alcove.

"What happened to you?" Aurelia whispered, her mouth slightly agape.

Yari considered her question for a moment. If Aurelia truly believed that Arlando had whisked her away on some romantic trip, then perhaps she didn't know the truth about what he was up to. And if that were the case, then Aurelia was as much her ally as Turi.

"Your cousin happened to me," Yari said bluntly, her tone sharper than she intended.

"What does that mean?" she scoffed, looking just as confused as Yari felt. "Are you two fighting or something?"

Yari shook her head in disbelief. "You really don't know anything, do you?"

"Uhh, you're going to have to enlighten me, magdalena." Aurelia set her hands on her hips expectantly.

Yari knew it was a risk talking to Aurelia like this, but it was a risk she had to take if she wanted to navigate escaping the Keep. She inhaled a steadying breath and said, "Arlando is not who you or I think he is. He's a monster."

Aurelia scoffed and waved her hand dismissively. "If this is about the demons, I already told you, they're a necessary evil—"

Yari felt like she was going to burst. She clenched her hands into fists and yelled, "I'm not talking about the fucking demons, I'm talking about the fact that Arlando raped me!"

"How can it be rape if the two of you are mates?" Aurelia asked, her tone dripping with sarcasm.

"It's rape if I said 'no.' It's rape if I begged him to leave me alone. It's rape if he didn't listen to me and took what he wanted anyway. It's rape because I say it's rape."

The smirk on Aurelia's face slowly faded, and her features twisted in horror. "What? I don't understand. That's not Lando. He—"

"You said he sent you looking for Tomás? But Tomás is dead. I saw Arlando shove his fist into Tomás' chest and rip out his still-beating heart."

Aurelia's face twisted with confusion.

Feeling bold, Yari added, "Don't believe me? There is a cabin in the woods somewhere to the west of here. You'll find Tomás' body and his empty chest right where Arlando left him. If the beasts of the woods left anything of him behind, that is."

Aurelia slowly stepped closer so that she stood directly below Yari. "He did something to my mother, didn't he?"

Yari's heart went out to her. She barely remembered her own mother, but she still ached for the comfort of her warm embrace and her soothing voice as she hummed a lullaby. "I don't know, but I think he had something to do with it."

Aurelia grabbed fistfuls of her own hair, and an agonized cry ripped from her throat. She sank to her knees as she cried.

Yari couldn't bear to watch her in so much pain. Feeling like she had formed a kinship with the woman, she slipped from the alcove and slowly made her way across the beam, down the shelves, and tiptoed up to the grieving woman.

She placed a timid hand on Aurelia's shaking shoulder, willing the mere contact to provide the comfort she needed.

Aurelia wiped her eyes and sniffed loudly. She slowly got to her feet, and her silver eyes caught on Yari. She gasped at whatever she saw, covering her stomach with her hands. "I'm so sorry," she said, reaching out a hand to Yari, but deciding against it, she dropped it to her side. "Shit, I have to get you out of here."

Yari stepped back and balled her hands into fists. "No, I won't leave Turi and the others behind."

"The others?"

Wow. Aurelia really was clueless. Yari explained, "Arlando captured his brothers and one of your cousins. They're in the dungeon. He's using them as bait to draw their mates here."

Aurelia's eyes widened. "That bastard. He told me he found another way to end the curse. A way that didn't sacrifice the mates."

It didn't really matter to Yari what lie he'd told Aurelia. It was clear that he'd been using his cousin for his own gain, and that was enough to bond Yari to her. "I can't leave without them. Two of them are the mates of my best friends, and one of them is the mate to my old Commander in the Demon Corps."

Aurelia's mouth dropped open. "You wouldn't happen to be talking about a certain Commander with curly red hair, eyes like ice, and a heart of stone, would you?"

Yari's mouth fell open in shock. "You know Solana?"

Aurelia cursed under her breath. "Do the names Kiki and Luna mean anything to you?"

Yari's heart leaped into her throat. "They are my best friends!"

"Fuck," Aurelia scowled. "Take me to the dungeon. We have to get the hell out of here and now!"

Yari started to move but paused. "I'm not allowed down there; I can't get past the guards. And I can't leave now, not without Turi. I won't leave while he's away with Arlando. If they come back and Arlando sees we're gone, he could take his anger out on Turi. I can't let that happen."

"Why the hell not? Don't any of you and your friends have any concept of self-preservation?" Aurelia growled.

Yari straightened her shoulders. Though the temptation to leave right away was strong, she'd never forgive herself if she left Turi behind. "I've survived this long. A little while longer won't make a difference to me. He can't do anything more to me that he hasn't already done."

Aurelia scowled and ran her hand through her hair, shaking her head with a rueful smile. "Your whole group, all of you, are a bunch of loyal idiots who are going to get me killed one day, you know that?" She shook her head again. "Fine, we'll do it your way. Erasmo is going to owe me the biggest suite in La Aguilera for this shit."

Chapter Twenty

Solana

The manor was the definition of organized chaos as everyone worked to get the house in order for the visiting leaders and their respective second-in-command.

Solana strutted through the grand dining hall, her every step echoing off the walls of the marble-floored chamber. Everywhere around her, men and women scurried about in a synchronized frenzy—setting up tables, chairs, and benches into one massive circular formation as she watched with a curious eye.

No one could be seen as superior to anyone else tonight. The circular seating would help to create an equal environment for all. Without a head of the table, no one could claim they were inferior or superior.

Though the Ozeteros called her La Reina Suprema, tonight she was Solana Ramirez, Commander in the Demon Corps. Bernat's status as her mate was a side matter. One that would earn her no favors if that were her only qualification.

Though the manor was coming together and everything was going according to plan, she couldn't shake the uneasiness in her stomach, like the feeling of butterflies, their wings lightly brushing across her skin.

She didn't normally get nervous before a battle, but she supposed this was a different kind of combat. A fight for resources, human capital, and weapons.

Not every territory leader had agreed to attend tonight's meeting.The leader of Las Muertas territory had sent back a beautiful gift wrapped in black paper with geometric decorations cut out and tied with a red silk ribbon.

But upon opening, Solana had found a rather disrespectful gift of horse shit. A clear rejection. They would be a problem for another day.

Three other territories had claimed neutrality in the conflict, while one other cited their own dispute with Las Muertas. Understandable.

Three more territories hadn't deigned to respond, leaving three out of the eleven territories contacted.

Three leaders of their own lands would be coming to La Aguilera, but their attendance at this meeting didn't guarantee their participation. It was merely a sign of their curiosity and, more likely, an attempt to create a deal that would benefit their people. Also understandable.

She'd been so far inside her own mind that she didn't notice where her feet had taken her until she heard the sound of metal clashing against metal.

The training yard was full of those from Yasir's group. They'd progressed an impressive amount in the last couple of weeks, and they'd learned to rely on tools rather than the shift, but there was still much for them to learn.

A flash of black drew her eye, and she turned to see Kiki standing in the middle of a sparring ring, her fists clenched and eyes locked on her partner.

She faced off against an impossibly large man, taller than even Bernat and wider in the shoulders. His thick neck bulged with spidery veins, and his fists looked more like two ham hocks than actual hands.

Suddenly, Kiki lunged forward, her fist aiming for the man's face, causing him to bring his arms up in a block, but Solana had noticed where Kiki's eyes had been focused, and she waited to see if she was right.

As predicted, Kiki turned her attack into a feint, dropped down into a crouch, and swiped her foot across the man's ankles, taking him down in a swirl of snow.

The small crowd gathered around the pair hollered at the man, teasing him for getting taken down by Kiki.

Solana strolled up, her voice cutting through the hecklers. "You're first mistake is underestimating her because she is small."

Kiki spun around, her mouth open in shock.

Solana resisted the urge to roll her eyes. Kiki always acted so shocked whenever she extended a compliment. Though she knew herself well enough to know that she wasn't one to dole them out like sweets on graduation day, she gave them when they were earned.

She turned to face the men who still were whispering jeers to their peers. "Beneath her small frame and pretty eyes is the mind of a skilled warrior, with years of battle under her belt, countless kills to her name, and a reputation that precedes her. She isn't called the Sicario for nothing, friends." She gave Kiki a wink which earned her another slack-jawed response.

She set her hand on the hilt of her machete. "Allow us to demonstrate the might of the Demon Corps, gentlemen." She turned to Kiki. "Shall we?"

Kiki shook herself out of her stupor and grinned. "I've been waiting for this my entire life."

"Trust me, I know," Solana said, allowing herself the small jab.

Kiki was easily angered and could be goaded into a fight with little provocation. It made her swift attacks fierce, but it also made her easy to read.

Solana pulled her machete from its sheath, and Kiki grabbed hers from her weapon's belt that she'd put to the side while she sparred hand to hand.

Once armed, they faced off in the sparring ring. The air around them was charged with tension.

Solana was grateful for the distraction that physical activity provided. Already, she felt her muscles relaxing, the tightness in her shoulders easing as she mentally and physically prepared to spar against Kiki.

They circled each other, sizing up each other, waiting for the perfect moment to strike.

The small crowd that had gathered to watch Kiki earlier grew until everyone training in the yard had gathered to form a circle around them.

"Fifty gold marks says Kiki wins," Yasir's voice pierced the silence surrounding them.

"My money is on La Reina Suprema," said Ramón, the man she'd put in charge of the logistics group. She gave him a grateful nod, but this wasn't about competition.

On any given day, Solana could have sparred against Kiki while in the Corps. She'd avoided doing it for a few reasons.

One, she didn't want to injure Kiki's already easily bruisable pride. Two, she didn't care if she won or lost, but her subordinates would, and so would her fellow Commanders. She had a reputation to uphold more so than any other person for the sole fact that she was the youngest Commander to ever rise through the ranks. Three, and this was the honest truth; she wanted to spar Kiki when she felt they were true equals. Their fight wouldn't have been fair, and any victory would have felt cheapened by that fact.

No, if she won or lost, it would be because they were the two best warriors to ever survive the Demon Corps, and that was a worthy feat in itself.

Kiki lunged forward, her machete aiming for Solana's neck. Solana easily dodged, and Kiki quickly recovered, swinging around to deliver a cut to her side instead. She jumped to avoid it and parried with a sweeping arc that made their obsidian blades ring.

Kiki was relentless in her counterattack, coming at Solana with skill and agility. She blocked each strike with finesse, retaliating with a powerful counterattack that forced Kiki back. The crowd erupted in cheers and claps as she sent Kiki stumbling back.

Solana took the opportunity to press forward, her machete pounding against Kiki's in an effort to send her rival back. With each move, she felt the fire of determination grow stronger within her chest until each blade connected with a metallic clang that echoed throughout the yard.

Kiki gritted her teeth and pushed herself harder, pushing Solana back as well and rallying for one final strike to win the fight. But Solana had other plans; she ground her own teeth and prepared to deliver a powerful strike of her own that would force Kiki back and end the fight.

With one last burst of strength, she charged forward, all her energy focused into one move—sending a wave of energy into her strike.

Kiki seemed to pick up on her intentions and fired back with a similar maneuver.

Time seemed to slow, and Solana saw how the fight would end before the final blow was even struck.

She aimed her strike at Kiki's neck, leaving her left side open and vulnerable. Kiki moved in, arcing her machete in a twin motion.

The crowd gasped, and a hush fell over them as the blades of both women paused at the other's neck.

Kiki and Solana stood facing each other for a moment, their breaths sawing in and out of their chests.

"Commander," Kiki said with a slight tilt of the head, acknowledging the tie.

"Slayer," Solana replied with her own bow of her head, also accepting the tie.

Together, they lowered their blades, and Solana felt a smile tug at the corners of her lips.

The fight was over, and they had emerged victorious together.

The crowd erupted into cheers once again, this time louder than ever before.

Kiki gave Solana a final nod of respect before turning away to accept the accolades from those who had watched them battle it out.

As Solana sheathed her machete, she turned to Ramón and gave him a pat on the shoulder.

He pounded his chest in salute as she walked out of the training yard, her mind at ease and ready to face the visiting territory leaders that night.

The tables were arranged with precision. Turquoise and silver platters were piled high with chiles rellenos, mole, carne asada, and mountains of warm tortillas.

Crystal decanters full of sangria, tequila, and pulque glinted in the hue of the setting sun.

Solana often felt guilty for indulging in such abundance when she knew that the Yearlings, Attendants, and Slayers in the Demon Corps were likely dining on soup that had too much water and not enough meat.

Once the curse was broken, she made a vow to herself to see the rest of Ozero equally supplied and fed. She knew the pain of being hungry all too well, and she was loathe to see others endure such a lack of resources when, clearly, there was enough to go around.

Beautiful decorations of papel picado were strung from the rafters, their floral and geometric patterns allowing the fading light to cast a kaleidoscope of colors into the hall.

All that was missing were the guests.

Solana sat in silence with Kiki and Luna seated on either side of her as they waited for the visiting dignitaries.

Kiki's knee bobbed up and down, her need to constantly move evidence of her anxiety. Solana didn't blame her. A lot was riding on this meeting.

Though the concept of high stakes wasn't unfamiliar to Solana, the Corps was rife with life-and-death situations. It was their current circumstances that felt deeply personal.

An attack from demons wasn't construed as tactical because they were senseless beasts. But an attack from the creatures at the orders of an invisible enemy? Now that they all took it personally.

Arlando had revealed his hand, and she wasn't about to let him succeed in his disgusting plans.

"Remind me again who is coming," Kiki muttered, her eyes darting around the room.

"The territory leaders of Maravilla, Esmeralda, and Las Víboras," Solana replied, reaching for her glass and taking a long sip of water. She wanted to keep her mind sharp and had no plans to partake in the alcohol served tonight.

Kiki's hands trailed over the tlazons strapped to the bandolier across her chest. "Got it. So, can anyone explain to me why the other territories have such cool-sounding names, and we're the Eastern Territory?"

Yasir sat on her left and chuckled. "Technically, we're the Deleste Territory."

"Same difference," Kiki scoffed. "Which territory sent us the shit again?"

"Las Muertas," Solana and Luna answered in unison.

"Even the heathens have a better name than us," Kiki grumbled.

Solana understood Kiki's need to run her mouth at any opportunity she got. She even understood that it provided a distraction while everyone waited to see if the leaders would even show.

That didn't mean that Solana enjoyed the incessant chatter.

Finally, mercifully, anything to stop Kiki's running commentary on the lameness of the nomenclature adopted by the Ozetero family, the doors opened, and a group of five people entered the hall.

The man in the center of the group was tall and lean, his curly brown hair tied neatly behind his head. He wore a somber expression on his handsome face, his amber eyes zeroing in on Solana immediately, as if he could sense that she was in charge here.

Solana stood from the table and extended her arm toward the seats she'd reserved for him and his party. "Xavier López, leader of the Maravilla Territory, welcome."

Xavier gave her a polite nod before taking his seat.

Next was a woman with luxurious waist-length blonde hair and deep brown eyes wearing an emerald cloak with white fur trim.

"Giselle Maroto, leader of the Esmeralda Territory, House Ozetero welcomes you."

The woman slid the cloak from her shoulders, revealing an intricate emerald dress with gold embroidery. "Your message seemed desperate. Naturally, I couldn't resist seeing what Erasmo Ozetero has gotten himself into this time. Where is the prince anyway? It's been ages since we last saw each other."

The sly lilt of her lips and the way she cooed Erasmo's name hinted that she and Erasmo may have had an intimate relationship in the past.

Solana wasn't the only one to notice. Next to her, Kiki curled her hand into a fist, her other one reaching for the machete at her waist. Solana jammed her foot into Kiki's ankle, causing her to choke on her drink.

"Calm down," Solana muttered through the side of her mouth.

Kiki set her drink down with a loud thunk but kept her mouth shut.

Thank the Saints for that.

"Your presence is much appreciated," Solana said. "However, Erasmo isn't here. And he is no longer the leader of the Deleste Territory; his eldest brother Bernat has returned. Yet, he, too, is also not here. That's why we sent the message."

"Hmm, consider me intrigued," Giselle purred, choosing a seat opposite from the leader of the Maravilla Territory, where she proceeded to wink suggestively at him.

Xavier merely turned to his party and started a hushed conversation with them.

Last to arrive was a stocky man with a barrel chest and a thick black beard. He wore a deerskin vest adorned with silver and obsidian. His hair was unkempt, and he let the long tresses fall down his back.

"Juan Martín de la Cavallería, leader of Las Víboras, welcome," Solana said, giving him a respectful nod of her head.

The burly man looked around the room, grabbed the first crystal goblet he saw, and took a long swig. When he was done, he set the glass down harshly and said, "There better be some buñuelos, or I'm out of here."

He unsheathed a large wooden sword with obsidian blades embedded throughout the circumference and set it clattering on top of the table. Then, he threw himself down in a chair and began piling his plate with savory empanadas and mountains of carne asada.

So much for decorum, Solana thought to herself.

She made a motion with her hand, and a servant rushed up to her elbow. "Please ask the staff to prepare some buñuelos and bring more sangria. We're going to need it."

Seeing that Juan Martín had started in on the food, the other dignitaries followed suit.

"Are we supposed to call him Juan Martín or just Juan," Kiki whispered, reaching over Solana for the pan dulce.

Solana swatted Kiki's hand away from the sweet bread. "Eat some real food first," she chided.

Kiki curled back her upper lip in a scowl but grabbed herself a serving of chicken-filled enchiladas instead.

The tension in the room was palpable as each territory spoke quietly amongst themselves, not even trying to speak to the others in their midst.

Solana broke the silence. "I want to thank you all for coming tonight. As you may be aware, we have recently discovered that the demons that have been attacking our territories are being controlled by an entity within our borders."

Giselle leaned forward, her emerald dress shimmering in the candle-light. "And you believe this entity to be from within one of our territo-ries?"

"No," Solana replied. "We know where the person is located. We need your help to put an end to this threat."

Xavier spoke up, his amber eyes intense. "Who is 'we' exactly? You say the word like you are an Ozetero, but you most certainly are not." He gestured to the other territory leaders. "None of us have heard of you, *Solana Ramirez.*"

Solana could appreciate Xavier's tactical mind, even if that mind was pitted against her. She knew there was no way she could move forward with the real purpose of this meeting without explaining who she was and where she had come from.

So that's exactly what she did. She explained her rank as a Commander in the Demon Corps. How she had crossed the Cicatrix with Bernat. How he had reunited with his family and how he'd been taken captive by Arlando.

Though she had done her best to keep the story brief, by the time she was done, everyone's plates were empty.

"So you're Bernat's mate, then?" Giselle asked as she twirled a strand of blond hair between her polished fingers.

Solana nodded. "I am."

Xavier thrummed his fingers against the table in a rhythmic pattern. "And since Bernat is the rightful King of Ozero, being his mate makes you our queen." He said it with a note of finality rather than a question.

"You're welcome to think of me in whatever terms you need. I couldn't care less. So long as I can count on your help in ending this conflict," Solana said, mindful to keep her tone steady and her face free of emotion.

She meant what she said. She truly had no desire to rule or be anyone's queen. But it was the role that had been asked of her, and she would perform her duty to the best of her ability.

Xavier studied her for a moment before asking, "And why should we help you? What's in it for us?"

Solana took a deep breath before answering. "Because if we don't stop this, it'll only be a matter of time before your territories are attacked as well. You're aware of the curse?"

Xavier exchanged a look with his people. "We've heard rumors," he said vaguely.

"Then you understand the importance of working together to fight the source of the demons and break the curse on our land," Solana said.

Giselle leaned back in her chair, a contemplative expression on her face. "It's a fair point that working together to defeat this enemy has a greater chance at succeeding. However, I'd like to know what it is we're up against. Who is the cause of the increased demon activity?"

"We've discovered that Arlando Ozetero has been using blood magic combined with ancient spells to somehow control the demons."

Juan Martín belched loudly, then wiped his mouth on his sleeve. "This is a family matter, yet you haul out your dirty socks for us all to see. Take care of this problem amongst yourselves, the way it should be done."

"If we could, we would," Solana said, her tone grave. "But the demon army that Arlando commands is too large for Deleste to take on alone."

"It's clear Deleste needs Maravilla's army, but why does Maravilla need Deleste? So, I ask again, what is in it for us?" Xavier asked, his amber eyes sharp.

Kiki's fist pounded the table as she stood in a rush. "You don't get it! You get to keep your lives. That's what you get out of this, you arrogant ass," she snapped. "If Deleste takes on Arlando alone, and we will regardless of whether you join us or not, and when we fail, which we will, then guess who is next? You. And when you're all dead, he'll go after Esmeralda. Then he'll swallow Las Víboras and all the rest of the territories who were too cowardly to be here tonight."

"You always have such a way with words, Xochicale," Solana muttered, giving Kiki a deadpan glare.

"There's no point in mincing words," Kiki snapped back. "We will all die if Arlando gets his way. The curse lives on, and more people die. It's simple, and so is the solution. We fight."

Giselle flipped her luscious curls over her shoulder. "Who is this delicious little spitfire that speaks for you?" Her brown eyes traveled up and down Kiki's form, brazenly making her interest clear.

Kiki frowned back at the woman, confusion written all over her face.

Solana jerked her chin in Kiki's direction. "This is Kiki Xochicale, she and Yasir lead our military efforts."

Juan Martín pounded his fist against the table, drawing everyone's eyes. "Las Víboras demand more than pretty words to raise our macuá and go against the will of Los Espíritos," he said, raising his large weapon off the table and jerking it in the air.

Giselle rolled her eyes. "Not this again."

"You mock the spirits, but you have not seen their power, have you little girl?" Juan Martín growled.

"Careful who you call 'little' old man," she sneered.

"Play nice, children," Xavier chimed in, earning him twin glares from Giselle and Juan Martín.

Juan Martín shook his macua, the wooden sword with sharp obsidian blades embedded into the edge. "Los Espíritos have allowed this curse to ravage our land as penance. When they are satisfied, the curse will lift, and Mama Quilla will rise."

At that, Luna leaned forward. "You know about the lunar mother?"

"Sí," Juan Martín replied with a reverent nod. "She is our goddess, and we await her return. She will come with the star-tipped spear and beat back the darkness once and for all."

Solana blinked at the resolute way Juan Martín spoke about these deities. She had no knowledge of other deities aside from the Saints.

Luna stood in a rush and grabbed a book that she'd had tucked at her side. Solana recognized it as the volume she'd been painstakingly trying to translate with Guille.

She opened the book feverishly and sped through the pages, stopping at one before turning it toward Juan Martín. "Is this the star-tipped spear you're talking about?"

Juan Martín's mouth fell open. "Mama Quilla," he said reverently upon seeing the image. He made a series of movements with his hands over his face before clutching the pendant at his neck and pressing his lips to the silver surface. "Where did you get that?"

"We found it in the archives here in La Aguilera. Do you know where this is?" she asked, flipping to another page with the map they couldn't decipher.

Juan Martín rose from his seat slowly and walked around the table to get a better look. "May I?" he asked, holding his hands out for the book. She passed it to him, and he studied the page with awe.

"We haven't been able to figure out where this is," Luna said, pointing to the map. "It isn't anywhere on our maps."

The bear of a man chuckled. "That is because it is not a map that you can look down on. It must be looked at from the side. Here, I will show you."

He began to grab goblets, silverware, and bowls and rearranged them on the table.

"Lovely, now he's playing with the food," Giselle complained.

It seemed clear that Juan Martín would ally himself with House Ozetero now that Luna had something that captured his interest. But Solana had to be sure. "Juan Martín, will you join us?"

He grunted as he lugged a platter of tortillas towards himself to continue making his display. "Fine. Las Víboras will join. But I will have a say in how my people fight. I don't want any of your fancy tactics getting in the way of our brute force."

"Done," Solana agreed.

While Luna worked with Juan Martín, Solana turned to the remaining territory leaders.

Crossing her arms over her chest, she said, "You've heard our request and our argument. Now it's time for you to decide."

Xavier took a moment to consider before nodding. "Very well. Maravilla will offer our support."

Giselle smiled coyly, her eyes sparkling in the candlelight. "Esmeralda will join you under one condition." She stood up slowly, her exaggerated movements showing off her curves as the emerald dress flowed around her. "I want one night with her," she pointed directly at Kiki.

Kiki choked on her drink again, and Solana patted her hard on the back, making her scowl.

"Excuse me?" Solana asked, arching a brow.

Giselle's eyes were trained on Kiki. "You heard me. One night. What do you say, volcánita?"

Solana didn't understand what this woman was playing at, but she wasn't about to extort Kiki for the sake of their cause. "She is not for sale," Solana said, her voice taking on a sharp edge.

"Done," Kiki blurted at the same time.

Now it was Solana's turn to gape at Kiki.

Kiki gave her a shrug.

Giselle smirked. "Excellent," she said, her eyes twinkling like a pit viper before it strikes.

A loud commotion outside the hall broke their conversation as the doors burst open. Everyone inside jumped to their feet, drawing weapons and bracing for attack.

A wild-looking woman with sun-kissed brown skin, her long brown hair cascading down her back, and amber eyes that burned like bright stars in the night sky stood with an axe slung over her shoulder.

"Am I late?" she asked, looking around with a confused expression at everyone poised to defend themselves.

Xavier made a choked sound that drew everyone's attention. He ran a hand over his face before letting loose a long-suffering sigh. "Everyone, meet my sister, Xylia, leader of Las Muertas territory."

"Didn't you get my gift?" Xylia asked, brows knitting together.

"You sent us a pile of shit," Kiki spoke up.

Xylia looked around the room as if she saw nothing wrong with this. "Yeah, but it was in a beautiful box."

"Lia, you didn't," Xavier groaned, dropping his head into his hands.

"What? It's symbolic," she protested, still looking around with confusion. "You know, we're going to shit on the enemy."

"How did we share a womb for nine months?" Xavier grumbled.

The ridiculousness of the situation hit Solana, and she couldn't help it; she started laughing.

At first, the sound was muffled by her palm as she tried to contain it. But before long, her laughter had taken over, echoing through the room like a peal of bells.

Everyone stared at her in shock, but Solana barely noticed. The tension in the air had been so thick that it felt good to just laugh freely for a moment.

"See?" Xylia said to her twin. "She likes it!"

"Oh, Lia," Xavier muttered, hiding his face as if full of shame.

The room burst into peels of laughter, and Solana wiped tears from her eyes. She hadn't had a good laugh in so long. It was a welcome moment of respite.

Once everyone had settled down, Solana raised her hands to call for silence. "Now that we're all here, let's talk battle plans."

Xylia raised her ax in the air and grinned. "Let's kill some demons!"

"**G**ood night, everyone," Solana said, bowing her head as she ducked out of the dining hall.

They'd had a good strategy session up until Yasir suggested they start playing a drinking game. Thankfully, they'd gone over the bulk of their plans to confront Arlando, and the rest could be sorted out later.

Now, the dining hall had become a courtyard to play some game that had everyone running around, stumbling over one another. The object of the game was to get a rubber ball into a basket set in the rafters. The players could use any part of their body except for their hands.

While Solana had enjoyed watching the others play like children for a little while, she quickly tired and desired the peace and quiet of solitude.

Once inside her suite, she sat on the bed to unlace her boots.

Kiki and Luna had explained how the mate bond had brought their mates to them during their sleep. She'd been secretly envious because she had yet to encounter Bernat.

While Kiki and Luna had both reported that Bernat was doing fine, according to his brother and cousin, she still felt the need to confirm that information.

She'd spent the last six years of her life in Bernat's company in some form. The first year, when she had just risen to the rank of Slayer, she and Bernat spent a lot of time together on Watch, on missions, or training.

Even back then, if she were being honest with herself, she found the man to be intriguing. But the age difference had prevented her from ever acting on those feelings, and she knew that up until a year ago, he hadn't reciprocated those feelings himself.

Despite being the same rank and then eventually surpassing him in rank, she was still five years younger than him.

Now that she was twenty-two, that age gap didn't seem so large. But she was grateful that he hadn't ever seen her in such a way before.

With Bernat so far away, all she could think about was him. Butterflies swirled in her stomach at the mere thought of him. She was anxious to see him again, to hear the familiar timbre of his voice. To kiss his lips and feel the warmth of him wrap around her.

With Bernat, there was no such thing as walls. He'd seen the fortress that she'd built around herself and leaped over them as if they never existed.

With Bernat, she felt safe and at ease.

She missed that feeling.

After removing her leathers and wiping them down with a soft cloth, she folded them neatly and set them inside a dresser drawer.

It was only now that Bernat wasn't here that she could actually care for her leathers the way she was supposed to. Normally, they'd end their nights here, with their boots and leathers and bracers scattered across the floor or hanging off some piece of furniture.

A spark of lightning ignited inside her chest at the memory of those passion-filled nights.

She blew out the candle at her bedside and settled under the fur blankets, letting her mind drift to thoughts of him and him alone.

*S*he stepped carefully along the well-worn paths of the Norceran Demon Corps base camp. Her gaze swept across the rows of tents, their canvases bleached from the harsh northern sun. Not a soul stirred in the camp as if the inhabitants had long since moved on.

She made her way to the Commander's tent, hoping she'd find someone to explain where everyone was.

Ducking inside the tent, she stepped into the warmth and faint glow of several candles and lit lanterns.

She found Bernat with his eyes focused on a map sprawled open on the table, but as soon as she slipped into the tent, his gaze snapped to hers.

"Mi sol," Bernat whispered, his eyes widening in surprise. "It worked!"

He rushed forward and pulled her into his arms. She gratefully melted into his embrace. "What worked?" she asked, her voice muffled from her face pressed into his chest.

"I was determined to make it happen, so I concentrated on you, just you, nothing else. No thoughts about escape, no worries about anything else. I just thought about you, and here you are."

"I did the same," she said, relief soaking her words. "I've been so focused on getting everything in order."

"I've heard," he said, pride tinting his voice. "La Reina Suprema," he hummed. "It suits you."

She grimaced. "I wish they wouldn't call me that. I'm not anyone's queen."

"You're my queen," he responded, pulling back enough to gaze into her eyes. "Always have been, even when I didn't know it."

She shook her head ruefully. "You're a fool," she said softly, leaning up to angle her lips over his.

"For you, always," he said against her lips before he pulled her tightly against him and attacked her mouth.

Heat engulfed her, swamped her, released the tension she'd been holding for so long, and she gave herself over to it.

Bernat lifted her into his arms and carried her to a pallet of fur blankets and soft pillows tucked into the corner of the tent.

Her mind was still reeling from the kiss when Bernat gently lowered her to the pallet and stretched out beside her.

She reached up to trace the line of his jaw, the curve of his cheek, and he closed his eyes to savor her touch. When she shifted up onto one elbow, he opened his eyes to watch her.

"I love you," she whispered, lowering her mouth to his.

It was a different kind of kiss—tender, sweet, reverent—but no less passionate. As they slowly explored each other's mouths, desire began to build again.

She traced the line of his jaw with her lips, down his neck, to the hollow below his Adam's apple, then lower, to the dip at the base of his throat.

Bernat's breath caught when she reached the top button of his shirt and slowly, carefully undid it.

His fingers trembled as he pushed the hem of her blouse away from her waist and slowly slid his hands up her back.

He gently tugged her shirt free from her pants and traced his fingers across the sensitive spot at the small of her back.

She shivered with longing at the contrast of his warm skin against hers. She missed him so much that she felt a pang in her heart. She wanted more than this tender exploration, though. She needed him to shift into the role he assumed when they were intimate. She needed it like she needed air to live.

She quickly sat up and lifted her arms so that Bernat could remove her shirt. When he returned to hover beside her, she pulled the shirt over his head and tossed it aside, impatience bubbling in her blood.

The weight of leadership took its toll on her, and she'd been noticing more and more signs of exhaustion. Though she was accustomed to the daily strain of command thanks to her time in the Demon Corps, the stakes were so much higher now. What she needed was a release from all of that responsibility.

She released his belt buckle, unzipped his pants, and tugged them over his narrow hips as he kicked them free.

She reached for the button on her pants, and he covered her hands with his to still them.

"Let me," he whispered, leaning over to kiss her again.

He pulled her pants from her body, tossing them aside in an impatient motion. His gaze was hooded, and the flame of desire that sparkled in her eyes sent a shiver of excitement up her spine.

Once free of all their clothes, they came together again, skin to skin, chest to chest, hip to hip.

They held one another for a moment, basking in the sensation of finally being in each other's arms.

"Mi sol," he whispered, kissing her neck, her jaw, and the corner of her mouth before lowering his mouth to hers.

She arched into him, her body consumed by fire at the heat of his lips on her skin.

The desire between them blazed, and Bernat's dominant side began to take over. He moved her onto her back and pressed himself against her, his hands exploring every inch of her body as he kissed her more deeply.

She moaned in pleasure, pressing herself closer to him, wanting—no needing—to be even closer still. Her hips rocked beneath him, entreating him to give her more.

"Your body is begging for me," he whispered, his hand trailing down the planes of her stomach.

"I don't beg," she panted, feeling his hands sinking lower and lower.

A devilish glint lit up in his eyes. "Oh, you will. For me, you'll beg."

Saints, she loved this side of him. She'd do anything the man said, just to feel him exert his power over her, just to have the joy of knowing she pleased him.

"Make me," she moaned when his fingers found her clit, slipping through her slick folds. "I'm yours to command," she said again when he pushed a finger inside her.

Her hips rose off the pallet, seeking more. He slid another finger inside her and began to work them in a slow, deliberate rhythm.

"Please," she cried, her hands grasping his shoulders as she rocked against his hand.

He slipped his finger out of her and brought his hand up to his mouth to lick the wetness off his fingers. "Please, what?" he asked, his voice rough with desire.

"More," she breathed, her body tense with need. "Please, I need more."

"Say it like you mean it," he growled, rising to his knees to remove the rest of his clothes.

His command made goosebumps prickle her skin, but she could tell he was holding back. She needed him to dominate every inch of her. Pound her into complete submission. She knew she'd have to push him to that ledge.

"Please," she gasped, stretching her arms over her head to emphasize her need. "Give me your cock!"

Bernat lowered himself beside her again, pulling her closer to him, guiding his cock to her waiting, slick pussy.

When the tip of his cock brushed against her clit he groaned and placed his hands on either side of her head, pushing himself up so he could see her face.

"Tell me what you want," he moaned.

"Fuck me," she growled, grinding her hips against him, every bit of her wanting him inside her.

"As my queen commands," he said, flexing his hips to push a little further into her.

She raised her knees and wrapped her legs around his waist.

"More," she demanded again, her voice hoarse with need.

"So greedy," he said, a smile breaking out over his face. "You're going to have to earn it," he said, pulling back again.

She grinned at the coarseness in his voice. He was so close to losing his control. With a sharp jerk of her hips, she stared him in the eyes and said, "Fuck you."

Bernat's hands slammed to the inside of her thighs, his grip tight as he spread her open. Sparks ignited along her body as she internally celebrated her victory. "What was that?" he asked, a mischievous glint in his eyes.

"I said, 'fuck you,'" she huffed as she slipped her hand down past her navel and dipped her finger into her own slickness.

His hand lashed out and grabbed her wrist. "Don't mind if I do," he purred as his tongue darted out and licked her juices from her fingers. "This pussy is mine."

"Then take what's yours," she whispered, her voice on the verge of cracking with need.

"Trust me, I will," he growled, yanking her closer so he could line up his cock with her entrance; then he thrust into her, filling her so completely that she cried out.

"Yes," he hummed. "Whose queen are you?" he asked as he began to thrust into her, his chest rippling with each movement.

"Yours," she whimpered, loving this feeling of being completely seen—being owned and safe enough to let go.

"All mine," he growled and picked up the pace, his cock slamming into her, fucking her at the pace he desired.

"Yes, Bernat, please," she begged, her orgasm pressing closer.

"What do you want, my love?" he moaned as he thrust, watching the pleasure move through her. "Use your words."

"I want to come," she cried out, the pressure building almost unbearable. "Please!"

"Not yet," he growled, his rhythm slowing. "But soon," he panted, his body tight with need. "You'll come when I say," he demanded as he continued to thrust into her with agonizing slowness.

"Bernat, please," she cried out.

It was the sweetest torture when he edged her like this. She both hated and loved it at the same time.

"I love it when you tell me what you want," he growled, pulling out of her so quickly that she gasped at the loss of him.

He grabbed her knees and flipped her over onto her stomach.

"On your hands and knees," he commanded.

She did as he ordered, her breath rushing in and out of her lungs in harsh pants as excitement made her pussy throb with need.

"You love it when I take you like this," he said, and with two strong hands, he pressed her shoulders to the pallet.

"Yes," she admitted, her body singing.

"You like to give up control," he said, grabbing her arms and wrenching them behind her back, holding her wrists at the base of her spine.

She whimpered at his words, her head pressed into the furs. Her hips lifted, and she arched her back, offering herself to him.

"I'm going to fuck you senseless," he said as he knelt behind her.

"Yes," she cried out, her hips gyrating in anticipation of his possession. "Splinter me on your cock."

Then he was there, the head of his cock brushing against her slick lips.

"Say it again," he said, his voice so rough with need that she could barely make out the words.

"Please," she whimpered. "I need you. I need your cock inside me."

"You're so wet," he growled, his cock slipping against her clit. "So fucking wet," he panted as he teased her with his tip.

"Yes. Please, yes," she sobbed, her body coiling like a spring.

He growled as he thrust into her, and her body shuddered in pleasure at the feeling of him filling her. He slammed into her again and again, driving her to the brink of insanity.

"I'm going to make you come," he growled. "Tell me you want to come."

"Yes, please," she sobbed, so close she could feel it. "I want to come."

She could feel her orgasm just barely out of reach like it wanted to wash over her and consume her whole but was waiting for permission.

"Come for me," he growled.

That was all her body needed. She shuddered as she gave him what he demanded. Her orgasm crashed over her in waves that made stars dance in her eyes, her moans muffled by the furs.

He rode out her orgasm, giving her everything she needed. Then, as her body stilled, he continued to fuck her, his pace as steady as his breathing.

"Tell me. Tell me you're mine," he growled, his hands tightening on her wrists.

"Yes," she panted, her body tightening again. "Yes, I'm yours."

"You feel so good," he ground out through clenched teeth. "So fucking good."

His pace quickened as he grew closer and closer to his own release.

She wanted to feel him come, to feel when Bernat fell over the edge of his own control and lost himself to her. There was nothing more empowering than knowing she was the reason he lost control.

"Come inside me," she whimpered, her body on fire once again as she was stretched to accommodate his girth. "I want to feel you come."

"Then come with me," he growled, his fingers digging into her skin.

The realization that she was truly his hit her like a wave of pleasure.

She screamed as another orgasm claimed her, her body shuddering with each spasm.

He groaned as he ground against her, as her body milked his cock, taking everything he had to give.

She felt his cock jerk as his cum spurted deep inside her, then overfilled her, spilling out from her pussy and dripping down her inner thighs.

"My queen," he hummed as he released her wrists and collapsed beside her, both panting and slick with sweat. "My beautiful queen."

"My king," she whispered, sliding her sweaty hand up his chest.

His lips kissed her shoulder, and she sighed as his hand moved over her stomach, her hip, her thigh—his touch so warm and tender.

"Sleep," he murmured as his hand moved up her body and cupped the swell of her breast. "My beautiful queen."

"Yes," she sighed, feeling herself fade into sleep. A small smile played on her lips as she realized that Bernat took every bit of her, and in return, she took every bit of him.

"Mine," she murmured, her eyes drifting shut.

Chapter Twenty-One

Turi

Snow flurries whipped across Turi's cheeks, sending a prickling sensation down his spine and seeping into his very bones.

The village was frozen in time. Just like the others he and Arlando had visited over the last several weeks.

Demons lurched around the village, their movements staccato and their sulfuric scent tainting the air.

I don't think I can take this any longer.

You must. If he is with us, then he is not with her.

Turi winced, knowing that the beast was at least right about that.

But saving Yari from Arlando's presence and further abuse came at a greater cost than Turi had anticipated.

No cost is too great! The beast snarled. **She is the only thing that matters to us. We will do anything to save her.**

He palmed his face in annoyance. He was also getting tired of the beast that lived just beneath his own skin. Always talking and coming up with horrific ways to end Arlando's life. And the sexual fantasies were getting darker and darker. It made him nauseated.

My fantasies are yours. I merely have the courage to speak them.

Shut up!

A piercing cry of terror ripped him back to the present. He turned in time to see a demon pulling a woman by the hair from one of the buildings.

Her eyes were wide with fear, and she clawed at the hand fisted in her hair.

He stood in shock at the woman. He'd never seen someone not fall to Arlando's spell when he cast it over an unsuspecting village.

"What do we have here?" Arlando cooed as he strolled up to the struggling woman. He bent at the waist to look into her eyes, and a smile tugged at the corners of his lips. "She's an immune," he said, turning to Turi.

"An immune?" Turi asked, trying to keep his face neutral.

"It's exactly how it sounds, brother," Arlando sneered, his face twisting into one of disgust. "Surely you're not that dense."

"I'm new to all of this," Turi hissed, his patience wearing thin. "Which, of course, you're well aware of."

He knew he was treading on thin ice with Arlando by speaking so boldly against him. But the beast within had a short temper and was easily riled.

Don't blame me. The beast interjected. ***This anger is yours and yours alone.***

He bit the inside of his cheek to keep from screaming. *I told you to shut the fuck up!*

The beast shook out its fur before curling into a circle, its muzzle resting on its front paws. But it didn't say another word, and for that, Turi was grateful.

"I don't like your tone, brother," Arlando said, his eyes sharpening into daggers. "And here I was going to offer you this gift, but perhaps I won't."

"Gift?"

Arlando gestured to the woman who was now sobbing. "You have no mate of your own, and surely this immune can act as entertainment in the meantime."

We do have a mate. You took her from us!

The beast wasn't wrong about that, either. Turi had yet to figure out how Arlando had managed it. Still, after seeing his blood magic's power, Turi didn't have to wonder too hard.

Turi straightened his shoulders and looked down his nose at Arlando. "I don't seek such wanton pleasure. I have a mate, and I will wait for her."

Arlando rolled his eyes and sighed heavily. "You may never find your mate. Take this woman instead. She has a nice face, and her body is adequate."

Turi hid the disgust that bubbled within his gut at the dismissive way he spoke about the poor woman. She was a person, and he spoke about her like she was nothing more than cattle that he was purchasing.

"Just let her go, and we'll be on our way," Turi said, turning on his heel to walk away.

"You know I can't do that, little brother," Arlando said, his tone darkening.

Turi whipped around to see Arlando yank the woman away from the demon; his hand curled in her hair. With a violent yank, he exposed her neck, and his fangs lengthened, his jaw expanding until his mouth was a macabre blend between bear and human.

Arlando's eyes lit up with a mix of excitement and hunger as he slowly leaned in and clamped his teeth into her soft neck. She let out a piercing scream that echoed through the vacant street, her arms flailing and legs kicking as she fought to the very end.

Silence enveloped them as her eyes rolled to the back of her head, and her body went completely limp, her once-tanned skin now a sallow grey, all the blood drained from her.

Arlando's powerful hands unclasped from around her throat, and she dropped to the ground like a rag doll. The corner of his lips was stained red with a mixture of blood and saliva, and he hastily pulled out a crisp white handkerchief from inside his jacket pocket, dabbing at the edges of his mouth in an attempt to clean away the evidence.

Turi opened and closed his mouth, at a loss for words. Bile crept up his throat, and he swallowed it down as he forced his shaking hands to still.

Arlando approached Turi with quick, deliberate steps, his long white coat billowing behind him. He reached out and pressed the bloody handkerchief into Turi's chest, his eyes narrowing as he spoke. "Next time, don't be a spoiled brat and accept my gifts when they're offered."

The tension in the air was thick as Arlando turned on his heel and walked away, leaving Turi standing there alone.

Once Arlando was out of sight, Turi snuck off to a darkened alley and puked his guts out.

We will make him pay for this.

Yes, we will.

Chapter Twenty-Two

Yari

"You can't stay in your little hole all day," Aurelia pulled Yari's hand as they walked down the castle's corridors toward the sitting rooms on the main level.

Aurelia's pet raven stood with its long, ebony wings tucked behind it. The bird's ink-black feathers glimmered in the morning light as Aurelia walked, and it seemed content to remain perched on her shoulder.

As they moved through the castle, Yari did her best to ignore the demons that stood guard at evenly spaced intervals, their raspy breaths the only sound that could be heard aside from the soft whisper of her slippers against the marble floors.

"I really don't understand why I can't go back to my alcove. I feel safer there," Yari said, her voice little more than a whisper.

Aurelia sighed as if annoyed but gave Yari a smile anyway. "Arlando and Turi aren't back yet, and the demons won't do anything unless Arlando orders them to. So it's like we're here by ourselves, basically."

"I think you're forgetting the part where your cousins are trapped in the dungeon," Yari said, glancing over her shoulder to ensure the demons weren't following them.

"About that, I sent Zuzu down there to check things out." The raven cawed at its name. "He said it looks like the demons have been ordered to feed the guys, so they're okay for now."

Yari hadn't gotten used to Aurelia's relationship with her pet, nor the fact that the silver-eyed woman somehow could communicate with it. All Yari ever heard was a series of squawks and caws. Either Aurelia really could talk with the bird, or she was delusional. Yari supposed it didn't matter if Aurelia was hallucinating; she made Yari feel less alone, which was something Yari was desperate to cling to.

If Zuzu was to be believed, the state of the dungeon and its accommodations didn't change the situation. Yari said as much. "They're caged like animals. That is hardly okay."

Aurelia shrugged. "I've been in worse situations, to be honest. So don't mind me and my lack of empathy. At least they're not being tortured."

"Small mercies," Yari muttered.

Aurelia pushed open the door to the sitting room where Yari's easel and paints still sat, waiting for her.

Aurelia pulled Yari toward the easel and positioned her right in front of it. "Now, in order for our plan to work, you have to convince Arlando that you're on his side. That you've forgiven him and have come to your senses."

Yari didn't like Aurelia's plan. But it was the only one they could come up with that created the perfect opportunity to get into the dungeon, break Aurelia's cousins out of their cages, and escape with them and Turi, all in one shot.

"So," Aurelia continued. "You need to go back to doing whatever you did before Arlando beared-out on you."

Yari winced at the reminder. She knew Aurelia wasn't trying to be insensitive, but the wounds of that night were still raw.

She nodded, moving to the blank canvases lined up along the wall, and picked the nearest one up.

She'd once thought it had been so thoughtful of Arlando to let her have all of these supplies. She had never once thought that she was merely decorating her own cage.

Yari picked up a paintbrush, feeling a sudden wave of despair wash over her. She had been so foolish to trust Arlando, to believe that he truly loved her. But now, as she stared at the empty canvas before her, she couldn't even remember what it was like to feel free.

Aurelia watched Yari for a moment before speaking softly. "I know this is hard, but we have to be strong. We have to find a way out of here, and we can't do that if we're too scared to try."

Yari nodded, trying to focus on the task at hand. She dipped the brush into the paint and slowly filled the canvas with black paint.

A sudden wave of anger washed over her. She'd been so foolish to trust Arlando—she grabbed the spatula and picked up some red paint, then made a slash through the black.

How did she ever believe that he truly loved her—she mixed white and grey and smeared it onto the canvas.

As she worked, her mind drifted to her friends. She wondered what they were going through, if they were afraid, or if they were holding onto hope like she was.

She didn't know how long she painted for, but eventually, she realized that Aurelia had left the room.

Alone in the quiet, Yari allowed herself a moment of weakness. She set the brush down and let out a soft sob, tears streaming down her face.

She couldn't bear the thought of being trapped in this castle only to be sacrificed like she was some animal for slaughter, never again to see the only family she had in this world, Kiki and Luna.

But Aurelia was right. She had to be strong. She had to bide her time so that they all could get out.

Wiping her tears away, Yari picked up the brush again and continued to paint. The colors on the canvas began to take shape, forming a brutal scene of a golden eagle, blood dripping from its talons, and a serpent clutched between its beak.

As she worked, she realized that painting was no longer just a way to pass the time but a way to escape. In this small way, she was free to create something beautiful, to express herself without fear.

For a moment, Yari forgot about the demons, the castle, and her trapped friends. She was completely absorbed in her art and lost in the colors and shapes.

Out of red paint, she set down her palette and grabbed an unopened tube of crimson. The seal was hard to open, so she grabbed the small razor-tipped tool she used to cut the canvas when stretching it.

But in her haste, she cut too deep, and the blade's sharp edge sliced into her finger.

She yelped and dropped the knife, watching as a drop of blood inched down her wrist.

The smell of her blood seemed to fill the room, and a low growl filled the air before she could do anything.

Yari's heart began to race as she saw something move in the corner of her eye. She looked up and saw a giant demon standing in the doorway, its red eyes fixed on her with an intensity that sent shivers down her spine.

Without warning, it charged towards her. Yari screamed and scrambled for the door, but it was too late. The creature leaped onto her back and pinned her with razor-sharp claws.

She screamed for help, struggling against it as it tried to sink its teeth into her neck.

"STOP!" she yelled.

The words seemed to reverberate off the walls, and time seemed to stand still for a moment. Yari realized with amazement that the creature had stopped attacking her.

Slowly, she looked up at the demon and saw it was standing perfectly still, its eyes focused on her with an unwavering intensity. A feeling of awe washed over her as she realized it was listening to her command.

She gently pushed it off her and got up from the floor, her limbs shaking with adrenaline and fear. She stepped back cautiously, but the creature stayed still, watching her every move.

"Sit," Yari commanded.

The demon did as she bid it.

Suddenly, there was a loud crash from outside, and Aurelia exploded into the room, brandishing a sword.

Aurelia paused her attack when she saw the demon listening to Yari. Her sword was still pointed towards it as she took in the situation.

Yari was standing in the middle of the room, blood dripping from her finger. The creature was not moving, its eyes still locked on Yari.

The silence stretched out until Aurelia finally lowered her sword and spoke. "What did you do?" she asked, her voice tinged with fear.

Yari shook her head slowly, still unable to believe what had just happened. "I-I don't know," she said, "but I think I might be able to control it."

"How?" Aurelia asked, her eyes darting between Yari and the demon.

Focusing on her intention, Yari gave the demon a simple command. "Leave us."

The demon bowed its head before turning around and left the room.

Aurelia stepped forward and said, "For your finger," as she passed over a handkerchief from her pocket.

Yari wrapped her finger with the cloth to stop the bleeding.

"Hey," Aurelia said, reaching up toward Yari's face. "Have you always had this little silver streak in your hair?"

Yari moved to the mirror in the room and stared at her reflection. Tucked beneath the layers of her hair was a streak of silver hair.

It reminded her of Arlando's hair.

She swallowed the lump in her throat. "No. It's new."

She removed the cloth from her finger and stared at the cut that had bled. She couldn't help but admire how powerful she felt when she realized she could control the demon—power she'd never felt before.

CHAPTER TWENTY-THREE

KIKI

A blizzard raged outside, forcing everyone to remain inside the manor until it died down. Kiki wouldn't have minded the day off if she were still in the Demon Corps. In fact, she probably would have celebrated by burrowing into her bed with a book in her hands.

But time was barreling forward, and the lack of action was starting to wear on her.

Plans had been made, and Juan Martín had sent messengers back to Las Víboras to muster his army. Still, with his territory being the furthest away, their plan hinged on waiting for his soldiers to arrive.

Soldiers from Maravilla and Esmeralda were due in a day or two, while the Lloronas of Las Muertas would arrive a few days after that.

Kiki lay sprawled on a plush green velvet sofa as she tossed a ball into the air to occupy her hands.

Since she had nothing better to do, she had decided to come into the study where Luna, Guille, and Juan Martín were still trying to decipher the map.

The flicker of a candle cast an eerie glow on their faces, and the howling wind outside only added to the sense of foreboding.

"What about this ridge here?" Luna pointed to a faded line on the map. "Maybe that's an old river that's dried up now?"

Juan Martín nodded in agreement, "Hmm, that would explain the landmarks not matching up."

Kiki blew out a frustrated breath. "I thought you had figured out that the map was supposed to be viewed from the side. What happened to your little food fort?"

Luna cut her gaze to Kiki, a silent warning to be quiet. "It was a good theory," she said, her tone defensive.

"Except it didn't work," Kiki mumbled.

"What was that?" Luna asked, her eyes narrowed.

Kiki knew Luna had heard her just fine and only felt a little guilty for repeating it. "Nothing," she drawled. "Nothing at all." She tossed the ball again, harder this time, and it hit the ceiling with a loud thud.

Luna gripped the edges of the table. "Would you be more careful? You're marking up the whole ceiling."

Sure enough, the ceiling was pock-marked with little smudges from some of her harder throws.

"Sorry," Kiki mumbled, tossing the ball again but with less force.

The trio continued to pour over the map, turning it and flipping it, holding it to the light, angling it to the side.

If Luna were in a better mood, Kiki might have made a joke about it. But, well, no one was in a particularly good mood lately, so she didn't push her luck.

However, after another couple hours of tossing the ball in the air and nothing new coming from staring at the map, Kiki huffed and threw the ball even harder, hitting the ceiling above. Again.

She winced and prayed that Luna was too consumed in her task to notice.

"Kiki!" she screeched.

No such luck.

Kiki sat up quickly and held her hands in the air. "Sorry, I'll stop."

Luna moved around the table to stand in front of her. "Look what you've done," she scolded, throwing her head back to examine the mess. "You've completely ruined it, how are we supposed to clean that—"

Luna trailed off all of a sudden, and Kiki darted her gaze between the ceiling and Luna's upturned face.

"I'll get Yasir to help me," Kiki said, trying to appease her friend. "We can do it tomorrow. Promise."

"Wait," Luna mumbled, her eyes still trained on the ceiling. "What do those look like to you?" she asked Kiki, pointing at the smudges.

Kiki turned her face up. "Dirt splotches?"

Luna waved her hand dismissively. "No, besides that. What else do they look like to you?"

"Uhh, I don't know."

"They look like stars," Luna whispered. "Saints, that's it!"

She rushed back to the map and held it above her head. "We've been looking at it all wrong. It's not a map of the land. It's a map of the sky! Or, more accurately, the stars!"

Luna passed the map to the two curious men, and she rushed forward and threw her arms around Kiki. "You're a genius!"

Kiki patted Luna's back awkwardly. "Usually, I'd take any compliment lobbed at me, but this time, I actually did nothing."

Luna laughed and released Kiki. "I know, but if it weren't for your constant need to stay busy, we'd still be staring at that map like idiots."

She wasn't wrong...

"I know where this is," Juan Martín announced, pointing a finger at the map. "We've had it this whole time," he added, a note of awe in his voice. "My people, I mean. This is in my territory."

"So now what?" Kiki asked.

The three map interpreters looked at each other skeptically, but Juan Martín broke the silence. "I will go back and retrieve it so that Mama Quilla may wake and banish the darkness."

Kiki resisted the urge to roll her eyes. She now understood why Giselle's eyes practically pointed toward the sky when Juan Martín was around.

He was rather rough around the edges, a trait she didn't mind too much. But his zealous faith in this moon goddess was a bit much to stomach in one sitting.

Kiki pushed to her feet and dropped the ball onto the cushions. "So, more waiting," she grumbled.

"Kiki," Luna said with a pleading tone.

"No, it's fine. I'm just going to take a walk. Around. Here. Somewhere." She ducked out of the study, the sound of excited chatter filling the room once she was down the hall.

She didn't mean to be in such a mood, but all this waiting around was starting to make her anxious. She needed action. She needed to punch something.

"Don't you look positively murderous," a feminine voice purred.

Kiki spun around and was faced with Giselle clad in an emerald bolero jacket and a matching skirt that flared out with white ruffles peeking from beneath the hem. Her eyes were lined in black, and she'd painted her lips a deep crimson.

Kiki had yet to fulfill her end of the "one night" bargain and had been avoiding being in the same room with Giselle since.

The woman hadn't clarified when that "night" should take place nor what such a night would entail. Though Kiki had agreed, she didn't see any harm in dodging her end of the deal indefinitely.

Giselle's lips curled into a smirk. "You've been avoiding me."

Kiki took a step back. "What? No, I haven't." She retreated another step. "It's just been so busy around here, and I haven't seen you," she said, her voice getting a note higher with each word.

"Come. Have a drink with me in my suite," Giselle grinned, grabbing Kiki's hand and tugging her along.

"If I have to," Kiki mumbled miserably.

Reaching her suite, Giselle opened the door and motioned for Kiki to enter.

With a groan, Kiki stepped over the threshold and paused mid-step as she took in the room.

Lush green fabric was draped over the windows and draped around the four-poster bed. Thick carpets of white fur lined the wooden floors, and golden trinkets with emerald inlay decorated the dresser and the vanity.

The sheer display of wealth made Kiki feel insufficient in her Demon Corps leathers. Saints, how many tlazons could be made from selling just one of those little golden combs sitting on that vanity over there?

"You can tell only warriors live here," Giselle said as she sashayed into the room and settled in a green lounge chair. She threw her legs up and laid back, letting her blond hair cascade over the high back. "Everything here is so utilitarian, no eye for beauty."

"Did you bring all of this stuff with you," Kiki asked, turning around slowly in a circle to take it all in.

"I always do," she said with a sigh. "No one has vision, and I refuse to stay somewhere without at least silk sheets. My skin is very delicate," she added, seductively sliding her fingertips up her arm.

Kiki palmed her face. "Look, I know I agreed to your deal, but I'm with Erasmo."

Giselle chuckled, the sound sultry and inviting. "Oh, I know he's your mate, known since before we even arrived."

Kiki's brows pinched as she quirked her head. "Then why—"

"Why did I make such a show about bargaining over you? Because I like to keep the others on their toes. Do the unexpected. I have a reputation to uphold." She toyed with a strand of her blonde hair. "Besides, rumor will spread about our deal, and when Erasmo is free, he'll hear all about it." She shivered as if the thought excited her. "He'll fly into such a jealous rage. I can already taste it."

Kiki raised a brow at her. Clearly, Mauricio wasn't the only psycho around. "So... that's it? I can go?"

"You can do whatever you like, volcánita. I'd rather share that drink with you, get to know each other better and all that." She grinned, her eyes roving down Kiki's form before she let out an exaggerated sigh. "But I'm not one to force my company on others. I do believe in consent, believe it or not."

Kiki pursed her lips. It was clear that Giselle found Kiki attractive, meaning she either preferred women or she enjoyed the company of both men and women.

Kiki's earlier suspicion when the woman first arrived rose from the ashes, piquing her curiosity. "How do you know Erasmo?"

"Oh, that killjoy," she rolled her eyes. "We went to school together. All the parents tried to keep the academy open even after the darkness, but with it being so far away and so many of the Ozetero males being taken by the curse, the other leaders decided to shut it down."

"I didn't realize there was a school here."

"Well, not here in Deleste. It's way down south in what's now known as the Paztla territory. They're a sort of intermediary between El Sur and Liebre."

Kiki vaguely recognized those names. She thought they might be the three territories that claimed neutrality in their current conflict.

She didn't see anything wrong with sharing a drink with Giselle, so she moved over to the velvet chair across from the blond. "So, how long did you go to school together?"

Giselle stood up and moved toward a table with a variety of glass decanters. "I'll tell you, but first, pick your poison, tequila or rum?"

Kiki shuddered at the thought of tequila. She still couldn't bear the smell of it without feeling sick. "Rum."

"My kind of girl," Giselle purred. She poured two crystal glasses dangerously full and passed one to Kiki. "Salúd."

Kiki repeated the toast and took a tentative sip, the alcohol burning on the way down.

Giselle settled back onto the sofa and flipped her hair over her shoulder. "We were at the academy until I was around fifteen, so Erasmo would have been sixteen at the time. Xavier was with us and most of the other territory leaders, too. God, I almost forgot how fun Xylia is. Did she really send a box full of horse shit as her response to your letter?"

Kiki nodded, remembering that night from a few weeks ago when they all learned that the woman had meant the gift symbolically and not as an insult. She stifled her laughter behind her hand. "She's something else."

Giselle leaned back along the sofa, kicking one foot up so that her other still rested on the floor. "Oh, that's nothing. You should have seen her when we were in school. Such a nightmare! Such fun!"

Kiki couldn't help but smile. Despite how forward Giselle was with her earlier, she thought that she might actually want to be friends with her. "What was Erasmo like?"

Giselle let out a huff of annoyance. "Much like he is now, a complete aguafiesta, such a wet blanket. Moody as hell and constantly trailing behind Arlando. I get that they are twins and all, but even Xavier and Xylia didn't spend every waking minute together."

Kiki chewed on the inside of her cheek. "The way he's talked about his brother, he made it sound like they weren't close."

Giselle shrugged. "That's probably because his brother is a fucking lying piece of shit, and it took Erasmo years to finally realize it. He always thought the best of Arlando, but the rest of us couldn't stand him. Have you ever met him?"

Kiki shook her head.

"A pretentious piece of work, and that's coming from me!" Giselle downed the rest of her drink. "He'd walk around all high and mighty like he was the rightful king or something. As if the rest of us just forgot all about Bernat or something. Such an ass."

"You knew Bernat too?"

"He was a few years ahead of us, four, I think. Anyway, he was like everyone's big brother when we were kids. Watched out for all of us, always happy to help, and often would take the blame for our mischief with the headmaster. Total king material, if you ask me. We all felt so lucky to go to school with the future king." Her smile faded as her eyes got distant. "We were really sad when we learned the darkness had killed him and their little brother. We had a memorial and everything. The future king was dead, and our kingdom was fractured." She blinked rapidly before pasting a smile on her face once more. "But it turns out Bernat and little Arturito survived after all! Cheers to that, am I right?" She lifted her drink to find the glass empty.

Kiki leaned over and passed her mostly full glass into Giselle's hand. "I didn't realize how much the curse had affected everything. Erasmo never talked about the academy."

"Probably because he and his brother had a huge falling out a few years ago. Rumor was that Arlando had finally jumped off the deep end and was going on about how he planned to abolish the territories and claim his seat on the throne. But, like, what throne, you know?" She scoffed. "Anyhow, I guess Erasmo had enough, and he led a mass exodus from the Winter Keep and led everyone here."

Kiki had surmised as much from the bits and pieces she'd gleaned from Erasmo and Mauri.

"What do you think about this plan to retrieve the star-tipped sword thing?"

Giselle chuckled darkly. "It's a bunch of superstitious nonsense, and that's coming from a girl who's seen demons straight up swallow people whole. But this whole Mama Quilla thing is idiotic."

Kiki stifled a laugh. "I agree. But I can't tell Luna that because she'll rip me a new asshole."

Giselle smirked. "I can see why Mauri is her mate. Don't get me wrong, she seems nice and all, but there's a darkness in her too. It's delicious," she said, closing her eyes as if she could savor the memory.

"I don't know about that," Kiki mumbled, "But she loves the psycho, so I guess he's okay. I just wish there was something more I could do. I hate waiting around doing nothing."

"What else do you propose we do?" Giselle asked, her head quirked to the side. "The plans are solid."

"I know, I just, I don't know—" Kiki stood and began pacing. "I just can't shake the feeling that we're missing something. Like we're going to go through all this effort, and then what? Rescue our people and hope that Arlando doesn't try again? Kill him and hope that ends the curse? I mean, we don't have any guarantee that will work!"

"So do something about it," Giselle said silkily.

"Like what?" Kiki scowled.

"You already know what you want to do, volcánita. You're just waiting for permission. But I say, fuck permission. Do what you want, and damn the consequences."

Kiki couldn't help but grin. Giselle was going to be a dangerous friend to have if she kept talking like this.

Sitting back down, Kiki rested her elbows on her knees. "I have an idea, but so far, everyone has shut it down."

Giselle leaned forward, intrigued. "Go on," she hummed.

"What do you know about the Spirit Woman?"

Giselle's lips curled into a feral smile. "How much do you want to know?"

S he stared at the map unfurled on the table. "It took us five days to get to Arlando's territory on horseback, and we didn't even go all the way." She moved her finger across a river and a line of mountains, tracing the path to the Spirit Woman.

"We'd have to cross the river here," Giselle pointed out with her finger, her nails painted green. "Then come back down south to take this pass through the mountains. My estate is right here, at the bottom of this mountain." She pointed to a spot at the opening of the pass, west of the mountain range. "It's about a two-day trip from here to my home, less if the weather is nice."

"So it'll take us another day and a half to get to the Spirit Woman?" Kiki asked.

Giselle nodded. "We can rest at my estate for the night before going further down to see her."

Sitting back in the lush chair, Kiki frowned. "Have you met her?"

"No. Not personally. I've heard of her, obviously, and some of my people have sought out her help, but if I'm being completely honest, I think she's a load of superstitious nonsense, too."

Kiki shook her head in disbelief. "With everything you've lived through, I'd think you would be more ready to believe in this stuff."

"I believe in what I can see," Giselle clarified. "I don't think there is such a thing as prophecies. We create our own destiny."

Kiki retraced their proposed path again with her eyes before asking, "I'm guessing you don't believe in the whole mates' thing then?"

Giselle's lips curled into a smirk. "Mmmm, yeah, that's a no from me. It's a spell, like any other spell. I'm sure it feels real enough for you and don't get me wrong, I would be the first person to jump at the opportunity to have a little magical help in the matchmaking department. And, even though I much prefer you to that spoilsport, Erasmo, at the end of the day, it was a spell that bound you two together."

Kiki crossed her arms over her chest. "Why are you helping me if you don't believe in any of this?"

Giselle shrugged. "Because I feel like it. And maybe because I'm not-so-secretly hoping that you'll take me up on my offer to give you the ride of your life," she added with a seductive wink, making Kiki blush.

"Giselle..." Kiki warned.

The other woman playfully flipped her hair over her shoulder. "What? A girl can dream. And, if nothing else, I'm doing it because Erasmo doesn't want you to see the Spirit Woman, and I am openly protesting that whole concept. Besides, I so enjoy seeing him mad. Honestly, it's one of my favorite pastimes. He makes it far too easy."

Kiki shook her head ruefully. "He's going to hate that we're friends."

Giselle reached out and grabbed Kiki's hands, holding them to her very full chest. "I know! Isn't it divine!" she squealed, her smile bright with glee.

Together, they completed their travel plans, and when the candles had burned down low, Kiki rose to leave.

"I'm beat," she announced, rubbing her eyes with her palms. "I'm heading to bed."

"Well, if you change your mind, my bed is always an option," Giselle purred coyly as she stood up to see Kiki out.

"Night, Giselle," Kiki said, opening the door.

"Chao, muñeca, see you in the morning." She blew two air kisses before closing the door behind Kiki.

Returning to her level of the manor, Kiki shook her head. Even if she was an unapologetic flirt, Giselle was harmless, but she liked the woman and saw their friendship blossoming.

She hoped the mate bond would bring Erasmo to her tonight. All of Giselle's teasing had only served to make Kiki want Erasmo all the more.

She slipped into the room she shared with Erasmo, his belongings still leaving the room with his lingering scent. She inhaled deeply.

It had been so long since she'd seen him in her dreams last, and she wanted to taste his skin under her tongue more than she wanted to eat, which was saying something.

Peeling off her clothes, she imagined it was Erasmo's hands brushing across her skin, slowly removing the form-fitting leather. She laid her leathers across the back of a chair and climbed into the bed.

Grabbing his pillow, she clutched it to her chest and willed herself to dream about him.

"There you are," a familiar deep voice said from behind her.

A pair of thick-muscled arms wrapped around her shoulders and pulled her close.

"Erasmo," she whispered, her heart full of joy at hearing his voice again.

"Kiki," he hummed, nuzzling his nose into her hair. "Fuck, I've missed you."

"Are you okay?" She hated asking that question because it was stupid. Of course, he wasn't okay. He was being kept hostage by his own brother. But she asked it anyway because she couldn't bear to think of him suffering.

"I'm fine. Arlando hasn't been back for a while."

"And Yari?"

"I'm sorry," he murmured. "I haven't seen her again since that first day."

Kiki scowled in frustration. Knowing where Yari was only helped to assure her that her best friend was alive. But knowing that Yari was in Arlando's grasp didn't comfort her and only made her worry more. "Saints, I hope she's okay."

"Didn't you say that Yari is your best friend?" Erasmo asked, quirking his head.

"Yes," she snapped. "What's that supposed to mean?"

Erasmo's lips thinned. "Nothing other than the fact that if she's your best friend, then she's most definitely okay. She has survived this long without you by her side. She's tougher than she looks."

Kiki shook her head. "No, she's all the good things in this world. Sweet, kind, caring, empathetic. She's soft and tender, and she's all alone—"

Erasmo rubbed her back in slow, comforting strokes. "She may very well be all of those things, my love. But she's also been through a lot since you last saw her. She most likely won't be the same person when you see her again."

Kiki shook her head more violently this time. "No. Yari will always need me."

Erasmo sighed heavily. "What is this all about? Hmm? Why are you so upset right now?"

She wanted to tell him that the lack of action had been wearing her thin and that she was taking things into her own hands. But she didn't want to admit that she had made plans to visit the Spirit Woman, especially because he had voiced his disapproval of such a plan since day one.

"I'm just tired," she said instead. It wasn't a complete lie.

Erasmo's lips curled into a mischievous grin. "Maybe I can help you relax."

His fingers rubbed her shoulders, the motion releasing the tension that lived there.

A moan slipped past her lips at his expert hands and their talent for making her melt.

"Keep that up and see what happens," Erasmo growled.

"Or what? You going to punish me?" Kiki asked, peering up at him through her lashes.

Erasmo quirked a brow. "You never know when to keep this smart mouth shut, do you?" he said, running his thumb over her lower lip.

"Nope," Kiki grinned as she gently bit down on his thumb.

"I can think of a few things you can do with this mouth," he whispered, his voice husky.

"Yeah? Why don't you show me?" she teased, feeling extra bold.

She loved the look on his face. It was a mix of surprise and pleasure. It made her feel powerful and strong.

Kiki reached up to tangle her hands in his hair as she brazenly kissed him. She swallowed his surprised whimper of pleasure and then moaned at the taste of his tongue in her mouth.

Erasmo broke off, his breathing labored. "You little brat, I've missed you so fucking much. I just want to fuck you senseless."

"Is that so?" she asked sweetly, playing the innocent as she slid her hands down his muscular chest.

"I'm going to fuck you so hard and deep that your sweet little pussy will beg me for a break."

A thrill shot through her at his words. Kiki felt herself become wet at his growled promise.

"Then what are you waiting for?" she asked, challenging him with the fire in her eyes.

Erasmo grabbed the zipper of her leathers and yanked it down, exposing her breasts and the flesh of her stomach.

Growling, he nipped at her nipples before covering her mouth with his own.

She could taste the night air on his lips and the fire in his blood.

He groaned into her mouth, the sound of appreciation only spurring her on.

"You taste like heaven," he whispered.

A whimper slipped past her lips, and Erasmo chuckled as he trailed his mouth down her jaw, along her neck, down the center of her chest to the top of her navel.

"Hurry up and fuck me already," she growled, her pussy throbbing with need. "You always make me wait," she complained, pulling the leathers down her arms so she could wriggle her hips out.

"And you're always so needy for my cock," he teased, his hands sliding down her body, helping her peel the leathers from her legs and tossing them to the side. "Fuck, you're so beautiful," he said, holding her at arm's length so he could take her in fully.

"Yes, yes," Kiki said, her tone full of impatience. "Now get on your knees and lick my pussy."

"Your wish is my command," he said with a devilish grin.

His fingers deftly slipped under her panties before he slipped them down her legs and tossed them to join her leathers.

Kiki watched as he kneeled at her feet, his shoulders flexing and his hair falling into his eyes as he parted her pussy lips with his fingers.

"I've missed how wet this pussy gets for me," Erasmo moaned.

"Stop messing around and eat me!"

"My pleasure," he said, burying his tongue between her pussy lips and lapping at her wet softness.

His tongue shot past her entrance and swirled around her clit before sliding back down to her opening.

The feel of him against her sensitive skin made her moan and shudder under his touch.

She tangled her hands in his hair as he dragged his tongue up her slit and swiped across her clit again.

"More," she groaned, her grip on his hair tightening.

He wrapped his arms around her thighs, his hands firmly on her ass, her pussy spread open for him.

He looked up at her, his eyes sparkling with mischief. "Don't come yet."

He buried his face between her thighs and fucked her with his tongue.

Kiki moaned as he lapped at her clit, his talented tongue flicking against the sensitive nub, driving her insane with need.

"Please," she moaned, feeling herself riding that wave to climax.

She rocked her hips forward to meet his mouth and pulled his face into her pussy, holding him in place.

Erasmo chuckled, the sound vibrating through her pussy as he backed off, gently licking her clit, driving her wild with need.

Deciding she'd had enough of his teasing, Kiki pushed him to his back. She climbed up his body and yanked at his belt buckle, whipping it through the loops of his pants and discarding it to the side.

"Someone is impatient," Erasmo grinned.

"When am I ever patient," Kiki snapped as she yanked his pants down his legs to free his mouth-watering cock.

He hissed as the cold air hit his skin.

She swirled her thumb around the head of his cock before she leaned down and lapped at the pre-cup from the tip. Taking him into her mouth, she swirled her tongue around the underside, teasing him. See if he liked his own medicine for once.

Erasmo moaned as he threaded his fingers through her hair and gently pulled.

"I won't last five seconds if you keep that up," he growled.

She hummed around his cock and then released him from her mouth, her hand pumping him slowly.

"Fuck, baby," Erasmo groaned.

"I love it when you melt for me," she murmured as she released him from her grip and climbed the rest of the way up his muscular body to straddle him.

"For you, always," Erasmo said, his eyes bright and full of love for her.

She lifted up and angled her pussy over his cock, teasing the tip before she slowly slid down, letting him fill her to the brim.

A soft moan escaped her lips as she let her body adjust to his size.

His cock stretched her inner walls and filled her up.

Kiki rocked her hips, her movements slow and measured. Her eyes connected with his as she slowly rode him.

His hands landed on her hips, his touch gentle, letting her set the pace.

"You feel so fucking good," he groaned.

"Mmhmm," Kiki moaned as she started to bounce up and down on his cock, sliding up in a smooth motion and then slamming back down, just enjoying the feeling of Erasmo filling her pussy. "I've missed this cock," she moaned, her voice rough with desire.

"Fuck," Erasmo cursed. "So tight and wet."

"Mmm, I'm all yours," Kiki said, leaning forward to kiss him.

His arms were wrapped around her, hands on her ass, helping her move over him.

Trying to make him lose control, she ground down on him, grinding her clit against his pelvis and speeding up her movements.

"Fuck," Erasmo gasped. "I'm so close."

"I'm going to come," Kiki whispered, her breath hitching at the impending orgasm.

Her head fell back, and her hand slipped between her legs.

She rubbed her clit for a moment before she thrust her fingers inside her wet pussy, her walls clamping down on her slim digits.

Her movements became jerky and erratic as her body tensed up, her pussy clenching on her fingers.

Her orgasm hit her hard, her pussy milking her fingers as she rode out the waves of pleasure.

Moaning, Kiki collapsed on top of Erasmo, her body ridden with after-shocks.

Erasmo rolled them over, his cock still throbbing inside her, as he leaned down to kiss her softly.

His movements were slow and deliberate as he fucked her.

Growling, she wrapped her legs around his waist, encouraging him to fuck her harder.

He thrust into her, his movements becoming erratic and uncontrolled.

"Come for me," she whispered, her voice rough with desire.

"Fuck, I'm so close," Erasmo said, his eyes on her as he fucked her.

His hands moved to her clit, rubbing the sensitive nub, and she moaned, her walls clenching on his cock even more.

A few more thrusts and Erasmo tensed up, his cock throbbing inside her as he came, filling her with his seed.

He collapsed on top of her, his head on her shoulder, and she panted under him.

"I love you," he whispered against her skin.

"I love you, too," she said, kissing his forehead.

They lay like that for a few moments, enjoying the tingling ecstasy of the post-orgasm bliss.

Kiki's breath caught when she felt the tip of Erasmo's cock slide out of her pussy.

She settled into his side as he pulled the blankets over the two of them.

"Why haven't we sealed our bond?" she asked as she snuggled into his chest, an ugly feeling crawling up from the darkest recesses of her mind, fueled with insecurity and doubt. "Is it because you secretly think the mate bond is just part of some spell and what we have isn't real?"

He shifted her off of him so he could prop himself up on his elbow to fix her with a dark look. "I just fucked you into oblivion, and that's really the first thing that comes to your mind?"

"Sol and Bernat sealed it, and so did Luna and Mauri. I just was wondering why we haven't."

"Bernat didn't know what he was doing, so it wasn't really Solana's choice. Luna made her choice so she could save your life." He reached out and tipped her chin up. "I've wanted to seal it since the moment I first saw you. But it's your choice, Kiki."

Kiki tugged her chin from his grip. "Okay, that's nice and all, but why didn't you ever bring it up?"

"Because that would have been easy."

Kiki scowled.

A chuckle rumbled in Erasmo's chest. "Remind me again what you did when you first learned about the mate bond."

Kiki huffed and turned her face away.

He nuzzled his face into her neck, his lips slanted in a smirk. "You stormed off and decapitated a training dummy, imagining it was me. Or don't you remember?"

Kiki really didn't like where this conversation was going. "I changed my mind. I don't want to talk about this anymore."

He pulled her into his arms, ignoring her half-hearted attempts to push him away. "All of this," he said, motioning to her wriggling away, "is why I didn't bring it up. Because you have a talent for either running headfirst toward your problems with your machete in hand, or you run the opposite direction like your life depends on it."

Kiki stopped fidgeting long enough to look him directly in the eyes. "So it's not because you don't want this?"

Erasmo's face softened as his gaze danced across the features of her face as if he were memorizing every detail. "I've wanted this with you my whole life, Kiki."

Relief flooded her veins at his admission. She sagged against him, melting into his touch. "Good," she murmured.

"My little demon slayer, what's got you so worked up?" he asked, caressing her head.

"Nothing," Kiki lied, knowing that she couldn't tell him she was nervous to see the Spirit Woman. "I just miss you, is all."

"I miss you too, muñeca." He kissed her forehead. "How are things coming along? Who ended up answering our message."

Kiki bit her lip as she tried to recall the territory names. "Maravilla, Las Muertas, Las Víboras and Esmeralda."

Erasmo chuckled, "So the old gang is back together."

"Mmhmm," she hummed. "Your friend Giselle is interesting, to say the least."

"Gods, not that tyrant. You know, she's the reason I stopped asking Mom and Dad for another sibling after Turi."

"You wanted more siblings?" Kiki asked, propping herself up on his chest so she could see his face.

"Just a little sister. I had this fantasy that a little sister would be sweet and cute; she'd look up to me, and I'd get the pride of looking after her."

Kiki thought she knew where this was going, especially after meeting Giselle, but she wanted to hear the story anyway. "What happened?"

"Giselle happened," he said, wincing. "She used to rig all sorts of little traps for me. I never knew if walking to my next class was safe or if I was going to get a macua hurtling toward me. She was such a little nightmare."

Kiki couldn't help but giggle at his expense. "I like her."

"Of course you do," Erasmo deadpanned. "The little pit viper, slithering her way into your heart."

That wasn't the only thing Giselle was trying to slither into. She felt her cheeks warm at the thought. Kiki couldn't deny that she found Giselle attractive, but that didn't change the fact that she was loyal to Erasmo and would never put herself in a situation that compromised their relationship. Giselle was her friend. And only her friend.

Kiki said, "She's funny, and I like her confidence, I can see us being good friends."

Erasmo palmed his face. "Please don't. I'll never have a moment's peace."

"Too late," Kiki grinned. She considered telling him about the deal she made with Giselle in order to secure the Esmeralda territory's alliance, but she thought better of it. Clearly, the idea of her and Giselle being friends was torture enough for Erasmo.

He groaned and covered his eyes with his arm. "I don't know what's worse, being locked up in Arlando's cage or knowing that I'm going to have a lifetime of Giselle haunting my home because my mate likes her."

Kiki smiled and pressed a kiss to his chest. "Only one of those situations has me in your bed every night, so think about that before you start complaining."

Erasmo's lips curled into a grin. "You should add 'naked' to that. Naked and in my bed every night has a better ring to it."

Kiki rolled her eyes and leaned down to press her lips to his. "I wish this was real. I wish you were really here."

Erasmo caressed her cheek with his fingers. "Me too."

Kiki could feel the pull of the dream ending and didn't want to see him fade away from her.

So she closed her eyes and held him tight until her arms were empty, and all she had was his fading scent on his pillow and a rebel tear streaking down her face.

Chapter Twenty-Four

Yari

She dipped her brush in more red paint and stared at the canvas. Her painting of the eagle with the snake in its talons was nearly complete, but she felt like it was missing something.

The composition was solid. Her best work yet if she were being completely honest with herself.

Art had always been a means to communicate the inner storm within. She'd often found refuge in a scrap of charcoal or even the calming practice of drawing with a stick in the dirt.

If she had to thank Arlando for anything, it was that he'd provided her with the tools she needed to bring to life what was in her mind.

But Arlando didn't deserve her gratitude, so she scrubbed that thought from her mind entirely.

She added more black to the red on her palette and twisted her lips in dissatisfaction.

She couldn't seem to make the right shade of red. Blood had a certain quality to it that she couldn't seem to replicate with her paints, no matter how hard she tried.

In frustration, she set down her pallet and brush.

So consumed in her thoughts she noticed too late that she was no longer the only person in the room.

The very hairs on the back of her neck stood on end. Her heart began beating against her ribcage. The blood rushed in her ears so loud she was sure that the person standing behind her could hear it.

Only one person in the world could yank such a visceral reaction from her. Only one man she could sense by the tainted smell in the air as he walked in.

She swallowed the lump in her throat and pressed her shoulders back. Reaching for the pallet again, she grabbed the sharp spatula she used to mix colors and set to working on the red again.

"You're back," she said, breaking the unbearable silence.

Though he still stood behind her, she could sense that he'd drawn closer, and she swore she could feel his self-satisfied smirk.

The heat of his body suffocated her as he stopped a hair's breadth away. "Did you miss me?" he purred.

His cold fingers snaked across the bare skin along the nape of her neck, and she had to resist the urge to flinch away.

She refused to let him see her cower. She'd done enough of that.

But she also had to play along. Pretend that everything between them was alright. That she was on his side.

"Of course." The words tasted like ash in her mouth, and her stomach roiled in revulsion.

"I take it you forgive me then?" There was a dark note to his voice, an underlying threat, and promise of violence if she didn't respond to his delight.

Swallowing the lump in her throat, she said, "I understand, now, what you're doing and why. I'm sorry that I didn't earlier."

Arlando continued to move his fingers across her skin, his attention rooted to the fine, downy hairs at the nape of her neck. "I had hoped you'd come to your senses. I'm so glad to see that you have."

He leaned down, pressed his lips behind her ear, and inhaled a deep breath. "You smell divine," he breathed, his voice shifting into something even darker. Lust.

Her heart raged within her chest, and she continued to focus her attention on the task of mixing the red and black paints and adding hints of blue to get it right.

But her hand stilled when he wrapped his arm around her waist and pulled her against his body.

She felt the evidence of his arousal pressed against her spine, and her stomach twisted.

"Get off me, you bastard," she growled. She almost didn't recognize the sound of her own voice. She'd never heard herself sound so strong before. It was as much a shock to her as it was to Arlando.

She wrenched herself from his grasp and knocked her painting to the floor in the process.

"Don't touch me," she hissed, taking a step back, her pallet still in one hand and the sharp paint spatula clutched in the other.

Arlando's eyes blazed with blue fire as his lips curled back in a snarl. "So you thought you could play me. Is that it?"

She narrowed her eyes, feeling justified fury warm her cheeks and flushing them with color. "I thought I could endure your presence for long enough to drive a dagger through your black heart. But it turns out I can't stand to be around you for more than a few seconds."

Arlando made a tsking sound with his teeth. "I guess I'll just have to teach you a lesson. And keep teaching it to you until it sinks into your empty head."

Yari was mentally kicking herself for showing her true feelings so soon. This wasn't the plan that she and Aurelia had concocted. It was too soon. Everything wasn't in place yet for them to safely escape the castle.

Turi and Arlando's arrival was supposed to be the genesis of their plan because, without Turi, Yari refused to leave.

Arlando's presence meant that Turi must also be back, but what if he wasn't? What if Arlando had left him and come back alone?

She couldn't dwell on those questions for too long, though, because she had a much larger and much worse problem to deal with.

She squared off with Arlando, her retreating steps angling her toward the door.

She knew she didn't stand a chance if she ran. Arlando would catch her in a heartbeat.

She would only have one shot at this, and then he'd know the truth.

She adjusted the spatula in her hand, letting the sharp edge press into her palm until it hurt.

Arlando quirked his head. "What are you doing?" He advanced, his strides long and filled with terrible purpose.

She wrenched the spatula across her palm, and blood spilled onto the rich white carpet.

Turning to the door, she raised her bloody palm to the demon that stood sentinel and yelled, "Protect me!"

The demon quirked its head, its neck snapping with a grotesque pop before it quickly spun and launched itself onto Arlando.

The two collided with a thunderous crash as if they were two mountains at war.

Arlando let out a roar of fury as the demon's claws raked down his skin, drawing blood.

"How dare you?!" Arlando growled, his face contorted with rage. "I order you to stand down!"

The demon ignored him and swiped at Arlando with its razor-sharp talons.

Arlando took the blow to his face, crimson blood streaming down his white suit. "What did you do?" he asked, his eyes pinning Yari to the spot. "Answer me!"

Realizing that she was frozen to the spot, Yari forced herself to step back. The demon angled itself and took a defensive position in front of her.

"How are you doing this?" Arlando seethed as talons extended from his hands, and his body surged as he began to shift.

She shook her head and whispered, "I don't owe you an explanation."

As much as she wanted to stay and see if the demon could defeat Arlando, she knew deep down that it wouldn't prevail and that she had to get out. Now!

Spinning on her heel, she raced out of the sitting room and bolted through the halls in search of Aurelia. They had to get out of the castle before Arlando could stop them.

She could hear the sounds of the fight behind her, the demon's snarls and Arlando's curses echoing through the castle.

"Aurelia!" she yelled with all her strength. "Turi!"

She called for them as she ran through the castle, heading for the front door.

This wasn't the plan. They were all supposed to get out together.

She ran past a pair of demons in the hall and held her still-bleeding palm to them. "Protect me!"

They both considered her for a moment before they turned and began lurching toward the sitting room.

Yari bent over her knees and inhaled a deep breath. She wasn't in the same kind of shape she had once been, and she was now paying for it. The sides of her ribs ached, and her back was spasming from the sudden exertion. But she knew she couldn't stop.

Using the wall for support, she stood back up and began to run.

The sounds of fighting drew nearer, and her heart felt like it was lodged in the back of her throat.

"Yarixa!" Arlando's voice boomed through the castle.

Damn it. Damn it. Damn it.

She threw herself around a bend in the hallway and skidded to a stop when she saw the hulking figure hunched in the middle of the hall, right in front of the entrance.

Arlando had shifted partially, his body remaining human, but his head had become that of a grotesque bear, and his chest was covered in white fur. "Did you really think you could outrun me, little mouse?"

She turned to go back the way she'd come, but Arlando was too fast.

He launched into the air and drove her into the marble floor.

She grunted at the impact. "NO!"

Arlando wound his hand into her hair. "Now, I'll teach you that lesson."

He dragged her up the grand stairs of the castle, unbothered by her nails clawing into his hands as he held her by the hair, nor did he seem to care that she screamed with all her might and cursed him to hell and back.

When he reached his suite, he kicked open the door, the wood splintering, and threw her inside.

She fell sprawled across the floor, her body bruised and sore.

Her eyes darted to the bed, and revulsion churned in her stomach. Fear spiked in her chest, and her throat tightened, preventing the scream of terror that desperately begged for release.

No. Not this again.

"You're a stupid girl," Arlando growled while his fingers deftly unbuttoned his bloody jacket.

Yes. I am stupid. Stupid for trusting you.

Fight him. A voice from deep inside her said. **Fight him.**

Yes. That's what Kiki would do.

If Kiki were in this position, she'd fight until she had nothing left. Until she had no breath in her body, and even then, she'd come back to haunt him.

Remembering her oath to herself, she called forth all the anger and hatred she could hold. It spun wildly in her stomach, spreading to her chest, filling her with courage that wasn't natural to her.

"Do what you want with me," she spat. "But I promise you this: I *will* kill you. Even if it's the last thing I do."

Arlando's sharp laughter echoed off the walls, and he took a menacing step forward. "I see my little mouse has grown a backbone."

His tongue excitedly ran along his lengthening canines as his power surged through the room.

He pounced on her in a single, swift movement, driving her to the ground with a loud thud. His fingers dug painfully into her wrists, tugging them up behind her head until she was completely immobilized beneath him.

He leaned in close to her ear and spoke softly but forcefully. "I can't wait to break it."

"Get your hands off my mate," a deep voice rumbled.

Arlando paused, and Yari saw Turi standing in the doorway, his eyes red with fury.

Turi launched himself at Arlando with a roar. Their bodies clashed like titans on a field of battle, the echo of bones cracking and skin tearing as talons burst from Turi's hands, the skin and sinews making an awful wet sound.

His body burst into jet-black fur that bore streaks of silver scattered throughout. His nose lengthened into a muzzle, and his teeth transformed into hand-length canines.

Hunched on all fours, he stood with her safely at his back, his focus completely on Arlando.

"So you figured it out, little brother. What gave it away?" Arlando's voice was taunting, and his half-shifted bear form grinned with malice. "You can't defeat me, Arturito. And since I don't need you for the ritual, I'll just have to kill you for your defiance."

Arlando's neck cracked at a grotesque angle as his body inflated, and he suddenly burst into black smoke. As the smoke cleared, revealing the terrifying demon bear haunting her nightmares for the last two years, Yari screamed.

Turi let out a primal roar and charged Arlando. The very ground shook beneath Yari, and she feared the entire room would come crashing down on them.

A surge of pride filled her chest at seeing Turi fighting Arlando. His bear form was considerably larger than Arlando's, which she didn't think was possible, considering the all-white behemoth was terrifyingly massive.

She understood why he hadn't transformed completely at the cabin. He would have ripped it to shreds with his size alone.

Which is why her heart soared at seeing Turi's bear towering over Arlando.

A flicker of hope sparked in her chest. This could all be over with one good swipe of Turi's talons or a good bite to the neck with his fangs.

Aurelia skidded into the room and screeched to a halt, her jaw dropping open as she took in the spectacle of Turi battling Arlando.

"I'm not even going to ask," Aurelia said, rushing over to help Yari to her feet.

A pained roar filled her ears, and she turned to see that Arlando had delivered a brutal blow to the side of Turi's face. A set of talons slashed across his right eye and down his muzzle, red blood streaming from the wound and pooling onto the floor.

The sliver of hope that had blossomed in her chest quickly puttered out.

Though Arlando was smaller than Turi, he had the advantage of speed and experience. While each blow he landed was devastating, Turi was not as agile.

"We've got to go." Aurelia bodily hauled Yari out of the room just as the two bears crashed right through the spot they'd just been occupying.

The walls shuddered, and cracks burst along the ceiling like a spider-web.

"Thanks for that," Yari huffed, nearly breathless from her race through the castle and the wind being knocked out of her when Arlando tackled her to the ground. "Is everything ready?" she asked, running alongside Aurelia as they dashed down the stairs and made their way to the dungeon.

"Not even close, but it'll have to do. Are you ready?" Aurelia asked, casting Yari a skeptical look.

Yari's chest filled with the warmth of determined anger. "Yes. I can do this."

"Good, because now's your chance."

They flung themselves around the corner of the hall and came face to face with the demons left to guard the entrance to the dungeon.

Upon seeing them, the demons began scuttling forward, their fangs bared, their talons clicking against the marble floors.

Yari shoved her hands in the pockets of her dress only to realize that her little spatula wasn't there. She must have dropped it when Arlando tackled her.

Aurelia took a hesitant step back. "Any day now, cupcake," she said, her voice turning singsong in her nervousness.

"I lost my blade," Yari said, patting her body wildly as if the little spatula would suddenly reappear. Her eyes frantically searched their surroundings but found nothing she could use.

"You what?" Aurelia whipped around, her eyes wide in horror.

Yari stopped patting herself and glared at the wound that had stopped bleeding in her hand. "I'm not going to die here," she said aloud, more to herself than to Aurelia.

She steeled her spine and lifted her palm to her mouth. She clamped down on her skin hard. The coppery tang of blood immediately assaulted her tongue.

Holding her hand out, blood leaking from her lips, she turned her focus on the demons hurtling toward them. "STOP!"

The demon's eyes widened, and they slowed to a crawl before they halted completely. The five demons looked at one another as if confused before focusing back on Yari.

Yari took a tentative step forward, and when the demons didn't move to attack, she turned to Aurelia. "It worked!"

"Good, because I really don't think I taste all that great."

Yari knew Aurelia tended to joke when she was afraid, much like Kiki did. But she couldn't muster the energy it would take to even pretend she thought the joke was funny. She pointed in the direction of where they'd been hiding their supplies. "Now go, set of the charges. However many you can and then get back here."

Aurelia nodded and raced back the way she'd come to set off the second part of their plan—to draw the demons away from them and keep them distracted or contained long enough to escape.

Yari turned to the demons, confident in her absolute control over them. "Open the door and take me to the prisoners."

The demons complied, their movements slow as if they were moving through honey.

"I don't have all day! Move!" Yari shouted, holding her hand up.

The demon closest to her turned its head and snapped at the air.

Yari's heart leaped in her chest. Maybe her control over them wasn't as absolute as she thought.

A wild idea popped into her head, and without thinking too much about it, she smeared her other hand into the blood seeping from her wound.

Taking her bloody handprint, she smeared it across the demon's face. "You will obey my every command and do so quickly."

That seemed to do the trick because the demon began walking faster, its long strides taking it to the door of the dungeon.

Turning to the other four demons, she repeated the same process.

Her hand ached from reopening her wound over and over again. With a whimper, she cradled it to her chest as she waited impatiently for the demons to comply.

She could feel the effects of her blood loss, her steps unbalanced, and her head feeling light, but she pushed on. This was her part of the plan, and she could not fail.

With the door open, she carefully made her way down the stairs of the dungeon and grimaced at the acrid smell that greeted her.

At the sound of her entry, the three men were already up and waiting for her. They clearly hadn't expected it to be her, though, because Bernat was the first to speak when she emerged from the shadows.

"Yari?" His voice was full of shock, and his brows were raised to his hairline. "What are you doing here? What's happened? Whose blood is that?" He berated her with questions before she could even get a word out.

Her heart swelled at his obvious concern for her welfare, and she had to choke back a sob of relief at seeing him again.

"There is no time to explain," she said in a rush. Turning to the demons, she held out her bloodied hand again. "Open the cages."

The demons didn't move. They didn't attack but didn't move to obey her order either.

Frustration bubbled in her chest. How much blood was she going to have to spill in order to get them to obey?

She grabbed the nearest sharp object from Arlando's table of horrors and angled it over her wrist.

"Yari, what are you doing?" Bernat shouted in alarm. "Stop!"

But she had to see this to the end. Because she refused to live in this twisted castle for a minute longer.

The men in these cages were the mates of her best friends. Kiki and Yari loved them. Solana too.

If she died setting them free, then that was just the price she'd pay. Though deep down, she really hoped not.

But desperation could make even the best of people resort to terrible means.

Yari drove the dagger into her wrist, pushing past the bone and through the other side. An agonized scream ripped through her throat, echoing off the stone walls.

At the scent of so much blood, the demons directed their attention to her.

"OBEY ME!" she ground out through the pain. "OPEN THE DAMN CAGES!"

The five demons stepped forward and placed their clawed hands on the bars of each cage, forming a chain between each other.

The cages immediately began to hum and crackle with black lightning.

"They're absorbing Arlando's spell," Bernat announced, his eyes wide with awe. "Stand back," he said to the two men in the cages next to him.

"Raz, the blood," one of the men choked. His hair was all black, and he had a feral red gleam to his eyes as he hobbled away to the farthest corner of his cage.

The other man she didn't recognize cast a worried glance at the other, then turned to Bernat. "The second these cages open, you and I have to rush him. He's been without blood for too long. The hunger is taking over."

"You handle him. She's my priority," Bernat snapped, his bright eyes igniting with blue flame.

The man they called Raz growled but didn't argue.

Yari didn't understand what half of what either man said, but she didn't really care anymore. All she felt was a glimmer of relief at knowing that the demons had finally listened to her and seemed completely compliant. That she'd succeeded in her task. The one thing she'd been trusted to do, and she'd done it.

No screw-ups. No Kiki to race to her rescue and make things right.

She'd done it by herself. And for that, a feeling she'd never felt before settled over her shoulders.

It felt a lot like pride.

She slumped against the table, her head feeling too light, and she sagged to the ground.

"Hold on, Yari!" Bernat bellowed.

Her eyelids fluttered as she drew in a ragged breath.

The air seemed to grow thick with power as the bars of the cages vibrated. With a final shudder and a burst of black smoke, the demons erupted, their black ichor splattering throughout the room, and the bars of the cages blasted open.

Bernat ran for Yari first, sliding to her side. He gathered her limp body in his arms. "I've got you, little one."

The corners of her lips lifted in a smile as she gazed upon her Second in Command. A man she'd always trusted to look after her along with the rest of her squad.

"You have to go," Yari whispered, her voice suddenly weak.

"We're not leaving you here," Bernat said, gently pushing her hair out of her face. "You're the reason we came into the Cicatrix in the first place."

"I am?"

"Of course you are. Kiki refused to let you go. Besides, she'd never forgive you if you don't hang on. She'll drag you from the depths of the underworld just so she could yell at you for it."

Yari could almost see the scene that Bernat painted, and it made her smile widen. "She would do something like that."

Bernat ripped the bottom of his shirt and made it into a strip. "I need to take this out," he motioned to the dagger still embedded in her wrist. "And stop this bleeding, okay?"

She nodded. She didn't think it would make much of a difference, but she didn't want to be the one to crush Bernat's hope.

Bernat swiftly removed the dagger, and a spurt of blood splashed across his face.

"Just one sip!" a wild voice roared.

The other two men were free from their cages, and the one with the wild eyes was being held back by Raz.

"Get a hold of yourself, you fucking bastard," Raz growled as he tackled the man to the ground.

"Just a taste, I promise, I'll stop. Just a little!" The man whined.

"That is Luna's best friend, you idiot!" Raz struggled to keep the other man down. "Mauri, listen to me, think about Luna. Luna. Your mate. What would she think if she knew you fucking ate her best friend?!"

That seemed to make the man called Mauri stop struggling altogether.

"Good," Raz said, patting the man's back as if he were comforting a child. "That's it, push the beast away. There you go, breathe."

As Raz coached Mauri into a calmer state, Bernat packed Yari's wound and then wrapped it tightly with another strip of cloth from his shirt.

"There, this will have to do for now." Bernat cradled her in his arms and lifted her from the ground. "Is he good?"

Mauri grunted. "Get your fat ass off me, Erasmo, before I claw your face off."

Raz, or rather Erasmo, as Yari realized the first was merely a nickname, rolled his eyes. "Yep, he's good."

Erasmo released Mauri and helped him up.

"Come on, let's get out of here," Bernat said, jerking his chin to the stairs that would lead them out of the dungeon.

No. Aurelia hadn't shown up yet. Where was she?

Suddenly, the dungeon shuddered, and loose stones fell from the ceiling.

"Aurelia," Yari breathed, a smile tugging at her lips. She'd done it. She'd set off a series of charges that would serve as a distraction. They hadn't managed to make enough charges, but what they had would be enough to drive the demons away and keep them trapped, unable to come after them all.

"What about that conniving little snake?" Erasmo asked, looking down at her.

"Friend. Help," Yari managed to say. Each word came with great labor, as did each breath.

"You're saying Aurelia helped you break us out?" Erasmo asked, his brows furrowing.

She nodded slightly.

"Fuck me," Erasmo growled, running a hand through his black hair that bore a single silver streak near the front. "Bernat, you and Mauri get her out of here. I'll go look for our slimy cousin."

Relief flooded her, but she quickly added, "Turi," before he could run off.

"Turi?" Erasmo sneered. "That fucking rat betrayed us. What about him?"

"Friend," Yari whispered.

"No," he shook his head, his lips pressed in a thin line. "You've lost a lot of blood. He stood by and watched as Arlando tortured you. He's not your friend."

Desperation flooded her eyes. She darted out her hand and gripped the collar of Erasmo's shirt in her fist. "Friend."

"FUUUUCKKK!!" Erasmo growled. "Fine. I'll get him, too."

Erasmo ran ahead of them, and by the time Bernat carried her out of the dungeon, the grumpy man was nowhere to be seen.

Yari just hoped that he would find Aurelia and Turi quickly because she didn't think she'd last long enough to see whether they made it out.

"You're going to be alright," Bernat consoled. "Just hang on for a little while longer."

Yari didn't know if she nodded her head in agreement or if she was imagining things. Her eyes fluttered closed, and an overwhelming sense of peace washed over her.

This wasn't so bad, either.

CHAPTER TWENTY-FIVE

LUNA

"I don't like this," Luna said, leaning back in her seat and crossing her arms over her chest.

Across the table from her, Kiki's fists clenched as she pouted. "Why not?"

Luna shared a glance with Guille, seated at her left. The man had been her constant companion since returning from their foray into the north, and she was grateful for his presence. He was a gentle spirit who shared her passion for healing and magic.

She had never known the joy of having a sibling, let alone a brother, but she imagined that if she did, her relationship with Guille was close enough.

His brown eyes were wary as he subtly shook his head. He was a little afraid of Kiki.

To be fair, who wasn't?

He rarely voiced his protests against Kiki in public, as was the case in this moment. Luna didn't mind being his conduit, especially when they were of the same mind.

"Besides the obvious?" Luna snorted. Kiki was still looking at her with a bewildered expression, and she rolled her eyes. "Wipe that innocent look off your face, Kiki, it doesn't suit you."

Kiki's eyes narrowed as she glowered.

Luna pointed an accusatory finger at the map. "If we ignore the dangers of the journey, there is still the fact that this so-called Spirit Woman demands payment for her assistance. And from what we have learned from others, her supposed help isn't always very helpful. So, please, tell me why you are so focused on going?"

Kiki turned to Solana, effectively dodging Luna's question. "You've been awfully quiet, Commander. Care to share your thoughts?"

Solana blinked slowly at Kiki before releasing a heavy sigh. "Despite the clear risks, I do agree with you, Xochicale. There is a lot we do not know about the nature of the curse. It would benefit us greatly to have a clear answer about how to end it that doesn't involve our own deaths."

Kiki pounded her fist against the table with a whoop of joy.

"But," Solana interjected. "You will take Healer Luna with you on your journey."

Luna and Kiki whipped their heads to face Solana at the same time. "What?!" they shouted in unison.

Solana shifted in her seat and pressed a hand to her lower back as if it pained her. "Luna is skeptical of this Spirit Woman. She will provide balance to any discussions you may enter."

Luna didn't appreciate being ordered around to babysit Kiki when she had plenty of work to do on her own. She stood up and pressed her palms onto the table. "I'm still working with Guille to translate Juan Martín's book. I can't just leave."

"Guille will join you," Solana said with a jerk of her head.

"I will?" Guille piped up.

"Yes," Solana said. "You and Yasir helped us when we were attacked by the demons not long ago. I would send Yasir too if I didn't need him to continue his work with our fighting forces."

Luna lowered herself back into her chair. "Do I get a say in this?"

Solana cut her ice-blue gaze to Luna. "Of course, but I'd ask you to consider the possibilities if you're not there when Kiki engages with this woman."

Luna winced at the thought of sending Kiki in to negotiate anything, let alone something this important. Meanwhile, across the table, Kiki protested, saying, "I don't need a babysitter."

Solana shared a knowing look with Luna that almost made her burst out into laughter.

"I wouldn't call it that exactly," Solana admitted, her lips tugging at the corners ever so subtly.

Now it was Kiki's turn to cross her arms over her chest as she sat back down with a petulant huff. "Fine. I'd like the company anyway."

"What does that make me, I wonder? Offal?" Giselle purred at Kiki's elbow.

The leader of Esmeralda had offered to escort Kiki and offered her own estate as a waypoint while they journeyed to meet the Spirit Woman.

It was clear Giselle was smitten—no—obsessed was a better word to describe the way Giselle looked at Kiki. Luna might have been worried that Giselle was hiding behind an agenda if she didn't genuinely think that Giselle had simply taken one look at Kiki and fallen for her friend right then and there.

"Stop pouting. You know I didn't mean it that way," Kiki mumbled, still throwing a fit worthy of a toddler.

"It's settled then. Pack up and head out today. The sooner we get answers, the better." Solana dismissed the room, and everyone slowly filed out.

Solana rose from her chair and groaned, placing a hand on her lower back again.

"You alright?" Luna asked, moving around the circular outline of the tables.

Solana nodded. "It's nothing. Just a little ache. Probably from sitting around all day and not out training enough."

"Perhaps," Luna said, sending a tendril of her power to scan the Commander. "I'd feel better if you let me examine you before I go."

Solana seemed primed to object but finally relented. "Very well."

Luna directed Solana to sit on the table and face her as if she were performing an examination back in the Healer Corps.

A part of her missed the days when life was a lot simpler. When her focus was on healing people and nothing more. When there weren't dark forces threatening to consume them all. When their lives weren't in constant peril.

Nothing about the Demon Corps was safe, but at least it had been predictable.

She placed her hands on Solana's shoulders and sent a thread of magic into the Commander's body, letting the tendrils of her power slowly work from her head and down through her chest. Solana's heart rate was higher than usual, but Luna dismissed that as a symptom of increased stress. She moved her magic down through Solana's spine, paying careful attention to the muscles that wrapped around her lower back, noticing that they were under more strain than usual. Then she curled her magic around the Commander's abdomen—

Luna paused when she felt a distinct shift in energy and a flutter.

No. It couldn't be. How was that—

The energy in Solana's abdomen shifted again, and the distinct beat of a heart echoed in Luna's mind.

She flicked her gaze to Solana, who was staring out the window as Luna performed her exam.

Another beat joined the first and then a third.

Luna pulled her hands back and said, "Well, the good news is that you're in perfect health."

"And the bad?"

Luna chewed her bottom lip. "I mean, it's not bad necessarily. Maybe not ideal timing—"

Solana's lips tugged into a tight line. "Out with it."

"You're pregnant."

Solana's face didn't shift to show Luna that she'd heard. She just kept staring at Luna as if she were frozen in time.

"Commander? Did you hear me? I said you're— "

"Pregnant," Solana whispered, a note of awe in her voice. She moved her hands to her lower abdomen and gently cradled it.

Luna considered how to tell Solana that wasn't all.

"Tell me," Solana commanded. "There's something else, isn't there?"

Luna nodded, feeling unequipped to deliver such news. "I don't know how else to say it, so I'll just come out with it. You're pregnant with triplets."

Luna expected the woman to start freaking out now. Because if Luna were in her shoes, that's exactly what she'd be doing.

Instead, the Commander's face softened as she looked down at her belly. "Triplets?" Her lips curled into a full smile.

Luna had rarely seen Solana smile, but this was something new altogether. It was akin to wonder.

By Luna's estimation, the children were at about twelve weeks of gestation. This would explain the aching in Solana's back as her body changed to accommodate the growing life within her womb.

"Are they healthy?" Solana asked.

Luna chewed the inside of her cheek before she answered. In general, the developing babies seemed healthy. The heartbeats were strong if not a little fast. But that wasn't what made Luna pale. "I think you're pregnant with bears."

Solana's eyes widened. "Excuse me?"

"I may be able to offer an explanation," said a shy voice.

Solana and Luna turned at the same time to see Guille standing at the entryway leading into the dining hall.

Guille cleared his throat and rubbed the back of his neck as he came further into the dining hall. "Pregnancies with men who are cursed in our family are slightly different than regular human pregnancies."

"How different?" Luna asked, her brows furrowing.

He tried to smile, but the act looked forced, and he shifted from foot to foot in nervousness. "Well, as you've already noticed, gestation is unique. Like bears, there is a high chance of multiple births, similar to that of bears and their litters, which explains your current situation." He fiddled with the ring he wore on his hand and focused his attention on it as he added,

"The children are more likely to be all males so that the curse passes on to them. And since they are most likely male, then they fall under the curse the same as any of the others."

Silence filled the air as he let Solana and Luna let the news sink in.

After a few moments, Guille cleared his throat. "The children will be born human and won't undergo the true shift until they reach puberty, but while in the womb, they'll shift their forms often."

Solana took all of this information with her usual stoicism. She simply nodded and scooted off the edge of the table. "Aside from those differences, will the children be healthy?" she asked, turning her stoney face to Guille.

His hands fluttered at his sides. "Oh yes, very healthy. The healthiest, even."

She seemed to file that bit of information away and inclined her head at them both. "Well then, that's all I need to know." She made her way out of the dining hall, her steps sure and confident. "Safe travels to you both," she called back to them.

Luna stared after the Commander with bulging eyes. She felt like her entire world had been turned upside down. In fact, she needed to take a seat. The world was starting to tilt.

"Did that really just happen?" she mumbled, more to herself than to Guille, who stayed with her. "How could she take that so calmly?"

Guille shrugged. "Maybe she's happy that she's pregnant. Though I wouldn't really know, I think I've seen her smile only one time."

That made Luna snort. "You're not the only one." She ran a hand over her face.

She supposed that it didn't matter how she felt about Solana's pregnancy. It wasn't her body, so any opinions she had on the matter were irrelevant.

Still, she couldn't imagine being a mother yet. She felt too young to take on so much responsibility. She realized that she and Mauri had never discussed the topic of kids.

She felt the color drain from her face. What if he wanted a litter like his own family? She thought she was going to be sick.

"You alright? You look like you're going to throw up."

Luna swallowed the bile rising in her throat. "I was just thinking about how I don't know if Mauri wants a big family."

Guille patted her on the shoulder. "Mauri wants whatever you want, Luna. I've seen him with you. He's different with you and you alone. You've filled a part of him that he's been missing for years. You don't need to worry."

Luna gave Guille a grateful smile. It soothed her heart hearing Mauri's cousin talk about her in such a way. She knew no one else understood the mate bond or why it clicked between two people and not others.

She was fully aware that the two of them seemed like polar opposites on the outside. But when she was with him, everything felt right.

She felt safe and at ease. She'd felt that way since the first day she'd met him.

That feeling of home wasn't something that could so easily be tossed to the side. She cherished it, and it was the whole reason she was so determined to find a way to break his curse.

Getting to her feet and smoothing her blue dress, she said, "Let's get packed up before Kiki takes off without us."

Chapter Twenty-Six

Erasmo

Erasmo knew they had to act fast. Aurelia and Turi were somewhere in the castle, and he had no idea where to look first.

An earth-shattering roar echoed through the castle, causing even the strongest pillars and walls to tremble. Erasmo sprang into action, his feet pounding on the marble floor as he sprinted towards the West Wing; his heart pounded in tandem with every frenzied step.

Mauri raced alongside him as they charged through the damp corridors of the castle. Their footsteps echoed off the walls as they pushed their bodies to run faster.

Erasmo risked a glance over his shoulder, keeping an eye out for any lurking demons.

He came to a sudden halt when he smelled the familiar, overwhelming scent of demons nearby. Peeking around the corner, he spotted a group of them congregating in the hallway ahead. They were snarling and snapping at each other with razor-like teeth, their eyes glowing with a fiery intensity that could only mean one thing—they were hungry for blood.

Erasmo cursed under his breath and signaled to Mauri to hold back. They needed a plan of attack.

"We can't catch their attention," he whispered.

Mauri nodded in agreement, and together, they slipped down another corridor to skirt around the horde.

Slithering shadows and wispy whispers surrounded them as they tip-toed past doorways guarded by menacing demons. They hugged the walls as they crept forward, cautious with their footfalls and the rustling of their clothes.

Mauri accidentally dropped the ball of cum-filled hay, and the scent of soured milk wafted into the air.

"Saints, that thing stinks so bad," Erasmo grunted, his back pressed against a wall as they waited for a pair of demons to lumber past.

Mauri gave him a self-satisfied smile as he scooped the ball up from the floor. "I know," he said, his tone full of pride. "I'm going to leave it on Arlando's pillow."

Erasmo shook his head. "Remind me again how we're related."

Mauri sneered. "You're just jealous that you didn't think of this first."

"I promise you, that is not what I'm thinking at all," Erasmo said, resisting the urge to plug his nose.

Mauri shrugged, and they continued silently creeping through the castle, slinking past statues and demons running around in a frenzy.

"What is that smell?" Mauri asked as they rounded a corner, the loudest fighting sounds here.

Erasmo looked at the ball of cum and hay in Mauri's hands and raised his brows, "Really? You're just now noticing it?"

Mauri tilted his nose skyward and inhaled deeply. "Smells like smoke."

He mirrored his cousin's actions and picked up the scent of smoke as well.

"Aurelia," they said in unison.

She was the only one in the family with a penchant for fire, and if she was truly in league with Yari, then whatever plan she'd hatched had something to do with the burning scent wafting through the halls.

"Split up or stay together?" Erasmo asked, knowing full well that if they stuck together, they might not get Aurelia and Turi out in time. Splitting up was the wiser choice, but he wouldn't make the call without Mauri's insight.

Mauri chewed at the inside of his cheek momentarily before saying, "Fuck, split up. I'll go after Turi and drop off my gift along the way. Leaving you to get Aurelia."

"Agreed." They clasped hands before running in opposite directions.

The smoke grew thicker as Erasmo neared what must be the original blast zone. The sounds of fighting also grew louder, and he could hear the snarls of demons and the metallic clang of a sword.

The smoke was thick and acrid, obscuring his view. But then he spotted a short woman surrounded by demons with horns, wings, and claws. He watched in awe as she swung her sword in one hand and held a shield with the other, parrying their attacks.

Without a second thought, Erasmo charged forward, his claws extended and glinting in the dim light.

He charged into the snarling crowd of demons, his talons ripping through demon flesh and his kicks sending them flying across the room.

Aurelia's face lit up at the sight of Erasmo, relief clear in the way her body sagged as if she'd been fighting the demons off for quite some time.

"Erasmo," she gasped as she bent over and braced her hands on her knees. "Where's Yari?"

"There's no time to talk. But Yari is safe," he said, grabbing Aurelia's arm. "She sent me to get you. I've done that, and now we must get out of here."

She gave a quick nod, and Erasmo stepped in front of her, blocking the demons' advances with powerful swings of his fists. They moved like a storm through the creatures, Erasmo using brute force while she trailed close behind, dodging weapons and ducking out of the way of slashing claws. Finally, they reached the courtyard—a scene of utter chaos with burning demons screaming and writhing in pain as their skin melted off their bodies until only heaps of steaming flesh remained.

"Where is your mother and Sergio?" Erasmo asked, searching frantically through the chaos.

Aurelia shifted her weight and glanced down at her sword. Erasmo saw the metal blade smeared with a sticky mix of black demon ichor and dried crimson blood.

"Is that human blood?" he asked, pointing at the scarlet smears across the sword's edge.

Aurelia looked up at him, her eyes glassy, like those of a scared animal. Her voice shook as she whispered, "He turned them. They—Their eyes were black, and they had all these sharp teeth. They weren't—they came at me—"

Erasmo grabbed his cousin by her shoulders and shook her gently. "Get ahold of yourself and tell me what happened."

Tears rimmed her eyes. "Arlando turned them both. They were half demon and half human."

"Who?" he asked, his ire rising.

"Mamá and Sergio. They weren't human anymore," she sobbed.

Understanding washed over him. "Arlando experimented on them."

She nodded sadly. "Mamá—she didn't recognize me. She came at me, and I had no choice." She glanced down at the red blood dripping from her sword and winced.

Erasmo realized then that Aurelia had been forced to defend herself against her own mother and their old caretaker, Sergio.

No one deserved to be experimented on, least of all by Arlando. But a deep pain yawned open in his chest at the thought of his poor aunt and her broken mind having to endure more trauma and his old mentor suffering.

With more gentleness in his voice, he lowered himself so he could be at eye level with Aurelia. "Your mother and Sergio weren't themselves anymore. If there was any part of themselves buried beneath their new forms, then you paid them a kindness. They wouldn't have wanted to live that way."

She nodded slowly, but Erasmo knew she'd be reliving those moments for a long time, if not for the rest of her life.

He couldn't imagine the pain of killing her own mother, turned half demon or not.

"We have to go now," he said, pulling her forward and skirting around the wailing demons.

"Yari? Is she okay?" she asked, her voice hollow.

"She's with Bernat; he should be miles from here by now."

As they walked away from the castle, he looked back for Mauri. *Come on, get out of there.*

Suddenly, a bear with silver and black fur barreled through the entrance. Following closely behind him was a flock of demons snapping their teeth in pursuit.

"Oh fuck." Erasmo grabbed Aurelia's arm and yanked her forward. "Time to run."

Together, they raced across the courtyard, ducking under fallen stone arches and leaping over crumbled pieces of fallen wall. Mauri matched their pace in less than two long bounding strides.

"Where's Turi?" he yelled, his legs pushing harder than he'd ever run before.

Mauri growled at Erasmo and skidded to a stop. *He stayed behind to hold off Arlando. Stupid fuck.*

Erasmo paled at the thought but didn't have time to consider the implications. He grabbed Aurelia by her waist and tossed her onto Mauri's back. She buried her hands into his fur and pressed herself against his nape.

"Don't let go," Erasmo warned her and pushed at Mauri's flank, sending them racing ahead.

With Aurelia and Mauri rushing ahead, Erasmo began to let the shift take over him.

A roar from behind made him turn on his heel as a pair of bears—one all black and the other completely white—crashed into the courtyard, their jaws snapping and paws swiping.

Seeing him, Turi roared, baring long white fangs. *Get Yari out of here! Keep her safe.*

Turi's voice rang so clearly and so full of desperation in Erasmo's mind that he didn't think twice. He shifted and bounded over the stone wall to join Mauri and Bernat.

Chapter Twenty-Seven

Kiki

The sun reached its peak in the midday sky, sending rays of warmth splashing across Kiki's skin. Ordinarily, she'd relish the feeling of such a treat, but she was in a foul mood.

Kiki directed her horse to avoid a boulder in their path, drawing her closer to Luna.

After several moments of silence, Luna heaved a long-suffering sigh. "What's the matter?" she droned.

"Nothing," Kiki quipped. Only she hadn't seen Erasmo in her dreams since the night before they left, and she was both worried about him and sexually frustrated.

The man was like a living and breathing treat to her. She needed him like she needed air, and she wasn't too proud to admit it—well, to herself, anyway. She'd never say as much to his face. He had a big enough ego as it was.

Luna sighed heavily. "You've been quiet this whole trip, and you act like you're upset about something. It can't possibly be because you didn't get your way because we're here, aren't we? So what is it?"

Kiki should have known better than to try to keep anything from Luna. She was an open book to her friend, even if she was sometimes unwilling.

Kiki bit her bottom lip before asking, "Have you seen Mauri in your dreams at all?"

A blush bloomed across Luna's cheeks at the mention of her mate. "Not since we left La Aguilera."

"And have you sensed anything...off?" she pressed.

"You mean through the bond?" Luna frowned. "No. Why?"

Kiki huffed. "I haven't felt anything either. So I was just wondering."

"If we feel nothing, then that's a good thing. It means Arlando isn't torturing them."

Kiki rolled her shoulders to release the tension that had been slowly building there. "I guess. I'd just rather know for sure than guess and hope."

Luna made a clicking sound with her teeth. "If we didn't have hope, we'd have given up a long time ago."

Kiki had to admit that Luna had a point.

She looked up to where Giselle and Guille rode ahead of them. Kiki had to admit that Guille had a sereneness to him. He was shy and quiet, but he was also incredibly smart, and she respected his breadth of knowledge when it came to all things magic.

They rode for another hour when Giselle pulled her horse to a stop. "We're here," she called over her shoulder.

Kiki's heart kicked into double time. This was it. The moment she'd been waiting for.

Through the trees, Kiki could make out a small adobe hut with terracotta tiles lining the roof and earthen pottery filled with green herbs. A green-leaved lime tree spiced the air, its stalks bowed under the weight of fruit. Wicker baskets hung from the rafters; bunches of sage and dried peppers lay inside. Deep-red bowls overflowed with bronze yarrows, their seeds spilling onto the ground and mingling with the dirt.

They all dismounted and walked their horses the rest of the way. Once they secured their horses to a nearby tree, Kiki strode up to the door and raised her fist to knock.

There was no way that the Spirit Woman hadn't heard them approach her home. Unless she was very old and couldn't hear that well.

Kiki hesitated before striking her fist against the weathered wooden door.

In nervousness, her stomach flipped over itself, and her palms suddenly felt sweaty. Shaking off her anxiety, Kiki blew out a frustrated breath and knocked hard.

She listened carefully for the sound of someone moving inside to get the door but heard none.

"Maybe she's not home," Luna suggested.

"Oh, the old bat is home, alright," Giselle pointed at the roof and the white stream of smoke from a chimney.

Kiki didn't like being ignored. She knocked again, banging her fist against the door. "Spirit Woman, we know you're in there. I have a question to ask and am willing to pay your price. So open up."

The moments slipped by, and Kiki's frustration grew. Just when she was about to kick open the door and demand the Spirit Woman talk to her, the door slowly swung open, revealing a woman in her late forties, her midnight black hair extending past her waist and plaited neatly into a braid.

Kiki blinked at the woman, her mouth falling open in shock as she took a stumbling step back.

This couldn't be real. Kiki felt like she was looking in a mirror as she stared at the small woman standing before her.

"Kiki?" Luna asked as she pushed in closer to look at the woman. She looked back and forth between the two of them and cursed under her breath.

"What is it?" Giselle piped up, clearly not understanding what was happening.

Kiki barely understood it herself.

This couldn't be possible. This must be a dream.

No. Not a dream. A nightmare.

Kiki swallowed the lump in her throat. "Mom?"

"Mom?!" Giselle and Guille said at the same time, their brows shooting into their hairlines.

The woman sighed and opened the door further, motioning with her arm for them to enter. "I knew you'd find me someday. The Spirits told me as much."

Kiki felt like she'd been punched in the gut. The air whooshed out of her lungs, and a gnawing ache yawned open in the space where her heart should be.

"Wha—how?" Kiki stammered.

The woman motioned again for them to enter. She didn't seem shocked at all and jerked her head almost impatiently as if she wanted this interaction to hurry up and be done. "Come inside. There's no use in you all standing out in the heat."

Luna gently nudged Kiki forward, and she took a stuttering step forward, then another, each movement feeling hollow as she entered her mother's home.

"Sit, you all look like you've had quite the journey," her mother said, motioning to a wicker sofa and matching wicker chairs.

Luna took Kiki by the elbow and guided her to a spot on the sofa.

"Would anyone like some coffee?" her mother asked, looking around expectantly.

Guille cleared his throat and glanced apologetically at Kiki, seeming to understand that this situation was weird and only getting weirder. "I'll take some," he said, forcing a smile.

"I think we all should," Luna said, still holding onto Kiki's arm. "I think we're all in shock."

Kiki gaped in disbelief as her mother nonchalantly added ground coffee beans to a metal decanter filled with water before carefully placing it over the low-burning fire in the center of her home.

Kiki still didn't understand how any of this was real. How was her mother here? Why was she here? And why was she acting like they all had just shown up for their weekly cup of coffee? As if this was something they did all the time?!

Her mother poured the coffee over a sieve, letting the brown liquid pour into a pitcher before filling the cups. "I ran out of cream the other day, so you'll have to take it black," she said, placing them on the table one by one.

Kiki hesitated before picking up her cup, unable to take her eyes off her mother. Her thoughts raced as she stared at the brown steaming liquid. On one hand, she wanted to pepper her mother with questions, but on the other, she couldn't wrap her head around her mother's seeming apathetic attitude to Kiki's arrival.

Perhaps it had been foolish to dream, but Kiki had often imagined what it would like like if she were ever reunited with her mother again.

They shared more than just the same name, Quirera. But clearly, they also shared the same face, the same voice, and the same straight black hair.

"So, you said something about asking me a question," her mother said as she sat in a nearby chair and pulled her feet up to sit cross-legged.

The room fell into silence, and Kiki could feel everyone's eyes on her.

Kiki's hands gripped the cup so hard she thought she might shatter it into a million pieces.

Anger roiled through her body like a forest fire.

Though she looked like her mother, it was clear that was where the similarities ended. How could her mother act so calmly?

Kiki was sure that if she opened her mouth, she'd only burn everything in her path.

But there was another emotion that was searing through her veins, one that made her heart ache. The feelings of abandonment, the ones she often fought so hard to push away—those feelings were driving daggers into her heart.

"What are you doing here?" Kiki finally asked between clenched teeth.

Her mother sighed deeply as if she found this whole ordeal tedious. "I think we're going to need something a little stronger in order for me to answer that question." She proceeded to get up and grab a bottle of amber liquid from a shelf and began pouring it into palm-sized wooden bowls.

When she got to Kiki, she took the cup of coffee from her hands and pressed the bowl into them instead.

Kiki could smell the sharp tang of tequila the moment the bowl touched her hands. She reeled back in disgust. She couldn't handle tequila, not since she'd drank so much as an Attendant that she'd thrown up all night because of it.

Kiki set the bowl down and rested her elbows on her knees, trying her best to remain calm and not run rampant in fury. "I asked you a question."

"You may not like the answer," Quirera responded, her eyes emotionless.

Kiki balled her hands into fists. "Any answer is better than what I've been running through my head for my entire life."

Her mother—Quirera, as Kiki decided to call her because a mother would display more emotion than this woman currently was—moved to stand over the fire, her eyes focused on the dancing flames. "Did your wela ever tell you anything about me?"

Kiki's nostrils flared. "She told me you were foolish. That you never told her who my father was. That you ran off after him and left me with her."

Quirera huffed with disbelief. "Of course she did."

"Was it a lie?" Kiki growled. "Did you not run after my father?"

Quirera shook her head. "It's the way she told it."

Kiki clenched her teeth so hard that her jaw hurt. "Well, now is your chance to tell your side of it."

"I was very young when I learned I was pregnant with you," Quirera said as if that alone was explanation enough for abandoning Kiki. "I thought I could raise you, but I didn't know what I was doing."

"So you thought it was better to just run off when I was four-years-old?" Kiki hissed. "Better to let me wonder what I did to drive you away? Let me cry for you every night as I went to sleep? Huh? Is that it?"

Quirera had the sense to avert her gaze. "That wasn't my intention. I was going to come back."

Kiki bared her teeth, feeling as if her chest was compressing and her lungs were fighting for space. "Well, you had plenty of time before the Cicatrix ripped through the kingdom. What stopped you?"

Her mother closed her eyes tightly. "I was afraid."

Kiki threw her hands in the air. "Wow. You were afraid. Imagine how I felt when the darkness swallowed our village whole. Imagine what it was like for a six-year-old to lose the only person she had in this world in a matter of seconds. Imagine the terror and agony I felt when the darkness devoured wela's home, and I realized I was all alone in this world!" she yelled, feeling her face heat with anger.

She hadn't realized she'd stood up and advanced on Quirera or that she had started to shout. She stood toe to toe with Quirera, looking down her nose at the woman.

"Can you imagine that? Or are you too selfish?" Kiki sneered.

"I was selfish," her mother said, swallowing hard. "But your wela was selfish too. She wanted you for herself, to make up for the years she wasn't there for me."

Kiki snorted impatiently as she stepped back, shaking her head in disgust. "Now you're going to blame your mother, my wela, for your mistakes. Classic."

Quirera's brown eyes lit with flame. "Did you know she was a Spirit Woman before I became one? No, I didn't think so. The thing about our magic is that it is matrilineal and can only be passed from mother to daughter. That's the way it has been for generations in our family. Each woman would bear a daughter for her mother to raise while she took on the mantle and served the people. While she traveled to distant lands to right the wrongs and injustices of the world. Then, when her daughter bore a girl, she'd pass the mantle on and get the chance to be a mother again."

"You're lying." Kiki shook her head and turned away so she didn't have to look at Quirera. "You expect me to believe you're some kind of saint, traveling the world, helping people?"

Quirera cast her eyes to the floor, and her shoulders slumped forward. "I was so young, and my heart was broken. You're father—"

Kiki rushed her mother until mere inches separated them. "Put the blame on a man that I have no knowledge of one more time and see what happens."

Quirera hefted her chin higher and met Kiki's stare with an intense glare. "Fine. I'll tell you the truth then. I wanted revenge," her mother hissed. "I didn't want the magic so I could uphold its calling. I wanted to punish him for breaking my heart. And your wela was only too willing to give it up to me."

Kiki's upper lip curled back. "So you took it and sought out your revenge. You abandoned me for some man. A man who apparently didn't want me or you. Yet you still chose him."

Quirera shrugged. "I'm sorry. That's the truth of it," she said, her tone matter of fact.

All the pain in Kiki's heart felt like it was bursting. She turned away from her mother, drawing her machete, the metallic clang of it being freed from its sheath echoing through the small home. She swung at the first thing she saw: a shelf full of little earthen jars.

Her scream filled the room as she continued to swing, needing to get this pain out of her body before it could take root and consume her whole.

She didn't notice that Luna had been calling her name or that she'd been yanking on her arm, begging her to stop. She only stopped when Giselle stepped in the line of her next swing.

She stopped the arc of her machete right before it reached the other woman's neck.

"Calm down, dulzura," Giselle purred, her eyes pleading.

Kiki heaved a deep breath, and Luna rubbed her back in small circles.

Giselle crept closer, her steps heavy with worry, and slowly raised her hand to gently rest against Kiki's cheek. "Are you with us again, muñeca?" Kiki leaned into Giselle's touch, craving the refreshing coolness of her palm, and nodded in response to the question.

Kiki spun around to face Quirera, pointing her machete menacingly. "You are no one to me," she growled. "You and I may share a face, but that is all."

Her mother sighed heavily, her voice tinged with something that sounded like regret. "I know."

Wiping the sweat from her brow, Kiki moved to her seat and dropped herself onto the red cushion. "Now, you will answer my questions."

Chapter Twenty-Eight

Erasmo

The snow flurries were like icy water raining down on Erasmo. He pulled the fur cloak he was wearing tighter, securing the fragile woman in his arms.

Mounted on Bernat's back in his bear form, he clung tight as his brother rushed through the surroundings at lightning speed, blurring everything together.

Erasmo wasn't a fan of riding on his brother's back, but it was the only option that made the most sense at the time.

Bernat was the largest and fastest of the three men, and he'd be less encumbered by the extra weight.

A chorus of vengeful roars and vicious snarls reverberated in their wake, and he dared to cast a look over his shoulder to find three hellish demons still hot on their trail, dispatched by Arlando to form an unholy legion hunting them down.

Aurelia clung to Mauri's back in his bear form. Her fingers clenched tightly around the coarse fur, knuckles white with tension. Her eyes were wide and wild, constantly darting over her shoulder and the demons snapping at their heels.

Yari had passed out before they could escape the castle, and since Aurelia wasn't mentally able to help anyone, it fell to either Erasmo or Mauri to hold onto Yari as they raced back to La Aguilera.

Since Mauri was still battling his own blood lust and Erasmo really didn't like the idea of putting so much temptation right under his cousin's literal nose, Erasmo had volunteered to hold her safe.

He had to admit that Bernat was indeed the fastest of them. Mauri's heavy strides lagged behind by several feet, his fangs bared and his muscles straining as he shot through the air with each powerful leap in his attempt to keep up.

As they crested a hill, the spires of La Aguilera's towers jutted across the horizon. The wind carried the smell of baked bread and cinnamon—a welcome scent from the ovens of his home.

"There it is," Erasmo pointed, calling out to Bernat and Mauri.

Bernat opened his mouth wide and unleashed a thunderous roar reverberating through the earth like an unstoppable force. Erasmo was shaken to his core by the sheer power of it, which seemed to shake every fiber of his being.

Yari's head bounced softly against his chest, and he spared a glance down. Her face had grown pale, and her hair was slowly turning ashy white, her brown curls seemingly being drained of life the way a flower wilts and crumbles with the first frost of winter.

He could still sense her heartbeat, though, as faint as it was. He hoped that Luna hadn't exerted herself recently because her friend was going to need every ounce of strength the Healer could lend.

Behind them, he heard Mauri give a warning growl at the demons on their heels.

Just ahead was the bridge that would carry them over the deep ravine surrounding La Aguilera.

Turning just enough so Mauri could hear him, Erasmo shouted, "Mauri, take care of the demons. We can't let them through the gates!"

Mauri didn't need to be told twice. Any chance he got to tear off something's head was like allowing him to binge on dessert.

Aurelia let out a startled cry, and Mauri flung himself back to take on the three demons intent on getting to the small woman in Erasmo's arms.

Knowing that Mauri would finish the job, he focused on Yari.

"Hang in there, hermanita. You're almost there. Kiki will be there. Hang on for her. For Luna. Keep fighting for your life."

Beneath him, Bernat's chest rumbled with his agreement.

The cries of La Aguilera's scouts rose from the ramparts in warning, calling for the gates to be opened and for the soldiers to ready their weapons against the demons. The thunderous crack of the gates being thrown open reverberated through the air.

Bernat bounded over the deep crevice and the ravine below, soaring over the distance with grace and ease.

Erasmo's stomach jumped into his throat at the sudden suspension into midair, and he let out a relieved grunt when Bernat's paws touched back on the ground on the other side.

"Show off," he muttered to his brother.

Bernat responded with what very much sounded like a chuckle, and he was grateful for the momentary distraction from their very present and perilous circumstances.

Bernat slid through the open gates and came to a screeching halt in the center courtyard, where people were already gathering to lend aid.

Erasmo's cousin Ramón reached them first and held his arms open for the sleeping woman. Erasmo gently passed her down before sliding off Bernat's back.

Once free of his passengers, Bernat shifted into his human form, and his blue eyes scanned those gathered around with obvious anxiety.

Bernat scanned the area, his eyes flitting left and right until they finally settled on the one person he cared about.

Solana descended the stairs in her typical slayer leathers, the material molding to her body, showcasing her lean muscle and statuesque build.

Erasmo knew that the women came from a place of scarcity, and it warmed his heart to see that Solana had begun to gain some weight during their absence. Her cheeks were fuller, and her hair more vibrant. She looked healthy, and the sight made Erasmo's heart lurch in longing for Kiki.

Solana's fiery red curls fell around her shoulders, and for a moment, Erasmo thought she looked every bit the part of a queen.

Warmth filled his chest at the thought. When this was all over, Bernat would finally take his rightful place on the throne, and Solana would join him.

He could think of no better duo to shoulder such a heavy burden. No other pair could take it all on and not crumple beneath its weight.

It was one of the reasons the territories existed in the first place. When the kingdom fell into ruin, the territories were drawn up to help manage and administrate such vast holdings.

Erasmo wasn't a fool, though. Not every territory leader would want to return to the old ways, nor did he think they should. There was a middle ground in there somewhere. He just hadn't really given it much thought until now.

Bernat politely pushed his way through the crowd and bounded up the steps until he collided with his mate. He lifted her off her feet and pulled her into what must be a bone-crushing hug as he lowered his mouth to hers and attacked her lips.

The sight sent a shiver up Erasmo's spine as he, too, looked for Kiki.

He scanned the crowd gathered in the courtyard but couldn't find his little demon slayer. He reached out through the bond, and he instantly knew the answer to his question, and he curled his hands into fists.

She wasn't here. He followed the bond, letting it guide him in her current direction. She was to the southwest, and she was pissed. No. This was more than that. She was brimming with anger and indignation. Whatever she was doing wasn't going how she had expected.

Panicked shouts followed by the parting crowd drew Erasmo away from his thoughts. Mauri slid through the gates, his talons screeching across the cobblestones, with a harried Aurelia still clinging to the fur on his back.

When Aurelia didn't immediately get off his back, he released a feral growl and violently shook his shoulders as if trying to dislodge her. A group of cousins quickly rushed forward, pried her fingers from his fur, and took her away.

Mauri shifted back to his human form, his chest heaving for breath as he stormed up to Erasmo. His entire chest was covered in black demon ichor, and he wiped a glob from his face, sending it flying in the air.

"Where is she?" he roared, his eyes red with blood lust. His eyes were trained on Bernat and Solana, who were still in the middle of their reunion.

Erasmo stepped in Mauri's path and grabbed him by the shoulders. "Calm down, you psycho, they're not here."

"Don't you think I know that?" he hissed, violently breaking Erasmo's hold.

Solana broke away from Bernat and faced their cousin. "Luna went with Kiki to seek the aid of the Spirit Woman."

Erasmo froze, and he and Mauri shared a look of dread.

No. Not the Spirit Woman.

He had expected her to be busy, perhaps coming up with a plan with one of the delegates from the southwestern territory, but now he knew exactly where to pin his anger.

"Giselle," he growled. He should have known when Kiki told him she'd befriended the little monster. The two women were a dangerous pair. Impulsive. Clever. And unpredictable. "That little beast. Just when I think I get rid of her, she just keeps coming back."

He didn't get the chance to stew too long in his thoughts, though, because Ramón approached Solana and whispered something in her ear.

Solana frowned and followed him back inside the manor.

Erasmo took that as an invitation to follow, and he, Mauri, and Bernat trailed on her heels down to Guille's lab.

Ramón had placed Yari on a cot in the laboratory, and she was lying motionless. Her chest's gentle lift and fall was the only proof that she still lived.

Solana rushed to Yari's side and knelt over her. "Oh, Yari, what happened to you?"

Bernat gave his mate a quick rundown of the events that led to the escape. He told her how Yari had used blood magic to control the demons but that her control was only temporary, and the demons slipped her grip. That she had stabbed herself in the wrist to draw as much blood as possible, making the demons open the cages, but at the cost of her own wellbeing.

Erasmo felt a pang of guilt pierce his chest at the memory of seeing her limping up to their cages, the hopeful gleam in her eyes as she looked upon them.

Yari had a quiet strength in her that he wasn't sure Kiki saw. But he did. And he respected the fuck out of it.

Who else would willingly sacrifice themselves for others?

Not many.

Solana gently pushed Yari's silver-white hair out of her face. "What happened to her hair?" she asked quietly.

"We don't know," Bernat replied. "She already had some silver strands here and there when we first saw her. But it started to turn after what she did to set us free."

Solana nodded and looked at Ramón. "What can be done?"

Ramón brows pulled toward the center, and his lips flattened into a thin line. "With Healer Luna away and Guille accompanying her, we only have the most base treatments available."

"She's lost a lot of blood," Solana said, her tone cool and observant. "What can we do for that?" she asked, looking around the room expectantly.

Ramón answered, "Someone can give her blood, but there is no guarantee that her body will accept it."

Solana let a long moment pass before asking, "How can we ensure that her body accepts it?"

Silence filled the space, and Ramón shifted from foot to foot uncomfortably.

Solana took their non-answer for what it was—none of them knew. The only sign that she didn't like their response was a slight twitch of her lip.

Erasmo admired the hell out of her external control. If a snowstorm raged inside her, she didn't show it.

"So we have no options," she finally stated, her face made of stone as she gently wrapped her hand around Yari's.

Kiki clearly didn't see the Commander's subtle tells. But he did.

Her shoulders were tense as she looked at the smaller woman lying on the cot. Her eyes were full of emotion, and her words were crisp and precise so as not to betray her true feelings.

She was a wreck over Yari, as much as all of them were. She just had a more level head about it.

"Let me taste her blood," Mauri blurted, startling them all.

"Not this again," Erasmo growled, moving in front of his cousin to hold him back if needed.

Mauri gave him a glare that could kill. "You don't taste the difference in the blood, but I do. Some blood tastes the same. If I know what her blood tastes like, then someone with her blood can give it to her." Mauri rolled his neck as if relieving the tension there, and a series of pops filled the air. "Besides, Luna told me that if two people have the same blood, a transfer between the healthier and unhealthy people can occur. And since my mate is a Healer, I'm going to take her word over anyone else's."

Erasmo shared a dumbfounded look with Bernat. It wasn't often that Mauri made a lot of sense, and there was something a bit terrifying about that.

"We don't have time for this," Mauri growled, pushing past Erasmo. "This is Luna's best friend, yes?" he asked, his eyes wild as he stared Solana down.

The Commander didn't balk at him for even a second. She rose from her kneeling position with the grace of a queen and nodded. "Yes. And she's in charge as a member of my squad. She's my responsibility."

That's all Mauri needed to hear. He dropped to his knees and untied the linen wrapped around Yari's injured wrist.

He placed his mouth to the wound, and Erasmo had to look away, the beast within waking at the scent of a fresh meal. Erasmo pushed the beast back down, but it was more of a struggle than usual, and he knew that he'd need to feed soon to satiate the monster within.

Mauri's lips popped off Yari's wrist, and he quickly wrapped it back again with the linen.

"Well?" Erasmo asked, pushing forward to stand next to his cousin.

"Her blood tastes like mine. I'm a match."

Without explaining further, Mauri bit into his own wrist, and blood gushed past his lips and streamed onto the floor in a puddle. He pressed his wrist to Yari's lips, and Erasmo cried for him to stop.

Bernat and Solana surged forward to yank Mauri away, but they all froze at the sound of Yari's hands slapping against Mauri's arm as she dug her fingers into his flesh.

Her eyes flew open, revealing two blackened pools with no whites in sight.

Erasmo staggered backward in horror, his mind racing to find words to describe the sight before him.

Mauri hissed as Yari's fingers curled and dug deeper into his skin, her throat bobbing as she guzzled down his blood.

"I think this one might have been a viper in a past life," Mauri winced as he used his free hand to brace the one Yari was feeding on.

Erasmo didn't know what to think as he watched the tiny slip of a woman command Mauri with such ease. Anytime he tried to wrench his wrist away, her grip tightened, turning his skin white with the force.

Mauri blinked slowly, his eyes going cross. "I don't feel so great," he slurred as he slumped the rest of the way to the floor.

"She'll drain him if she doesn't stop," Erasmo said, his voice laced with panic as he grabbed Mauri's arm and tried to pry it away from Yari.

But she wouldn't let go, and a feral growl slipped past her lips.

Solana darted back to Yari's side. "Yarixa Canahuate, listen to me. That's enough. You've had enough. Let Mauri go."

But Yari didn't seem to hear Solana. Or maybe she did, and she didn't care.

Erasmo couldn't let her kill Mauri, and he shouted for Yari to stop. He yelled all kinds of things that he thought might make her stop.

That she was no better than Arlando if she kept going. That she was safe now and could let go. He started to get desperate and begged her to release Mauri. His best friend. His family. He couldn't lose someone else, not after everything.

"Kiki will never forgive you if you kill him!" he yelled, his eyes winced shut as he still struggled against her vice grip on Mauri.

Her lips made a popping sound as she released Mauri's wrist, and together, Erasmo and his cousin went tumbling sideways.

Mauri's skin had grown ashen, and he'd long since passed out, but his heartbeat was strong and his breathing even.

Erasmo couldn't help but feel like they'd gotten dangerously close to the point where the curse would no longer heal him.

Panting from the effort, Erasmo slowly stood up and turned to face the woman who'd nearly killed Mauri.

He expected her to be awake, but when he turned around, she lay in the bed peacefully, sound asleep. Her skin had regained its golden brown glow, and her hair seemed to be a deeper shade of gray now than before.

"What the fuck was all of that?" he seethed as he tried to reign in his anger.

Bernat gaped at him, his mouth opening and closing as if he were, too, at a loss for words.

It was Solana who spoke up. "I'm long past expecting easy answers at this point," she stood to her full height and stretched out her back.

When she pushed her hips forward to lengthen her spine, Erasmo swore he noticed that her lower abdomen seemed a bit swollen.

He quirked his head at the sight, and when he flicked his gaze back to Solana's eyes, he found her staring right at him as if straight into his soul.

She gave him an almost imperceptible shake of her head, and he knew what she was saying without her having to say it.

"Say nothing," her eyes commanded.

He narrowed his gaze and flicked his eyes to Bernat. She'd have to tell his brother sooner or later that he was going to be a father, but it wasn't his business to tell, and he had too much respect for her to go against her wishes.

He gave her a quick nod in response, and he almost missed the tiny quirk of her lips, the ghost of a smile.

Everyone filled out from Guille's lab, save for a few members of the family who volunteered to stay with Yari until she woke.

Once back upstairs and in the dining hall, Erasmo immediately took note of the circular pattern of the tables and smirked.

He took one look at Solana and surmised that she'd decided on the layout, knowing that the other territory leaders needed to feel like they were equals in the looming problem of Arlando and the curse rather than subordinates.

Once again, he felt a blooming appreciation in his chest for the Commander. Though she was younger than him, she displayed wisdom beyond her years, and she matched that wisdom with a level-headedness that he admired.

Yes. She'd make a great Ozero Queen. Perhaps the best that would ever live.

He only hoped they all made it that far to see such a happy day.

Solana ordered food to be brought out despite the fact that dinner wasn't for another few hours.

La Aguilera ran on a strict schedule. The nature of its inhabitants necessitated such regimentation. However, he was grateful for the bending of the rules.

He, Mauri, and Bernat had quite literally just escaped their own version of hell.

But even he could admit that he needed to recuperate as much as possible because there was a more pressing matter at hand.

Kiki.

Bernat took a seat to Solana's right, and Erasmo tossed himself into a chair across from them.

"I didn't think this day could get weirder," Erasmo drawled. "But here we are."

"What happened? How did you escape?" Solana asked, leaning back in her chair.

Erasmo grabbed an empanada from a tray and bit into it, savoring the earthy flavors before saying, "Bernat will have to fill you in on that bit because I can't stay."

Solana arched a brow at him.

"What do you mean?" Bernat asked.

Erasmo grimace. "Once Mauri wakes up, we're going after our mates. Before that witch can bind them in a deal, they'll regret."

Chapter Twenty-Nine

Kiki

A lone quetzal bird sang a sweet melody as Kiki watched the sun slip past the horizon.

She tilted her head to the sky and watched as the soft purple hues of darkness spread and engulfed the remaining orange splashes.

Heaving a weary sigh, she crossed her arms over her chest and double-checked the location of the protection runes surrounding the Spirit Woman's home.

Though Quirera assured Kiki and the rest of the group that no demon could slip past her wards, Kiki didn't want to make the mistake of trusting the woman who'd abandoned her over fifteen years ago.

She hadn't anticipated the pain of encountering her mother again after all these years. She'd harbored so much resentment toward the woman that it had shaped her entire outlook on life.

Her fear of being left behind had not only weighed on her heart, but it had nipped at her heels like demons thirsting for flesh.

She knew it would be better for her if she let the past live in the past. But that was easier said than done.

Though she wasn't a little girl anymore clinging to her grandmother's leg for fear that she'd, too, leave, it didn't change the fact that Kiki felt betrayed. And for what? For power. For revenge. For a man.

She scoffed and kicked at a rock, sending it flying past the wards and skittering into the woods beyond.

To make matters worse, Quirera refused to answer any questions that related to the curse, citing that the spirits demanded payment first before delving into the spirit realm for answers.

What a load of horse shit.

A set of light footsteps in the grass alerted her to someone approaching. But all the tension in her body faded as she recognized her best friend's gait and how it felt in her heart when Luna was near.

Luna stopped at Kiki's side, and she could feel her friend's eyes scanning her face without even turning to look.

"Spit it out," Kiki grumbled.

"What's your plan?" Luna asked, her tone gentle and lacking any trace of the bitterness Kiki felt swirling inside herself.

She frowned and glanced at Luna, meeting her dark brown eyes. "I expected you to tell me that this whole trip was pointless and that we should return to the eyrie."

Luna shook her head solemnly. "Even if I did, would you listen?"

Kiki dropped her chin to her chest and toyed with the bear-tooth pendant she still wore—Yari's necklace. "Probably not."

Luna smirked at that and looped her arm through Kiki's, pulling her near. "I'm close to completing the translation of the book, and I think I know a way to end the curse. But I also know that is not enough for you. You want assurances. Guarantees."

"Don't you?" Kiki whispered. "We're talking about the fate of the entire kingdom. What if we get the spell wrong? What happens? We don't know. Arlando has Yari and has been spinning his plan for years. Long before we even crossed the Cicatrix. We're up against someone who has been several moves ahead of us at every turn."

"There's no such thing as a guarantee that something will or will not work. I'd rather try with our resources than trust a woman who extracts payment from those she claims to help." Luna held her tighter as she added, "And I don't trust anyone who'd willingly give you up. She may have been young, but that's hardly a good enough reason for her foolish-ness. Because that's what she is, a fool for leaving you. You're worth more than any vendetta. I hope you know that. Everything you've done for Yari, know that if roles were reversed and you'd been taken, Yari and I would have searched the world for you."

Kiki's shoulders bowed forward, feeling a swell of emotions washing over her. She didn't know how much she needed to hear Luna say such a thing until she'd said it.

Kiki's eyes stung as fresh tears pooled along their rims. "It still hurts," she choked.

"I know," Luna whispered as she tucked a strand of Kiki's hair behind her ear. "Just know that you're not alone. You built a new family for yourself, one full of people who admire you, love you, and put up with all your hot-headed nonsense." She said the last bit with a grin, and Kiki mirrored her friend.

Luna pulled Kiki into a hug, and she felt herself melt in her best friend's arms. "Sometimes the family we choose is stronger and more loving than the family we're born into. But it's you who gets to choose which of the two you'll listen to. Which one you're going to put your faith in."

Kiki felt something inside herself shift as if there had long been a piece of a puzzle that had been missing, and it had finally slid into place.

With a sigh, she pulled away and held Luna at arm's length. "I don't know what I'd do without you."

Luna's eyes crinkled with mischief. "Oh, I do." Kiki quirked her head in surprise. "You'd run around hacking heads off with your machete and ask questions later."

"I thought I already did that," she smirked.

"True," Luna shrugged. "But you do it a lot less than you would if I weren't around."

They shared a glance before bursting into laughter.

"Let's go home," Kiki said once they recovered.

It was a bittersweet moment for her to admit that La Aguilera had become her home and that the one thing she'd been searching for her whole life, a connection with her mother, was not what she'd thought it would be.

A part of her was glad to know the truth of it. Even if that truth hurt like absolute hell.

As she and Luna walked back to her mother's cabin to turn in for the night, she smiled.

The family she'd chosen was the balm that had been healing her broken heart, and it was that family she would fight for until the end.

A loud pounding at the door to the cabin ripped Kiki from a restless sleep.

Next to her, Luna sat bolt upright, and her lips curled into a grin.

"Mauri," she breathed with reverence as she quickly pushed the blanket she'd been sharing with Kiki off her legs.

Giselle slept on Kiki's other side and rubbed her sleep-crusted eyes. "What the hell?" she grumbled. "What time is it?"

But Kiki didn't answer the other woman as she, too, peeled the blanket off to rush to the door. She quickly pushed her night dress down so it fell to her feet and joined Luna.

Just as Luna opened it, Erasmo came rushing in.

His eyes were wild as he searched for Kiki, and as soon as his blue gaze settled on her, a rush of heat pooled in her belly.

Erasmo growled as he took her in, his eyes not failing to miss how her nipples were visible through the linen gown. He stormed up to her and attacked her lips with his own.

Still lying on the floor, Giselle groaned. "Great. You're here."

Erasmo broke away from the kiss and glared at Giselle. "I'll deal with you later," he snarled.

Giselle's eyes glittered with mischief. "Don't be mad at me just because I could give Kiki what she wanted and you couldn't."

Kiki winced at the obvious innuendo, and she held Erasmo in place as he moved to lunge for Giselle.

"You brought her here against my express wishes," he hissed.

A tremor of annoyance ruffled against Kiki's skin. "Excuse me, I make my own choices, Erasmo Ozetero, and don't you forget it."

Erasmo cut his gaze to hers, and his eyes turned molten as a growl rumbled from deep within his chest. He seemed at war over wanting to throttle Giselle and fuck Kiki where she stood.

Kiki would rather he do the latter, just not here inside her mother's home. And definitely not in front of everyone.

"If you're going to act like a beast, then I suggest we go outside where the beasts live," she growled, her eyes trained on his, her invitation heavy with double meaning.

Erasmo gathered her in his arms and pressed his lips to her ear. "Call me a beast again and see what happens."

Kiki's skin tingled as his breath curled around the shell of her ear. Desire pooled low in her belly and traveled further south to her pussy.

"Beast," she whispered back in challenge.

Erasmo growled and flung her over his shoulder before storming from the cabin.

Kiki couldn't hide her giggle as he grumbled under his breath about showing her exactly what a beast could do to her and something about making her beg.

She liked the sound of that.

Before she lost sight of the cabin entirely, she caught sight of Luna clinging to Mauri's front with her legs wrapped tightly around him, their lips moving in a frenzy as he blindly carried her into the woods as well.

Erasmo deposited her in a clearing and removed the leather bracers strapped to his forearms.

"You're going to pay for not heeding my warning about the Spirit Woman," he growled.

Kiki retreated a pace, a feral smirk twisting her lips. "Is that so? How are you going to make me pay, I wonder."

He advanced on her and slammed his lips to hers, his kiss leaving her breathless. "You say you don't answer to me, but that's where you're wrong, my love. And I'm going to prove it when I make you come on my cock as many times as I wish."

A thrill raced up her spine at his dirty words. "Do I look afraid?" she taunted.

Erasmo's pupils blew wide, and he hefted her off the ground as she lifted her dress up enough to wrap her legs around his waist. His hands cupped the bare swell of her ass, and he groaned as he squeezed her cheeks hard.

She whimpered at how close his fingers were to her bare pussy. "Seal the bond with me," she panted. "Make me as yours. Forever."

A growl rumbled through Erasmo's chest at her words. "Yes," he purred. "Your heart is mine. Your soul is mine. You are mine."

He slammed her against a tree as he ripped his cloak off and tossed it to the side before claiming her lips again.

A moan escaped her as his hard cock pressed against her throbbing pussy. She ground her hips against him to relieve the pressure, to give herself some relief from this burning need to have him inside her.

His hands were everywhere at once as he groped her breasts through the fabric of her dress, the linen scratching against her touch-sensitive nipples. He palmed her ass with reverence, pulling her thighs tighter around his waist.

She clung just as desperately to him, her nails digging deep into his shoulders. She loved that he didn't hold back. Erasmo showed her exactly what he wanted, and he didn't apologize for it. It made her feel wanted, cherished and loved. She felt completely and totally accepted by him. She didn't fear he'd walk away from her, not when he looked at her like she was his entire world. Not when he kissed her like he'd never get enough.

She clawed at his shirt, lifting it over his head before diving in to nip at his neck.

He shivered as she nibbled on his ear. "I fucking need you," he whispered, his voice cracking as she moved her lips to the juncture between his neck and shoulder.

"Then take me," she teased as she leaned back and lifted her dress over her head, exposing her breasts and bare pussy.

Erasmo grunted when she ground her pussy on his hard length.

Kiki's lips quirked in satisfaction.

"You like that, do you?" He said in a rough growl. "You like rubbing your hot little pussy on my cock?"

A thrill rushed up her spine at his words. "Mmm, yes," she moaned, her eyes half-lidded.

"What else do you want, Kiki? What do you want me to do to you?" he muttered against her skin.

She could no longer speak, so she swiftly reached between them to unfasten his belt to free his cock.

Erasmo's breath caught when she wrapped her hand around his length and pumped his cock up and down, her eyes never leaving his as she did it. She loved watching the erotic ways his face changed as she displayed her wanton disregard for his control.

She enjoyed the fact that he couldn't tear his eyes away from hers.

"Say it," he demanded. "Say what you want."

"Fuck me," she moaned, the command spilling from her lips. "Fuck me like you'll never get another chance. Like we're going to die tomorrow."

Erasmo's eyes flashed wide before he snarled and lifted her up so he could notch himself at her entrance.

He slammed into her hard, her back pressing into the rough tree bark.

She moaned loudly, her eyes fluttering closed at the delicious sensation of his cock and the pleasure that flowed from it.

"That's it," he whispered against her lips. "Take it all, Kiki."

He leaned into her, the hand that wasn't bracing her around the waist skimming over her breast, tweaking her nipple. "You're so fucking tight, Kiki," he growled as he buried himself balls deep inside her. "I could spend all fucking night inside you and never get enough."

She whimpered as he withdrew and thrust hard, her pussy tightening around his cock like a vice grip. "Don't hold back, Erasmo. I want everything you can give me."

Erasmo's eyes glittered with lust as he caught her lips in a possessive kiss, the kind of kiss that said he'd never let her go. His hands moved to grip her ass tight as his hips found a rhythm.

Her breasts jiggled as he pounded into her over and over.

She'd never get enough of this. This feeling of being so fully loved. She'd long thought that finding her mother would fill the hole that her absence had created. But now Kiki understood that only she could repair that kind of damage. That filling it with training for the Demon Corps, her mission to find Yari, and even her determination to end the curse wasn't the answer.

Instead, she realized that she was already whole, and any additions she made to her life made it that much sweeter.

With Erasmo, she felt like she'd found her equal in every possible way and was willing to do anything to defend that.

She screamed his name as he slammed into her again, the thick head of his cock pressing hard against the spot that could drive her over the edge.

"I'm close," she moaned as his hips slapped against hers.

"Come for me," he groaned and pressed his forehead to hers, his hips pistoning back and forth. "Come all over my cock."

That was enough to send her flying over the edge. She yelled Erasmo's name as her pussy spasmed around his cock, her orgasm rolling through her body like a tidal wave.

He didn't relent. He kept on fucking her through the orgasm, keeping his promise that he'd make her come as many times as he wished.

Kiki felt a second, smaller orgasm build inside her. She grasped his shoulders and held on as he slammed into her relentlessly.

"Do it," he whispered harshly. "Come for me again. Let me feel it."

Kiki mewled in pleasure as his cock rubbed against that spot deep inside her, sending stars bursting in her vision.

The knot in her stomach tightened, and her pussy clenched around his cock.

She came hard and fast, her mind shorting out just as her body did.

Kiki's eyes fluttered closed as she rode out her orgasm, feeling the last of the tension flow from her body.

"I love you," he whispered reverently.

Kiki wished she could just believe that everything would be alright. That they'd end the curse, and they'd all get to live happily ever after.

She wished she could believe that this would all end without tears.

However, she knew there was too much outside of her control. And she knew that if it came to it, she'd defend her family, the family she'd built if it meant saving them all.

"I fucking love you," he growled as he slammed into her once more and froze as his cock swelled and throbbed before spurting thick jets of cum inside her.

Erasmo's groan was low as he collapsed against her, his hands tightening around her as his cock continued to twitch and pulse within her.

In that moment, Kiki felt something deep inside her shift. The connection she'd felt with him deepened, spreading throughout her body, sending sparks of lightning zinging across her skin. The mate bond sealed around her heart as if it were a tangible thing, bringing with it a feeling of completion. A rightness. It flowed through her, filling her with a lightness of being and a certain sense of peace.

He leaned heavily against her, his head resting on her shoulder. His lips moved against her neck, his tongue licking her salty skin.

"I don't think I'll ever get tired of this," she said breathlessly.

"I'm counting on it." Erasmo chuckled against her neck. "Your satisfaction will always be my priority."

Chapter Thirty

Solana

The morning sun filtered into Solana's room, casting bright rays across her face. She shifted her nose under the fur blankets, too content to leave the warmth of Bernat's body pressed against her back.

His arm circled her waist, and his breath was hot against her neck.

She let herself sink into the feeling of safety that she only ever felt with him.

That feeling of wings fluttering in her stomach made her place her hand over her lower belly. Her belly felt swollen, but it wasn't very noticeable yet.

However, she knew Erasmo had figured it out when his eyes caught on the slight change in her physique.

Bernat hadn't noticed; if he had, he had likely attributed what little weight she'd gained to the improved food options in La Aguilera.

In fact, she'd noticed that both Kiki and Luna had begun to fill out more too. Their cheeks looked flush with life rather than that sunken quality expected in the Demon Corps.

She knew she needed to tell Bernat about the pregnancy soon, but there didn't seem to be a good moment with everything going on.

Last night, when she and Bernat had retired for the night and entered their suite, the first thing he did was pin her against the wall and kiss her until she was breathless.

She pressed her fingertips to her kiss-bruised lips and felt the corners of her lips lift into a smile.

"I've missed you, mi sol," he whispered when he finally broke away, his chest heaving for air.

"I don't have to tell you how relieved I am to see you again."

He curled his finger into a red curl of her hair and gave it a gentle tug. "No, you don't. But I expect you to be a good girl, get on her knees, and show me."

A shiver of anticipation raced up her spine at the look of hunger in his eyes.

Without saying a word, she lowered herself to the ground and knelt, her palms pressed to the tops of her knees.

Bernat ran a hand through her hair, and she leaned into it. "That's right, my sun. Show me how much you burn for me."

She flicked her gaze up and reached for his belt, unfastening the buckle and tugging it through the loops on his pants before tossing it into some corner of the room. She didn't break eye contact with him for a second, and the prolonged silence only made the room temperature spike.

Everything Bernat wouldn't tell her about his experience as a captive filled his eyes, and right now, she could see what he needed.

He needed to be grounded once more in who he was. In who they were together. He needed to take control the way he liked when they had sex, and he needed her complete submission.

She was more than willing to give it. Bernat was her only solace. She knew he'd be right there to catch her in his warm embrace, the safe haven where she could truly be free and fall.

She pulled his pants down, freeing his already hard cock. She leaned in and ran her tongue up and down his length slowly. Bernat let out a low groan, his fingers tangling in her hair.

"You're so good at this," he breathed, his voice thick with desire.

She took him deeper into her mouth, using her tongue to swirl around the head of his cock. Bernat's hips bucked, and she felt his fingers tightening in her hair.

The sound of his groans filled the room and only spurred her on. She loved the way he tasted and how he felt in her mouth. She loved that he responded to her like this. She felt in control without having to take the reins of that control. Even on her knees, she still commanded every fiber of his being.

She pulled back, leaving him hanging on the edge, his chest rising and falling with deep breaths.

"Stand up," he commanded, his voice rough.

She stood up, her eyes locked on his as he pushed her back onto the bed. He crawled over her, his lips trailing down her neck.

"I'm going to take what's mine," he whispered, his voice like velvet.

He ran his hands over her body, his fingers grazing her nipples, making them harden under his touch.

When he reached her pussy, he slipped a finger along the hood, his finger just grazing her clit.

"You're wet for me already." It was a statement, not a question.

He bit her lower lip, and she moaned, the sound muffled against his lips.

"Roll over," he growled.

She quickly followed his order.

"Put your hands behind your back," he commanded.

She did as she was told and felt the cool leather of his belt wrap around her wrists as he pulled them tightly together.

"Is that too tight?"

She shook her head. "Make them tighter," she whispered, feeling bold.

A chuckle of approval rumbled through Bernat's chest as he tightened the belt even further. "How's that?"

She wriggled her wrists, the leather cutting into her skin just enough to pinch. "Perfect."

"You're so beautiful," he said in response before he lifted her hips into the air and pushed her head into the soft mattress.

He'd never tied her up before during sex, and the newness of it made heat rush through Solana's skin. Trussed up like this made her feel safe because she knew the man who'd done it would never do anything to harm her.

She loved that Bernat knew what she needed as much as she knew what he needed. When it was just the two of them together, they could let all their walls drop and be completely accepted for who they were, desires, and all.

"You look so fucking good like this, mi sol," Bernat said roughly as he rubbed his hand over her ass cheek.

He lifted his hand and brought it back down with a hard slap.

She couldn't stop the small squeal that escaped her lips as he smacked her ass again. She jerked forward from the momentum, the pain quickly fading into pleasure as her pussy clenched.

"You like that, don't you?" he asked.

She nodded as she bucked her hips, seeking friction where he offered none.

"Use your words, Sol."

"Yes," she whispered. "Give me more."

He ran his hand over her ass again.

She didn't have time to brace herself before he smacked her again.

"So good," she said, her head still pressed into the mattress.

"Good girl."

Once more, the pain turned into a red-hot fire that burned straight to her pussy. She let out a groan of frustration.

"If you want more, you'll have to tell me exactly what you want."

She shook her head, the words on the tip of her tongue, but lost as Bernat began to rub her ass again.

She relaxed into the mattress, knowing the next blow would sting harder. She thought if he hit the same spot again, she might just come from that alone.

Her thighs were slick from her own arousal, and her breaths rapidly sawed in and out of her lungs.

He slapped her ass again, and she moaned. She was so close—

With every smack, he pushed her closer to the edge, and when his hand came down on her ass again, she couldn't stop the moan as the pleasure found its way to her pussy, making her clench hard.

Her orgasm flashed through her light lighting, making her toes curl.

He quickly grabbed her wrists and hauled her to her knees so that her back was pressed against his chest.

"Do you want my cock, Sol?"

She nodded, the pain and pleasure mixing into a heady cocktail of emotions. She felt hot all over and wanted more.

"Say it. Tell me what you need. Say it like you mean it."

"Please, Bernat, please fuck me," she begged, trying to pull her wrists apart so that she could touch him.

With one swift motion, he freed her, letting her arms fall to her sides.

She didn't have time to savor the relief of being able to move because he pushed her head down on the bed and entered her from behind.

She felt his cock push into her, slowly spreading her wide. He filled her to the brim, and she moaned as her pussy clenched around him.

"I want you to tell me what you're feeling," Bernat said, his voice low and gravelly as he drove forward.

"It feels so good. I love the way you fill me up," she said, panting.

Solana turned her head and caught his lips in a kiss as he began to move inside her.

His cock slid in and out of her, hitting every pleasure point over and over again until she couldn't hold back any longer. He slammed into her hard enough to knock the wind out of her, and she dug her nails into the sheets as she whimpered into his mouth.

She felt his hot breath on her neck as he nipped at her skin with his teeth.

"Come for me, Sol. I can feel how close you are," Bernat said.

"Fuck, yes," she replied.

He slammed into her again, his hand reaching underneath her body to pinch her clit.

She felt like she was falling backward as the pleasure coursed through her body.

"Don't stop!" she cried out.

"Never," he grunted, picking up his pace.

Every thrust pushed her higher until she was so close she could almost taste it. Her body felt like it was electrified with sensation, the tension coiling tighter and tighter until she thought she might explode.

She felt Bernat's fingers press past her folds as he inserted them inside her, joining his cock. He curled his fingers, teasing that sweet spot that would make her fall apart.

"Bernat," she said, panting, her head falling forward, pressed into the sheets. "Oh, God, Bernat."

As if her body was his to command, she felt herself come apart at the seams, the orgasm so powerful it made her see stars as her pussy convulsed and milked his cock for all it was worth.

He thrust into her once, twice, three times before he, too, succumbed to his orgasm, his cock throbbing as he came inside her.

She felt him slump against her as he caught his breath, their bodies already entwined.

"I love you," she said, her voice barely louder than a whisper.

After a long moment, he pushed himself up, gently removing his fingers from her pussy. He kissed her neck before he slipped out of her and then rolled onto his back.

"And I love you, mi sol."

"I don't know what I'd do without you, Bernat."

He kissed her on the lips tenderly, lovingly. "We're a team, mi sol. I'd be lost without you, too."

She felt her cheeks flush with color at the memory of last night. Though she knew they had a lot of work to do, she couldn't resist the temptation to stay in bed all day with the gorgeous man sleeping soundly behind her.

She pressed her thighs together in a poor attempt to quench the heat spreading through her pussy. Rolling over to face him, she found that his eyes were open and looking right at her.

"Someone's being naughty," he teased, his eyes taking in the color staining her cheeks.

She nuzzled closer to him, inhaling his scent deeply as if she could take him in completely and never be apart again. "I don't know what you're talking about."

"Is that so?" he said, his tone teasing as he lifted up and rolled her onto her back. He caged her between his arms, part of his chest pressing into her, keeping her pinned to the bed.

He traced her lips with his thumb before he trailed his hands down the line of her jaw, down between her breasts, down her stomach, and dipped his hand between her thighs.

His eyes lit up when his fingers slipped through her wetness, and his chest rumbled with an appreciative growl.

"Did I not satisfy my queen well enough last night?" he asked, his eyes hooded and his fingers still slipping through the wetness and the folds of her pussy.

She squirmed beneath him, her breath starting to come out in desperate pants. "We have work to do."

He chuckled as he pushed two fingers inside her and spread them apart, stretching her.

She let out a startled moan and felt herself arching up off the bed.

Bernat grinned. "I can think of a million things I'd rather do that involve just you and me and those little sounds you make when I make you come."

He slammed his lips to hers, and she responded with the same force.

She'd never get enough of him.

He pushed another finger inside of her, warming her up so that she could take him with ease, but then came a hard knock at the door of their suite.

"Mi Reina, come quickly." Ramón's familiar voice echoed through the hall.

Bernat growled, his eyes narrowing at the door as he shouted at his cousin. "Not now, come back in a few hours."

"A few hours?" Solana smirked, wondering exactly what he had planned for her. She could only begin to imagine, and that thought made her ache for it.

"I'm sorry, cousin," Ramón said. "But this can't wait. Arlando is here."

Solana exchanged a worried look with Bernat before they broke apart and began throwing their clothes on.

She was dressed first and flung open the door while Bernat was still rooting around looking for his belt. "Give me a second," he growled, crouching down to look under the bed.

She rolled her eyes at him and turned to Ramón, who saluted her with a fist to his chest. "Give me all the details."

"Arlando is here, and he has a demon army at his back. But he's not alone." Ramón glanced into the room where Bernat finally found his belt and was looping it around his waist. "He has your little brother with him. Arturo."

Bernat froze and slowly looked up, catching Solana's gaze, the worry plain to see in the way his eyes crinkled at the corners. "Is he," he swallowed hard and continued. "Alive?"

Ramón's mouth twisted, and Solana felt her gut lurch. If Turi was dead, it would devastate Bernat. Just when he'd been reunited with his family, only to lose one.

"He is, but—just come," he finally said. "You'll want to see it for yourself."

Together, the three of them rushed through the manor out to the courtyard, where there was already a buzz of activity as everyone was getting prepared for an attack. Yasir stood on a wooden crate, orders spewing from his lips as he took command of his army.

Solana nodded at Ramón, knowing full well that he'd orchestrated the organization of this. She had been right to appoint him head of logistics.

Ramón led them through the courtyard and into a side door that led them up a series of stone stairs that opened up to the ramparts of the wall that protected the eyrie.

The gates were closed shut, and the wooden bridge that crossed the deep ravine below had been pulled back to prevent crossing. But sure enough, across the ravine was a demon army that made Solana pale.

She'd never seen so many demons in one place, let alone organized and taking orders from a single person.

Arlando sat astride a white stallion at the front of the army, and behind him was a cart that hosted a single wooden pole to which Turi was strapped to.

His hands were bound behind his back around the pole, and his head hung limply against his chest.

His body was covered in blood and open cuts as if Arlando had taken his anger out on his little brother and hadn't bothered to consider if it would kill him.

Next to her, Bernat inhaled sharply, and he stepped forward, resting his hands on the stone railing, his knuckles turning white as he took in the full extent of Arlando's crime against Turi.

"That bastard will pay for this," Bernat seethed, his voice dark and heavy with rage.

"Oh good, you finally decided to grace us with your presence," Arlando called to them.

"Let Turi go," Bernat growled, the skin along his knuckles breaking as his talons slowly extended.

Arlando laughed, and a fiery rage seeped through Solana's veins at the sound.

She knew Arlando didn't come just to hand over Turi. This was a demonstration of his power. And she was short her best demon slayer and her best healer at the moment.

She had to find a way to stall.

"What do you want?" Solana yelled as she stepped forward.

Arlando cocked his head at her. "You're going to let a woman speak for you?" he asked Bernat, his tone disgusted.

Bernat's nostrils flared, and he seemed ready to go down there if she didn't get things under control.

Solana lifted her chin into the air. "Bernat is the rightful king of Ozero. You are speaking to her queen," she announced.

That caught Bernat's attention. He flicked his gaze to her, and she could see how proud he was of her at that moment.

"Queen," Arlando scoffed. "The last queen fucked us with the curse. I think I've had enough of queens."

Solana pushed down the impatience bubbling in her chest. "I ask again, what do you want?"

Arlando frowned, seeming to truly despise how she was taking command of the conversation. She knew he liked to run his mouth, but she didn't want to give him the chance to do so now.

She had no idea what his plans were, and that was the first problem she needed to solve. Whether or not she'd give him what he wanted was another thing entirely.

Arlando's lips curled in a snarl, and he turned his head to look directly at Bernat. Clearly, he had no intention of addressing Solana any further.

Arlando shouted. "Give me Yarixa and turn your mate over to me, and I will return this pathetic excuse of an Ozero Prince over to you, brother."

"That'll never happen," Bernat yelled, his voice booming as he was mid-shift.

"That's too bad," Arlando said with an exaggerated shrug. "I thought family meant something to you. I guess I have no further use for this sack of meat then."

Arlando flicked his hand, and a group of demons stepped forward; their snarls echoed in the open space.

"NO!" a familiar voice rang out.

Solana turned in time to see Yari running along the ramparts, still dressed in the clothes she'd been brought in, still covered in a mixture of her blood and Mauri's.

She had a dagger in her hand, and she flung it in Arlando's direction.

Solana knew that there was no way such a throw would ever make it that distance. Even if it had been a tlazon meant to travel greater distances thanks to its shape and weight, there would have been no way it would travel over the ravine.

However, Yari hadn't thrown the dagger with her strength alone. A line of blood dripped from the hand she'd used to throw the dagger, and it soared over the open space like a perfectly aimed arrow.

Time seemed to slow as the dagger hit Arlando square in the chest, knocking him from his horse and tumbling to the ground.

For a moment, Solana stood there with her mouth open in shock.

Arlando howled in pain, hands clutching at the dagger buried in his chest. But to her dismay, he gathered himself up, snow clinging to his all-white jacket and pants as he clumsily climbed back onto his horse and started to retreat.

Yari gripped the stone ramparts, her eyes narrowed with rage as she watched Arlando turning away. Her lips curled back in a snarl that surprised Solana. She'd never known Yari to harbor such strong emotions, least of all such hatred.

As if sensing Solana's stare, Yari met her gaze straight on, her lips pulled into a thin line before she stormed off. Solana hoped she was going back to Guille's lab to rest. She'd have to look in on Yari soon.

But Bernat was her main concern at the moment. Seeing the opportunity before him, Bernat launched into a run and began ordering the guards to open the gates and calling for the bridge to be lowered down.

He raced down the stairs, and she quickly rushed after him.

"What are you doing?" she shouted when she caught up to him. "He's retreating."

"I'm getting Turi away from him and ending this once and for all," he growled.

"Did you not see that demon army, or am I the only one, Bernat?" she asked, bewildered at his line of thought.

"I don't care. I have to try."

"No, not this way," she grabbed Bernat by the arm and twisted it back, bringing him to his knees as he let out a cry of shock.

Solana quickly countered his orders and instead told their people to reinforce the gates.

"If the demons attack, we'll pick them off from the ramparts," she announced to Yasir, who came to a screeching halt at her side. "The ravine will give us an advantage, but prepare to be overrun. They *will* make it over the ravine, and they *will* scale the wall."

Yasir took her orders and began to ensure their execution.

Meanwhile, Bernat struggled against her hold on him. "WHY, SOL?" he howled. "I could have grabbed him. I could have saved him!"

"That was a suicide mission, and you know it," she retorted. "There is a demon army out there. What did you expect to do? Just stroll out there, pluck your brother from right in front of them, and make it back without a scratch?"

Bernat stopped struggling, and she released him. Cautious, she knelt before him and lowered her head so that she was at eye level with him. "Tell me that's not what was going through your mind."

When Bernat finally met her gaze, his eyes were brimming with tears. "Did you see what he did to Turi? He looked like he was barely breathing."

"I did see. But I couldn't let you do it, Bernat." She grabbed his hand and placed it on the small bulge in her lower abdomen. "Not without you knowing what you were leaving behind."

His eyes rounded at the corners as he slowly understood what she was saying.

"You're—We're—" he stuttered, the words failing him.

"You're going to be a father," she said, the relief of finally getting to tell him washing over her.

He pulled her into his arms and slammed his lips to hers, his mouth punishing as the fire within him burned down her throat and consumed her whole.

She let herself drown in that feeling of being completely owned by him.

When he broke away, he pressed his palms to either side of her face. "A father?" he whispered, his voice so full of hope.

She nodded. "Now, do you understand? I wasn't about to let you throw your life away on a doomed mission."

His brows knitted together as he winced, the agony of his loss so great that she felt a twin pain in her own heart. "We have to save him," he said, his voice breaking at the end. "He's the reason we made it out of there. Why I'm here. If it weren't for him, I'd still be there in that cage."

Solana knew the dangers of making a promise she couldn't keep. She wanted to rescue Turi as much as he did, but the odds didn't look good.

For now, Arlando was injured. She owed thanks to Yari for that.

Though she couldn't tell from the distance, she had initially thought the dagger had pierced his heart. But no one could get back up after being stabbed in the heart, so she had to assume that Yari had missed. But barely.

His wound was clearly bad enough that he was forced to retreat. But for how long? That was the real question.

"We'll do everything we can to save him," she said, meaning every word.

She would do everything to return Bernat's family to him. But not at the expense of Bernat's life nor her own or anyone else's for that matter. Especially if that meant a doomed mission.

Defeating Arlando and breaking the curse was the priority. She had a feeling Turi would understand her choice. He must have known what he was doing. She had to trust that and trust his wishes.

He'd wanted to see his brothers free, even if that came at the cost of his own life.

She wouldn't waste his sacrifice if it came down to it.

Chapter Thirty-One

Yari

Yari stood in the center of the room, surrounded by a smattering of cheers and loud applause.

She didn't know what to feel. On one hand, they had repelled Arlando and his demon army. But the cost was great—and he had gotten away.

She still felt weak from the blood magic she'd used to help the others escape Arlando's castle. So, she'd gone out to investigate when she'd woken in some kind of infirmary, alone and full of questions.

She hadn't expected to walk in on utter chaos. Soldiers ran at their commanders' orders, weaponry exchanged hands and calls for order filled the air.

She had found her way up onto the ramparts and had done so without being stopped. She supposed there were bigger things for the soldiers and guards to worry about than a blood-stained ghost of a woman wandering around.

Yet, her heart had stopped when she'd looked across the landscape to see row upon row of demons, neatly organized and ready for battle.

At the head of it all had been Arlando sitting atop his white stallion, and at his side, strapped to a pole and carried by a cart, had been Turi.

She felt her stomach turn as the vivid memory of Turi battered and broken assaulted her. The sight of his near-lifeless body, a pool of blood congealing at his feet, made her want to scream. His chin rested against his chest like a fallen angel, his wrists bound together with rope soaked and dripping with blood.

She didn't know what overcame her at that moment. She'd been filled with rage and despair at knowing that Turi hadn't made it out with her and the others.

She'd failed him.

Her blood boiled beneath her skin, and she'd grabbed a dagger from a soldier standing watch along the ramparts.

"Hey!" he cried in shock, seeing her for the first time. "What are you doing?"

The blade glinted in the pale light as she lifted it above her right hand. She pushed the sharp edge into her skin with a determined grip and gritted teeth. A bright red line blossomed in the center of her palm, and crimson droplets clung to the metal. She ran her fingers along the handle, smearing the blade in a thick coating of her blood.

She tightened her grip on the dagger, raised it high above her head in a powerful arc, and locked eyes with Arlando. Her energy crackled the way the air trembles just before a storm as she poured every ounce of her being into a vengeful oath, declaring that if Arlando did indeed possess a heart, it would be pierced by her weapon and all the force of her seething wrath.

The dagger wasn't the same as a tlazon, and she was horribly out of practice—not that she'd ever been a very good shot to begin with—but she put her faith in the magic she'd just begun to wield. Trusted that it would respond to her intention. Prayed to any Saint that would listen to help her succeed.

With a flick of her wrist, she flipped the dagger so that she held the blade between her thumb and forefinger and hurled it across the expanse.

It seemed to hang in the air for an eternity, each rotation revealing a glint of its razor-sharp blade, a lethal rose sailing toward Arlando with deadly grace.

Arlando's eyes widened as he saw the silver glint of the dagger arc through the air towards him. He tried to twist away, but it was too late—the blade embedded itself in his chest, knocking him off his horse.

A cruel smile twisted up the corners of her mouth as she watched him crash to the ground, arms flailing and eyes wild.

Knowing him, he would take the blow straight to his sensitive pride.

She hadn't meant to miss. She had meant to strike Arlando in his heart and end him once and for all.

Yet, she'd failed and, in doing so, had also failed Turi.

Rage coursed through her veins like liquid fire, and all she could think about was the retribution it would take to finally bring her justice to life.

Despite Arlando retreating several hours ago, the memories continued to plague her as the residents of La Aguilera rejoiced.

The crowd celebrating the victory over Arlando's retreat started to disperse, leaving Yari sitting alone at a table tucked in the corner.

Bernat stepped forward and pulled her into a hug, but Yari felt nothing. She had no energy left for emotions. Instead, she could only think about the fact that Turi had been left behind.

"Why?" she said finally, pushing Bernat away. "Why did you leave him?"

Bernat's eyes were sad. "It wasn't my choice," he said. "Mauri said that it was Turi's decision to stay, to hold Arlando back. To give us all a chance to escape. Turi thought it was the only way."

Yari had passed out after asking Erasmo to find Aurelia and Turi. So she hadn't been awake to see just how dire the situation had become.

Still, it didn't make Yari feel any less guilty.

"I'd like to be alone now," she said quietly, her voice barely audible over the din of the crowd.

Bernat nodded and squeezed her hand before leaving her alone.

Yari sat at the table, staring blankly at the spilled beer on the wooden surface. Her mind was a mess of emotions and thoughts. She wished she could have done more to save Turi, to save everyone. But she couldn't change what had happened.

Yari stood up from the table and made her way out of the dining hall. She didn't know where she was going or cared to know, for that matter. She wanted to be anywhere but here.

As she rounded a corner, she heard quiet sobs inside a room. She hesitated for a moment before pushing the door open. Inside, she saw Aurelia sitting in the corner of the room, her head buried in her hands.

Yari's heart broke at the sight. She could only imagine the pain Aurelia must be feeling. She'd overheard talk about what Arlando had done to her mother, Pilar.

Without a word, Yari walked over to Aurelia and sat beside her. Aurelia didn't look up, but Yari could see the tears streaming down her face.

"I'm so sorry," Yari whispered, touching Aurelia's shoulder. "I wish I could have done more to save your mother."

Aurelia shook her head, her voice muffled. "It's not your fault. You didn't know. How could you?" She wiped her nose on her sleeve. "You saved us from Arlando."

"But I didn't save Turi," Yari said, feeling the weight of her failure. "I don't know if he's even alive."

Aurelia lifted her head, her eyes red and puffy. "He's alive. For now," she said, her voice shaking. "Arlando will use him. Though, for what, I can't even imagine."

Yari felt hopeless inside. She couldn't help but think of all the ways Turi could be suffering, all the ways she could have saved him if she'd just been strong enough.

Commotion from outside the manor made her and Aurelia look up. A horn blared, and shouting ensued.

"Another attack?" Yari asked, already getting to her feet to find something to defend herself with.

Aurelia tilted her head to the side and listened to the horn. "No. Someone's returned," she said, her voice lifeless.

Yari's heart skipped a beat. She wondered who could have returned and whether it was good or bad news. She followed Aurelia out of the room and down the hallway, past other soldiers and survivors who were also curious about the commotion.

As they reached the manor's entrance, Yari saw a familiar figure approaching.

She blinked a few times to make sure that her eyes weren't playing tricks on her.

Kiki let the grumpy man named Erasmo help her down from her horse. She wore her Slayer leathers and was outfitted in weapons from head to toe.

Yari's heart swelled with relief at the sight. For months, she'd wondered about her best friend. Hoped that she was safe. Cared for. Healthy.

And now, here she was.

Yari didn't realize that her feet had started moving. But before she knew it, she stood just behind Erasmo, a mere few feet from Kiki.

Kiki didn't recognize her at first, her eyes scanning over her before snapping back to her face.

"Yari?" Kiki breathed, her voice soft and her mouth open in awe.

Yari nodded, tears streaming down her face. "Kiki," she said, her voice choked with emotion. "I thought I'd never see you again."

Kiki rushed forward and hugged Yari tightly. "I'm sorry," she said, pulling back to look at Yari's tear-streaked face. "I'm so sorry for every-thing!"

Kiki's arms were bands wrapped around Yari's shoulders, strong and reassuring. "I promise to never leave your side again," she whispered into Yari's ear.

Yari pulled back and looked at Kiki, marveling at her friend and the clear changes in her. It was clear to her that Kiki had found whatever it was that she'd been missing, and she was now whole.

"Don't make promises you can't keep," Yari whispered. "You're not the only one that's changed since we last saw each other."

Kiki twirled her fingers in a strand of Yari's now silvered hair. "I can see that," she muttered, her eyes filling with tears.

"Where's Luna?" Yari asked, her throat tightening with emotion.

"Right here," Luna spoke up, the unhinged man, Mauri, standing right next to her.

Yari threw herself into Luna's arms, and she began sobbing all over again.

She had missed her best friends so much that it felt like a part of her had been missing ever since they were separated.

Luna hugged her tightly, tears streaming down her own face. "I can't believe you're really here," she said in a soft voice, squeezing Yari's shoulders gently.

"Me neither," Yari said as she pulled away, wiping the tears from her eyes.

Erasmo and Mauri watched the women in quiet understanding, both too emotional to say more than a few words of welcome.

Finally, Kiki stepped forward, her voice full of emotion as she pulled Yari and Luna into another hug. "It's so good to finally see you safe and sound."

"It's good to be here," Yari said as she gestured around the manor courtyard. "Though, this place looks like it has seen its fair share of trouble."

Yari let Kiki usher her back into the manor and a sitting room where everyone took seats and listened as Kiki filled Yari in on everything that had happened since they had last seen each other: how she'd come after Yari with Luna and Turi in tow, how they'd met Aurelia, how they'd come to La Aguilera, how they'd planned to confront Arlando, how Kiki had almost died, how they'd been fighting to free Bernat, Erasmo, and Mauri, and how they learned of Yari's whereabouts and the depths of Arlando's scheming.

Yari filled Kiki and Luna in on what had happened when Arlando tried to attack and how she'd wounded him, driving him back in surrender.

Kiki's face fell at the mention of Turi and the state he'd been in.

"Was he... alive?" Kiki trailed off.

"Yes," Yari confirmed. "But barely."

Yari's fists clenched in anger and frustration. She couldn't believe Turi was still suffering because of Arlando's cruelty.

Erasmo shifted in his seat. "I'm sorry I couldn't get him out."

Yari snapped her gaze to Kiki's mate. "You mean how you left him."

Erasmo flinched, and Kiki frowned. "Turi stayed behind to give everyone else a better chance at escaping. Don't blame Erasmo for Turi's decision."

Yari averted her gaze but said with determination in her voice, "We have to save him."

Kiki nodded. "We've been working on a plan," she said, looking at Luna.

Luna took a deep breath and began to explain what they had come up with so far.

"So this star-tipped spear is supposed to be used for what exactly?" Yari asked.

Luna faltered and glanced at Mauri. "Well, we're not entirely sure yet. I haven't finished translating the book yet."

Yari nodded solemnly. She didn't want to say it out loud, but she felt like her friends were holding onto a prayer, nothing solid to actually work on.

"Can I see the book?" Yari asked.

Luna frowned in confusion but reached into her satchel and pulled out the old tome.

Yari took the book from Luna and opened it. She immediately noticed the strange dialect written in faded black ink.

"This is an ancient language," Yari said, turning the pages slowly.

Kiki and Luna exchanged a glance, but neither said a word. They had explained how they all had been trying to make sense of the words, and none of them had been successful.

Yari furrowed her brow in concentration as she continued to examine the text, and then suddenly, an idea overcame her.

But she didn't want to test her theory here with everyone watching.

"Can I keep it for now?" Yari asked. "Just for the night?"

Luna nodded her head, her brows still furrowed. "Sure, if you really want to."

"I do," Yari said, standing up and leaving them in the sitting room, no doubt watching her walk away with dumbfounded expressions.

Once she reached the makeshift infirmary in the bowels of the manor, she sat on her cot and opened the book in her lap.

She reached for a piece of splintered wood nearby and pricked her finger on it. She used the blood to draw three symbols on her palm - symbols that she didn't know how she knew, but it was like it was written on her very bones.

Once she'd finished drawing them, Yari's eyes clouded, and her vision cleared when she looked back at the text.

She began reading aloud from the book, translating each sentence as she went along.

The star-tipped spear had been created to beat back the darkness of the world and could only do so when it touched that darkness directly.

The book explained a powerful ritual that would cleanse the darkness from those affected. Still, there was only one problem: the ritual demanded the willing sacrifice of a repentant person. Someone who had done much wrong and wanted to make it right.

The only person she could think of that fit that description was Arlando himself, but he'd never admit that everything he'd done had been wrong.

Still, this was something and much more to work off of than what Luna had deciphered.

Yari closed the book and tucked it safely under her cot. She knew that this was something she couldn't do alone. She needed Kiki, Luna, and even Erasmo if they were to succeed in rescuing Turi and defeating Arlando for good.

The night was long and restless as Yari tossed and turned, her mind racing with thoughts of the ritual and how they would carry it out. But eventually, exhaustion overtook her, and she fell into a deep sleep.

The next morning, Yari woke up feeling revitalized and more determined than ever to save Turi and put an end to Arlando's tyranny. She returned to the dining hall and found Kiki, Luna, and Erasmo already up and ready to start the day.

"Good morning," Luna said with a smile as she poured Yari a cup of hot coffee.

Yari took the cup gratefully and sat down at the table. "I think I know how to end the curse and defeat Arlando."

Chapter Thirty-Two

Luna

Luna's eyes widened in surprise, and the coffee she poured sloshed over the cup's rim. Kiki reacted quickly, grabbing the carafe and deftly tipping it back upright to stop the hot liquid from spilling across the table.

The sun shone through the window, making Yari's silver-white hair sparkle like a star. She stood confidently and raised her voice to be heard over the clamor of conversation in the room. "I know how to break the curse," she said.

A chorus of gasps and questions swept the room like a powerful wave.

Yari seemed unaffected by the raised voices and theories being thrown her way. It was as if she'd created a shield around herself, letting each inquiry aimed like a tlazon fall to her feet in a heap.

After the shock and seeing the seriousness in Yari's eyes, Luna shouted over the chaos. "Quiet! Yari is the only one who should be talking right now. The rest of you, keep your mouths shut."

Everyone in the hall began muttering to each other, and Mauri pounded his fist against the table, shaking the plates and silverware. "Don't make her ask you again. You won't like the results," he threatened, a low growl rumbling through his chest.

Luna felt a surge of appreciation for his interference, especially when those mutters trickled into silence.

Smoothing down the front of her dress, she clasped her hands before her. "The floor is yours, Yari."

Yari gave her an appreciative nod and turned to face the rest of the people in the hall. "I've been studying the text that Luna has been working to translate, and I believe I've found the answer—"

Juan Martín stabbed his fork into the wood of the table. "Who is this frail little girl standing before us?" he asked, his stern gaze meeting Luna's. "I do not know this child. Where did she come from? Where has she been this whole time that we've been interpreting the ancient text?"

Luna didn't blame Juan Martín for his harsh reaction, but she knew he'd trust her word. "To answer your first two questions, Juan Martín. This is my friend, Yari," Luna began to explain. "She was taken captive by Arlando and escaped with Bernat, Mauri, and Erasmo." She met Yari's gaze and tilted her head in curiosity. "As for your third question, we'll have to get the answer from Yari directly."

Yari inhaled deeply and began unwrapping the linen bandage around her left hand. She held her palm up when the dressing was off for all to see. In the center of her palm were the fading scars of multiple slashes through her skin.

Luna's mouth fell open at the sight of the scarred-over skin. She'd bound that hand herself just days ago when Yari first arrived. There was no way she could have healed so quickly.

"During my time as Arlando's prisoner, I learned a little about the blood magic he uses." A collective gasp of shock and fear rolled through the room. "Magic that I used to stab him when he was at our gates," Yari added, accentuating each word.

The room erupted in incredulous murmurs, and some people even began backing away from Yari.

But Luna could see the fierce determination in Yari's eyes and knew that she wasn't done yet. "You have every right to fear blood magic and to fear me," she said, raising her voice. "But you must trust me to end the curse and defeat Arlando once and for all."

"What does blood magic have to do with breaking the curse," Giselle spoke up, her eyes narrowed on Yari.

Yari tilted her chin in the air and continued. "Blood magic is the key to ending the curse. For it was with blood magic the curse was created, and it can only be broken with blood magic."

She continued, "I used this magic to interpret the text last night, and you've been on the right track with the star-tipped spear. It has the power to contain the darkness within. But it needs to be wielded by someone with blood magic in their veins."

Luna didn't like the sound of using the same magic that Arlando used. Nor did she like that Yari had taken the book last night and hid her intentions. Luna knew that Yari had endured a tremendous amount of trauma while she was Arlando's prisoner, but she hadn't realized how much her friend had changed until this moment.

Her heart ached at seeing the physical changes that Yari had under-gone—clearly, those changes weren't just superficial.

Yari turned slowly on her heel so that everyone could hear. "But the spear isn't enough. The prophecy states, 'For love was sacrificed at the start, so too shall love be sacrificed at the end.' Arlando has taken this to mean that he and each of the Ozero princes must sacrifice their mates to break the curse. But he has already met the conditions set forth by the prophecy."

"How?" Kiki asked, her tone sharp.

"The curse can only be broken by a sacrifice of love," Yari said softly. "But it doesn't have to be a sacrifice of romantic love. It can be a sacrifice of any kind of love."

Yari closed her eyes and took a deep breath. "Arlando betrayed his brotherly love for Bernat, Erasmo, and Turi when he chose his wicked path. He knowingly deceived and tortured them to fulfill his plan," she continued. "He is blind to all the pain he has caused and is single-minded in his goal. In effect, he has sacrificed his love for them in favor of his own desires."

There was a moment of stunned silence before Kiki spoke up. "If the conditions of the prophecy have been met, then why isn't the curse broken yet?"

Yari's lips turned up at the corners the slightest bit. It was a motion so faint that Luna almost didn't recognize it. "Arlando must die for the curse to be broken."

Gasps of shock and astonishment went all around the room as Yari's words sank in. Luna felt her heart drop at the thought of taking another life, even if it was Arlando's. She looked around the room and saw that the same fear was reflected in the faces of the others.

Arlando was powerful, and killing him would be no easy feat.

"But how do we kill him?" asked Mauri, his voice low and dangerous. "As much as I hate that fucker, he isn't easy to bring down. Trust me, I tried."

Yari looked at him with a steady gaze. "That's where I come in. I know a way to harness the power of the star-tipped spear to weaken him enough for me to land the killing blow."

Luna felt a shiver run down her spine at the thought of using the same magic that had caused so much destruction against the one who had unleashed it.

Again, The room fell silent, this time with a weighty sense of finality. Luna could see the emotions that flickered across everyone's faces - shock, disbelief, and a tinge of fear. But even amidst the heavy silence, she could sense a growing determination, a sense of purpose that was slowly building up within everyone.

This was the answer they'd been looking for. And here it was, laid out for them on a silver platter.

"We need to act fast," Yari said, her voice ringing out with a newfound conviction. "Arlando is not one to sit idle. He will be coming for us soon."

"You're right," Mauri said, his voice low and determined. "We can't let him catch us off-guard."

Solana, who'd been silent up to that point, stood up and pressed her palms into the table. She looked at each territory leader one by one. "Prepare your people. We attack in the morning."

CHAPTER THIRTY-THREE

KIKI

The air was heavy with anticipation, and the heavy fog in the air made the bristling emotions that ran through their army even more magnified.

What they were about to embark on was no simple feat. Laying siege to Arlando's castle and taking his demon army head-on was no mere skirmish. The consequences of success or failure would echo for generations to come.

The importance of their task weighed heavily on them all. This was more than just a life and death matter. It was a matter that would forge the destiny of the entire Ozero kingdom and all who called her home.

Kiki tried to keep her mind focused on the future task at hand. Break through the front lines and get Yari in front of Arlando.

Their entire plan hinged on giving Yari the opening she needed to trap Arlando with the star-tipped spear and then start the ritual that would end the curse for good.

Or at least, that was their desperate hope.

Luna hadn't stopped combing through the book of rituals, even after Yari had completed her translation. Kiki knew that anxiety rode her friends, and they just wanted to ensure they hadn't missed anything.

The fabric of their very existence was riding on an accurate translation of the ritual and Yari's execution of it.

Kiki stole a brief, furtive glance at Yari to her left as she rode a tall gray mare, her posture confident and dignified. Her gaze was set ahead, her expression unreadable and unyielding.

She didn't share Kiki's last glance.

Her hands held her horse's reigns loosely, and the star-tipped spear lay strapped across her back.

She wore a new set of leathers that hugged her petite figure. Her pale silver hair was divided into twin braids that cascaded down her back and ended just above her waist.

Kiki felt a pang of regret knowing the old Yari, her once timid and often easily scared friend, was gone.

Yari had entered the Cicatrix as one person and had evolved into another.

Kiki didn't know if she had any right to mourn the loss of that girl. Rather, she grieved for her friend and the suffering she'd endured. Suffering that had changed her.

There was one undeniable thing, though. Yari had a choice: to either shatter under her circumstances or to rise from the ashes of her abuse and become something truly fearsome.

She'd chosen the latter.

And now, she was a sight to behold.

Kiki had always seen Yari as someone she had to protect and shield.

But today, Yari was the dagger they were sending into the heart of darkness itself. Aimed to kill and destroy.

And she certainly looked the part.

"We're ready," Yasir's voice broke Kiki out of her line of thoughts.

She turned to Erasmo's sandy-haired cousin and did her best to give him a reassuring grin. But it came out more like a grimace, and she decided to drop the pretense. Yasir was a warrior like herself. He didn't need false assurances.

Kiki maneuvered her horse so that she came to Solana's side.

"It's time," she said, tone heavy and serious.

Solana glanced to her right, where Bernat sat proudly atop his own horse.

He wore the traditional demon slayer leathers, complete with some additional bandoliers full of obsidian tlazons, an extra pair of obsidian machetes strapped cross-ways to his back, and a bow and quiver full of arrows slung over his shoulder.

Solana bore just as many weapons, if not more. Her leather pants bore modifications that housed several obsidian throwing knives.

Kiki felt a surge of pride rise in her stomach at seeing the Commander outfitted so heavily with weaponry.

She never thought Solana had cared much for her. Had been convinced that the Commander only had it out for her and wanted to torture her.

But over the last few months, she'd grown to respect the woman with ice in her veins.

Everything Solana Ramirez did was for a reason. Her moves were carefully calculated and weighed, then re-weighed. She never acted out of spontaneity and always had an endgame in mind.

Kiki could finally see that everything Solana had done in the past was to mold Kiki into a better demon slayer.

Because of this woman's faith in her that Kiki had grown to become one of the fiercest demon slayers to live. She had earned the name 'The Sicario.'

And finally, Kiki could admit that if she survived this day, it would be because Solana had trained her to endure and persevere.

"Commander," Kiki whispered. She didn't know if she'd have a chance to say this later and didn't want to regret not doing so. At least once.

Solana cut her ice-blue eyes to Kiki, her brows raised expectantly.

"Thank you," Kiki said with a bow of her head and a fist raised to her heart in salute.

The corners of Solana's lips lifted in a smile, and the corners of her eyes crinkled. "You're welcome."

A moment full of emotion passed between the two women and all the things they didn't have time to say and the things they may never admit to one another.

Solana gently tugged the reins and maneuvered her horse so that she was facing their army.

"Today, we make history as our very actions on this day will reverberate through the entirety of Ozero. Our mission is far from simple, but it can be boiled down to one basic premise. Defeat the demon army and grant an opening for Yarixa to infiltrate the castle so that she may perform the ritual that will end the Ozero Curse."

The army bristled with anticipation, and many of the soldiers shared glances with those next to them in silent exchanges of encouragement.

"Today we take the battle to Arlando, and we will end this day in victory," Solana roared, her ice-blue eyes blazing with fierce determination as she unsheathed her machete from its leather scabbard and brandished it in the air. Sunlight glinted off its edge as she yelled, "Now, who is with me?"

The army responded by drawing their swords, metal ringing against scabbards. They banged their weapons against their shields and roared their agreement.

"Let's kill some demons," Solana snarled as she guided her horse to face forward and led the charge across the countryside.

Kiki shared a glance with Erasmo and felt her heart soar at the look of pride on his face. This was their queen they were following into battle, and she'd never felt more proud in her life to be part of something. Not even when she'd been in the Demon Corps.

This was different. This was a fight for the very bonds that tied them all together. The threads that wove through their lives in a messy tangle of destiny.

With a battle cry of her own, Kiki urged her horse into a run, and together, she and Erasmo led their team across the barren plains that would lead them to Arlando.

The horses' hoofbeats echoed in time with her heart as they galloped towards Arlando's towering castle.

The air was pregnant with excitement from her soldiers as they drew nearer, but it was also tempered with a healthy dose of fear.

They'd win nothing today if they went into this with raging egos and didn't look after themselves and each other.

The castle came into view, its looming silhouette making their approaching army seem like a horde of ants.

She raised her machete over her head and pointed it forward as if she could pierce the castle's battlements and raze them to the ground in a single swipe.

She shouted a cry of defiance and determination that was taken up by her group of soldiers and echoed back as far as the last rider.

It was time to lay siege to Arlando's castle and end this.

As if Arlando had anticipated their attack, a massive army of demons poured out from the castle's main gates.

Demons quite literally skittered out of the castle from any available outlet. Their twisted forms seemed to slide out from every crack and crevice, emerging from windows high above and slithering out of small side gates. The air was filled with their terrible screeches and the smothering smell of sulfur.

Her heart raced as a flicker of fear sparked in her chest. There were so many. She quickly pushed it aside as she signaled for her team to form a tight line behind her.

The demons charged towards them, their eyes glowing with an infernal light. Kiki took a deep breath, steadying herself for the fight to come.

As the demons closed in, she sprang forward, meeting them head-on. Her machete flashed in the sunlight as she swung it in a wide arc, cleaving through demon flesh like it was water.

The two sides of each army clashed with ferocity, claws, and talons clashing against armor in a dizzying array of shrieking and snarling.

The air was filled with screams and cries as both sides fought for survival.

Kiki glanced at Yari to find she was holding her own just fine. Yari had always been timid in the way she fought. But no longer.

Yari bared her teeth in a fearsome snarl as she swung her twin machetes with such fervor that she cut through a pair of demons at the same time and sliced the heads off two more in her recovering upswing.

Nearby, Erasmo shifted partially and tore through the demons with his fangs.

Together, their team held their own against the onslaught, pressing forward inch by inch.

The demons were relentless, with their grotesque forms and warped features. Kiki's machete sliced through their flesh easily, but they kept coming. She began to feel overwhelmed at the sheer number of them.

Kiki wiped the sweat off her forehead as she fought off a horde of demons. The stench of blood and decay filled her nostrils, churning her stomach. She was surrounded by chaos, screams, and the sounds of weapons clashing.

"This is taking too long," Erasmo shouted, coming up close to Kiki as he swiped his talons across the neck of an oncoming demon.

She knew he was right. They needed to get Yari inside the castle. That was their team's purpose.

But a window of opportunity had yet to open up that would grant them the chance.

"Leave it to me," Yari shouted as she plunged her machete into a demon's chest, and it exploded in a cloud of black ichor.

Flicking the excess demon blood from her blades, she sheathed her twin machetes and drew a dagger from her belt.

Kiki realized what her friend had in mind too late, and she lunged forward. "No, Yari!"

But she wasn't fast enough.

Yari sliced the dagger across her palm, and a great pulse shook the air around her, sending Kiki and Erasmo tumbling back.

Kiki scrambled to her feet to see that Yari had cut a path through the demons leading right to the castle gates.

Yari spared Kiki one last glance, her eyes full of determination right before she dove through the opening she'd created, and it closed with demon bodies.

Kiki was cut off from her friend as a demon hissed and went for her neck.

Kiki dispatched the demon easily, but she'd lost sight of Yari.

"What the fuck?" Erasmo growled.

She was still in shock over losing Yari through the horde. This wasn't the plan. They were meant to breach the castle together.

"That wasn't the plan!" Erasmo added, his voice hoarse from shouting over the snarling and snapping jaws edging closer.

No. It wasn't. She just hoped that Yari knew what she was doing and that she'd succeed.

"We'll catch up with her," Kiki said, turning to her soldiers. "Cut down as many as you can, but we must push forward."

Her team fought through the demon army with renewed vigor, leaving a trail of black demon ichor behind them.

Chapter Thirty-Four

Yari

She'd always been faster than Kiki. That was one advantage of being the one who was always afraid. She'd learned how to duck and dodge better than anyone else.

She raced through the path she'd created and shoved her way through the front doors of the castle that were partially left ajar, likely from the demons that Arlando had sent out to meet her and the army from La Aguilera.

If there was one thing she knew about Arlando, it was that he was arrogant. He wouldn't expect anyone to make it through his demon army. In fact, he'd be so confident in his impending victory that he'd leave the castle's interior defenseless.

Just as she suspected, the main hall was empty. Not a single demon in sight.

She made her way to his office, where she knew he'd be standing on the balcony, watching a safe distance away from the battle he had orchestrated below.

Though she didn't see any demons, she knew Arlando to be a treacherous, devious snake and kept to the shadows anyway.

Reaching the top of the stairs of the West Wing, she moved on silent feet as she neared the door to his office.

Peeking through the open door, she found him exactly where she knew he'd be.

She hadn't expected to find Turi's broken body in a heap in the corner of the room.

Her heart leaped into her throat at the sight.

His shirt was a shredded mess that hung from its threads alone. His pants were hardly better, the dark color stained with the telltale signs of blood.

His bare feet were covered in dirt and blood as if Arlando had made him walk in the snow without any boots.

Anger rose in her chest at the thought.

She quickly went over the ritual in her mind, knowing she couldn't get any details wrong.

She took a steadying breath and steeled her spine as she crossed the threshold into the office.

As soon as she did, Arlando whipped around, his eyes blazing with blue fire as he took her in. The only sign that he was, in fact, surprised to see her was the way his eyes rounded in the corners.

He hadn't expected her. Of course, he hadn't. He expected an easy victory today. He likely thought he'd capture her and her friends and sacrifice them as he had always planned.

Why would he ever fear Yarixa?

She was nothing to him.

He'd broken her. Both in body and in spirit.

Or so he thought.

She couldn't help the smirk that lifted the corners of her lips. She liked knowing that she'd become a pest in Arlando's carefully laid-out plan.

As she slipped further into the office, the star-tipped spear in hand, Arlando chuckled.

"Have you come to kill me, little mouse?"

Her lips curled back in a feral grin. "Yes," she hissed, her steps light as she moved around his desk, stalking him like a predator would its prey. "You'll suffer for everything you've done. For the pain you've caused. For the lives you've taken. For what you did to me. You'll die today, that I promise you."

Arlando clapped his hands slowly. "And my brothers sent a little mouse to do all that? They must have been really desperate if you're their only hope."

She was done listening to him. She lunged forward with the spear, aiming for his heart.

Arlando dodged her attack with a growl.

"I see you've forgotten your lessons," he sneered. "Perhaps I will give you a refresher."

She tightened her grip on the spear and circled around him, ready for his next move. She knew he was powerful, but she also knew he was arrogant. And that would be his downfall.

Arlando lunged at her with surprising speed, but she sidestepped him and struck his back with the tip of her spear.

A cry of pain slipped past his lips as the spear cut across his chest, leaving a tear through his white jacket and a line of blood beneath.

He stumbled forward, but quickly recovered and turned to face her again.

"You think you can defeat me?" he spat, his eyes glowing brighter. "Do I have to remind you how powerful I am?"

Oh, but she was counting on it. The spear would only work if he shifted.

Rather than waste her breath responding to his taunt, she lunged at him again. This time, he was ready for her, and he caught the spear between his talons as they shot through his skin.

"You really thought this needle could kill me?" Arlando hissed. "I'm going to enjoy sacrificing you to end the curse, Yarixa. You've disappointed me so terribly."

She eyed his claws as they slipped along the spear. That wasn't enough. She needed him to fully shift.

She had to find a way to rile him up even more. Get him truly angry.

With a sudden jerk of her arm, she freed the spear from Arlando's grip and stalked around him.

"Before you do that, I think you owe me an explanation for what you did to me. For why you made me fall in love with the ghost of you. Why did you take your brother's mate for your own? Why did you betray Tomás." Arlando's eyes narrowed, and a derisive laugh slipped past her lips. "Didn't think I knew about that, did you? You see, things didn't add up. And while you had me locked in your room waiting to know my fate, I had a lot of time to think about Tomás coming after me. Want to know what I couldn't understand? Why you killed him. He said he did everything you asked. You could have continued your little charade with me had you not shown your true colors that day. So why? Why kill him?"

Arlando glared at her but remained silent.

"Answer me!" she shouted. "After everything, I think I at least deserve to know why you did any of it."

"I will tell you why and sate your curiosity, my little mouse. And then I will bend you over that desk there and destroy you from the inside out while your mate watches." He flicked his gaze at Turi and spat in his direction.

Yari didn't take her eyes off Arlando for a second. Still, a faint groan from behind her confirmed that Turi was at least alive, even if he was barely hanging on.

"Even now, the fool thinks he can save you," Arlando taunted. "Such arrogance."

Yari scoffed. He was one to talk. "Answer the questions, Arlando."

He rolled his eyes as he took a slow step to the left, forcing her to move to the right to keep him directly in front of her.

"I had a mate of my own once. She was everything I could have ever desired. She had so much faith in me. Her love—" he inhaled deeply as if he could smell the remnants of his mate. "Her love was so innocent. She was pure. Like you, she was so trusting. So ready to look for the good in others. But I knew I had to end the curse. And since none of my brothers were willing to offer the necessary sacrifices, I tried to do it alone. Even though a small part of my soul died at just the thought of causing her harm." His face twisted into a mask of agony. "So I muted our bond as much as I could—even at the end, she still looked at me with so much trust. So much love. Right up until I ripped her heart out."

Yari felt sick to her stomach. She could see through him now. He'd brutally murdered his own mate for his foolish faith in the prophecy, and since she was gone, he'd tried to fill that void with Yari.

"And Tomás?" she asked.

"Tomás was a loose end that I couldn't keep around anymore. And you were asking too many questions. You were starting to lose your trust in me. I thought if I recreated the events that earned me your trust in the beginning, you'd stop prying."

Yari shook her head. After he rescued her from the demons, she felt filled with gratitude toward him. In her eyes, he'd been her savior. He'd fed and clothed her and made sure she had everything she could possibly want.

He'd given her the bare minimum and she'd soaked it all up as if he'd showered her in silver and gold.

"But your plan didn't work," she growled.

Arlando bared his teeth, and she noticed that his canines were lengthening as his shift slowly took over.

"No. You were horrified," he scoffed. "Instead of falling into my arms with gratitude, you were ready to run from me."

"Then you raped me," she said, her voice steady despite how her stomach roiled at the painful memory.

"I own you, little mouse. You're mine to do with as I please."

"I never belonged to you, Arlando," Yari hissed.

Arlando's eyes flashed to Turi in the corner, and she stepped in his line of sight to shield him.

"Turi may be my mate, but that doesn't mean I belong to him either," she said, pointing the star-tipped spear at the center of his chest. "I belong to no one but myself."

"That's what *you* think," Arlando bellowed, and Yari braced herself for his attack.

She refused to let him see even a hint of fear. She bared her teeth at him, her determination stronger than ever.

He shifted mid-air, his body bursting with white fur as he tackled her to the ground.

Arlando chuckled as he pressed her into the ground. "You are weak, little mouse. You always have been and always will be."

"You're wrong," she grunted at his weight on top of her. She angled the spear and drove it into his side, slipping the tip between his ribs and puncturing his lung.

Arlando screamed in agony as sparkles of golden light encircled the gash on his side. He fell back, contorting and shifting until his body returned to its human shape. But still, the wound remained wide open.

He fell onto his hands and knees and vomited black demon ichor.

"What did you do to me?" he gasped between bouts of retching.

"I trapped you in your human form and pierced the darkness that lives in you, holding it under control," she said as she began to push the furniture out of the way.

She no longer needed to fear Arlando. He was as good as dead. Now, she needed to perform the ritual, and this would end.

"No, you can't," he panted, his eyes wild as he tried to hold his wound closed. Already, wisps of darkness were swirling out of him. "That's not possible."

"You're not the only one who can use blood magic," Yari said as she grabbed him by his arm and dragged him into the center of the room. "You'd be amazed at the wealth of knowledge you can find in a book."

"The Spirit Woman, she said—"

"The Spirit Woman gave you an answer. But there is more than one way to end this curse." She knelt down before him and sneered. "You killed your mate for nothing. For the words of a bitter and lonely woman."

Arlando let out a pathetic keening sound as he cradled the wound in his rib.

Commotion from outside the office made her snap her head up.

Perhaps Arlando had sent for backup after all.

She pushed up to her feet and unsheathed her twin machetes, ready to face any number of demons that might pour through that door.

She had to finish this.

This was her battle to end.

The door crashed open revealing Kiki, Erasmo, and Yasir covered in black demon ichor.

Kiki took one look at Arlando cowering on the floor, and she lowered her machete. She opened her mouth to speak, but her eyes said it all. She was proud of Yari.

"Brother," Arlando pleaded, crawling forward on his hands and knees toward Erasmo. "Save me. Don't let her do this. We can still end the curse. We'll find another way."

Erasmo crossed the room and gathered Turi in his arms. "What did he do to you?" he asked Turi, his voice laced with agony and concern.

"Brother!!" Arlando keened. "Help me!"

Erasmo hefted Turi into his arms and returned to Kiki's side. He looked down on Arlando and shook his head solemnly. "The curse has taken everything from us, even our brotherhood."

Arlando's face twisted in anger. "You fool!"

Kiki stormed up to Arlando, placed her boot on his face, and pushed him onto his back. "No, Arlando, it's you who are the fool."

"You should go," Yari jerked her chin to the door. "You won't want to see this." She spared Erasmo a glance, and Kiki nodded.

"The demons have scattered. We're chasing them down before they get too far," Kiki said. "We'll take care of Turi."

Yari nodded, and her best friend left the room. She spared one last glance before shutting the door behind herself.

Yari sheathed one of her machetes and used the other to reopen the wound in her palm.

Fresh blood blossomed, and she began to paint the runes into the floor in a circular pattern around Arlando.

"Please don't do this," Arlando pleaded.

"Funny, I recall begging you not to rape me with those same words. You didn't listen to me then, so I won't be listening to you now. Besides, you're getting exactly what you've always wanted. An end to the curse."

She continued her work before approaching him.

She drew a symbol in the center of his forehead and leaned back on her heels.

"You loved me," he said, his voice ragged and his eyes crazed. "Admit it. You did love me."

Yari shook her head. "I loved the idea of you. But it was a lie," she said, adding another symbol in blood to his left breast. "The thing about me that you took advantage of was the fact that I've always been considered weak for how willing I am to see the good in others. For being too trusting. For being quiet and shy." She added a third symbol to his right breast. "I trusted you, and you betrayed that trust. That was your first mistake."

She began to draw the needed symbols on her own forehead and shoulders, mirroring the ones she drew on him.

"Your second mistake was underestimating me. People like you always misjudge people like me. You think that just because we seek the light doesn't mean we know what it is to walk in the dark." She quirked her head as she re-checked the symbols. "What you don't realize is people like me know the darkness very well. It's in the darkness that we can be our true selves."

She sheathed her machete and positioned herself directly in front of him. "I suppose you saw yourself as the hero in the story you wrote for yourself."

Arlando's eyes flared with anger, and his lips curled back in a snarl.

A faint smile curled the corner of her mouth. "But every hero has a villain."

Before he could anticipate her next move, Yari plunged her hand into his chest. The same way she'd seen him do to Tomás. The way it had felt when he'd betrayed her in body and mind.

Arlando's eyes widened as she held his still-beating heart in her hand.

She leaned forward and whispered in his ear. "You made me your villain."

His hands reached out to grab her by the shoulders, but before he could touch her, she yanked his heart from his chest, leaving a gaping oozing cavity in its place.

Arlando stared at her as if he were in shock. Even in death, he still underestimated her.

His body slumped, and he fell to his side, his eyes still wide open and his mouth gaping.

Taking the heart, Yari murmured the words of the spell that would end the curse once and for all and replace it with a gift instead.

As the last words left her lips, she raised the bloody heart to her lips and sank her teeth into it.

This wasn't part of the spell that Luna had deciphered. Still, it was part of the spell that Yari had created to protect Ozero and the Ozetero men she'd come to know to be good, faithful, and loyal men. Men who'd have many challenges ahead of them as they rebuilt their kingdom.

This was her gift to them and to herself.

Chapter Thirty-Five

Kiki

Kiki's eyes scanned the battlefield as the sun fell over the horizon. The smell of sulfur and rotten eggs was fading away, and the remaining demons in Arlando's army had long since burst into clouds of black ash.

Soldiers were already combing through the carnage, seeking their wounded friends to take the infirmary tent or to remove their lifeless bodies from the field.

She felt a pang of sorrow for the fallen soldiers, but she knew that each one of them had been willing to give their lives for a chance at defeating Arlando. Like Kiki, each soldier had made their choice willingly.

They had done what was necessary in order to protect their people and the rest of Ozero from Arlando's tyranny. And now, with his army defeated, the inhabitants of Ozero could live without fear.

The burst of energy that had been pumping through her veins was fading, and exhaustion was settling in. She made her way back to the tent Luna had set up as the infirmary.

A long line of soldiers waited outside the tent, all wounded and tired. Most were sitting on the ground, trying to tend their comrades' wounds that didn't need a Healer right away, while others passed around flasks of alcohol and made conversation—anything to lighten the mood.

Though they'd won the battle, the atmosphere was still heavy as the cost of such a victory weighed on everyone's minds.

Solana exited the infirmary tent and motioned for Kiki to follow her.

"What can I do for the Supreme Queen?" Kiki asked, trying to keep her tone light and teasing. She rested her hand on the hilt of her machete. Though the battle was over, she felt comforted by the feeling of her weapon wrapped in her fingers.

"I want you to find Ramón and gather our people near those trees over there," Solana said, pointing to a grove of trees near the Winter Keep. "It's time for us to honor our dead."

Kiki was relieved to be given something to do. She hated feeling like she was useless.

The crowd began gathering before dusk with torches and flags in hand. Bernat stepped forward and raised his hand for silence.

His face was solemn, and his lips were pressed into a thin line. "What we accomplished today is nothing short of a great victory. Our kingdom has been freed of the darkness that has plagued it for more than a decade. It is not lost on me that I was not present at that time, and I thank each and every one of you for answering the call to arms when it came to your doorsteps. Ozero will forever be grateful to you and your sacrifice."

Soldiers began raising their fists to their chests one by one in salute to their king. Bernat acknowledged them all with a bow of his head before he continued. "It is also not lost on me that in our gravest moment, when my brothers and I were taken captive, the mantle of leadership fell to another. This person organized our efforts, strategized our plans, and ultimately led us to victory today. It seems only right that she be the one to honor our fallen warriors." He held out his hand for Solana to take.

Gripping his hand, she began to speak, her voice heavy with emotion.

Her voice was heavy with emotion as she began to speak. "Tonight, we honor those we have lost," she said solemnly. She paused for a moment, giving everyone time to reflect on the lives that had been taken that day before continuing. "We may not have known everyone by name," she continued, "But they are our brothers and sisters who fought alongside us today. We will never forget their sacrifice for the sake of Ozero's freedom from the curse that plagued it." She signaled for Kiki to step forward, and she did so with heavy steps.

Kiki handed Solana a torch that shone brightly in the night sky, its flaming orange light casting Solana's face in a beautiful glow. Solana turned to Bernat and lit his torch with her own, a spark of flame bursting to life. Bernat turned to Erasmo and repeated the process as every soldier held a flaming beacon one by one.

The reverence was palpable as everyone stood there for some time, watching their torches flicker in the night breeze and feeling an immense sense of respect for all those who paid the ultimate sacrifices.

Finally, when each soldier had lit their torch, Solana spoke again. "Let us never forget."

The soldiers responded in unison. "We will never forget."

The ceremony ended, and the crowd slowly began to disperse. Kiki caught up with Erasmo, and they walked silently for a few moments, each lost deep in their thoughts.

Finally, Kiki spoke. "How does it feel?" she asked. She knew Yari had broken the curse, but there had been a lot demanding their attention. Now, with the battle over, they could take the time to talk about the victory they'd won.

Erasmo's lips tugged into a smile. "It feels like freedom," he said, his voice tinged with relief. "I don't feel like I have something living under my skin, feeding my deepest, darkest, most depraved thoughts." He held out his hand and extended his talons past his knuckles. "It doesn't hurt anymore to do this."

Kiki's heart swelled at seeing the relief in Erasmo's eyes. "Are you happy with it though? You're not mad at Yari for what she did?"

"Mad?" Erasmo asked, his brows furrowed. "I'm overjoyed. I get all the advantages with none of the negatives."

She felt the tension in her shoulders ease up. "I'm relieved to hear you say it. I was afraid you'd be upset that you still had the shift."

Erasmo pulled her into his arms. "I've lived with the shift for longer than I haven't," he said, nuzzling his nose into her hair. "I think Yari did the right thing. She gave us a choice, one we didn't have at the start. Now, if we want to shift, we can. And for those who don't, they never have to."

Together, they approached a large tent that served as their central command center. Erasmo held the canvas open for Kiki to duck inside.

"There you two are," Bernat said as they entered.

Mauri and Luna were already inside, seated next to a low-burning fire. Turi sat propped up in a cot in the corner with Yari seated near his feet.

Kiki frowned at the intimateness she saw between Yari and Turi. She had never known the two of them to be so familiar, and a weird pang of—something—blossomed in her chest. She quickly shook the unwanted feeling away.

"What's wrong?" Erasmo asked, his black brows furrowing. "Did something happen?"

Bernat clapped his hands on Erasmo's shoulders and grinned. "No, all is well, brother. I just wanted you here. There is something important that I must do, and I want my brothers here to witness it."

Erasmo exchanged a curious glance with Kiki, but they didn't have to wait long to learn what Bernat was up to.

Bernat took Solana's hand in his and dropped down to one knee. "Solana Ramirez," he began. "You are the most magnificent woman I have ever met. You've shown me what it means to be strong and courageous against all odds. You've been my guiding star through all of my life's trials, and I cannot imagine my life without you. Will you do me the highest honor and become my wife?"

Kiki liked to think she was impervious to getting emotional, but seeing Bernat on one knee and the obvious glee blooming on Solana's face, she let herself get swept away in the moment.

She knew Solana would say yes. The Commander's feelings for Bernat were the Demon Corps' worst-kept secret.

Kiki felt a flutter of joy in her heart seeing Solana so happy. She tucked away the memory of this moment because she doubted Solana would ever publicly display so much emotion again.

"Yes," Solana gasped, her voice choking on what Kiki thought could be a sob. "A hundred times, yes!" she cried as she bent over and kissed Bernat fiercely.

Kiki stifled a laugh at the sight, and Erasmo wrapped an arm around her shoulders, and she let him pull her close. Leaning down, he pressed his lips to hers as they basked in the happiness emanating from Bernat and Solana.

"Get your own tent," Mauri growled with Luna tucked tightly at his side. "None of us want to see that shit." Luna jabbed him in the side and whispered something to him.

When Luna pulled away, Mauri's face had drained of color, and Kiki knew she'd have to catch up with Luna and force her friend to spill whatever secrets she held.

Bernat ignored Mauri, and Solana actually laughed as she said, "I think we might just listen to you for once, Mauri."

When Bernat and Solana left, Yari left Turi's side and nudged Kiki.

"Can I talk to you?" she asked, her soft voice a clever mask for the power that bubbled beneath her skin. She cast a glance at Erasmo and added, "Alone?"

"Sure," Kiki responded, allowing Yari to lead her out of the tent. "What's going on?"

Yari's face was serious as she said, "I have something to tell you that I haven't had a chance to share yet."

Kiki crossed her arms over her chest, that weird feeling from earlier worming its way into her heart. "Alright," she said warily.

"Before I tell you, I want to make myself clear that no matter how you react, it's not going to change anything."

Kiki's shoulders bowed forward as if she'd been punched in the gut. Kiki felt like Yari had just slapped her in the face. She wasn't used to this new version of her friend. It wasn't that she didn't like it; it was just that Yari was usually less assertive.

Recalling her promise to Luna that she'd try to listen better before reacting, she reached out and wrapped her hands around Yari's upper arms. "I promise to listen and not freak out like I usually do. It's something I'm working on."

The corner of Yari's lips quirked into a soft smile. "I know you are," she said fondly, her eyes sparkling.

"Whatever it is, it isn't going to change the fact that you're my family. My sister. So just tell me. I can handle it," Kiki said, forcing a note of confidence in her voice even as that green feeling continued to wrap around her heart.

Yari stared at Kiki silently for a long moment before saying, "Turi is my mate."

Kiki's mouth fell open as that feeling tightened around her heart and squeezed. "What?"

"The simplest way I can explain it is this: Arlando masked the bond I had with Turi and mirrored it to redirect to himself. He had already murdered his own mate and needed leverage to get you and Luna to cross the Cicatrix. I was the easiest target."

Or so he thought, Kiki thought with murderous glee.

Yari must have been able to read the intention in Kiki's eyes because she smiled again. "I know this news is probably awkward for you. It's a little strange for me as well—"

Kiki realized that the feeling coiling around her heart was that of jealousy. The feeling was foreign to her, and she fought against it, not wanting the emotion to dig its claws further into her heart. It was a strange feeling to have, and she realized she didn't want to feel it.

Yari and Turi had both been through so much. Of all people, they deserve to find some measure of happiness. Who better to find that happiness than in each other?

Kiki had been drawn to Turi because he was kind and attentive. But she suspected that even Turi could admit they'd had a stronger friendship than a romantic one.

Kiki didn't want Yari to feel awkward or keep things from her. She admired the courage her friend had to say the truth outright.

She cut Yari off with a fierce hug. "I'm happy for you," she whispered, tears welling in her eyes. "Truly, I am. You deserve all the good things this world has to offer. You deserve to be cared for, cherished, admired, and, above all, loved. Thank you for telling me. I wish you both all the happiness."

Yari melted into Kiki's embrace, and that little green feeling faded away, releasing Kiki's heart so that all that was left was pure love for her friend.

CHAPTER THIRTY-SIX

SOLANA

The morning sun filtered into the room, reflecting a ray of light across the mirror Solana gazed into.

She ran her hands down the silk bodice, her fingers tracing over the golden embroidery, and stopped at the swell of her growing belly.

Her hair cascaded around her shoulders in a curly riot of fire, and a gold coronet sat atop her head.

"You're almost ready," Yari said as she approached with a lace veil in her hands.

Solana couldn't explain the nervous feeling that was swirling inside of her. She knew today marked an important milestone for the new Ozero, but she would have preferred a smaller affair.

Instead, all the territory leaders and the Protectorate leaders of both East and West Ozero had been invited.

"You look like you're going to puke," Kiki said from where she lay sprawled on the bed. She was dressed in a blood-red gown with silver embroidery embellishing the skirt and bodice. She wore her short black hair down, and a silver coronet circled her head, denoting her status as a princess of Ozero.

"Kiki," Yari hissed, twisting to scowl. "You're not helping."

Luna rearranged Solana's dress, making sure that it didn't wrinkle. "You *are* looking a little green, Sol. Are the babies okay? Are you in any discomfort?"

"I can probably loosen the bodice here a bit," Yari offered, placing her hands on the sides of Solana's waist.

"I'm fine," Solana said, her eyes still taking in her reflection in the mirror. She couldn't recall a time when she'd ever looked at herself and found what stared back to be stunning. But now? She was speechless.

She'd been fighting her whole life. And though there was plenty to fight for, for the first time, she didn't need to carry her machete with her.

"Are you sure?" Yari asked, already kneeling to start undoing a seam. "Because I can be quick about it with a little help."

Solana knew Yari meant with a little help from her blood magic, but she still didn't like how comfortable Yari was with using it.

As it was, Solana liked the surety of things she understood and could control. She hadn't touched her own magic since the battle at Arlando's castle, and it wasn't something she wanted to use again.

Solana swatted their hands away. "Stop fussing over me. I said I'm fine."

"Better listen to her majesty before she bites you," Kiki drawled.

"You're getting yourself all wrinkled laying there like a drunken cat with your legs all sprawled," Luna bit out.

Kiki shrugged and shared a knowing look with Solana before continuing to play with a loose thread in the sheets.

Solana let Yari place the veil over her head and couldn't resist the urge to smile.

Here she was, on her wedding day, with the three women she'd grown to trust the most and had put all her faith in.

Together, they'd beaten all the odds.

Solana hadn't known what a family was like before the Cicatrix. And she'd filled that hole in herself with the camaraderie of the Demon Corps. But this, here, with these three women, this was different. This was family. United in spirit and blood.

Her hand unconsciously drifted to her belly, where she felt a flutter of movement and smiled. That family would soon be growing.

Getting up from the bed, Kiki came to stand behind her.

"You ready?" Kiki asked, a playful smirk on her lips. "I have our leathers ready if you change your mind," she added with a wicked gleam in her eyes.

Solana grinned at the joke and reached for Kiki's hand, gently squeezing it. "I'm ready."

If anyone had asked her months ago if she could have predicted that the canyon that separated her and Kiki Xochicale would ever close, she'd have told them they were delusional. But now? Now, she and Kiki had come to respect each other as much as they cared for the other.

With a smile and a quick nod, Kiki squeezed her hand back and left the room to arrange the beginning of the ceremony.

The inner courtyard had been completely renovated for the sake of today.

The maze of hedges had been razed to the ground and blossomed a lush garden full of flowers and singing birds in its place.

In the center of it all, an arch stood proudly with flowers and vines draping the trellis.

As Solana made her way down the aisle, her eyes caught on the man standing there under the arch—waiting for her.

He was dressed in a blue jacket and matching pants that hugged his muscular frame in the best way possible. Golden embroidery in the same pattern as her dress embellished his pants' legs and the sleeves' sides. Atop his head was a crown identical to hers, glittering in the sunlight.

From the start, Bernat always had a way of taking her breath away. She'd been fond of him and fallen in love with him long before she knew he reciprocated her feelings.

And even then, she refused to act on them as his commanding officer despite being years his junior. Fraternization was frowned upon, and she upheld her vow to the Corps more than she did her own heart.

She would have never guessed that she'd get to live the kind of life where she could express her love for him freely, let alone in such a public and ostentatious way.

But here she was, free from the restrictions of the Demon Corps, marrying the love of her life. A man who also happened to be the King of Ozero.

Upon reaching him, he took her hands into his and squeezed them reassuringly.

She loved that he knew how much she hated all this fanfare. But this wedding was about more than just herself and Bernat.

In the wake of the grief and uncertainty that followed the fall of the Cicatrix, their union offered the kingdom a symbol of hope and the chance for renewal.

She quickly looked out at the crowd, noticing the many faces she didn't recognize.

It had been decided that their wedding should be a grand affair and that all the territory leaders and the Protectorate of East and West Ozero leaders should be invited to attend.

As she scanned the faces, she made note of those that were familiar. Giselle sat next to Aurelia, her orange dress a shade that perfectly complimented Aurelia's blue suit.

She didn't think the pairing was a coincidence, and she fought the urge to smile. It was a relief to see people forging bonds of friendship in the aftermath of so much grief.

Seated behind them were Xavier and Xylia, their shoulders bumping and their lips a blur as if they were in the middle of a heated fight. She didn't doubt it. The twins had a knack for fighting over the slightest provocation.

To the left of the aisle sat Juan Martín and Ramon, their hands intertwined and a content smile on their faces.

She gave the subtlest nod to her logistician, and he returned it with a knowing grin.

The courtyard was filled with palpable joy, such that La Aguilera hadn't seen in over a decade and a half.

All the guests were dressed in their finest apparel, and more people had showed up than Solana had thought would.

A throat cleared, and Solana turned to face Guille. He wore a simple black jacket and matching pants, with grey embroidery embellishing his shoulders and chest.

He gave her an expectant look, and she nodded for him to begin the ceremony.

"Today, we gather to join Solana Ramirez with Bernat Ozetero. Their love is a light that shines even brighter in the darkness. As we've all seen, they have survived the trials and tribulations that come along with the world of magic. They've overcome insurmountable odds, fought their way through battles, and made their way to one another. And now, they stand here today, ready to take the next step in their journey together. To all those gathered here, I ask that you join me in blessing this union. May their love for one another continue to grow stronger with each passing day. May they face any challenge that comes their way with strength, courage, and an unwavering trust in one another. And may they never forget the joy and happiness that they feel on this very day."

Solana felt her eyes well up with tears as Guille continued with the ceremony. She looked over at Bernat, her heart full of love and gratitude for him. He was her rock and shelter, and she knew she could face anything with him by her side.

As Guille spoke, Solana found herself lost in thought. She couldn't help but think about how far she had come, how much she had endured to reach this moment.

It wasn't just about the wedding or the importance of their union for the kingdom. It was about the journey that had led her here and the people who had helped her along the way—her family.

She looked around at her loved ones, her eyes lingering on Kiki, who had a small smile on her face.

Kiki had been a thorn in her side from day one. Yet, when they'd needed each other, they'd stood back to back, ready to face the oncoming challenges headfirst.

And then there was Luna, who had been her confidant. She had faced danger and death alongside Solana and had always been there to offer support when she needed it most.

And she couldn't forget Yari, who'd given so much and risked so much to ensure that they could all be here today, free of the darkness and the man responsible for tugging on the threads of their lives.

As Guille pronounced them husband and wife, Solana felt a rush of excitement, knowing that they would be able to build their lives together, free from the constraints of their pasts.

Bernat pulled her into his arms and kissed her lips tenderly.

As they parted, a loud roar of approval erupted from the guests. Solana felt her cheeks warm from the overwhelming emotion. Bernat smiled down at her, his eyes alight with happiness.

"Shall we?" he asked, extending his arm towards her.

Solana took his arm, slipping her hand through his elbow. Together, they began to make their way back up the aisle.

The guests threw flower petals as they walked, cheering and clapping. Solana felt her heart swell with a sense of fulfillment she'd never felt before.

Solana grinned, her heart overflowing with love and happiness. She knew that they had a long journey ahead of them, but with Bernat by her side, she felt confident in their ability to face anything that came their way.

As they entered the reception hall, Solana couldn't help but laugh at the sight of it. The tables were overflowing with food and drink, and people were already dancing and mingling.

Settling into their seats, surrounded by the people she'd come to love, she felt a sense of peace wash over her. For the first time in a long time, she felt truly happy.

Bernat leaned in close to her ear, his breath warm on her skin. "I love you," he whispered.

Solana turned to him, gazing into his bright azure eyes. "I love you too," she said, her voice low and husky.

They shared a kiss, lost in the moment. The rest of the night was filled with laughter, dancing, and celebration.

As the night dwindled down and guests began to slowly trickle out, Solana found herself alone with Bernat in their chambers.

She stood before him, her heart racing with anticipation. He pulled her into his arms, kissing her deeply. She moaned into his mouth, unable to contain the passion that had been building within her all day.

He pulled back, gazing down at her with a hunger that mirrored her own. He began to undress her slowly, his hands moving over her curves with a reverence that took her breath away.

She'd never get enough of this. Of him. And now, with the end of the curse and the birth of their new kingdom, she'd never have to.

CHAPTER THIRTY-SEVEN

KIKI

The bride and groom had long since retired, and the afterparty had slowly petered out to Kiki's group of friends and a few of the territory leaders.

Kiki sat back in her chair with a contented sigh. It had been a few months since the Battle in the North, the Ozero curse's end, and the Cicatrix's fall. But none of that stopped Kiki from training in the yard each day with Yasir.

She never thought she'd see the day when she'd cling to the routine she had grown accustomed to in the Demon Corps. Old habits died hard.

Though the Cicatrix had fallen, there were still demons roaming around Ozero. Not as many as there once had been, especially now that Arlando wasn't alive to convert whole villages into mindless beasts. But, still, the demons that remained were out there. She didn't think she'd really rest until every last one of them burst into smoke and ichor.

But tonight wasn't about considering the problems of the future. She could think about them tomorrow.

Erasmo slipped into a chair beside her and kissed her temple. "So, what's this I hear about you and Giselle and some deal about 'one night.'"

Kiki blinked at him in shock and opened and closed her mouth.

"Don't try to wriggle out of this," he said sternly, a glint of mischief in his eyes. "Apparently, in order to secure the Esmeralda Territory's participation, you bargained yourself off to Giselle."

A blush ran rampant across her cheeks at the reminder. "So what if I did?"

Erasmo flicked his eyes up, and Kiki realized Giselle was standing on her other side. They were boxing her in, and she felt like prey between two predators by the look in both their eyes.

"What's going on?" Kiki asked, sitting straighter in her seat.

Giselle's blond hair fell over her shoulder as she leaned down and caged Kiki in further by placing her hands on both armrests. "You could say that Erasmo and I have come to a little agreement, volcánita." With Giselle bent over like this, Kiki caught a full view of the other woman's very round and full breasts.

The scent of rose, vanilla, and amber filled her nose with notes of sultry smokiness. She inhaled again, the scent sending a pulsing thrill right down to her pussy.

"What kind of agreement?" Kiki rasped, a flurry of emotions washing over her at Giselle's nearness and Erasmo's hand slowly trailing up her leg toward her inner thigh.

Erasmo's hand darted out and caught Kiki's chin between his thumb and forefinger. "I've seen how you look at her," he whispered against the shell of her ear. "Did you think I wouldn't notice? Did you think I couldn't smell your arousal when she was near?"

Kiki squirmed in her seat, and her fists clenched in her lap. She didn't know what game the two of them were playing, and only a small part of her was afraid to find out.

It was true; she was attracted to Giselle, and if Erasmo weren't her mate, she likely would have taken full advantage of her 'one-night' deal with Giselle.

But she and Erasmo were mates and had sealed their bond. She didn't know how this would work.

"I know what you want, Kiki," Erasmo whispered. She felt his lips ghost across her throat, his other hand winding into her hair as he gently tugged at the roots. "*We* know what you need."

"Do you know what you need, volcánita? Have you thought about it?" Giselle purred as she leaned in closer and pressed her soft lips to Kiki's other ear.

"Y-yes," Kiki breathed. "I want you both."

"Then you'll have us both," he said, the sound of a growl rumbling in his chest. Erasmo stood abruptly from the chair, and Giselle gave Kiki's arm a squeeze before releasing her.

"Wait," Kiki hissed. "All three of us? Together? I thought you hated each other."

Erasmo and Giselle shared a look with each other as if they understood the punchline to a joke that had gone over Kiki's head.

"Oh, we do," Giselle said softly, brushing a tuft of hair behind Kiki's ear. "But we both want you, and we know you want both of us. So we're willing to share you."

"Share me?" Kiki gulped. "For how long?"

Erasmo chuckled. "For as long as you want, princess. It can be one night like you agreed in your bargain. Or it can be more. All I want is you, but I can see you want her too. That doesn't bother me. I know I have your heart forever." His warm breath ghosted across the shell of her ear as he added in a husky voice. "But your happiness and *satisfaction*, is something that I am always willing to bend for."

Giselle wound her fingers through Kiki's "Come, let us show you how much we want to make you happy."

Erasmo grabbed her other hand, and together, they led her out of the dining hall and through the dark manor house. Most of the partygoers had retreated to their rooms throughout the house, and the halls were quiet save for the hissing of candles as they burned down to the wick.

Erasmo opened the door to their shared bedroom and closed it quietly behind them.

Giselle slinked alongside Kiki and nuzzled her nose into the crook of her shoulder. "I've been dreaming of this since I first saw you."

A shiver ran up Kiki's neck at Giselle's warm breath fanning across her skin, and a moan slipped past her lips. Giselle's smile was pure sin as she leaned in and kissed Kiki's lips fiercely.

Kiki melted into the kiss, moaning in earnest as Giselle's tongue slipped into her mouth and began teasing her own.

Erasmo's hands slid up and down Kiki's sides, sending tiny shivers of pleasure through her. She felt his lips against her neck as he whispered, "Do you like that?"

Kiki hummed in her throat and tilted her head back to give him better access. She only realized he'd unlaced her dress when his warm fingers brushed the underside of her breast.

"Fuck, these tits are perfect," he muttered as he palmed both breasts in his large hands.

Kiki gasped into Giselle's mouth when he began rolling her nipples between his fingers, but the blond didn't give her time to ask questions before her mouth was taken in another hungry kiss.

Giselle's hands found their way to Kiki's ass, and she began kneading in greedy handfuls, leaving Kiki to push her back to Erasmo's waiting chest. Kiki responded in kind by grabbing handfuls of Giselle's breasts and massaging them. She could feel Giselle's hard nipples through the fabric of her dress and wanted nothing more than to see them for herself.

Erasmo slipped Kiki's dress off her shoulders, allowing it to pool in a silken puddle at her feet.

"Look how perfect you are," Giselle breathed, leading Kiki to stand before the mirror.

Kiki stared at the reflection before her. She was completely naked, her breasts heavy and a flush running across her chest. Her cheeks were red with need, and she could feel her own slickness as she pressed her thighs together.

Behind her, Erasmo continued to kiss along her shoulders, his hands trailing down her waist.

Kiki was about to ask how this would work exactly with three people when she felt a hot, wet tongue stroke up the inside of her thigh. She gasped and glanced down at Giselle on her knees as the other woman continued to drag her tongue up the inside of Kiki's thigh.

"You're so wet. I want to taste you," Giselle murmured as she licked Kiki's pussy from bottom to top, slipping the tip of her tongue into Kiki's entrance.

Kiki gasped in surprise, her hands flying into Giselle's hair, and had to bite her lip to keep from crying out.

Erasmo reached down and spread her legs wider, giving Giselle better access. "I'm going to take your sweet little ass while she sucks on your pretty pussy until you scream," he whispered in her ear. He lifted his fingers to her mouth and said, "Get them wet for me."

Kiki took his fingers into her mouth and sucked them, getting them lubricated for what was to come. Her head fell back against Erasmo's shoulder as he spread open her ass cheeks with one hand and began to spread her saliva around her asshole. Her thighs began to quiver as a tingling sensation began to grow in her belly.

Giselle's held Kiki's thighs open; her tongue and lips attacked her pussy as she lapped at Kiki's clit, teasing that bundle of nerves until Kiki's knees began to give out.

Kiki moaned as she let one hand drift from Giselle's hair and wrapped it around Erasmo's neck. She felt his lips curve into a smile as he nipped at her ear. She turned her head toward him, burying her hand into his curls, and allowed him to capture her mouth in a searing kiss. Her body ached with need. She wanted him inside her.

Giselle popped off Kiki's clit with a moan and massaged her legs. "She's close," she announced to Erasmo.

"Is she now?" he asked, a self-satisfied chuckle vibrating in his chest. "My little demon slayer knows not to come until I say so."

Giselle stood up, pulling the straps from her dress down and pushing the fabric down her ample curves. Her skin was smooth and tan, her nipples brown and erect. Kiki wanted nothing more than to suck on them, to lick them until Giselle felt the way Kiki did in this moment.

"Really?" Giselle asked with a grin. She pressed her lips to Kiki's mouth. "Are you a good girl, Kiki?"

Kiki couldn't help the whimper that escaped her throat. She nodded earnestly as Erasmo pulled his fingers away and guided her to the bed.

Erasmo slipped off his pants and prowled toward Kiki, his eyes smoldering as he reached out and cupped her face in his hands. "Are you ready for me, princess?"

Kiki took a shaky breath as Erasmo's cock sprang to life between them. It was glorious, long and thick, and pointing right at her. Her mouth watered at the sight.

Saints, she wanted a taste.

Erasmo chuckled as if reading her mind. "Show Giselle what a good girl you are, and take every inch I give you." He climbed onto the bed and pulled Kiki on top of him, turning her so that her back pressed against his.

"Oh fuck, that's hot," Giselle groaned as she slipped her dress the rest of the way off her body.

Kiki's eyes trailed of their own accord over Giselle's body, taking in her round, soft ass and the tiny pink slit between her thighs. Kiki wanted nothing more than to reach out and touch her, but her eyes were drawn back up to Giselle's face. The look there was primal, her pupils blown wide and her cheeks flushed red. Her desire for Kiki was clear in how her tongue darted out, moistening her lips.

Giselle sat on the edge of the bed and watched as Erasmo pulled Kiki's hips down and guided his cock to her ass. The head of his cock pressed against her tight entrance, and Kiki took a deep breath and dug her fingernails into his forearms.

Erasmo nudged her entrance with the head of his cock and smiled at Kiki. "You ready?"

Kiki nodded, and Erasmo gently pushed forward, slipping the tip of his cock into her asshole. Kiki moaned and held tightly onto his arms as he slowly lowered her down his length, her eyes closing in bliss.

Giselle crawled up the bed and nestled between Kiki's thighs. She skimmed her fingers across Kiki's clit, sending a jolt of lightning through her body. Kiki reached between her legs and threaded her fingers through Giselle's, her eyes greedily watching as the other woman rubbed her own clit in tight circles.

Erasmo curled his hands around the backs of Kiki's thighs and began lifting her up the length of his cock before letting her come slamming back down.

Kiki threw her head back and moaned. "Oh, fuck!"

Giselle licked Kiki's pussy in small, teasing licks, drawing a low groan from Kiki.

"That's it, princess," Erasmo growled. "Ride my cock." Kiki didn't need to be told twice. She arched her back and pushed her pussy toward Giselle's mouth, rocking her hips against the object of her desire.

Kiki's head fell back, and she let the ecstasy wash over her. Every nerve in her body was on high alert, and she could feel herself beginning to tighten around Erasmo's cock.

"Who do you belong to?" Erasmo growled in her ear.

Kiki angled her face toward his and moaned. "You," she gasped. "I belong to you."

"Fuck," Erasmo hissed and began pounding into her at a maddening pace.

"Harder," Kiki begged as she unwound her fingers from Giselle's and replaced them in her blond curls, holding tightly at the roots.

Giselle's grip on her thighs tightened, her fingerprints leaving red marks along her skin.

Erasmo growled low and picked up the pace again, the sound reverberating in Kiki's ears. Heat began to pool in her belly, and her pussy ached with a need to be touched. Giselle was making a living hell out of keeping her just on the edge of orgasm.

Giselle looked up at Kiki and grinned. "Such a good girl. Look how wet you are for us." She brushed her fingers over Kiki's clit, and Kiki arched into her touch.

Giselle lifted up and grabbed something from the bedside table. She held it up for Kiki to see. It looked like a cock that tapered at the bottom and curved into another cock.

"What's that?" Kiki asked, her breath coming out in labored pants.

"It's what I'm going to fuck you with," Giselle purred as she spread her legs wide and pushed one of the cocks into her glistening pussy.

With the one cock nestled deep in her pussy, Giselle slowly crawled between Kiki's legs, the other cock bobbing as she neared.

Giselle moistened the tip of the cock by rubbing the soft surface of it against Kiki's slick pussy before pressing the head to her entrance. "Have you ever been fucked by two cocks, volcánita."

Kiki shook her head, anticipation building in her belly. "No."

"Do you want to be?" Giselle asked.

"Yes," Kiki hissed.

"Then take it," Erasmo growled.

Giselle gently pushed the tip of the cock into Kiki's pussy, and Kiki groaned as her muscles squeezed around it. Giselle stilled and looked up at Kiki.

Kiki took a deep breath and nodded. "Yes. I want it."

Giselle grinned and pushed the cock in deeper. The stick of the cock jolted through her body, quickly eased by the pleasure of being fucked by Erasmo as Giselle filled her up. The feeling of being fucked by both of them caused her to gasp for air.

Giselle watched her closely as she began to rock her hips mercilessly into Kiki's pussy, working in tandem with Erasmo, matching his rhythm.

Kiki pressed the back of her head against Erasmo's chest as she tried to control her breathing. The way this was going, Kiki would lose it long before either of them told her to.

"Come for us, Kiki," Giselle murmured as she dipped her head and pulled one of Kiki's sensitive nipples into her mouth and sucked hard.

Kiki nodded her consent and let the sensations rush over her. She felt her orgasm building quickly, and Giselle dove her hand between them as she slowly circled her clit. Her whole body was hot and sensitive to every single thing that was happening to her.

"Oh, fuck," Kiki cried out as her orgasm washed over her in waves of pure bliss. She felt Erasmo's cock twitch and stiffen in her ass, and Giselle quickened her pace, thrusting in and out of her.

"You're so fucking sexy when you come," Giselle moaned as she rode her own orgasm, her hands squeezing Kiki's breasts as her body shook.

Kiki moaned and bucked against them, trying to ride out the waves of her orgasm. Her heart raced, and her breathing grew shallow. Her vision went dark around the edges as her orgasm continued to rush over her.

She was vaguely aware of Erasmo's hands on her hips as he helped her to ride through it.

"I'm going to fill your ass," Erasmo growled. He wrapped an arm around her waist and pulled her as close to him as possible. He began to pump his cum into her, and Kiki moaned loudly as she felt every ounce of his cum.

Kiki rested her head against Erasmo's shoulder and took a deep breath. Her pussy ached, and her nipples were rock hard.

Giselle gently pulled back, and Kiki gasped at the loss of fullness. Erasmo lifted her limp body from his lap and gently laid her on her back.

"Stay with us," Kiki said as Giselle began to crawl off the bed.

Giselle shared a look with Erasmo, and he took a deep breath before nodding his consent.

Giselle grabbed the blankets from the end of the bed and spread them over the three of them until they were all tucked in.

Erasmo pressed his body against Kiki's spine and draped an arm around Kiki's waist as Giselle nestled into her from the front, both of them snuggling close to her.

Kiki smiled contentedly as she felt their warmth and reveled in the afterglow of great sex. She closed her eyes and let out a satisfied sigh as their bodies cuddled together in contentment, basking together in pleasure.

Before she let sleep overcome her, Kiki said, "This doesn't feel like a one-night thing."

Erasmo pressed a kiss to her shoulder. "I didn't think it would be," he said, his voice husky. "Sleep, my little demon slayer."

Giselle pressed her soft lips to Kiki's forehead and pulled her closer. "We've got you."

CHAPTER THIRTY-EIGHT

YARI

Yari watched with amusement as Giselle and Erasmo led Kiki out of the dining hall. Not that it was any of her business, but she was happy for her friend.

Kiki had a lot of love to give, and it seemed, somehow, right, for the trio to explore what that meant exactly.

Yari smiled nostalgically, reflecting on the journey she had been on since she first met Kiki. Before her, Yari cowered in the corner of the orphanage. She cried each night for her mother and cried even harder when her tummy ached without enough food.

But then Kiki swooped Yari up, like an eagle taking flight, and everything changed. Kiki rubbed Yari's back until she stopped crying. She shared her portion of food and fought off anyone who thought to steal it away. Under Kiki's watchful eye, Yari felt safe and cared for. She happily hid behind the towering might of Kiki Xochicale and followed her friend wherever she went. As the years passed, Yari saw Kiki as more than just her savior but also as her protector, her confidante, her sister.

They had been inseparable.

Until they were ripped apart by Arlando's schemes.

Yari had promised herself that she'd survive everything that Arlando did to her if she pretended to be more like Kiki.

Somewhere along the way, Yari had stopped pretending, and she now could appreciate that in putting on a brave face, she'd been pulling from something deeper within. A place where her strength had always resided.

Yari stood up to leave the dining hall, turning out of the doorway to wind through the manor until she reached the garden. In the past few months, she'd come to love being outside. Between the bitter cold that killed all tender life in the Norceran basecamp and her time in the Winter Keep, a lush garden was a luxury that she wasn't accustomed to.

She caught a glimpse of Turi standing under the trellis where Solana and Bernat had been married earlier that day.

He'd made a full recovery since the battle but had been distant from her in the months that followed.

She didn't know what torture he endured at Arlando's hands and hadn't wanted to press him to open up to her.

She understood too well the dark places the mind could spiral into and decided to give him space to battle the demons that plagued him.

But seeing him standing there, his face turned up to the sky, his brown curls floating in the wind, she couldn't help herself.

As Yari approached Turi, her heart fluttered with a mixture of anticipation and anxiety. As if sensing her presence, Turi turned to face her, his eyes full of curiosity and trepidation.

Yari couldn't help but take in the beauty of Turi's face, and she suddenly felt overwhelmed with emotion. It had been so long since they were just two ordinary people—so much had changed in their lives—so much had changed between them.

"Turi," she said softly as she brushed a strand of silver hair behind her ear.

"Yari," he said, a hint of relief in his voice.

"How are you?" she blurted out and bit her lip, worried that he'd think she was pushing him too quickly. What if he wasn't ready to talk? What if he wanted to rid himself of the mate bond? What if—

Turi reached out and captured her chin in his hand, his thumb reaching up to release her bottom lip. His eyes were molten blue, and for a moment, Yari could see the intensity of his desire, his need for her.

"I'm better now that you're here," he said, his voice husky and low.

Yari felt her body responding to the intensity of his gaze, her heart pounding in her chest at the heat of Turi's touch. She had always been drawn to him, even before the mate bond, but she had never acted on her feelings. Now, as they stood alone in the garden, she felt a surge of courage.

"I've missed you," she said, her voice barely a whisper.

Turi's eyes darkened as he pulled her closer. "I've missed you too," he said before quickly retracting his hand. "Sorry," he muttered, casting his eyes to the side.

She felt a surge of courage as she darted her hand out and grabbed his wrist. Her breath caught in her throat as she pulled his hand to cup the side of her face. "You don't have to be sorry."

Turi shut his eyes as if he were in pain. "Yari," he whispered, his voice breaking. "I can't be near you."

A sharp pang pierced her heart, and she let his hand drop. "Why not?"

His eyes snapped open, and the look in them was full of so much heat that she felt it wash over her like a lover's embrace. "I don't trust myself to be around you."

Yari frowned and took a tentative step closer. "Why?" she asked, angling her head to look up at him through her lashes.

Turi retreated a step, but his movements were stiff as if the act of pulling away from her brought him physical pain. "I hoped that when the curse broke, the beast's thoughts would go away. But he was right. His thoughts were my own."

Yari ventured another step closer. "What thoughts?"

Turi groaned and turned his face away. "Don't you know how much I want you?"

Her heart soared at his admission, and she closed the distance between them. "Did you ever think that I might want you too?"

He inhaled sharply, his pupils dilating as he scanned her face, drinking in her features. "I thought you wouldn't—" he paused and swallowed the lump in his throat. "After everything."

He wouldn't say it aloud. That Arlando had raped her. But she would. Because refusing to voice something didn't make it go away. To Yari, that only gave it more power. Power that was hers to take back.

"I was raped. Brutally. By your brother," she said, courage fueling her as she stood taller. "I know what happened to me just as much as I know what I want."

"I'm sorry—"

"I don't need, nor do I want, your apology, Turi."

"Then, what do you want?"

"I want you to trust me enough to be honest with you. To believe me when I tell you that I know my own mind. To have faith in me when I tell you that I don't want my rape to define the rest of my life. I refuse to let my body, my sexuality, my very soul be the victim of someone else's actions."

She licked her lips, a surge of courage coursing through her veins as she said the words she had been too afraid to voice before. "I want you to accept me as I am and help me reclaim my body for myself." She paused, her breath shallow as she waited for Turi's response.

Turi finally met her gaze, and his eyes were full of an emotion that made Yari feel like she could do anything, be anyone without fear.

He stepped closer and gently brushed the back of his hand against her cheek before lightly pressing his lips against her forehead. "I'm here," he said softly, his voice filled with such tenderness that Yari felt tears well up in her eyes.

"Help me erase the memory," she whispered, her lips inches from his chest as she reached up and placed her palms over his beating heart. "Seal the bond with me and erase the past."

"Anything," he murmured, his arms tightening around her waist. "I'm yours. Today. Tomorrow. For eternity."

Her lips tugged into a smile. "And I am yours," she said softly before pulling him down to meet her in a sweet kiss of promise.

Turi pulled away and studied her eyes as he asked, "Are you sure?"

"I've never been more sure of anything in my life."

He leaned in and captured her lips in a searing kiss.

Yari felt his hands trail down her back, and she shuddered at the sensation of his calloused fingertips tracing the curve of her back.

Her lips parted with a moan as Turi pulled her closer, his other hand tangling in her hair. There was no denying their chemistry, their connection, their bond.

She melted into his embrace, allowing herself to be swept away by the passion that had been building between them since learning about their bond.

Turi's hands roamed over her body, his touch sending shivers down her spine. She moaned softly as he lifted her up, her legs wrapping around his waist.

Yari responded eagerly, wrapping herself around Turi, her fingers tangling in his hair. She could taste the heat and hunger on his lips, and it set her entire body on fire.

They broke apart, panting and staring into each other's eyes. Turi cupped Yari's face in his hands and whispered, "Tell me what to do. Tell me what you need."

Yari's heart raced as she met Turi's gaze. "Bite me."

Turi's eyes widened in surprise but quickly turned into liquid fire as a growl vibrated deep in his chest. His arms tightened around her thighs, wrapped around his waist.

She angled her neck to give him better access.

He lowered his head to her neck, the heat of his breath tingling against her skin, sending shivers down her spine. He pressed his lips against the column of her throat, his tongue darting out as he licked her flesh.

Yari let out a soft cry of pleasure as he gently pierced her skin with his fangs, his lips forming a gentle suction around the spot as he drank directly from her.

Yari's legs tightened around Turi's waist as she pulled him closer, grinding her body against his.

Turi released her neck and angled his throat to her. "Your turn," he rasped.

His words were the catalyst she needed to reach out, grab his hair, and yank his head to the side, baring his throat to her completely. She lowered her lips to his neck and relished in the sweet tremor that ran down the length of her spine as she opened her mouth and pierced his flesh with her teeth.

Hot, salty blood rushed into her mouth, and Turi shuddered as he released a tortured moan echoing in the air around them.

Yari pulled away, licking her lips. She could feel his blood flowing through her, sending a thrill of pleasure straight to her pussy.

She gazed into Turi's eyes and found them hazy with pleasure. His breath came out shallow as he stared at her, his eyes flicking down to her mouth and back up again.

Turi's blue eyes were hazy with pleasure. "You're so beautiful," he whispered. "Even more so when you're like this."

Yari's lips curled into a smile. "Like what?"

Turi's eyes glittered with desire. "When you let yourself free."

Yari's heart fluttered at the heat in Turi's gaze. "Fuck me, Turi. Claim me as I claim you. Mark me with your blood."

Turi growled and slammed his lips to hers, his tongue plunging into her mouth. His lips were salty with the lingering drops of her blood, but it was the sweetest taste Yari had ever experienced.

Turi continued to kiss her, his hands roaming and clutching at her body as if he couldn't get enough of her. She matched his kiss, her hands clawing into his chest as she ripped his shirt open.

She ran her nails down his chest, carving tiny cuts into his skin. Blood welled from the wounds and spilled over, staining his skin crimson.

The scent of their blood filled the air, making Yari's eyelids flutter as jolts of pleasure sparked along her skin.

There was something erotic about spilling each other's blood this way. The act was full of trust and ownership. A way to infiltrate one another in the basest way possible.

Yari ran her hand through the blood dripping down Turi's hard chest and spread it along her throat, effectively marking herself with his essence.

Turi lowered to his knees and sank back on his heels, keeping Yari securely in his lap. She felt his hard cock press against her pussy, and she let out a moan as she rocked her hips against his length.

Turi's lips were soft and hot as they grazed along her neck and down to her shoulder. Yari's knees quivered beneath her as Turi gently bit her shoulder.

"Oh, god," she panted when Turi's teeth sank into her skin.

Turi's fingers tangled in her hair as he pulled her against him, his lips leaving a trail of scarlet in their wake as he pressed his fangs into her neck again. His lips created delicious suction as she felt his fangs pierce her throat.

A flash of heat ripped through her body, making Yari's toes curl and her skin tingle. She writhed on Turi's lap, grinding her hips against his cock, trying to find some way to ease the throbbing ache between her legs.

"Now," she panted. "Fuck me now."

Turi grinned wickedly and threw himself back, dragging her down with him. "Then take me and do with me as you please."

Yari felt powerful with her dress bunched around her waist and her legs spread over his hips. She dipped her fingers into his blood and whispered an incantation she'd read about.

She'd learned a lot about blood magic in the last few months, namely that all forms of magic weren't inherently evil. Even blood magic, when wielded free of wicked intentions could result in miraculous wonders. She'd been relieved when she realized that she wouldn't slowly go insane.

She hadn't understood what purpose this particular spell could possibly have, but now—she had a perfect use for it.

As the last syllable left her lips, her clothes vanished in a black cloud of smoke. Turi's clothes were equally missing, leaving him wonderfully naked and sprawled beneath her.

She reached between them and gripped his hard cock in her hand. Turi's chest heaved, and his breath caught in his lungs, as she slowly positioned him at her entrance. With her eyes locked on his, she sank down his length, taking him deep inside her pussy.

Yari gasped, her eyes fluttering closed at the sensation of Turi filling her completely. She dropped her head back as his fingers dug into her hips, and he began to bounce her up and down in a steady rhythm.

Everything about Turi felt amazing. His skin, his scent, his taste, his blood. Yari's body hummed with pleasure as she rode him.

"Yari," he moaned, his eyes fluttering closed. He looked like a man who'd died and gone to heaven. "My dark rose... my heart... my soul... my life..."

His words sent a shiver down her spine as he surged forward and buried his face into the crevice between her breasts. He tugged one nipple into his mouth while his thumb and forefinger rolled the other between them.

He continued to move inside her, pushing her to the edge.

Yari threw her head back and moaned, her hands moving to his shoulders and digging into his skin as she rode him faster and deeper. Turi's hands moved to her hips to steady her as he thrust into her in time with her movements.

The feeling of his cock buried deep in her pussy and his mouth on her was too much. She felt herself on the edge.

She was so close. So close. Any second now—

She could feel the bond, the connection, the completion of it taking hold of her soul as magic surged through her veins like pure lightning. Turi whispered her name, his voice sweet and lyrical like a siren's call.

She felt the blood rush from her body, and the heat of his touch ignited her soul. Her fingers dug into his skin, her grip tight as she inched closer to the edge of release.

Suddenly, she was falling, plunging into a sea of ecstasy.

As her body reached the height of bliss, her magic danced between them, enhancing their pleasure.

She was barely aware of the sound of her own cry of pleasure as she spiraled out of control, her pussy muscles clenching around Turi's cock as he spilled his cum deep within her.

The bond between them flared, binding them together as one.

Yari rested her head against Turi's chest, and she could hear the deep thudding of his rapid heartbeat as her body continued to shake with the remnants of her orgasm.

"Yari," Turi whispered. "I love you, Yari. Now and forever." He captured her lips with his and kissed her with long, languish strokes of his tongue.

Yari pulled back and brushed a tender kiss against his lips. "I love you too, Turi," she whispered.

Kiki

Epilogue

Two years later.

"Get back here, you little beasts!" Kiki cried, sprinting through the manor as she chased after the trio of bear cubs.

Instead of the triplets going down for their afternoon nap, Kiki had fallen asleep in the rocking chair next to their cribs.

She woke when she heard the faint clicking of talons against the hardwood floors and caught the sight of a fluffy round tail as it slipped out of the room and scurried down the hall.

Solana and Bernat had put a lot of thought into their sons' names. The eldest was Salvador, his name meaning "savior" and a symbol of the fight Ozero fought and won against the darkness. The second to be born was named Valiente, a play on Bernat's mother's name, the late Queen Valentina. And, last but not least, was Maximiliano, meaning "great courage" -- more like a great pain in Kiki's ass. Though Max was the youngest by a mere 6 minutes, he was the most mischievous.

Although the curse had been lifted, along with its constraints on the Ozetero men and their inability to control their shifts without the help of their talismans, all Ozetero men still retained the ability to shift if they desired. What none of them had anticipated, since it had never happened before, was would become of children born outside of the curse. As it turned out, the little devils could shift at will and the triplets had a nasty habit of shifting quickly and annoyingly often!

"You had one job, Kiki," she muttered as she threw herself down the winding stairs, hoping to catch them before they reached—

A series of shouts and yelps echoed through the manor as the trio of bears made it to the main level.

"Damn it!" she growled, hitting the main level at a sprint and bowling straight into Luna.

"OW!" Luna stumbled back as she struggled to keep hold of the healing supplies piled in her arms.

"Sorry!" Kiki yelled over her shoulder, her ears pricking up when she heard the sound of pots clattering. "Gotcha," she grinned and bolted for the kitchen.

Sal, Val, and Max weren't like other children Kiki had ever encountered. They'd come into the world in their bear forms and were running around razing havoc five weeks after their birth.

They had a tendency to prefer their bear forms since they were faster with four legs rather than two.

Kiki burst into the kitchen, ready to grab Val and force the other two into compliance.

Val was the lover. He couldn't resist the opportunity for cuddles, and he only ever followed along after the other two because they were his brothers, and he didn't like being left behind.

Out of the trio, Val was Kiki's sweet saint of a nephew, and all she had to do was cajole him into her arms, and then it was game over.

She didn't expect to catapult right into Solana's towering frame and find the little miscreants crawling all over their mother.

Solana's fire-red curls cascaded around her shoulders as Val tucked his muzzle into her neck. Sal clung to her opposite shoulder, and Max burrowed into her chest. The cubs all had the same reddish-brown hair and shared Solana's ice-blue eyes.

"Sorry, Sol," Kiki said, gasping for air. "They tricked me into thinking they were sleeping."

Solana smiled warmly, her face softening with the gesture. "They did the same to Turi a month ago, don't feel bad about it."

Kiki knew that but thought she would have known better than to fall for their tricks.

Max made a grunting sound, and Kiki narrowed her eyes at him. The little hellion.

Kiki dragged her toe across the floor. "Does this mean you're kicking me off babysitting duty?" she asked, trying to mask the disappointment in her voice.

As much as the triplets drove her insane, she loved them dearly and cherished her time with them. She wasn't ready to be a mother just yet, but she was having a blast of a time being an aunt.

Solana gave Kiki a soft nudge against her shoulder. "No, Kiki, you're not being kicked off duty."

Kiki's shoulders bowed forward as she relaxed. "Oh, thank the Saints."

"Besides," Solana added as she pried her sons off of her and set them gently on the ground. "If I hadn't been here, you would have caught them anyway before they raided the pantry again."

Kiki winced, remembering the last time the trio had gotten free of their caretaker. If she never had to bathe a bear cub coated in honey again in her life, it would be too soon.

Sal and Max began playing a wrestling game, their tiny tails a blur as they tumbled over one another. Meanwhile, Val made pathetic mewing sounds at Solana's feet.

A poof of white smoke filled the air, and a second later, a sweet voice rang in the air saying, "Mama." Val wrapped himself around Solana's leg, his blue eyes looking up at her pleadingly. "When is Papa coming home?"

Good fucking question, Kiki thought to herself.

Bernat had taken Erasmo, Turi, and Mauri with him to visit the leaders of Eastern and Western Ozero. The Protectorate leaders of the East and West had yet to bend the knee and seemed loathe to relinquish their power over the kingdom.

Kiki didn't like the idea of being sandwiched between the East and West because she feared what would become of Central Ozero should the two ever go to war.

Bernat hoped to convince the Protectorate that bringing the kingdom together was of more benefit to everyone than remaining three separate entities.

The East seemed to be warming to the idea, especially with the promise of increased resources and the opportunity for real economic growth and prosperity for the people. However, the West was staunch in their belief that Ozero was no longer a kingdom and that they didn't need Bernat or the East to prosper.

The door to the kitchen opened, and Giselle came sauntering in. Her blond hair was braided down her back today, and she wore a decadent red pantsuit with golden embroidery embellishing the lapels of her bolero jacket.

"There you are," she purred, sidling up to Kiki. She pressed a kiss to Kiki's lips before Max hurtled around the corner of the kitchen island and poofed into his human form.

"Auntie Elle!" he shouted, jumping up and down, holding his arms up. "Up! Up!"

Giselle bent over and hefted the excited toddler into her arms. "Did you escape again?" she asked him, her tone playful as she tried to keep her face serious.

"Aunt Kiki fell asleep," he announced. "We're not tired," he added, his lower lip pouting.

True to form, Sal also poofed into his human form and began tugging on Giselle's pant leg.

Giselle's eyes filled with humor as she adjusted Max on her hip. "Aunt Kiki didn't get a lot of sleep last night," she said, her tone full of innuendo. She gave Kiki a wicked grin before masking it for Max's sake.

"Play with us," Max chirped as he bounced excitedly on her hip. "Play!"

"I'll play with you on one condition," Giselle said, holding her pointer finger up. "No biting. Even though I know you don't mean it, it still hurts."

Sal piped up. "But Aunt Yari doesn't mind!"

Kiki bent over and picked Sal up. "That's because Aunt Yari is a blood mage and can heal herself right away."

Max and Sal made a disappointed "awww" sound that did nothing to change Giselle's serious expression.

"Okay, Auntie," Max chirped. "No play biting."

Giselle motioned for Kiki to lead the way to the training yard.

Solana joined them as they walked through the manor.

"Any word from Yari?" Kiki asked Solana.

"She's fine, Kiki," Solana responded, her tone long-suffering.

"I know," Kiki quipped. "I was just asking."

Solana's lips tugged in a smile, and she added, "You don't have to worry about her anymore."

Kiki felt the truth of those words deep in her very soul. Yari was a powerful blood mage now. She'd been called to a distant queendom a few months ago to help with some sickness that was ravaging the people.

Yari had offered to go in place of Luna since La Aguilera couldn't be without a Healer. Turi had wanted to join her, but she'd been insistent that she go alone, fearing that he'd catch whatever illness was killing people in droves.

One of the benefits of being a blood mage was Yari's ability to cleanse her blood of any sickness. She was as good as immune.

Still, that didn't make Kiki worry any less. She resolved that she'd probably always have a seed of concern for her best friend. Her sister. Her family.

She couldn't change that part of herself—the part that needed to protect those she loved. She was born that way, and she knew the same family she had fought so hard to protect felt the same way for her.

"Telling me not to worry is like telling me to lay down my machete. I can't," Kiki whispered, her throat getting tight with emotion.

"I know, Kiki," Solana said, her eyes warm as she patted Kiki's shoulder affectionately. "We love you all the same."

ABOUT THE AUTHOR

Nicolette Elzie writes mythology-inspired fantasy romance with delicious, morally gray heroes and fierce heroines more likely to jump into battle mode with their swords blazing. She lives with her swoony husband, two children, and three fur babies. She can usually be found reading, re-watching her favorite shows for the millionth time, playing board games, and reminiscing on her past life as a dragon.

Nicolette's Newsletter

https://nicoletteelzie.com/newsletter/

Follow Nicolette on TikTok

https://www.tiktok.com/@authornicoletteelzie

Follow Nicolette on Instagram

https://www.instagram.com/nicolette.elzie/

Follow Nicolette on Facebook

https://www.facebook.com/nicoletteelziewrites

Visit Nicolette on the Web

https://nicoletteelzie.com

www.ingramcontent.com/pod-product-compliance
Lightning Source LLC
Chambersburg PA
CBHW020139170726
47995CB00003BA/600